THE PHANTOM ORACLE

VAMPIRE INNOCENT
BOOK FIVE

MATTHEW S. COX

DIVISION ZERO PRESS

The Phantom Oracle

Vampire Innocent Book 5

ISBN (eBook): 978-1-949174-90-8

ISBN (Print): 978-1-949174-91-5

CONTENTS

THE WORST SUMMER OF MY LIFE

S omber thoughts keep getting in the damn way of hanging out with my friends.

Like, seriously, brain. Leave me the hell alone for a couple damn hours at least. Here I am, at Michelle's place, trying to enjoy the last few days of the worst summer of my life—not an exaggeration, since my life technically ended, and well... I think being murdered qualifies as crappy.

But yeah, every time there's a quiet moment, I catch myself thinking about depressing shit. Like how my friends and I aren't kids anymore, our days of not having responsibilities are over, summer vacation's about done. And how college, work, and real life are going to pull my friends and I apart. That sort of crap.

And, honestly, it's total maudlin bogosity.

At least for me. I'll forever be eighteen. Chances are kinda slim I'll ever have a career. It's more likely Seattle will see seven straight days of sun—or the Seahawks will make it to the Super Bowl two years in a row. So, yeah... I'm sitting here with my two best friends, feeling like I'm standing at the dock while they pull away on a cruise ship I'm not allowed on.

Then again, Dad constantly rambles about how much he misses

his childhood and not having any responsibilities. What happened to me isn't that bad, honestly. Fate decided to pick a reasonably good place to kick me out of the simulation and enable the cheat codes. It would totally suck to be stuck as a *child* forever, like my siblings' ages. Even as a vampire, looking like I'm ten years old for the rest of eternity would create a whole crapload of problems. Couldn't exactly go wandering around a city at two in the morning without attracting attention. And, geez, I get the 'kid' thing bad enough now. I don't even want to think about how other vampires would react to me if this happened while I was that young. And, part of me hopes that never happens. It's too sad thinking about a little kid dying. Vampiredom has a rather steep entry fee.

On the other hand, at eighteen, I'm still physically young enough to get away with shit—and my Innocent bloodline making me look young for my age helps. I'm like Schrodinger's kid, stuck in some quantum state simultaneously adult and child while being neither. Also, I'll never grow old, complain about not fitting into clothes I used to look great in, watch my body slowly succumb to the ravages of time, and so on. Granted, I can't exactly go to my fortieth high school reunion without causing a fiasco. I'd be surrounded by people like Kurt Wimmer who'll no doubt be full of himself about becoming some high-powered corporate executive, lawyer, or some such thing, basically sweating money and power. I can just picture him bumping into me: 'Oh, Wright, what did you do with your life?'

I grin, imagining myself saying 'Not much, just decided to stay eighteen forever. How's it feel being fifty?'

Fun to think about, but I'm not that petty. Besides, who knows if Kurt will *stay* a jerk. Some guys do grow out of that.

"Ugh." Ashley flops back on the sofa. "I can't believe summer's over already."

"No shit, right?" Michelle stands and collects empty iced tea glasses.

"Heh." I flash a wry grin. "At least last summer *was* killer."

Both of my friends stare at me. Michelle shakes her head in an 'I can't believe you went there' sort of way while Ash's eyes redden.

I sit up from the mega-slouch I'd fallen into. "Sorry. Gotta laugh at that stuff or it'll drive me nuts."

"You've been in a mood all day." Michelle walks past me toward the kitchen. "What's bothering you?"

"Yeah." Ashley hops off the recliner and plops down next to me, arm around my shoulders. "It's only the end of summer vacation. Not the end of the world."

Her over-enthusiastic hug shakes me back and forth.

"It's mostly summer being over, but my brain is turning it into a metaphor for like the end of our childhood and stuff."

Michelle raspberries from the kitchen. "Come on, Sare. You can't honestly *want* to stay a kid forever. Personally, I can't wait for the freedom of not having to base everything I do on what my parents want."

I refrain from pointing out I have no choice in the matter. Staying a kid forever is exactly what I'm going to do.

"I'm gonna miss being able to hang out all day and do goofy stuff, too." Ashley smiles. "But, really… we haven't been able to do that for a couple years at least. 'Chelle's got a point, but it is kinda scary to think about leaving home."

"Who are you kidding?" I poke her in the side. "You're going to live with your mom as long as you can get away with it."

"Well…" Ashley puts on the same face she wore whenever her mother caught us raiding the cookie cabinet. "For one thing, Mom and I are really close. She's not overbearing like *some* parents who shall remain nameless."

"I heard that," calls Michelle from the kitchen.

"And," says Ashley, "have either of you actually *looked* at things these days? Kids our age—or the age we'll be when we get outta college—*can't* afford to live on their own."

"Sure we can." Michelle walks in with refilled tea for everyone. "Put in the required work, make the right choices, and you'll do fine."

"So the thirty-year-old professional who's still living in a one-bedroom apartment with a roommate while working fifty hours a week doesn't own a house in the suburbs with a pool because they're lazy?" Ashley rolls her eyes. "It's not like I'm studying to become a teacher or like majoring in philosophy or English. I'll make okay money if I make it to veterinarian. Just... why waste it on rent when I don't have to."

"Ouch," says Michelle, grinning. "Yeah, that was damn surreal finding Mr. Martin working at the mall."

"Yeah." I whistle. Seeing our sophomore year English teacher working retail at a clothing store in the mall had stabbed my childhood in the side for sure.

"But still. Do you wanna be 'that girl' who's still living at home? How are you gonna settle down with someone? Remember Mr. Dougherty? You don't wanna be that." Michelle shakes her head.

Ashley's face reddens. "I'm not gonna wind up a thirty-two-year-old math teacher living in their parents' basement, even if *my* mom can't afford to help me buy a house."

"You think my parents are just gonna buy me a house when I graduate?" Michelle leans forward, eyebrows up.

I keep quiet, as both my parents make decent money. Not quite as much as Michelle's, but definitely more than Ashley's mom.

"No, not 'buy you a house' but I'm sure they'll help you pay rent. You're not going ride a bathtub of money straight out the doors of law school." Ashley folds her arms.

Sensing the tension growing, I fling my arms up. "Guys! Chill. We have two days and a weekend more of summer left. Can we stop arguing like adults?"

"But we *are* adults." Michelle sighs and sinks back in the recliner. "Sucks, but we gotta grow up. At least two of us."

Ashley scowls at her.

I put a hand on her shoulder. "It's okay. She didn't mean it in a bad way."

"It bothers you though." Ashley stares at me like I'm some lost kitten on the side of the road. "You still look sad."

"I was starting to feel down about losing our childhood, my being 'outside the game' so to speak, and some other crap. But, I'm just being stupid. I *could* be dead. And technically, I still don't really have responsibilities. Life is a giant video game and I clipped through the walls."

"Huh?" asks Michelle.

"You ever play a game where you hit a glitch and fall out of the map?" Ashley grins. "That's Sarah. She's turned on god mode, playing outside the boundaries of the level."

"Oh." Michelle takes a few sips of her tea. "So why are you even going to college then? What are you gonna major in?"

"Phlebotomy," I deadpan.

Both of them stare at me.

I shrug. "Or maybe cryptozoology."

Michelle blinks, then laughs. "Are you for real?"

"No. I'm a fictional creature, and I suck at life."

Ashley groans.

"Seriously?" Michelle cringes. "You've been spending way too much time around your dad. You're way too young—and way too female—to make dad jokes."

"Yeah, that one was kinda lifeless, wasn't it?"

Michelle throws a pillow at me.

I get my hands up in time to catch it even though the rainy daylight is still bright enough to shut down my vampire-ness.

"Seriously though. Why bother?" Michelle gestures at me. "You don't need to work. Hell, you *can't* really work. Anything you want, you can just mind-whammy people into giving you. That Aurélie woman sure as shit don't work."

Ashley's eyes glaze over with a love-struck expression.

"Yeah, but she's older than hell. I dunno. I guess college is just to feel normal. Sometimes, I say it's because my parents always wanted me to go to college and I don't want to disappoint them. My not going would only remind them that I died. Maybe that's part of it, but it's starting to feel like an excuse."

"You're in denial?" Michelle grins. "Trying to pretend none of it happened?"

I raise an eyebrow. "You'd rather I sleep in a coffin, wear all black, and talk with a horrible Slavic accent?"

They both laugh.

"Ugh." I rake my hands over my hair. "I dunno. Going to college feels like what I should be doing. At least I'm still in the area, right?"

Ashley hugs me.

"Oh, you two should just stop fooling each other and admit you're madly in love."

"Hah!" Ashley bursts into giggles.

I know Michelle's kidding, so I laugh, too.

"For real though." Michelle wags her tea at me. "What the hell are you going to school for?"

"At the moment, I'm in the computer science/programming track. Could always work at home, and writing my own video games someday could be fun."

Ashley and Michelle both laugh.

"What?" I ask, biting my lip at a momentary surge of self-consciousness.

"You're not exactly an über math geek," says Ashley. "Nor *that* into video gaming."

Michelle grins. "Yeah, you're no Sierra."

"I'm not *that* bad at math. Just lazy. And, since my, umm, 'schedule change,' I've been playing more of them. Kinda hard to go out and do crap outside when it's fatal. Besides, if I can't keep up with the math, I might change to an English major."

Ashley stares at me like I just suggested we kill and eat her mom. "Umm, what? Did you say major in English?"

"Uhh, yeah," I say, involuntarily doing an impression of Bree Swanson. "I like reading."

"Why?" Ashley blinks. "The only thing you can do with an English degree—other than wait tables—is teach. And you can't go outside that early."

"Could be worse. She could major in art history." Michelle giggles.

I laugh. "Guys… it's not like my future depends on my ability to earn a living. I'm never going to work a real job. College, for me, is all about A: feeling normal and B: placating the 'rents."

"That's kinda weird you're having them pay for school and won't really use it." Ashley looks down, fidgeting at her pink Hello Kitty sweatshirt.

"I'm going to use it as much as I can. If I stick with programming, I can work from home like Dad. And, umm, English, I dunno. Maybe I'll write—or wait tables on the midnight shift at a truck stop diner."

Michelle starts choking on her tea, trying to laugh and drink at the same time.

"If she chokes to death, bring her back as a vampire," says Ashley.

Still unable to speak, Michelle raises a middle finger. Once she recovers, she sighs, shaking her head. "You can't make me into a vampire. My parents would kill me."

Ashley emits a tentative laugh.

"I can't make you into a vampire because I have no idea how." I shrug. "Wasn't exactly awake to watch when Dalton did it to me."

"Umm. You should learn." Ashley nudges me. "Like just in case we die. You know what kind of luck I have. I could wind up slipping on something and going head-first into the rear end of a horse and suffocating. Talk about a shitty way to go."

I can't exactly die laughing, but I come close.

Michelle cringes. "Okay, Ash, that is like the most disgusting thing I think you've ever said."

"Ash…" After the tears stop streaming from my eyes, I try—mostly failing—to take on the serious parent-to-kid tone like I'm about to discuss teen pregnancy. "If you suffocated to death with your head up the ass of a horse, I don't think you'd *want* to come back and remember that."

She sputters tea, giggling.

"And where the hell did that come from?" Michelle cringes.

"Oh, I was looking at the paperwork for the curriculum. They got a picture of this girl up to her shoulder. Her arm, not her head." Ashley mimics cringing away from something while reaching forward. "Not sure exactly what she's trying to grab in there… and the horse didn't seem too happy about it either."

We all crack up giggling.

"But yeah… it's not like I need to earn money for food. And I'm not demanding my parents pay for it. They want to, since I'm not 'scholarship girl' here."

Ashley sticks her tongue out at me. "You could be, but you're a slacker."

"I'm not a slacker." I smirk at her.

"Among nerds, you're a slacker." Michelle winks. "Our slackers are 'mere overachievers' in the mortal world."

I snicker. "Oh, come on. None of us are *that* nerdy… or we'd have been in college by fourteen and designing like new spaceships already."

"No…" Michelle takes on an air of reverence as if she were talking of fallen war heroes. "Those are *supernerds*. Nerds the likes of which we can only aspire to be."

"No capes!" shouts Ashley in a horrible accent.

Michelle tilts her head. "Was that supposed to be French or German?"

Again, Ash sticks out her tongue.

"Michelle," says Mrs. Gerard, while breezing in from the hallway. Her sand-brown raincoat is so drenched it looks like she went swimming in it. "Don't forget we have the bake sale at the church, Sunday." She smiles at me and Ashley. "Your friends are more than welcome to join us."

I bite back the urge to ask her why a church has to sell cakes to raise money if 'god' is supposed to provide. Guess their pastor wants a new car.

Ashley gets a case of the giggles, probably finding some irony in the woman inviting a vampire to a church.

"I didn't forget, Mom." Michelle looks off to the side, dodging eye contact with everyone. "I already invited them and they're both busy. Ash is working and Sarah's parents need her help with something."

"Oh. That's too bad." Mrs. Gerard sets her fists against her hips and shakes her head. "After God protected their daughter from that boy, they ought'a make time to thank him on Sundays."

"By selling cakes?" I blurt.

Ashley's eyes redden with imminent laugh tears.

"Mom..." Michelle sighs. "Remember how you agreed to ease back on the God stuff around people who aren't into it? Please... My friend almost *died*. Please don't turn what happened to her into a sales pitch."

Mrs. Gerard pauses, then sighs. "That's not how I meant it. But, all right."

Michelle's father enters from the hall, also rain-soaked, and carrying two enormous bundles of grocery bags. "Hey, girls."

We all wave and say hello as he goes by into the kitchen, lugging their haul.

As soon as Mrs. Gerard follows him and is out of sight, Michelle slouches forward, head down.

"What's wrong?" Ashley leans on me, but looks at her.

"Ugh," whispers Michelle. "I wish I could stop going without them disowning me."

I raise a finger. "Speak the words and reality shall bend to your will."

Michelle looks up at me. "Do not mess with my parents' heads."

"Hey, just saying it's an option. If you really don't believe in that stuff, it's kinda shitty of them to disown you for not going. So much for that 'love everyone and turn the other cheek' stuff, huh?"

"It's not that I don't believe. I'm not like you two and 'know' there's no God. I just... I dunno. The people there are all so superficial. Everyone smiles at everyone's face, but as soon as their backs are turned, it's shredding time. It's not about spirituality at all, just about *looking* right. If there *is* a god, my parents' church has nothing to do with him."

"Hang on there a sec," I say. "I don't *know* there's no god. I just don't make a habit of believing things people tell me are true just because they tell me so. Show me some proof and I'll be happy to change my mind."

"Guys," whispers Ashley. "Can we not do this again? Especially not with her parents so close? If they catch us questioning their faith, they'll tell her she can't be friends with us anymore."

Michelle stares into her iced tea. "If a defense attorney asks the prosecutor to prove their case, and the prosecutor gets pissed off and starts screaming... pretty good chance he doesn't actually have any evidence. I get what you're saying. But there's no discussing it with them. Why do you think I want my own place so bad? And I'm not quite where you guys are. Maybe it's real, maybe not. But... there's a big damn difference between those fake-ass people at that place and genuine spirituality."

Ashley sighs, downcast.

The Gerards still don't—nor will they ever—know that Ash is bi. I'm sure Michelle didn't intentionally refer to her parents as fake spiritualists, but we're all pretty sure they'd freak out. Considering Mr. Gerard often randomly blames societal problems on everyone and anything he deems 'ungodly,' we're avoiding the topic entirely. I mean, there have been a few politicians who spoke out against LGBT people until someone in their family came out of the closet, then they changed their mind. I suppose it is possible that the Gerards might accept Ashley since they've known her for years. But... that's a coin flip none of us—especially Ashley—are comfortable making.

Pretty sure watching that hate in action played a part in souring Michelle on the church—or at least the one her parents attend. She probably still believes in some kind of creator. I shake my head. Mrs. Gerard thinks some entity 'saved' me that night... yeah. Some entity did save me, and his name was Dalton, not Jesus. Whatever creator may exist didn't save me. He let me die.

But... I'm with my dad on that topic. Proof please. Hmm. I wonder if my existence as a vampire proves anything. Obviously, supernatural stuff exists. But, I don't need anyone to just take my condition on faith. I can show them fangs—at least when it's dark out.

And, yeah. I'm not wasting the last few days of summer on brain-crushing philosophy.

"So what do you guys wanna do with our last night of childhood?" I ask.

"That happened like three years ago before we had to get summer jobs." Michelle grins. "But... hmm. Movie? Girls night out?"

Ashley stretches one leg into the air, appraising the polish on her toes. "Movie would be dark enough to hide how badly I need to redo my nails. I don't really care." She again squeezes me. "Just glad we can do something together... and that you're not moving away to California."

A pang of homesickness hits me at the thought of California. "Yeah. Me too. I can't even remember where the idea of going to Cali came from. Probably would've hated it and come back after one semester."

Michelle scoffs. "Semester? More like one week."

"Give her *some* credit." Ashley elbows me playfully in the ribs. "She'd have lasted at least a month."

"Either way..." Michelle scoots forward out of her chair. "Unless you guys wanna wind up conscripted into baking all damn day, we need to go somewhere soon."

I glance down at the bright purple on my toenails. It doesn't look obviously in need of repair like Ashley's nails, so I shrug. "Whatever you guys wanna do is fine with me. Let's just have some fun."

"We could hit that augmented reality place?" asks Michelle. "Or a movie."

Ashley shrugs. "Okay."

"How about both?" I twirl a strand of hair around my finger. "It's our last night of freedom. We might as well stay up late."

2

CALIFORNIA DREAMIN'

C omfortable warmth surrounds me. I'm content and relaxed in silence. At least, until the din of voices and the occasional joyful squeal of a distant small child intrude upon my peace. Blackness fades to a blinding reddish glare. I haven't even opened my eyes yet, but the light is painful. A soft breeze brushing over every inch of me sounds alarm bells since I don't seem to be wearing anything. I briefly start to panic at winding up in a morgue again, but the creaking of a beach chair under me and the smell of sunbaked plastic causes my brain to halt. I raise an arm to shield my eyes, and open them to an impossible sight.

I'm smack dab in the middle of a huge beach, maybe forty feet away from the water on a big folding lounge chair. Sunglasses appear to be the only thing I'm wearing, but none of the people around me seem to notice or care. Two guys go by in USC T-shirts and swim shorts, both giving me 'hey what's up' nods.

That I'm stark naked on a crowded beach doesn't even register to my mind. I've got bigger problems: it's like high noon on a bright, sunny day.

I scream and jump up, flailing my arms while looking around for anywhere to take cover from the ball of fiery death in the sky. Pristine sand stretches an impossible distance in every direction except toward the water. It's like I'm at the edge of a desert that touches the ocean with nowhere I can go to escape incineration. Panic drives me into a short run, but I keep stopping and dashing in back and forth since it's the same endless sand everywhere I look—unless I dive under the waves. Finally, I catch sight of a giant umbrella and sprint.

An older couple who look simultaneously familiar and strange, peer up at me from their beach towels as I skid to a stop by the strut holding up their umbrella.

"Oh, hi, sweetie," says the woman. She's easily late seventies with ye-olde-standard white curly granny 'do. "Can we help you?"

"Umm." I finally notice that I haven't caught fire—and I'm not even smoking.

"Is something wrong, hon?" asks the old man, sitting up. Gah. He looks like a giant piece of fried chicken with body hair. Dude needs to lay off the tanning bed or invest in sunblock.

"I'm..."

Neither one of them react at all to my lack of a bathing suit, which is too damn strange. No concerned expressions or even inappropriate staring from the guy. A girl streaking the beach should at least be getting stared at. And on a college beach, probably applause... until the cops show up.

"Not burning," I mutter.

"Well that's good." The woman smiles. "Are you out of lotion?"

I bite my lip. "Not that kind of burning. I, uhh, usually take sunburn to the next level."

"Ahh, you're Irish?" The old man laughs. "No color at all to Maine lobster in five minutes?"

Okay, that's beyond weird. Why is he saying something Ashley always said about going outside in the summer?

Another pack of 'generically good looking young men' go by, all with USC logos on their shirts, hats, or coolers. Not one of them reacts the way I'd expect a boy to react to me standing around in my birthday suit. In fact, they barely give me a second glance.

I peer down at myself. Yep, still bare assed.

Even more bizarre, I'm not on fire.

Oh. Duh. I'm dreaming of California. Wow. This is really... strange. I don't remember ever having a dream that felt like this before. Meaning, real time, like I'm awake and thinking and stuff. Usually, my dreams are more like watching a movie from inside.

"I'm okay. Thanks." I shrug at the old couple. Might as well see where this rabbit hole goes. A bizarre dream is hardly the screwiest thing to happen to me in the past few months.

Since I'm no longer panicking about burning to ashes, I blush hard at being around so many people with nothing on. Still, I force myself to ignore that mortifying detail and walk back to my lounge chair. After all, this is a dream and no one is really seeing me. This dream probably doesn't mean I'm anxious about something or I'd be in the center of a bunch of people pointing and laughing at me for being naked.

The second my ass touches the overly warm plastic chair, my iPhone emits a *tweep*.

Wow. Even in dreams I can't get away from text messages. How messed up is that?

I wonder if the naked part is related to my waking up in the morgue, or from Ashley's joking around last night about the worst part of my being a vampire is we'll never go to a nude beach. Both she and Michelle had consumed a couple beers at that point, so it's anyone's guess where *that* suggestion came from. Ash had always been the shiest of our group. For her to suggest something like that was way outside normal. Of course, she *has* been kinda odd ever since her tryst with Aurélie. And okay, maybe I was a naughty vampire and helped people believe my friends' fake IDs.

A text on the screen appears from Sophia: ‹Sare, when are you coming home? I miss you. And Sierra's being a butthead. She keeps teasing me. Please come home.›

I notice a 99* on my little brother Sam's name, so I page over to his message stream, which is an endless repetition of ‹when are you coming home?›

The next page has a notification from USC that I failed a biology test.

"Wow," I mutter to myself. "Anxiety must be on overdrive. Sun. Public nudity. Guilt trips from my siblings *and* a test failure."

I hang my head and sigh. When I look up, I'm at a desk in a classroom... and I'm still naked. Still, none of the forty or so students around me nor the professor—who looks like Gandalf's older brother with rheumatoid arthritis—react to it.

Despite wanting to get up and leave such an embarrassing situation, I don't move. Something between the instinct to sit still because it's class and the fear that the instant I do anything abnormal everyone will notice I forgot my clothes keeps me seated. Reminding myself over and over again that I'm dreaming keeps me sane. I'd take notes, but the teacher's indecipherable. He's doing the 'wahwahwah' thing like from a *Peanuts* cartoon. Hours pass in what feels like mere moments. Every time I look over at the wall clock it's jumped by twenty minutes or so.

Finally, everyone gets up at the same time.

I don't have any books, bag, or anything to carry, so I sheepishly stand and follow everyone into the hall. A moment later, Ashley comes out of the crowd and pounce-hugs me, bursting into tears and telling me how much she misses me. No, it's not awkward at all having her wrapped around me in the middle of a crowded hallway while I have nothing on. At least she's dressed.

Before I can even think of what to do, she disappears into a cloud of smoke.

"This is one weird ass dream."

For no particular reason, I walk with the crowd, feeling like I have somewhere to be in a hurry, like a next class period. Okay, this naked thing has got to be a metaphor for vulnerability or being unprepared. I'm neither vulnerable nor unprepared. Well... maybe not vulnerable. College still makes me nervous, but the stakes are lower.

Ugh. That was bad.

I mean, if I fail out of school, I'm not ruining my life/career, just disappointing my parents.

And, I'm a vampire. I don't have any reason to be afraid of physical threats anymore.

By the time I reach the doors outside, I've somehow wound up in a sweatshirt, jeans, and sneakers. I can work with that. Paradoxically, now that I'm dressed, people start staring at me like I'm walking around naked. Probably because of the Seattle Central College logo across my chest.

"Hey," says a voice I never wanted to hear again.

I whip around to stare straight ahead—at Scott Deacon. He's still wearing his varsity jacket from high school, a red Solo cup in his left hand. He would've hated college if he actually managed to get accepted anywhere. While he wasn't quite the *king* of high school, he was in the top six 'dudes.' Going from that to a relative nobody would've driven him nuts.

"Let me guess, you're going to stab me," I deadpan.

Scott tilts his head in confusion. "Why would I do that?"

"Oh, I dunno…" I shrug. "Maybe because—"

His right arm flies out and embeds a giant knife in my chest.

I peer down at it and sigh. "Figures."

Scott disappears in a whorl of vapor. Frowning, I yank the knife out and throw it aside.

Everyone on the campus stops and stares at me.

"What? You've never seen a girl stabbed to death before?" I hold my arms out to the sides.

They shake their heads like I did something rude in public, and keep walking. I wander the campus for a little while until I realize I'm mostly retracing the steps from the tour I went on three months into my senior year.

"The hell am I doing?"

I blink, and find myself staring at the ceiling of my room in glorious black-and-white. The only spot of color is the alarm clock to my right. Tall numbers in green LED indicate the time at 2:37 p.m. Ugh. What a messed up dream. I sit up and habitually rub my eyes even though they don't crumb over anymore. Another mark in the 'no longer dreaming' column is my oversized T-shirt. I generally don't sleep naked—unless Hunter's here. I would do it more often for comfort but... I have siblings and a mother who walk in with little to no warning.

Although it hasn't been that long since I've been beholden to a schedule, realizing that I have a class at 7 p.m. makes me groan. Summer vacation's officially over. Hi. I'm a college student now. Ashley's right. I guess I do kinda qualify as a nerd, if a lazy one. I channeled my powers to coast through school with decent grades and minimum effort. Sure, I probably could've worked my ass off, taken AP courses, maybe even made it to college a year or two early. But... I was so not into that level of punishment. I liked my free time and having fun way too much.

And it's kinda dark of me to say this, but I'm glad I did. If I wasted the last four years of my life having no fun at all while working like hell for something I could never have now—a career—I'd be really pissed off. I had a social life, such as it was, and a lot of good memories. But, to Ashley's point, I can handle the programming track if I really want to. Computer stuff has never really grabbed me the way it did Dad or Sierra... but I can make it work. Truth be told, *nothing* really clicked with me. I'm jealous to a point of my friends, even my siblings. Ash always knew she wanted to do something like be a veterinarian. Michelle's been talking about law school ever since we met. Sophia's got dreams of doing makeup and stuff for Hollywood someday. Granted, she's ten, so who knows if that will change. Sierra wants to do something with video game development or computers. It's good and it's sad in a way. Ten- and eleven-year-olds shouldn't be thinking about their careers. At least my brother Sam acts like a normal kid. If he's got plans for what he wants to do as an adult, he's kept them to himself.

So yeah, we got the nerd gene from Dad. Along with the noodle gene. To be fair, Mom helped with that one, too. Her entire family is skinny. All three of my siblings have spaghetti strands for arms and legs. Surprisingly, Sophia's got the most defined muscles of any of us since she's totally into her dance class. I started to have a shape before I died. Undeath has taken away a few pounds, probably from internal organs or muscles shrinking or some such thing like that. Or maybe that's just the Innocent thing trying to make me childish. I asked Aurélie if she thought that might be the case. She laughed at first, but then found herself wondering, too. She told me Innocents are pretty damn rare, so no one really understands them. Almost every vampire she knows of wanted to be one. The youthful thing might be a defense mechanism. Her joke about how children are cute so their parents don't kill them out of frustration rang a bit too dark for me, but if looking cute and harmless prevents some Fury from tearing my head off for saying the wrong thing, I'll deal with it.

I check the iPhone for weather and determine it's cloudy-overcast today. Cool. After pulling my door open an inch to test light levels, I relax and head upstairs for a shower. The place is eerily quiet. Oh, it's so bizarre. All three of the littles are away at school. Mom's at work, and Dad—if he's home—is sequestered in his office working. He's unusually silent, so I change course from heading to the stairs to his study.

He's at the computer, reading from a book thick enough to qualify as a deadly weapon. Aha. That explains the lack of clicking. Not wanting to disturb him, I back away and go to the upstairs bathroom. The beach dream was so vivid, I feel like I've got sand all over me. It's nice not to have to battle for bathroom time, and actually enjoy a somewhat-too-long shower. Before I can even turn the water on, an explosion of tween voices goes off downstairs. I click the lock to avoid unwanted interruptions.

You know what else is cool? Not having to shave my legs.

My hair and nails only grow if I concentrate on wanting them to. Guess what I *don't* want. Of course, I haven't told Sophia that. She'd go nuts messing with my hair since I could grow it all back from a totally shaved head in about two minutes. Her using me as a cosmetics crash test dummy is fine. I'm *not* dealing with Edwina Scissorhands.

Sam shouts to Dad that he's going to Daryl's house. Giggling comes from Sophia's room across the hall from me, and the house experiences a mild catastrophic earthquake from the PlayStation in the living room.

Eventually, I drag myself out of the shower, wrap my hair in one towel, my body in another, and slip out into the hall. Two other girls are in Sophia's room, chattering away. I leave them be and head downstairs. Sierra's sitting on the floor in the living room next to her friend Nicole. Neither of them look up as I go by in my towel toga. I scurry to my cave in the basement, drop the towels, and throw on a long T-shirt until my hair finishes drying. While I wait, I flop at my desk and look over the school stuff for the thousandth time.

The more I study the maps, schedules, and student guide, the more I start to freak out. For no particular reason, I'm anxious about being late or getting lost. There's no detention anymore for missing class, just bad grades, failure, and the potential of wasting money. I already feel like I'm making my parents light dollar bills on fire sending me to school, but at least the local college is quite a bit cheaper than USC. Part of me still feels guilty about being accepted there and withdrawing. But, it really isn't like I chickened out or had a crisis of confidence... okay, maybe I did chicken out. I probably *could* have made USC work with late classes. But California sun and vampires really don't sound like a good combination. At least here, it's rainy enough that I can sometimes go outside during the day without too much pain.

I'm sticking with my 'health issues' excuse.

Anyway, my schedule isn't that bad. Classes five days a week. I'm not exactly killing myself credits wise. What's the rush, right? If I have anything, it's time... and I can't take classes too early in the day for obvious reasons. Monday's English Lit from 7 p.m. to 8:45 p.m. Tuesday is Intro Bio, same hours. On Wednesday, I have two classes: Comp Sci 101 from six to seven, and Intro to Calculus from eight to nine. Thursday is Philosophy/Sociology from eight to nine, and Friday is a repeat of Wednesday.

Wednesday and Friday are the riskiest days, since toward the end of the school year, I might run into sun problems on the way to school for a class starting at six. Still can now, but in another month or two once the clocks go back an hour, it'll be dark before I even leave the house. That will let me fly there, which drastically cuts my commute time from about a half hour to five-ish minutes. As far as driving in goes, there's a parking deck across the street from the school. Even on nights when I can fly in, it'll make for a good place to land.

I get up and fluff out my hair a bit with my hands to check for dampness. Satisfied it's dry enough, I change. Not looking to impress anyone, so it's a Nike T-shirt, jeans, and sneakers. Though, the sneakers can wait. I still have a little while left before I have to leave.

A few months ago, I killed an enormous troll with a giant iron spear. Why is the first day of school freaking me out?

Nah. That troll thing didn't really happen. We inhaled something funny deep in the cave, passed out, and hallucinated all of it. Yep. Ben and Cody Peters and I all had the same dream at the same time and nothing that bizarre really occurred.

I spend a few minutes staring at the pile of books I bought a couple days ago, especially the calculus one. Forget Kevlar… they should ship these bad boys over to wherever the heck they're fighting now and use them for armor. Cripes, this thing is like 500 pages. How do people without vampiric strength even cope with this? And whoa. College. No lockers in the hall. Wait, stop panicking. Only one (or two) classes a day. I don't need *all* the books with me *all* the time.

It's a little after four, so I've got three hours until my first class starts. Since I haven't quite worked out teleportation, I need to factor in travel time. First-day jitters plus not knowing how bad traffic is going to be now make me think I should head out the door around six. Allocating a full hour for a trip that ought to be around half that should be okay.

Were I alive, I'd head upstairs to eat something. I still could eat, but nah. No sense taking food away from the littles. It's one thing sitting down with everyone for dinner. For me, that's less about eating and all about spending time with them. Alas, given my class schedule, I'm not going to be attending too many dinners. The parents usually had food on the table around six… and that's when I have to leave. Though, there's still Thursday. That class doesn't start until eight, so I will be home for dinner. Tonight, I'll have to run out the door right as everyone's sitting down.

Sigh.

I've looked over these maps as much as I can. Gonna spend some time with the sibs before I leave. Ashley, Michelle, and Hunter are all working anyway. Not that we'd really be able to do *that* much in two hours. The littles have adjusted to the new normal of my not being dead. We haven't gone back to the old arrangement of me mostly ignoring them, Sophia being super clingy, Sierra being moody, and Sam being... well, Sam. The near miss with almost losing me *has* made permanent changes in our family dynamic. However, they've all dealt with what happened enough that normal has returned. Sophia's got friends over and is hanging in her room. Sam's off at his friend's place, and Sierra's invited Nicole over.

Okay, since they're spread out, I activate my powers of time budgeting. I pop in to check on Sophia and her two friends. Megan, the slightly chubby girl from her dance class and Priya, one of her school buddies, are sprawled on the rug, talking about stuff that happened at school. I don't quite remember where Priya lives, but I know it's far enough that someone will need to drive her home. She probably got off the bus at Sophia's stop.

"Hey." I lean in.

The girls all wave at me.

"What's up?" asks Sophia.

"Nothing specific. Starting school tonight, so I wanted to see you before I left. You'll probably be in bed by the time I get home."

Sophia peers up at me with this mixture of guilt and annoyance. I don't even need powers of mind reading to know she's realized we have limited time and her usual clinginess has started a fistfight with her want to hang with friends her age.

I slip into the room and sit on the bed. "Can't stay too long... but how'd it go?"

She leans against my leg. "It was okay. Didn't really do much today."

"Yeah." Priya scissors her feet back and forth while fiddling at her phone. "Kinda boring really. I heard Mrs. Pearson gives a lot of homework."

Both Sophia and Megan groan.

We chat for a little while before I start feeling like a fifth wheel and slip out. Sierra and Nicole are beating the crap out of each other virtually while discussing something that's either an upcoming video game or an anime movie they can't wait to see.

"Hey, Sare," says Sierra, by way of greeting.

"Oh, hi." Nicole's character grabs onto Sierra's character. She takes the few-seconds-long break from playing to twist around and wave at me.

Sierra growls. "I hate grapples!"

"So block them." Nicole twists, giggling as her character suffers a vicious mauling.

That explains why this girl is Sierra's bestie: being pummeled in a video game makes her laugh. Two kids who both became furious at losing wouldn't be a good match. While I don't think Nicole *lets* Sierra win, she doesn't care at all when she loses.

I sit on the couch to watch a few matches. Sierra's not big on public shows of affection—especially in front of her friends—but she repositions herself from sitting on the floor to the couch and leaning against me.

For her, that's clingy.

My 'is everything okay?' glance receives a nod and a smile back before her game face returns. She's being affectionate like a cat that hates being picked up but will sit next to you for hours. I soon learn that *Kuroi Tsuki* is an upcoming game with anime style art. Something mixing cyberpunk with ghosts. Sounds creepy and pretty cool. Might be a bit intense for an eleven-year-old, but sitting here, talking with these two, it's pretty easy to forget how young they are.

I say this like I'm an old maid at eighteen.

Really though, talking to Sierra… what kid her age considers character arcs and branching story paths and depth of narrative? Around 5:30 or so, a pallid ghostly form drifts silently down the corridor toward the kitchen. For an instant, I'm like *ugh, a ghost? What now…* then I realize it's just Dad.

"Ack. I need to get ready to head out," I say.

"Okay." Sierra un-leans from me, then gives me a playful punch to the shoulder. "Good luck on day one."

"Thanks." I pat her on the head—earning a small snarl—and head into the kitchen where Dad's staring into the fridge like Indiana Jones opening the Ark. "That bad?"

"Huh?" He peers over his shoulder at me.

"You look like you're expecting last Thursday's meatloaf to melt your face off."

Dad laughs. "I have averted my eyes from the Meatloaf of the Covenant."

"So…"

"Ehh, just trying to figure out what to get started for dinner. Your mother's going to run late again tonight." He glances down. "Forgetting something?"

I lift and lower my toes. "Still in the house. It's probably going to take more than one day of college to turn me into a hippie."

"Still a bit light out for you to fly. Remember, you can take the Sentra whenever you need it for school purposes."

"Thanks, Dad." I hug him. "I'd offer to help cook, but I gotta hit the road in like twenty minutes. Ugh, this makes no sense."

"What makes no sense?"

"How nervous I am. Everything that happened to me this summer, and I'm anxious about going to school. I'm not even out of state."

He closes the fridge and pats me on the shoulders. "You'll do fine, hon. Maybe after all this new stuff you've been exposed to, you're worried it'll be too mundane and boring there."

That gets a laugh out of me. "Maybe. It's my fault for never really thinking about what I wanted to do with my life… before I lost it. I picked this major more or less at random since it sounded reasonably fun and possible to work from home."

Dad grins. "New programmers don't usually get the chance to work from home. This is like my sixth different company since I hit the workforce, and it's a pretty sweet deal. Though, I imagine with your special talents, it wouldn't take much for you to convince a hiring manager to let you work from home right out of the gate."

"Wouldn't that be like unethical or something?" I ask.

"Altering the parameters of a job to sidestep what's basically a health condition you can't really talk about doesn't feel icky." He winks. "Now, compelling the guy to hire you in the first place, inflating your salary, stuff like that is another matter."

"Right... Okay. Gonna get going."

"You'll do great, hon." He kisses me atop the head.

Here's hoping.

3

DISAPPEAR

I t's a little bright yet, even at a couple minutes to six.

Nothing a hoodie, sunglasses, and gloves won't make bearable. I feel a bit like a basket of those rolls at the steak place they leave sitting under heat lamps, but the sun isn't making me squint too much that I feel unsafe to drive. I used to be happiest driving in bright, clear weather while dreading being on the road at night. Dying has flipped me to the reverse.

The ride into Seattle isn't bad, but I still find it frustrating to be moving so slow. No one gets a Nissan Sentra up to 140-ish MPH without fire winding up where it doesn't belong and serious bodily injury. Alas, until the sun is down, any comparisons to flying are kinda like using words greater than four syllables with Scott—completely pointless.

And, dammit. I really need to stop thinking about him.

I'm clearly not pining for him at all. Either his killing me has permanently burned him into my psyche, or I'm just that pissed. Being pissed off is a reasonable reaction, I think, for a girl to have toward the jackass who murdered her.

Eventually, I'm downtown on Harvard Ave. I swing a left into the parking garage and drive around for a little while until I find a space.

In another lifetime, the idea of walking alone from the school to this parking garage after dark would've terrified me. Maybe 'terrified' is a little strong, but I would've been on edge. As big cities go, Seattle's fairly nice… especially compared to some areas on the East Coast. No point worrying about it. Had I not wound up as a vampire, I wouldn't be attending night classes.

I sling my backpack over one shoulder, grab the map pamphlet, and head out of the parking deck. Left turn at the corner, half a block down, I head into the school building and try to figure out where I'm going. While I do see a couple other people my age, the majority are older. A few give me weird looks, but no one says anything. Of course, receiving weird looks makes me stop to make sure I didn't forget something trivial—like pants.

Nope. I'm not re-enacting my dream. Pants are intact.

Hmm. Guess I'm getting curious glances because I look too young to be in here. Do they all think I'm fifteen?

Sigh.

Or I look like a total dork walking around with a map in my hand. Yeah, that's probably it.

After five minutes of racing back and forth down the same hallway, convinced it's an exact match for the map, I realize I'm not seeing the right room because I'm on the wrong floor. One quick stairwell later, I find the number I'm hunting for on a wall plate and head into the classroom I'm supposed to be in for English Literature I. It's surprisingly austere, with minimal decoration that offers no clue what subject happens here. Though, I guess college-level English teachers don't hang the alphabet up on the wall, but geez, at least put up a Shakespeare poster or something so it doesn't feel like a prison.

This room is probably shared among multiple teachers and subjects. Bookshelves and whiteboards cover every inch of wall where there isn't a door or window. A square panel in the ceiling appears to be the hiding place for an overhead projector presently retracted out of sight.

Only two other people are in here at the moment, a woman in her early forties and a guy all the way near the back corner that looks like the delinquent from *Breakfast Club* after ten years at a soul-crushing retail job. Class starts at 7 p.m., and it's only 6:49. I pick a seat near the middle of the room, closer to the back by one row. No idea how different this is from high school, but I don't want to seem like a kiss-ass by sitting in the front, or like I'm uninterested by going all the way to the back. I don't exactly have any trouble seeing the board. Heck, once the sun is down, I could read the whiteboard from down the street.

I fidget with the textbook, which—like an absolute dork—I've placed dead center on my desk. The class came with a reading list for novels that we'll be using. Hopefully, the teacher's going to be okay with Kindle copies. Much easier to lug around, though I doubt we'll do any actual reading of the novels during class time.

More people file in as the clock nears seven. It doesn't take long before I feel like the youngest person in the room. One woman's gotta be in her sixties. Another guy looks like a stunt double for ZZ Top. They're all adults. I get a few more curious glances, but distract myself by fidgeting at the textbook, not paying attention to any of the motion around me. Random colognes, perfumes, and one waft of cigarette smoke go by. Not fresh, just the ghastly stink that clings to someone's clothing after they've smoked recently.

An odd floral fragrance catches me by surprise, more like someone's got a bouquet of flowers than is wearing perfume. I look up and around, hunting for the source. Three people closer to my age have joined the class, one of them the evident owner of said perfume. She's maybe a year or two older than me, sitting two rows to my right and one desk forward.

This girl is wearing an elaborate dress with black-on-black embroidery, puffy shoulders, a frilled collar and sleeves, and a long skirt. Her hair, light brown and quite long, doesn't really go with the look she's aiming for. I mean, I figure she's trying to do some kind of sparkle goth thing since she's hit the white face paint kinda hard. Even put it on her hands. Or… maybe she *is* that pale.

The woman catches me staring at her and returns this coy smile, like she's wearing that outfit on purpose to make people look at her. I return a 'hey, what's up' sort of nod.

A man in a long coat breezes in the door, his afro already fully grey despite him not seeming all that old. Figure the guy's around fifty and is probably the teacher. Or duh, this is college. They don't call them 'teachers' here.

"Hello everyone." The man sets a briefcase on the desk at the front of the room. "I'm Professor Robin Kendall, and welcome to Introduction to English Literature."

I start to find myself tuning out of his introductory spiel, but this isn't high school. Maybe I should, like, focus here. Of course, it's not as if I'm really going to *use* this degree. 'Sarah Wright' is going to disappear in fifty years or so. Can't exactly run around with a driver's license that says I was born in 1999 in like 2050 or so when I still look the same. By then, I'll have to get a fake ID... or maybe I'll reach a point I just stop caring and mentally influence my way past any situation where a normal person who appears to be a teenager would need an ID card.

While Professor Kendall hands a sign-in sheet to the kid in the front left desk, I glance again at the woman in the super-frilly dress. Kinda weird that she's not getting any strange looks. But, she's a little older than me, so maybe she's on her second or third year and people are used to her?

Meh. This class is about literature, right? Maybe she's just *really* into like, *Great Gatsby* or whatever. I've got more to worry about than some weird girl in a period dress. I'm going to school during the time slot where my friends—and boyfriend—are most likely to be not in school or at work. Except for Hunter. He works later at the restaurant. I doubt any of them would be up for doing much once I'm home after class since they've all got to wake up early.

Great. I'm in for a lonely nine-ish months.

Might as well focus on school. If nothing else, it'll fill up time.

And, time is something I have buckets of.

4

JOB SECURITY

Dracula gives me an idea.

I fly up to Hunter's window around ten, only I'm not there to bite him on the neck. Well, not unless he asks me to—and not with fangs. I hang outside the house, tapping on the glass until his face appears behind the reflection of the moon, peering out at me with a bewildered expression.

My attempt at an alluring smile makes him drop something that hits the floor with a heavy *thump*.

He pulls the window up, but there's still a screen in my way. "What are you doing?"

"I've come to drink your blood," I say in my best attempt at a Transylvanian accent... which isn't all that good. Okay, it's awful.

Hunter coughs. For an instant, he seems to think I'm serious, then cracks up laughing.

Bang!

I twitch and scream in surprise. When the shock of such a loud noise in near total silence wears off, I rotate a quarter turn to my right and spot a car plowed headfirst into a van that had been parked in front of Hunter's house. Not even any screech of tires.

"Who hit what?" whisper-yells Hunter.

"Why are you whispering? And some dude crashed into a van across the street."

"Because, Ronan's asleep. So's my Mom."

"Hang on. Gonna go check on them."

I drop straight down onto my feet, then dash over the lawn, past the old boat on the trailer, and over to a blue Cadillac. The airbag's gone off, but the middle-aged balding guy behind the wheel doesn't appear hurt. As soon as he sees me coming, he stares at me like I've got three heads.

Okay, that's unusual, and worth a peek into his thoughts. Oh, crap. He glanced over and saw me floating outside Hunter's window. And, staring at me, veered out of the lane and hit the parked van. I've never considered myself pretty enough to cause traffic accidents, but I suppose flying works better than a bikini.

Crap.

"Are you okay?" I ask, after pulling his door open—and doing a little memory surgery. He swerved to avoid a dog. Didn't see the van in the dark.

"Son of bitch," mutters the guy. "Yeah, I think I'm okay."

"Sounded like a pretty loud hit, are you sure?"

The man gets out of the Caddy and wanders over to look at the front end. It's not *too* bad. He couldn't have been going much faster than thirty or so on this road. Still, the fairly new Cadillac's plastic front end is going to need work. The van, however, is on the older side and laughed it off.

Lights flick on, illuminating the porch of the house that the van likely belongs to. A man in his earlier forties emerges, hastily pulling a sweatshirt on over a tank top. He runs over, eyeing the damage while a woman hovers in the doorway on the phone. The instant I look at her, my ears hone in on her talking to the police to report the crash.

Okay, this is handled. I should extricate myself from this before the cops show up.

"What the hell, man?" asks the homeowner. "You drunk or something?"

Caddy Man gestures at the road. "Damn dog ran out in front of me. Swerved. Didn't see the van."

Sweatshirt Guy looks at me.

"Just visiting my boyfriend across the street. Heard the crash. Ran over to see if the guy was okay."

Homeowner nods at me, then looks at the damage. Seeing his van largely unscathed except for a dent or two in the bumper, he calms down. "Wife's already on the phone with the cops. May as well do the paperwork."

"Dammit. I've only had this thing for three months." Caddy Man sighs.

"It ain't that bad. Insurance'll cover it. Mostly plastic bits these days." The homeowner pokes at a crumpled bit of the car's front end. "Nasty part will be replacing the airbag."

I back up unnoticed, and make my way to Hunter's. He's on the porch waiting for me.

"Well, so much for being smooth."

He raises an eyebrow. "How do you mean?"

I stuff my hands in my hoodie's front pocket and walk in. "Dude saw me floating there. Oops."

"Is he hurt?"

"No. Just his car."

"Hey, you didn't make him stare at you."

An almost smile manages to form on my face. "So... am I interrupting anything?"

"Just reading. Gotta slog through a hundred pages of *Paradise Lost*. You?"

I laugh. "You've got English Lit today, too?"

"Yeah, and history... and an Intro to Psych class."

"Holy crap. That's a lot."

He shrugs. "Nothing I can't handle. You get a lot of work?"

"Nah. Kendall wants us to read a bunch of Poe and write up a few paragraphs about our thoughts on how his style and stuff changed from the early works to the later ones. I, umm, only had the one class today."

We head up to his room, discussing our varying schedules. I can tell he's got a pile of work to get done before he goes to sleep, not having a lot of time after returning from his job waiting tables. As much as I want to spend some time with him, I don't want to screw with his life. If he fails a class, it's a lot worse than me, and not only due to the immortality thing. He's barely managing to afford it.

Hunter protests me saying I should get going so he can finish what he needs to, but I insist, hug him, and head out. A cop is still there talking to the two guys across the street, so I slip around to the back yard for takeoff.

Tonight's going to be boring and lonely.

Well, there's always Poe. Might as well get that done with.

I awake to a wonderfully gloomy day Tuesday.

Ugh. I suppose since I just referred to a rainy, overcast day as 'wonderful,' this whole being dead thing is turning me into an older version of Wednesday Addams. At least to a point. I mean, I'm not having homicidal thoughts toward my little brother. Rainy days always did soothe me anyway, so it's not like I'm *totally* missing out on beautiful weather. Ashley and I never were much for hitting the beach, though we did spend a reasonable amount of time doing 'outdoorsy' stuff... usually hiking in the woods. This one time when we were twelve, we got lost and both panicked thinking we'd never get home and die of starvation. In truth, we'd spent hours going in circles only like a hundred yards from the edge of the woods.

One thing about staying up until sunrise every night: being awake when everyone else is asleep makes it easy to avoid procrastination on homework. So, before crashing, I read a bunch of stuff and scribbled out a couple of paragraphs on how I think his style evolved from *Tamerlane* to *Annabel Lee*. I'm not exactly a massive book geek—nowhere near Mom or Sophia—but hopefully, I've come up with an essay that doesn't sound *too* much like guessing in the dark.

A brief round of text messages tells me Ashley and Michelle are both in class—they don't reply—and Hunter's walking between classes. We chat about randomness for a little while until the start of his next period.

By that time, the littles are home, so I head upstairs. Prior to my rather, umm, *pointed* breakup with Scott, a rainy day like this with everyone trapped inside would usually devolve into a shouting match by five or six. Hopefully, I'll have a little time to spend with them before someone's too pissed off to speak.

The area by the front door, Mom's demilitarized zone for shoes, is soaked. Puddles of muddy water are all over the small patch of linoleum, but by some miracle, nothing hit the rug. Judging by the wet pink socks also draped over the shoe shelf, it's either raining *really* bad out there or someone had an unfortunate encounter with a puddle.

Sierra comes down the stairs in black and red pajamas and fuzzy socks. Since she's usually too lazy to completely change clothes right after school, I'm going to assume everyone got drenched. If the look on her face is any indication, her fuse has been trimmed short. My guess is either she wanted to hang out with Nicole today and can't because of the rain, or she's the one who fell into a giant puddle.

"Hey." She plods past me, heading for the PlayStation in the living room, but stops short and spins around. "You got school tonight?"

"Yep." I hook my thumbs in the waistband of my sweat pants.

"What time?"

"Class stats at seven. Probably gonna leave here at six."

She makes a series of faces like she's doing math or is about to break wind. The aggression leaves her posture and she peers up at me with an almost sheepish expression. "You wanna maybe play a board game or something?"

I put a hand on her forehead. She must be feverish if she's actively choosing to do something not involving a video game.

Sierra raspberries me.

"Yeah, sure. Which one?"

She heads back to the stairs. "You pick one. Be right back." With that, she runs up to the second floor.

Hmm. That's odd. Only three things usually get between Sierra and video games: school, being grounded, and sleep—though the third one isn't an absolute. Mom's caught her a few times sneaking back downstairs when she should be in bed. Her being the one to suggest doing 'not video games' almost worries me.

I head over to the dining room and grab this 'adventure horror' type board game, *Stillwater Hollow*, where the players all pick different characters to explore a creepy town where weird stuff happens. It's kinda story driven, with an iPad app controlling the 'forces of evil,' so all the players wind up being cooperative. Dad said it's kinda like C'thulu mythos, only a bit tamer for a younger audience.

Sophia runs downstairs. She's barefoot in a plain pink dress, her hair soaked. "Hey, Sare. Can we have cocoa?" At the sight of the game box on the table, she pauses. "Ooh. This one's scary."

"Seems like a good day for it." I smile. "Not in the mood for scary?"

She shrugs and hops in a chair. "It's okay."

Sam, still wearing his wet T-shirt and jeans, rumbles down the stairs louder than Dad. I still can't understand how a nine-year-old boy makes so much damn noise. He's a twig like the rest of us, yet he sounds like Ashley's steamer trunk being dropped down the steps.

"You gotta change," says Sierra from behind him. "You'll get sick if you keep wearing wet stuff."

"Is it really raining that hard?" I ask, peering back over my shoulder on my way into the kitchen.

"No. Some butthead splashed us with his car," mutters Sierra.

"That was awesome." Sam jumps, thrusting his hands up.

"It was not 'awesome.'" Sophia shakes her head. "It knocked me and Sierra over. And some of my school stuff got wet."

I pause in the kitchen doorway. "Wait, what?"

Sierra scowls. "We were walking down the street from the bus stop, and this shithead in a hot rod swerved close to the side of the road. His car hit a puddle and threw up a wave that knocked me on my ass."

"Hey, easy on the language. Dad's home," I whisper.

"And his ears aren't gone yet," calls Dad from his office.

Sierra's cheeks pale with an 'oh crap' face.

"It was pretty funny." Sam peels his shirt off and runs upstairs. "Be right back."

"Not funny. We got *soaked!*" Sophia gags. "And I got muddy water in my mouth."

"Who was it?" I ask.

Sierra shrugs. "No idea. But if I see that car again, I'm gonna let the air out of the tires."

I raise an eyebrow. "What's it look like?"

"Some idiot your age. Car's white. Kinda old. Big tires, and one of those silver things on the hood. Why? You gonna go bite him?" Sierra grins.

Sophia covers her mouth to hold in laughter.

"Maybe." I wink, and head into the kitchen to fill the kettle.

A little while later, the four of us all have hot cocoa and we're trying to figure out what sort of monster is leaving puddles of slime around the 'sleepy little town' of Stillwater Hollow. Dad runs over to join us. The game isn't too scary until real life thunder rolls overhead like a giant boulder.

"Maybe you should stay home tonight?" Sophia smiles at me.

"Will lightning kill you?" asks Sam in a tone as casual as if he wanted to know my favorite color.

"No, it'll piss her off." Sierra rolls two dice for her move.

I cringe. "Umm. Not exactly sure, but I'm not in any hurry to find out."

"So, despite it being dark, I take it you'll not be flying in tonight?" Dad hands Sierra a map tile when she goes through an unexplored door.

"Nope. Not unless I stuff my clothes in a watertight bag and fly in a bathing suit."

Dad nods. "It's supposed to stop around six."

Sierra pokes the iPad screen, and a squid-faced monster pops up with a sudden, loud crash of dramatic music—too well timed with a peal of actual thunder.

Predictably, Sophia screams. Despite expecting it, I still jump. Dad nearly chokes on his cocoa.

Sierra goes wide-eyed and freezes stock still, staring at Sophia. Sam laughs.

My siblings have three distinct reactions to fear. Sierra freezes like a deer in the headlights, then—if whatever it was *really* scared her—she gets pissed off at it. Sophia screams. If something genuinely got her bad, she'll burst into tears when the screaming stops. Sam gets the giggles for quick jumps, but if he's genuinely frightened, he'll stop talking for a while and usually want to be alone. His laughter sounds genuine, so neither the monster on the screen nor the thunder bothered him at all.

"It's not that scary," mutters Sierra.

Sophia looks around. "I know. The thunder's just loud."

The game ends about twenty after four. Sophia spends a little less than half of it sitting in a ball on the chair half hiding her face behind her knees. We barely manage to beat the tentacle-faced monster. Sam and Sierra's characters are the only two to survive.

With the little town once again safe, we put the game away. Dad heads back to his office to keep working. I wind up on the sofa with Sierra on one side playing *Call of Duty*, Sophia on my other side reading on her Kindle, and Sam sitting on the floor in front of me waiting his turn at the controller. They are remarkably organized and civil. Once the first match ends, Sierra hands the controller to Sam without protest.

Now I'm starting to feel guilty. Like, my death totally changed my siblings. Being housebound on a crappy day would normally have resulted in a lot of screaming and two out of three grounded by now. Sierra often wound up on punishment first, Sam second—for making a wiseass comment. Sophia rarely gets in trouble. The few times she *has* been punished, Sierra hit her with nasty verbal barbs that hurt so much she snapped back in kind. Most of the time, she'll just start crying and run to her room.

So yeah. Shit's changed. I'm *not* in California having a nervous breakdown from homesickness and my siblings are like close or something. I'm still not completely convinced there won't be arguments, but that look Sierra gave me right before she suggested we play a board game said quite a bit. I practically saw her think 'I could snap and start a fight, but Sarah almost died...' then she probably thought about losing Sophia or Sam, too. And, yeah. She's not a cryer. When Sierra's sad, she gets clingy... and clingy for her is playing board games instead of video games, or sitting next to me on the couch instead of sitting on the floor. Sophia, she takes clingy quite literally. Seriously, I think Mom cheated on Dad with a block of Velcro the way that girl sticks to me sometimes.

Speaking of Mom, she walks in the door about ten after five and stands there staring down at the dirty floor. All four of us brace for it, but our mother doesn't bark at anyone. She wordlessly steps out of her sneakers—the heels live at the office—and steps onto the carpet. The woman looks so exhausted that for a second, I half expect her to simply fall forward and land on her face.

"Umm... sorry." It's dark enough out that I'm online already... so I fly straight up off the couch and land in front of her. "I'll get the floor. Some idiot splashed the littles on their way back from the bus stop."

Mom nods.

"Okay, what's wrong?" I walk up to her. "You don't look right."

"It's nothing... I hope." Mom bites her lip. "Rough day at work is all. Stress."

"'Kay." I zip to the kitchen to grab a sponge and a bucket.

"You've got school soon, hon." Dad walks in behind me. "I can get the floor."

I stand and lean close, whispering, "You should cook tonight. Mom's done. Besides. I'll be finished with the floor before you could even walk out there."

As fast as I can move, I run across a living room that appears frozen in time and mop up the dried dirty puddles. I'm back in the kitchen dumping the filthy water out before Dad even has all the stuff out of the fridge for dinner.

"Gah!" yells Dad, startled by my sudden appearance beside him. "Wow, that was fast."

"I could've gone a little faster, but I didn't want to spill the bucket. Okay. Time to get ready for school."

After a hug, I head downstairs to change. No real need to shower again since, while I still sweat, it's mostly for appearance. My metabolic processes aren't exactly normal. Takes me a couple days before even *my* nose can pick up any stink. Vampires like Glim, shadows, with *zero* attempt to appear alive, never bathe, or at least have no natural body odor.

I do the T-shirt and jeans thing again, then head upstairs to make the rounds of 'bye for now' hugs. Mom's not in sight, so I head up to the parents' room… and catch her crying.

Shit.

"Mom?" I ask, barely over a whisper.

She jumps and looks at me like I'd walked in on her doing something *way* more embarrassing than having a simple emotional breakdown. I ease the door closed behind me.

"Something you wanna talk about?"

Mom chuckles. "Welcome to opposite world. Shouldn't I be the one finding my teenage daughter upset over something and trying to get her to open up about it?"

"Well, there's my ex-boyfriend… I was dying to dump him for a while."

She blinks.

"Too soon?" I ask.

She blinks again.

"I'll take that as a yes. Sorry." I wander over and sit next to her. "So, what's wrong?"

"Honestly?" She chuckles. "It's my overactive worry engine running away with itself. Could be nothing at all."

"I've seen you cry three times in my entire life."

A humorless laugh comes out of her. "I'm just good at hiding it. Aren't you late for school?"

"No. I'm leaving plenty early. If it's important and you want to talk, I could skip the car and it'd only take me five minutes to get there. That would give me over an hour before I had to leave."

Mom takes and squeezes my hand. "It's not that bad. I've just gotten myself worked up over the outside chance I might be laid off."

"What?" I gawk. "Laid off? Are you serious? You're like the best lawyer on their team. How could they lay *you* off. What about that obnoxious guy with the super fake hair?"

She glances sideways at me. "That doesn't exactly narrow it down."

"The guy who hit on me at the last Christmas party because he had too much champagne and didn't realize I was seventeen?"

"Oh. Chad."

I laugh.

"What's funny about that?"

"There are some names that just work for the people who have them. Like the douchebag character in Dad's Eighties college movies is always named Chad, Kent, or something like that."

Mom laughs, then sighs. "There are rumors going around the office. Some defense contract for a next generation fighter craft has gone from definite to maybe-not-going-through. Boeing sank so much cash into the prototype to show off to the DOD, there are fears of cutbacks if we don't get the contract. I'm only worried because Fowler is fond of people who kiss his ass, and I can't do that. He gave me that look today like he's got a nasty surprise waiting for me. If he gets told to reduce staff, I'm probably first on his list because I don't take his shit, and after eight years of refusing to kiss his ass, I don't think any natural force on this Earth would change his mind."

Whoa. Did my mother just drop a not-too-subtle hint?

"Who's Fowler again?" I ask, peeking at her thoughts. And whoa—yeah. She *does* kinda hope I do something, but can't bring herself to 'break the ethical wall' of coming out and asking me directly.

"My boss. Cristian Fowler. He's the director of legal." She finally opens her coat buttons—or at least tries to. Her hands are shaking. "Except for his desire to have people constantly suck up to him, he's not that bad."

And, color me freaked out. Mom read me the riot act for using my powers of mental influence to encourage people to buy a box of Girl Scout cookies. That she's even contemplating asking me to fiddle with her boss' head is totally epic. In a bad way, I mean. She must really be scared of losing her job.

"Don't worry, Mom. I'm sure they'll get the contract. And Fowler would be a moron to get rid of his best lawyer."

She sputters at me, waving. "Please. I'm nowhere near their best."

I grab her in a hug. "Of course you are. You're my mom."

Mom gives me an 'oh shit what have I done' look. "I love you, too, sweetie."

Playing innocent, I stand. "Okay. Suppose I should get going. Got class in an hour."

"Drive safe… or fly safe. Whatever you wind up doing." She looks me over. "Did you eat yet?"

"Nah, I'll grab someone at school."

She just stares at me, unsure if she should laugh.

"Bye, Mom. See you later."

And speaking of grabbing, I nab a box of Thin Mints on my way out the door.

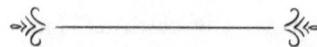

Tonight is Introduction to Biology with Professor Clark Connolly.

I don't know what the hell is wrong with my brain, but I went in there expecting a mountain of sexiness. Like Clark Kent crashed into Sean Connery. Alas, the guy looks more like the slightly-over-the-hill alcoholic police captain from a primetime cop drama. He's fiftyish, hair brown on top, grey over the ears, and has this quiet, unassuming demeanor that makes me think he'd just keep right on lecturing in the middle of an earthquake.

Once again, I feel like I'm at 'take your daughter to work day' more than in school. I'm the youngest person in the room, and the weird girl with the frilly goth dress is nowhere to be seen. The other students around me are all in their thirties, more than half still wearing various polo shirts or uniforms from their day jobs.

Depressing thoughts about my being denied the 'normal college experience' don't get a chance to take hold since Professor Connolly launches straight into it. No 'hey let's get used to each other since it's the first class period of the semester' for this guy. But at least science is interesting.

It keeps my mind occupied until first break. The class is an hour and forty-five minutes long, with two ten-minute breaks. On the first break, I follow a group of three to the ladies' room. The straggler, in her late-twenties and either Chinese or Korean, is absorbed enough with her smartphone that the other two go into stalls before her. Since there's no one watching, I barge right in behind her.

She jumps back, but before shock becomes anger, I overwhelm her mind, forcing her to stand there in a daze. To avoid any unwanted rumors, I float off the ground and keep my feet tucked up so anyone going by outside will only see one pair of legs in here.

I brush her hair off her neck and sink my fangs in, emitting a startled moan of surprise at the flavor of mocha coffee. Must be her 'Starbucks-green' shirt that implanted the idea. Either way, dangerously yummy. Gotta be careful. Usually, when people run into something like an alcoholic drink that tastes too good to realize how powerful it is, they wind up passed out. If I lose myself having a flavor-gasm, I could kill someone.

Careful only to take what I need, I back off once I'm full, then stare into her eyes to make her forget seeing me in the bathroom. The near-deafening clicking of fingernails on smartphone screens from two other stalls tells me exactly where the other women are. The space adjacent on the right is empty, so I float up and over the partition, flush, then walk out like I'd used that toilet.

The woman I fed from starts to leave her stall, then stops, realizing she hadn't done what she came in here to do yet, and ducks back in.

Well, I don't smoke, don't need a snack from a vending machine, and don't have any friends to hang out with here... so I head back to the classroom to spend the last four minutes of the break period sitting at my desk like a nerd.

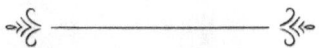

PROFESSOR CONNOLLY IS A NICE GUY.

Dreadfully boring and a complete failure at public speaking, but a nice guy.

I had an English teacher once, Mr. Martin. Same guy who I saw working in the mall at a clothing store that totally shattered my notion of teachers being these mythical beings of power. Anyway, the guy said something like 'There are people who make great teachers. There are people who truly understand a given subject. Finding someone who is both a great teacher and truly understands their subject is rare.'

Alas, Connolly falls into the second group—not the third.

No doubt he knows the material, but he could narrate a battle between two fifty-foot-tall robots with missiles and laser cannons and make it sound as dry as needlepoint night at the old folks' home. At least bingo occasionally involves a raised voice or a little excitement.

He almost puts *me* to sleep before sunrise.

Still, the material is interesting. I can't imagine taking this guy's class at eight in the morning, first thing. No wonder the school bookstore also sells pillows. Making it through the remainder of his lecture takes a good amount of concentration on the material rather than the voice conveying it. With my amped up reflexes, I could transcribe everything he says word for word into my notebook, but there's no point. I *do* take notes, but only important things that sound like test bait.

When class is over, I make my way out of the building. Fortunately, the rain's stopped by now, but the ground is still wet. There's enough of a group heading up the street to the parking garage that I would've felt reasonably safe as a normal girl. I don't really know any of these people, but it's still highly unlikely an entire group of like eleven students would conspire together to assault me.

The parking garage is another matter. It has numerous areas that appear like they'd probably be shadowy and dangerous. I'm guessing since I can't actually see darkness anymore. Still, they look like perfect ambush spots for creeps. By the time I get to the Sentra, I've been walking alone for at least a hundred feet. Then again, it's not like I'm in one of the bad metro areas.

I flop in the driver's seat and pull out my iPhone.

Hmm... Cristian Fowler, Boeing. Okay, Google, what'cha got?

Looks like he lives in a big-ass house on Garfield Street in Queen Anne. Damn. That's way close to center city Seattle. Guess this guy's doing pretty well for himself.

Whistling innocently, I grab the box of Thin Mints, get out of the car, and meander over to the edge of the parking garage. One casual look around to make sure no one is watching me later, I zip into the air.

It's barely two miles away as the crow—or vampire girl—flies.

Driving, more than ever, feels like a ball and chain slowing me down. But, it is a lot drier than flying on a rainy day. I glide in for a nice landing on the sidewalk in a nice, suburban area. The guy's house is huge. A set of concrete stairs leads up to the front porch along the side of a dirt mound covered in bushes. To the right of that, a two-car garage occupies a sunken area even with the ground floor, though half of it's embedded in the hill, so it's more like the basement is exposed on the right side than a two-story house.

Anyway, I trot up the steps, ring the doorbell, and smile like a tween-aged Girl Scout.

A skinny blonde girl in a teal top and yoga pants answers. She's maybe fourteen, and gives me this 'what are you supposed to be' look.

"Hi. Is your father home?" I wave the box of Thin Mints. "Delivering his cookie order."

"Aren't you kinda old for that?" asks the girl in a patronizing tone.

"My kid sister's the scout. I'm just running it around since it's a bit late for her to be out."

"Oh." She reaches toward me. "I can take it. Dad's watching TV."

I stare into her eyes, making her think I'm holding a clipboard. "That's cool. But I still need him to sign the form."

"Seriously? Why do you have to be so annoying?" She sighs at me like I've just thrown off the entire rest of her life with the massive inconvenience. Ooh. Entitled little brat. "Fine."

"Sec?"

The girl smirks at me.

As soon as she makes eye contact, I plunge into her mind. "You really could stand to be a bit nicer to people."

Her expression falls slack into a distant stare. Ten seconds later, her eyelids flutter and she just kinda stands there, clueless.

I wag the box of Thin Mints at her. "Would you please let your dad know I'm here?"

"Oh. Sorry. Hang on. I'll go get him." She zips into the house, leaving the door open.

Ahh. Wild abuse of vampiric powers. Fear me. *Rawr*—or something.

"Umm, Dad?" says the girl somewhere inside the house. "S'cuse me... there's someone at the door. She's got your cookies and says you have to sign for them."

"Something wrong, Andrea?" asks a man.

"No... Why?"

"Did you take something?"

I can just picture her shaking her head. "No."

Upholstery creaks, then the *thud, thud, thud* of someone walking across the house. A man in his later forties with slick black hair and a dark tan emerges from the living room in a Boeing polo and cargo shorts. His right eyebrow is attempting to embed itself into his hairline.

"Hi, Mr. Fowler?"

"Do I know you? You look kinda familiar..."

"No. I'm just dropping off cookies." I dive into his head. "Just need you to sign here."

I remind him of Mom, but he doesn't realize it yet. At least, not at a conscious level. *Mrs. Wright is the best lawyer working for you. You'd never lay her off. She's way too valuable for Boeing to lose.* I momentarily debate throwing in a raise, but nah. That's too much like stealing and I'm pretty sure Mom would be legit pissed at me for doing that. In his mind, he takes the clipboard from me and signs his name right next to his original signature where he agreed to buy one box of Thin Mints for $5.

"Thanks," says Mr. Fowler in a lifeless tone. He takes out his wallet and hands me a $10. "Keep it. Call it a donation."

Okay, that's all him. I didn't do that. Honest.

"Here you go. Thank you!" I chirp while handing him the box of cookies. *Remember. You would never lay off Allison Wright. Your team would fall to pieces without her.*

While I'm in there, I also tweak his memory of my appearance enough for safety. Black hair, blue eyes instead of brown, and hell... freckles.

"Take care, kid." Mr. Fowler waves at me and shuts the door.

Sierra's probably going to kill me for pinching one of her boxes of Thin Mints, but hey... she's got a whole case. I head a few houses down, slip into a nice dark spot, and leap into the sky for the flight home.

Oh, crap.

I forgot the car.

5

NO ONE ALIVE

Within seconds of my sneakers touching down on the parking garage deck, a dark figure walks out from behind a column.

I jump, startled by the sudden presence of another person, but relax when I recognize it's the strange young woman in the super frilly goth dress I saw in English Lit class. She gives me a Mona Lisa smile and keeps on walking. Okay, either she didn't see me fly in and land, or she did and—for reasons unknown to me—has no problem whatsoever with that. No freak out. No 'wow, that's so cool!' No confused staring.

Like this girl sees people climb in the side of a third-story parking deck all the time.

There's no way she saw me fly and has no reaction whatsoever. So either she didn't see me, or... she's a vampire, too. She glances back at me before disappearing into the stairwell. I manage a friendly wave. Her smile widens, though she doesn't slow down or stop. Hmm. Odd. If I had nothing better to do, I'd go chase her down and make sure she didn't see anything weird.

But, that would cut into my Hunter time.

And besides, no sane person sees a girl flying around and just walks off totally calm, right?

She didn't see me—or she's not sane. In which case, no one would believe her if she tells anyone. Screw it.

I jog across the garage, hop in the Sentra, and drive.

You know what's frustrating? Being stuck doing like forty miles an hour when I could be flying at 140. What's even more frustrating than that? Getting stuck behind a dump truck. What the hell is a dump truck doing on the road at like 9:30 p.m.? Argh. I shift positions, tap my fingers on the wheel, lean the other way, tap my fingers on the wheel harder.

Finally, after a few blocks, the truck turns off.

Less than a full minute after I finally get up *to* the speed limit, a cop comes out of nowhere behind me and turns his lights on.

Okay, seriously what the hell? I didn't do anything.

Most eighteen-year-olds being pulled over for the first time would be about ready to wet their pants. And okay, I experience about ten seconds of that dread, too, before I realize my parents won't be yelling at me for getting a ticket because no matter what happens in the next five minutes, I'm not getting a ticket.

I signal and pull over in the first open place to do so. The police car noses up behind me. A spotlight comes on, and… there we sit. Was I tailgating that truck? I don't think so… No way was I speeding. Mom told me once about how she used to get pulled over all the time in her younger twenties because rookie cops wanted to hit on her. Ugh. I hope that's not what's going on here.

Finally, after about four minutes, the police car's door opens.

The cop's a guy, later thirties probably. Big, with a shaved head. He walks up beside the car, looks in at me, flashlight right on my face. I squint.

"Who's car is this, sweetie?"

"My dad's."

"He know you took it? You a bit young to be driving?"

I sigh out my nose. Oh. Dammit. "I'm eighteen."

'Yeah right, this kid think I'm an idiot?' goes across his mind so loud I can hear it without even trying. "Eighteen, huh?"

"Yep. One sec." I fish my license and college ID out of my bag and hand them over. "Was I doing something wrong, or did you just stop me because I look like I'm fifteen?"

He examines my cards, glances at me, stares at the cards again, then squints. "Hold tight. I'll be back in a moment."

It's *so* tempting to just send him on his way, but I really am in the clear, so I merely nod.

The cop tromps back to his car. I amuse myself by picturing his increasingly desperate need to prove my IDs are fake crumbling. When that loses its appeal, I check myself in the mirror to make sure I haven't regressed any younger. This whole vampire deal is still new ground, so who knows what'll happen to me. Thankfully, I don't look any different. Someone seeing only my face could guess anywhere from thirteen to sixteen.

He finally returns and hands me the cards back. "Checks out. Sorry about that. You look young."

"No problem."

He leans his head partially in the window, peering around the car. "Wouldn't happen to be anything in there you don't want me to see?"

All the powers of an immortal vampire at my disposal—well, at least a somewhat watered-down version—and of course, having a cop looming over me turns me straight back into Follows Rules Girl.

"No, sir. Just my school stuff."

He nods, not even a note of suspicion on his face. Well, I guess that's one advantage to *looking* innocent. "Drive safe, hon."

"Thanks."

I wait for him to get back in his car, then signal and pull out into the road. Swear... if being pulled over for looking too young to drive becomes a trend, I might just get into the habit of sending the cops on their way without going through the whole routine. Honestly, I don't think I look *that* young. The guy probably just saw an 'under twenty' driving around at night and hoped he'd find alcohol or something.

To save time, I drive straight home, leave the car, and fly to Mi

Tierra. Fortunately, Hunter is working until 10 p.m., plus whatever time it takes him to finish up. The cop didn't steal *precious* time. Only about fifteen minutes of waiting.

It's not *bad* waiting, really. The rain's stopped, so I sit on the trunk of Hunter's car, lay back, and stare up at the moon and clouds for a while. Sometimes when I was a little kid, I'd look up at the sky and think of it as a massive, perfectly blue swimming pool, and daydream about diving in. That I *can* do that now is both amusing and sad. Though, the somberness only comes from thinking about myself at like eight or nine, and how I had no idea back then a boy I thought I liked would stick a knife into my chest. Hell, at that age, I didn't even have a concept that people could stab each other to death at all.

Still, watching the shadowy forms of clouds glide across the night sky is a net improvement in my mood. I really don't know why I find thinking about the past sad at all. Even if my life had continued in the normal way, it's not like I would've been running around with my friends all day long anymore. College, job, career, life… all that stuff is just as fatal to the carefree days of childhood as a giant effing knife.

I look at it in a new light. Dalton hit the giant pause button on my existence at just about the perfect time. I can do anything as a young-looking eighteen year old… except maybe rent a car. But who cares? If I feel like it, I can pass myself off as being too young for responsibility. When my mood shifts, I can act older. It's like being a kid and an adult at the same time. And, best of all, I'll never wind up in my forties wondering why my ass is twice the size it was when I'd been in high school. Or maybe not. Mom's not doing too bad in that regard. Guess there *is* an upside to my family's genetics. We might not rock athletic muscles or sexy curves, but we tend to stay skinny.

The moon beckons me like I could fly straight up and grab it. I think once Hunter's asleep, I'll go night flying.

A few minutes into my enjoyment of the quiet night sky, I get the sensation that someone's watching me. Expecting Hunter, I ignore it for a minute or two, but when I don't sense him getting closer to the car, I sit up and look around. In the weird sort of way the world is to my vampiric eyes, nothing—except for the sky—is dark. I see as far as a normal person can during the day even without any light at all, though in the absence of actual light, colors are super washed out and hard to distinguish. A handful of people wander the shopping center, though none are paying attention to me. The watched feeling continues, so I keep looking around, but can't figure out who or what is looking at me.

Eventually I give up and lay back down, my head against the car's rear window. I sigh at the Moon, but it doesn't help me figure out who's staring at me. After a while, the slow scuffing of shoes draws near. I smile, waiting for Hunter to walk around and scoop me up, kiss me, or say something cute and cheesy... but he hops in the car.

And starts the engine.

Really?

When we start moving, I roll onto my front, then glide up and over the roof, to peer upside down at him through the windshield.

"Holy shit!" shouts Hunter, slamming on the brakes.

The car stops short, but I don't go flying since he hadn't been going *that* fast.

I drift to the right, land, and let myself in the passenger side. "Wow, you must be tired. Didn't see me?"

Still clutching his chest, he shakes his head. "No... didn't see you. And yeah, little fried."

"If you need sleep, we can hang out later."

He reaches over and takes my hand. "Nah, it's cool. I really need some time with you to relax. Sleep's overrated."

"Don't go missing too much sleep or everything else will get worse."

Hunter leans into a kiss. I scoot closer, close my eyes, and enjoy the moment. Right when it starts getting good, the car lurches forward. He yelps and pulls away, jabbing on the brakes before we roll into a light post. "Whoa... Oops."

"Umm. Maybe we shouldn't make out with the car in drive."

"Yeah. Good idea. Are all college girls smart like you?" Grinning, he backs away from the pole, shifts, and steers around it toward the exit.

I laugh.

"Sorry. That was dumb of me. Should've at least put it in park first. Whenever I'm around you, it's like I'm in a dream... and I'm afraid of waking up."

A little warmth rushes to my cheeks. "Are you sure it isn't lack of actual sleep? Your first class is like at eight, and you work almost to eleven. When do you do homework?"

"Uhh, mostly on the weekend, or on my break here. I don't have an early class on Thursday either, so I have a couple hours then, too."

"Sounds romantic." I twirl some hair around my finger. "Working your way through college... like something our parents did."

He chuckles. "I wish. Financial aid is paying for most of it. I'm working more to help my mom cover the mortgage and buy food. It's not much, but it's making the difference."

"Oh... wow..." I blink, taken by sudden guilt... I don't even really know what going to school costs. My parents took care of all that stuff. But yeah, I guess it is way more than what a kid our age could possibly make waiting tables.

"Hey, don't look at me like that."

"Sorry. Umm. Like what?"

"Guilty." He gives my hand a squeeze. "You don't have to feel guilty for having two parents with killer jobs. It doesn't bother me at all. I used to worry your parents might not think I was good enough for you, but they're really cool."

"Hah! Yeah, they are kinda cool. But, this isn't the 1800s where you need to get my father's permission to date me."

Hunter wrings his hand on the wheel. "I know, but they still could've nagged at you about dating the poor kid from the wrong part of town."

That gets an eye roll. "You're not in the wrong part of town. And my parents like you." I draw his hand up to my chest and hug it. "Sorry your dad's the way he is."

"That's all on him. Not your fault."

"I could, umm... help out if you want, so you didn't need to burn yourself out going to school full time *and* working."

He sneaks a few quick glances at me while driving until a red light offers the chance for a longer stare. "Help? Sarah, you don't need to give us money or anything. We're doing okay."

"Not what I meant. I could, you know, maybe persuade someone to hire your mother at a better job or something."

"Oh." He looks forward again when the light changes. "That's an idea. But Mom still doesn't know about your, umm, special talents. Not sure how that would work. Wouldn't you need to be like with her in the interview or whatever?"

"Umm. Not sure. Never used my powers for sinister dolphins before." As soon as I say that, I blush again. Ugh, I am such a damn dork sometimes!

"No idea what you just said."

I cringe like someone caught me pushing on a pull door. "Something stupid I came up with when I was like eleven. My dad thinks it's hilarious, so it kinda stuck."

Hunter slows, and turns left into my cul-de-sac. "What, so like dolphin ninjas?"

"Hah. No... Nefarious porpoises." I cringe.

He stares at me, dazed.

"Oh, wow. You're tired. Nefarious purposes? Never used my powers for nefarious—"

"I got it. I'm not making this face because I'm tired. That was *really* bad."

"Well, I did come up with that when I was a kid." I fold my arms and look off to the side.

"It's cute." He grins. "I can see why your dad keeps using it."

"Sierra thinks it's lame. It makes Sophia giggle, and Sam keeps saying it to annoy Sierra."

Hunter laughs.

We get out of the car and make our way inside, pausing by the shelf to ditch our shoes.

"Hey, you two," says Dad from the couch.

Oh no. Please no. My father's deadpan serious tone is a portent of something super embarrassing coming out of his mouth.

"Hey, Mr. Wright." Hunter waves.

"And what are you two planning to do down there in the total privacy of my daughter's bedroom?" asks Dad, still not looking over at us.

Okay, I can do one of two things here: crawl into a proverbial little hole and try to stop existing, or throw the embarrassment back at him and say something really raunchy.

"We were gonna watch a movie." Hunter smiles. "But we might be going down there for sinister dolphins."

Or option three: *Hunter* says something mortifying.

Dad coughs and peers over the couch at us.

"Did I use that right?" whispers Hunter.

"Yeah." I grab him by the arm and pull him past the living room into the kitchen, and down the basement steps.

He follows without a word until we're in my room and the door's closed. "Sorry, was trying to be funny. Didn't know it was like something special."

"It's fine." I rest my head against his shoulder. "I'm not blushing because you said those words. You basically just told my father we're going to *do stuff.*"

"Sorry."

I finally manage to laugh at the look on my dad's face. "Don't be. He deserves it for all the times he embarrasses me."

He flops on the bed and starts surfing Netflix while I change into just a long T-shirt, then curl up beside him. The repetitive *ping, ping, ping* of him searching for a movie ends with him selecting some random indie comedy about drunk people at a college. I allow about a three minute wait before I start kissing the side of his neck.

"Hungry?" asks Hunter.

"Yeah, but not for that... I'm not gonna bite you."

He brushes a hand over my head, pulling me into a deep kiss. It's pretty obvious he's not fully into it, and I know it's not the movie distracting him.

"What's wrong?" I whisper once our lips part.

"Is your dad gonna come down here to check on us?"

"Nah. I doubt it. He likes to embarrass me with words... and old pictures. He doesn't want to see what he thinks is going on in here." I tease at his chin with my finger. "Besides. If he does decide to sneak up on us, I'll hear him before he's at the door."

The next hour or so goes by in a blur of movie, cuddling, kissing, increasingly intense pawing... and finally, off comes my T-shirt. Of course, by that time, he's only in his boxers... and they land on top of my shirt. Our hands roam, his lips go exploring. My amped up senses make even the texture of the sheets at my back an overwhelmingly intense experience. I can almost perceive the ridges of his fingerprints on the hand sliding up the inside of my leg.

It takes all I can do not to scream out in ecstasy when his fingertips make contact.

He continues kissing me while his touch sets off fireworks inside my head.

I'm so lost to the heat of the moment that I don't hear the patter of small feet crossing the basement until mere seconds remain. Fast as a blur, I twist around, grab the blanket, and pull a Count Dracula cape maneuver, covering us to the neck. It's so fast Hunter doesn't have time to react before Sophia opens the door and peers in.

"Sare?" She doesn't wait for an answer, slipping inside and closing the door. Yeah, she looks totes adorbs in her pink nightgown but I'm half tempted to stuff her in my clothes hamper at the moment.

Hunter freezes at the sound of her voice... and gradually removes his fingers. The sensation of them retreating triggers a shudder. Oh, wow. Just a wee bit awkward.

"Yeah?" I manage, trying to hide how wound up I am. My brain's jammed on the brakes, but my body is still going.

"I'm scared. I think there's something in my room." She sniffles.

"What's in your room?" I half-whisper.

"I dunno. Something scary. I think it's watching me."

I sigh, letting my head fall on Hunter's chest. "Okay. I'll check."

Sophia stands there.

"Umm. Gimme a sec?"

"I'm scared," whimpers Sophia. "I don't wanna be alone. 'Specially in the basement."

Ugh. Fine. Whatever. Not like she hasn't seen me naked before. My siblings have *amazingly* bad timing when showers are involved. I peer up at her. She's at least turned her back on the bed. I slip out from under the blanket and pull my giant T-shirt on so fast, she couldn't have caught me if she tried.

Alas, Hunter's excitement is still kinda obvious.

I pat the point of the tent.

He rolls on his side. "Oof."

"Sorry," I whisper.

"It's cool." He grins. "Go kill the closet monster."

I head for the door.

Sophia reaches to take my hand, but I dodge her grip.

"Hang on a sec. Wait here."

She blinks at me in alarmed shock.

I run out to the basement bathroom, wash my hands, then hurry back to my room. *Then* I take her hand. Fortunately, she doesn't ask why I did that. The house is dark. My parents rarely stay up much past eleven, so it's pretty late. I lead the way down the hall to the room that used to house both my sisters before Sierra moved into my old room.

No idea if my vampire upgrade came with extra senses, but I don't pick up on anything unusual. Sophia whines a little, but follows me in. Of course, to her, the room is pitch dark save for a bit of moonlight coming in the window.

"Where was it?" I whisper, mostly not to wake either of the other two sibs or the parents.

"I dunno." She gazes around. "Felt like someone was in here watching me, but invisible."

Motion near the floor catches my eye. One of Sam's frogs hops out from under the bed, then hops again, landing right on Sophia's bare foot. Shit! If she sees that, she's going to wake the entire neighborhood up. As desperate as if a flaming crossbow bolt flew toward my heart, I throw my reflexes to the max, diving to snag the little amphibian before she can finish looking down at the cold, slimy thing touching her skin.

I'm upright again with the frog held behind my back so fast she doesn't even perceive that I moved.

Still, she jumps back with an *eep*, stares at her foot for a second, then whines at me. "Something cold touched my foot! I think it's a ghost."

"Probably just a breeze. It's kinda chilly. Get in bed and be warm."

Ribbit.

Sophia cringes. Fortunately, she doesn't scream… but she does leap onto the bed and pull her feet in. "Where is it?"

Ribbit.

"I got him." I pull my arm out from behind my back, showing off the frog.

"Eww," whispers Sophia. "You're touching it."

"It's only a frog."

She sticks her tongue out.

"C'mon. Back to bed. There's nothing here."

"Did a frog wake me up or is there a ghost?" She scoots under the covers and pulls them up to her chin.

I shrug. "Could be either one."

She glares at me with a 'you're really not helping' expression.

"Look… if there is a ghost here, it can't hurt you." I hold up the frog. "Neither can this little guy."

Ribbit.

She pulls the blankets over her face. "Eww."

I stick my head into the closet just to be sure, then check under the bed. "All clear."

"Thanks for looking. Sorry to bug you."

"It's okay. If you're really scared, go ahead and bug me whenever you need to." I ruffle her hair.

Sophia sits up and clamps her arms around me. "You sure there's nothing here?"

"Yeah."

"Okay." She lays back down. "Tell Hunter I'm sorry. And I didn't see you guys kissing. It's dark."

I snicker. "Go to sleep."

She grins.

After Sophia closes her eyes, I creep across the hall to Sam's room, deposit the jailbreak frog back in his terrarium, and head back to my room. Hunter's lying on his side with his head propped up in his hand like he's posing for a Greek statue. I nudge the door shut, briefly complain about the lack of a lock, and pull my shirt off again.

"Sorry about that. Just a frog."

"A frog?"

I crawl into bed. His chest at my back is so warm I could just let him hold me for hours and be the happiest girl in the world. "Yeah... my brother's got a pair of them. They've been kinda creepy ever since we went to the caves. Feels like they're looking at me with intelligence way past what a frog should have sometimes."

"That's weird."

"Yeah... I've been feeling watched a lot lately. Those frogs did that to me, but it happened in the parking lot behind the restaurant before. Wonder if it's all in my head."

He kisses my ear. "There's no one alive who can sneak up on you."

I smirk. "That's exactly what I'm afraid of. If something sneaks up on me, it won't be someone who's alive."

"At least your sister's safe."

"Yeah."

I roll toward him and kiss him on the lips. "Now... where were we?"

We stare into each other's eyes for a moment.

"It's pretty late. You should spend the night."

"I have to be at school early."

"Really?" I raise an eyebrow. "You won't wake me up when you leave in the morning."

He cringes ever so slightly.

"Oh... sorry. I didn't even think about that."

"About what?" He tilts his head, genuinely confused.

"I look a bit creepy when I'm asleep."

"No, that's not it at all. You're still the most beautiful woman in the world, even then. Really, you don't look bad at all. Just a bit pale, not like a corpse at all."

"Aww, Hunter Lawrence, that's the sweetest thing anyone's ever said to me."

His grin says he wants to laugh at my remark but isn't sure if I meant it seriously. As soon as I start giggling, he buries his face in the crook of my neck and laughs. The mood returns, and we proceed to use my bedroom for some rather sinister dolphins.

6

NO SMALL AMOUNT OF SCREAMING

When consciousness returns to me, Hunter's gone, I'm somehow back in my T-shirt, and, oh yeah, it's Wednesday.

Heh. Hump day. Oops. Guess we did that a little early.

So far, vampiric life (such as it is) comes with the truly bizarre ability to go from dead asleep to wide awake in an instant. Except in one or two cases where I'd had my ass handed to me in a fight, my usual morning grogginess is a thing of the past. Given what Hunter and I did, I'm in sore need of a shower. I check the iPhone and grin at the little rain icon. It's 2:33, so I have a couple minutes before the littles are home from school.

With a clean set of sweat pants and a new T-shirt under my arm, I hurry upstairs and hop in the shower. I'd say I miss the normality of shaving my legs… but I don't. Flight still ranks tops on my list of 'why it's cool to be a vampire,' but the list of small minutiae I no longer have to deal with like shaving, tampons, having the slightest care about calories, are all strong marks in the 'win' column, too.

Shower done, I wrap my hair in a towel, dress, and head downstairs.

Dad intercepts me on my way from the bottom of the stairs to the kitchen. "Hey, Sarah?"

"Hmm?" I stop and smile at him. "What's up?"

"Do you think you could take Sam and Sierra to karate?"

I shrug. "What time? I have a class at six."

"It's from four to five."

Sierra and Sam both walk up behind Dad.

"Yeah I can do that. Be cutting things a bit close, but I don't really need a whole hour for the drive to school. And whoa... Sierra wants to go? I thought you lost interest. Too much time away from video games."

Sierra glowers at nothing in particular. "I don't want to be kidnapped again."

I almost make a joke about Bree Swanson kidnapping anyone is almost 'cute,' but don't. Despite that girl being relatively harmless, anyone under the influence of mind control is a threat. That entire situation *could* have gone way wrong. Hmm.

"Cool. I wonder if I should take karate lessons, too? Considering how things have been going for me lately, learning how to fight might not be a bad idea."

Sam shakes his head. "They're not teaching us how to fight with claws."

"You could look around for a place that has tiger style kung fu?" Dad attempts a horrible martial arts stance.

"Is that drunken monkey stance?" I ask.

"Ha. Ha." Dad relaxes and stops standing like a huge dork.

A frog lands on my head with a *slap*.

"Ow!" I cringe.

Ribbit.

It clings to my hair while I peer up at the stairway it leapt from.

"Sam..."

"Sorry!"

I snag the frog from my head and hold it up to stare into its beady eyes. That weird feeling of them watching me with real sentience is gone, but something strange is still going on.

"I can't tell if this is the same one, but a frog got out last night, too."
I hand it to my brother. "Are you feeding them enough? Why do they
keep escaping?"

"Yeah, they're eating enough." Sam nods. "Found a guide online
how to take care of frogs. I don't know why they keep getting out."

"Oh, speaking of tiger style." Dad wags his eyebrows. "*Bloodsport*."

"Not funny," I mutter.

"No… I mean next movie." He grins.

"That sounds gory." Sierra peers up at him. "Sophia's gonna scream
the whole time."

Dad pats both her and Sam on the shoulder. "Nah. It's not gory. It's
a martial arts movie. You guys will love it."

Translation: Sam will think it's cool. Sierra will roll her eyes the
whole time, and Sophia will be emotionally traumatized. Me? I'll
smile through it, grateful to still be able to spend time with my family.
Had I not died, I'd probably be in the rolling-the-eyes camp with
Sierra.

Anyway…

We each drift off to our own separate distractions for a little less
than an hour. I randomly munch on some pretzels because, hey why
not? Feels like I need to eat something right after waking up.
Eventually, Sam comes thundering down the stairs in his karate
uniform. Sierra, not having one, rocks a T-shirt, yoga pants, and ballet
flats.

"You have to get a uniform," says Sam.

"She has to decide if she wants to go more than once first," calls
Dad from his office.

Sierra shrugs. "I'm curious. I might remember why I stopped going
and hate it again."

I grin… and, after heading down to my room to grab my backpack
and books, usher the littles through the rain to the Sentra.

The karate place isn't too far from home, in a modest strip mall
barely half the size of the shopping center where Sophia's dance class
is. It's full of shouting tweens, a handful of parents, and six employees
all wearing karate uniforms. The smell of rubberized mats, old sweat,

and that weird wet dog fragrance that always saturates locker rooms is everywhere.

A small desk sits off to the left of the entrance with a middle-aged guy in a karate uniform standing behind it. Most of the place is wide open except for a few columns holding up the ceiling, all thoroughly wrapped in padding. Some parents sit on the radiator by the front window, which is pretty much opaque with fog.

Dad already made the arrangements for Sierra to take the 'free first class,' so I just need to sign her in at the front desk. She and Sam head out to the main floor with the other kids while I take a seat among the parents. It's similar to Sophia's dance class, but quite a bit louder.

I sit there listening to kids shouting as they perform a series of rehearsed punches and kicks at midair. This one chubby boy about Sam's age occasionally loses his karate pants whenever he tries to do a side kick, giving everyone a view of his briefs. Naturally, everyone laughs. He blushes a little but doesn't give up. One of the instructors checks the drawstrings, but the poor kid's unusual shape doesn't help. It's like trying to put pants on an egg. Still, he refuses to give up.

Half an hour or so into the class, the kids pair off, one holding a padded target while the other tries to punch or kick it. I'm *so* glad I'm dead. All these kids and teens shouting would give any mortal being a severe headache. I don't know how the heck the people who work here tolerate it.

Mostly, I focus on Sam and Sierra. He's totally into it, though he does ham it up a bit much… like he's the hero of a lame kung fu movie. Sierra spends the entirety of the fifty-minute class period with the same expression she had on when she first tried a Thai iced tea: part confusion, part disgust, part smile. She had to drink three of them before she decided she liked them. I guess that means she's going to want to come back at least a few times.

At the end of the class, the primary instructor, Dave something, has all the kids line up, bow, and give off a battle shout at the same time. Most of the parents around me are expecting it and plug their ears. Sam zooms over as the class breaks up, Sierra trudging along behind him.

From what I saw, I don't think this class is going to do me much good... unless I get attacked by a guy standing as rigid as a video game character and trying to kill me with a foam target.

The head instructor walks over and introduces himself as Dan—not Dave—Black. Since I'm not the parent, I don't get the full brunt of the sales pitch, but he does tell me how good he thought Sierra did for a first timer, and compliments her on picking things up fast. Surprisingly, he doesn't press us to sign anything tonight and leaves us with a, "Well, hope you had fun tonight and maybe learned something."

The kids grab their coats and we head outside across a downpour-saturated parking lot to the Sentra. Sierra runs faster and makes it to the front seat. Sam doesn't bother complaining, which probably annoys her on some small level, and slides into back. Both of them breathe heavily from the class and the dash to the car.

"So, what did you think?" I ask, starting the engine.

Sierra groans. "Ugh. That was a lot more work than I thought it would be."

I chuckle. "Wow. That didn't take long."

"No, I'm not giving up yet... just thought it would be more 'how to kick someone's ass' and less workout."

Sam shrugs. "This is basically yoga with more screaming."

Okay, so much for driving right away... I'm laughing too hard.

Sierra fans herself. "*More* screaming? There isn't usually *any* screaming in yoga."

"I went with Mom once, and this lady there screamed a lot. Sometimes bad words, too. She fell over a couple times."

Once I stop giggling to myself, I glance at Sierra. "So, you going to come back?"

"Maybe."

"Well, think about it. Mom and Dad will need to pay for... what is it three months or six?"

"Three," says Sam. "Or six. Or a year. It's cheaper the more you get at once."

Sierra's quiet the rest of the way home, lost in thought.

I pull into the driveway and stop, intending to let them out and go straight to class. Sam bolts for the door, but Sierra lingers. When she looks over at me, her eyes are a little red. Uh oh.

"What's wrong?"

"If you knew karate, would Scott still have killed you?"

And just like that, I'm stabbed in the heart for the second time of my life. "Uhh... Well, it happened kinda fast. Umm."

"Think it's a waste of time? I mean, we're all pretty skinny and weak."

I grin, ruffling her hair. "You're not overly weak. Just not strong."

She sticks out her tongue.

"Actually, it might have helped... but not so much because I would've been able to stop him from stabbing me. We were close together, I wasn't expecting him to get violent, and he moved so damn fast."

"What the heck else would karate do if it wouldn't have helped you stop the knife?"

I do my best impression of Dad's cheesy voice. "If I'd been studying karate—or anything really—for a couple years, I'd probably have had the self-confidence to dump him way before I did. And out in the open, not off in the woods alone with him."

"Okay, Dad. Thanks for the PSA." She rolls her eyes. "And knowing is half the battle, right?"

"Something like that." I laugh.

She grabs my hand. "Hey. Don't die again."

"It's only school."

"That's what I'm worried about." She swallows hard. "If someone goes crazy with a gun, I hope they wait 'til it's dark."

Aww, shit. How the hell am I supposed to discuss spree shooters with an eleven-year-old? I'm ready to cry as much as I'm furious with the world that a kid her age is even thinking such things can happen. I don't want to say 'that stuff doesn't happen here' because guess what'll happen if I say that? "Yeah. I do, too."

"If I die at school, please bring me back. I'd rather be a vampire than gone. You guys would be too sad."

And... I'm gonna be late for class. I grab her and burst into tears. Sierra sobbing as well makes it worse. This girl never cries. We sit there together in the running car, rain swirling in the headlight beams from the world weeping along with us.

7

EYE CONTACT

I t's dark enough that I consider taking the 'flying in a bikini' thing seriously.

However, with my luck, I'll pull a full-on Icarus. The rain will stop, clouds will part, and the sun will pluck my wings when I'm at a thousand feet doing 140 miles an hour. Aurélie warned me that if something 'killed' me while I'm exposed to sunlight, I'd die for real. Even if it's something—like a bullet to the heart—that wouldn't normally bother a vampire.

By extension, I'm going to go out on a limb and assume my body turning into a quarter-mile-long squish mark on the road would count as a fatal injury.

So... I drive.

It is dark enough that I'm online. Between superhuman reflexes, actual immortality, and the full intent to mentally command any cop who gets in my way to forget having seen me, I manage to arrive at school with three minutes to spare.

I didn't tell Sierra that I don't actually know *how* to make someone else a vampire. Nor did I mention that the idea of doing it to any of my siblings is heartbreaking... but if something else killed them already, I would absolutely do that. But yeah, I'm gonna just stop thinking about that scenario or I'm going to spend the whole rest of the night crying to myself.

Both of tonight's classes are in a different place, the "Science and Math Building," which is on the next block north, across the street from the main building. A quick flight from the parking garage allows me to reach the classroom on the second floor only a few seconds behind the instructor—a late-twentysomething Hispanic woman in a sharp navy pantsuit. The room's pretty much full, and of course the only seats left open are in the front row. Whatever. I'm dead. I shouldn't be intimidated by a teacher.

I take a seat and listen to the professor introduce herself as Olive Garcia, and go over the basics of what we'll be covering in Comp Sci 101. Since I'm—at least on paper—a programming major, this is a bread and butter course, so time to pay attention.

The class is only an hour, from six to seven, and feels like it went by in a blur. I like the teacher a lot. Friendly, professional, definitely knows her shit, and she has an easy mannerism about her that makes me think she fits into that small group of perfect teachers... the ones who are both experts in their field and also have a knack for communicating it.

Today's my first multiple class day. It's annoying for two reasons: first, the early start time at six. Second, I have a one-hour gap before my next class, Intro to Calculus, which runs from eight to nine. And the best part is... I get to do this again on Friday. Ugh. Anyway, I've got an hour to kill.

Might as well go grab a snack.

Seattle Central College doesn't exactly have a sprawling campus like what I'd always imagined I'd be running around in after high school. It's pretty much a couple of big ass buildings and a few not so big ass buildings in the heart of Seattle. While it's good for minimizing dealing with bad weather, it makes it a little annoying for me in terms of finding food. Like, whoever designed this place really didn't take the needs of vampire students seriously.

I *really* don't want to constantly ambush people in the bathroom. For one thing, that limits me to other women. For another, I don't want to develop an association between feeding and being in a public restroom. My life is screwy enough already without the sight of toilets making me hungry. That's a level of messed up I'm not prepared to tolerate. So... I head outside—or start to. Damn. It's still pouring. Heck with it. I can eat later.

The school has a little lounge-slash-arcade near the cafeteria. Of course, at this hour, it's mostly staffed by vending machines. Not that I'm upset at the lack of fresh, hot food. I could do the responsible student thing and get started right away on some reading I have to do for my Comp Sci class, since I need to have it done by Friday. However, the old arcade games are more appealing.

It takes me an embarrassingly long time to realize why the start button isn't working: this thing wants quarters. Like seriously? A video game that only lets you play if you put money into it? Wow. Dad talked about 'arcades' like they were the most awesome thing ever. He never said anything about money.

Blah.

Schoolwork it is.

Fortunately, the 'work' for that class is only reading. Fifty pages in two days is kinda annoying but whatever. I flop at a corner seat on the far end of the cafeteria and open the textbook... and find myself staring at meaningless marks on the page. It's in English, but I haven't found the energy to engage my brain yet. I am an immortal vampire. Any hope of a normal life for me is long gone. Why am I doing this again? Oh, right. To feel normal. To make my parents happy, which in turn makes me happy. Nothing to see here. I'm just an ordinary kid in an ordinary cafeteria reading an ordinary book.

Nothing weird about me at all.

The constant sound effects from the arcade games demo-playing themselves and a low murmur of conversation isn't too distracting. Not like when I stare right at someone and can perceive their muscles creaking. I tune out the world and focus on the book in front of me. A while later, the feeling like I'm a deer standing in a hunter's rifle scope comes back.

I look up from the book and cast a glance around, which is pretty easy considering I'm in the corner. That woman in the super frilly black dress catches my eye from the arcade area. She's wandering among the people in there—three of whom are playing the weird coin-eating games—and watching the screens like the same twenty-second loops are entertaining. No one in the area even bats an eye at her. Okay, that's weird. This girl looks like she should be on her way to a movie set or a theater.

Goth stuff is cool and all, but this girl's taking it to the level of mission statement. I'm surprised she didn't go all the way and dye her hair black.

She grows bored with a *Dig Dug* machine, pulls her gaze off the screen, and looks straight at me. We hold eye contact for about five seconds before she resumes drifting around the arcade. Something about her feels not quite right, so I keep on watching her. She doesn't seem to mind me staring at her, in fact, she smiles—and keeps smiling at me while walking out of the cafeteria.

Okay, that's a 'hey come up to my room' glance if I've ever seen one.

Not that I've ever seen one.

I mean, usually it's the girl giving that look to a guy, and I'm neither that girl nor likely to be on the receiving end of such a smile.

Except for right now.

Only... it doesn't give me the idea she wants to hook up. No, something weird is definitely going on here. Could she be another vampire and she's seen through my disguise? I try to think about my landing in the parking deck and if she would've seen me or not, but I'm certain she didn't step out from behind the column until after I'd been walking for a few seconds.

But, she might've been peeking around the side.

Grr.

Curiosity wins. I get up and trot after her, but stop in the hall when I don't see her anywhere. Damn. I look back and forth twice more without finding her. Not wanting to leave my stuff unattended, I hurry back to my table, annoyed and confused. My irritation is mostly coming from unanswered questions. But, really, if that girl wanted me to follow her, she'll come back when she realizes I'm not there.

I read for another ten minutes, then pack up and proceed to the room for my calculus class.

Admittedly, there's more than a little dread involved here. Calc is like the scapegoat subject for math being horrible, one of those super hard, super abstract classes that everyone has to take but only like five percent of people will ever use again once they're done with it in school. I'm not seeing much of a future at NASA for me, so I'm going to take a wild guess and say I'll be in the ninety-five percent who'll never see it again.

I'm early, so I have my pick of seats. I wind up again going for one near the middle of the room. More students—again mostly adults—trickle in over the next few minutes. The room's only about half full when the professor walks in. She kinda looks about Mom's age, though her face seems a bit young for all the grey streaks in her long dark brown hair. She introduces herself as Doctor Chelsea Mercer, and proceeds into this spiel about how she knows most of us here are only taking calc because it's required for our curriculum paths. She claims her class is tough but fair and she's willing to help anyone who struggles.

And she goes straight into a lecture, like we're midway into the school year and this isn't the first day. Hey, isn't day one supposed to be easy or something? Ugh. At least she's easy to follow… she speaks in a slow, precise manner, close to over-enunciating every word.

I take notes as best I can, trying to capture what's probably important to remember.

Over the course of the next hour, my mood swings wildly back and forth from 'I can do this' to 'I'm a vampire, screw college' over and over. No, really, I *can* do this. Question is do I want to? Yeah, I think so. While I can't say I ever *adored* math, I didn't mind it. Calculus is taking things a bit far, but I'm sure I can handle one intro course. Not like I'm a math major going for a PhD. Dad might be able to help me out at home and there's always visiting Doctor Mercer for some one-on-one coaching if I fall behind.

Or I could just mind control her to give me a B.

Nah. That's the opposite of normal. The entire point of me being here is to feel normal.

As if.

Dr. Mercer keeps right on lecturing past nine. Unrest stirs among the students, growing louder until at about ten after, when she pauses.

"I realize we are a little past time, however I'd ask you to bear with me a little longer to wrap up this concept." She resumes lecturing, picking up the pace to normal human speed. The squeak of her dry erase markers sound like screams for mercy.

Everyone—me included—scrambles to copy the formulas down since we're apparently going to need them for the homework.

At 9:28, Dr. Mercer finally caps the marker. "All right. Thank you everyone for bearing with me. Going late shouldn't be *too* much of a habit, though I do admit to perhaps speaking a bit more slowly than most of you are used to. For Friday, please read chapter three and complete the worksheet at the end." She smiles. "See you all in two days."

People shuffle around, repacking their bags, standing, and hurrying to leave. I toss the book into my backpack, sling it over one shoulder, and follow the crowd out the door, feeling pretty much the same as I did in high school other than the age gap. A group of men in their later thirties, who appear to know each other, chat amongst themselves, complaining that Mercer talks too slow and her classes always run long.

Great. I have the feeling this class is going to be *fun*. Note to self: don't make plans on Wednesday or Friday nights until this semester is over. The rain's backed off to a light drizzle, which is no big deal. Doesn't matter if I get soaked now, I'm only going home. Still, it's not exactly raining hard, so I don't rush.

Once I'm out of the Science and Math building, I hang a left and make my way down Harvard Ave toward the parking deck. A spot of black catches my eye on the right, across the street. Goth Girl is sitting on the steps of this church-type building. The place looks kinda old and maybe in need of some renovation. No idea if it's still a functioning church, but she doesn't look so out of place in front of it.

She stares at me as I go by on the other side.

Screw it.

I stop only a step past her, turn, and head straight across the road. She doesn't flinch or make any effort to go anywhere as I stroll right up to her. No one in all twelve years of my prior school career would ever have accused me of being shy. However, approaching a random person I've never met before to start a conversation because they looked at me is a bit unusual. Then again, I can't help but think she's been following me... somehow.

Up close, I'm certain she's not too far off in age from me. A year or three older perhaps. Despite the formerly heavy—and now drizzling —rain, she doesn't look like a drowned rat, barely damp if anything. All the multi-layered tiers of her dress are pristine, black, and new. It's a pretty sweet attempt at recreating clothing from the turn of the century with a more modern gothic tweak.

"Hi," says the girl.

"Hey."

"I'm Coralie Hall."

"Sarah Wright... just started this week. Freshman."

She giggles. "That's obvious."

"Umm, saw you in English Lit on Monday. Sorry for staring. Your dress kinda stands out."

"Oh, it's all right. I don't mind." She plays with the ruffles on her skirt. "I'm quite fond of it."

Yeah, obviously... or she wouldn't wear it every day. Of course, I'm not obnoxious enough to say that. "It had to be expensive. So fancy."

"It didn't cost that much, really."

Two guys walking by us give me a weird look. Their expressions are intense enough that I glance down to make sure my clothes haven't spontaneously vanished. I'm good. Hmm. Oh, this girl has to be like the school weirdo or something and I'm getting the 'why's she talking to the basket case?' reaction.

"So, umm... What's your major?" I hook my thumbs in my jean pockets.

"I'm only auditing the more interesting classes. I don't care about credits." Coralie stands up off the stairs—she's about an inch taller than me—and gives me a head-to-toe appraising glance. "I'm rather surprised to see you taking classes here."

"Yeah well..." I shrug, pausing to stare-joust at a dark-haired girl going by who's also looking at me like I've got a screw loose. "Life got a little complicated, so I have to take night classes."

Coralie covers her mouth and laughs. "I imagine so, since the sun would kill you."

I open my mouth to reply to what I thought she said, but wind up gawking when what she *really* said sinks in.

"Don't be so shocked. Your secret's safe with me. I *can't* tell anyone." Coralie reaches out and sticks her hand right *through* my chest, causing a tingly cold feeling. I think she's tickling my heart. "You're the first person out here to make eye contact with me in almost a century."

Oh, holy crap! No wonder people are looking at me funny. I'm not talking to the weird girl everyone avoids—I'm talking to a damn ghost! And geez, hasn't anyone ever heard of Bluetooth headsets? Seeing someone talking to thin air isn't exactly that strange anymore. Okay, talking to thin air while reacting to invisible people in front of a —possibly—decommissioned church is a bit weird.

"Umm. Wow. That explains why no one stared at your dress."

She sighs. "Yeah. I'm not wearing it for attention. It's what I died in."

"Sorry. That sucks."

Coralie makes a blasé face. "It is what it is. Happened long before you existed. Well, long before you look like you would've existed."

"Probably. Just happened to me last summer."

"Oh, you're a baby!" Coralie attempts, rather unsuccessfully, to hug me. "You poor dear."

I look around and try to stand in a way that makes me seem less crazy while talking to no one. "Did it happen around the school here? Is that why you're haunting the place?"

"No, nothing like that. I'm kinda stuck here. I can't leave." She looks off to the side and down, wearing perhaps the saddest expression I've ever seen on anyone ever.

Well, maybe not the saddest. That time Sophia somehow convinced herself we were getting a puppy or a kitten and it turned out not to be true beats it. Still, looking at this woman is making me want to cry.

"Is there anything I can do to help?"

Coralie's mood brightens back to normal. The tears running down her cheeks vanish like a special effect being removed from video. "I don't think so, but thank you for asking. It's really just nice not to feel so alone anymore. I rarely get the chance to talk to anyone."

"Well, I don't really have anywhere pressing to be for a little while..."

Her smile widens. "That would be lovely of you to spend time with me to talk."

"Least I can do..."

I have no idea if *all* vampires can see ghosts, though Glim seems to think so. Guess that means we don't typically hang around the school. Coralie's range is somewhat limited, so we can't walk too far. We wind up heading back toward the Science and Math building to hang out in the courtyard between it and the main building. A row of large block stones forms a bit of a wall around an area with a tree and tiny bushes. Beyond it, only bike racks. So, I make do with the stones for a seat.

Most of our conversation is about me, since she seems intrigued about how a girl my age wound up as a vampire. After I explain that I wound up as a vampire by accident, wanting to stay with my family, and attending night school because of sun reasons, I ask how she died.

"Kindred souls of a sort," she mutters in a tone like she's angry with someone else. "Late May, 1849, I'd been married for about three years. My former husband had a wonderful surprise for me—a beautiful necklace. He also gave me something to drink that he said would make our wildest dreams come true. A magical potion, if you believe in that sort of thing."

I bite my lip, thinking back to Garrett Alder living in the caverns. Part of me wants to chuck that whole experience aside as one giant nope, but I do kinda hope the potion he wanted to make works. Existence as a Beast sounds so damn lonely.

"Let' just say I don't *not* believe in them. Guess it didn't work... unless his dream was being single again."

Coralie rolls her eyes. "Not entirely. It did exactly what he wanted it to, but it didn't quite work out for him the way he hoped. Yes, it killed me, and yes he expected that would happen."

I gasp. "What an asshole. Did you know?"

"No. It rather surprised me."

"Guessing he's already dead."

"Oh, quite." Coralie looks up with a decidedly non-innocent gleam in her eye. "Alas, I did not cause his death. Perhaps I may have been able to warn him of it, though I chose not to do so. The man didn't linger around for very long. I suspect he tired of my being able to once again slap him. But, please... enough about me. Would you indulge me and tell me more of your family? So curious that you remain with them."

"Yeah." I smile at my lap. "I guess it is strange, but I couldn't do it to them, yanno? Let them think I died. And maybe I panicked a little and wanted the security of home, too."

"There is nothing wrong with that. If I hadn't been trapped here, I would have done the same, even if they couldn't see me."

Putting my arm around her shoulders doesn't work too well, and we both wind up laughing.

"Please don't feel sad for me. There's nothing you can do."

"Are you sure?" This woman sitting next to me looks so forlorn it feels wrong to just *not* do something.

Coralie nods. "You have already done the best thing anyone has done for me in a hundred years. I would be thrilled if we could talk again sometime."

"Yeah, no doubt. I'll be around here for the next couple of years a lot... and I usually head into town for food, so it's not a big deal to stop by."

"Thank you, Sarah Wright." She stands.

I get up too, tiling my head in confusion. "I didn't really do anything."

"Of course you did." She leans in close, whispering, "You saw me."

And with that... Coralie Hall fades away.

8

F THE UNIVERSE

Cops leave me alone tonight on the drive home.

I sit in the car for a few minutes checking over all the text messages that came in while I was chatting with Coralie. Normal updates from Ashley and Michelle, who are both no doubt asleep by now. Hunter sent a few 'how's class going?' and 'I love you' messages along with the occasional funny remark about annoying customers at the restaurant. This one guy sent his food back for not being seasoned enough. He left it under a warmer lamp for five minutes and brought it back to the guy—otherwise untouched—and it was fine.

Guess I'll go out for a snack and then deal with this calculus homework.

Without the burden of a car slowing me down, it only takes me a few minutes to get back to center city Seattle. I land in a dark alley and spend a little while exploring until I find a solitary guy in a black raincoat yelling at someone on the phone about marketing spend and throwing too much money at Europe. He's so into his conversation he doesn't notice me until I accidentally-on-purpose walk into him.

"Hey, watch where you're—"

The man's eyes glaze over the instant I invade his thoughts. He follows me like a good little mind puppet to a shaded alley between two high rises, standing motionless while I float up high enough to sink my fangs into the side of his neck. A rush of steak flavor fills my mouth. I've never actually had filet mignon before, but I think I'm tasting what I imagine it would be like. The guy reeks of money, and I'm really just glad I have no frame of reference for caviar. Blech.

A voice from his earbud repeats, "Mr. Strickland?" a few times before the line beeps off.

Ringing comes from his suit jacket pocket.

I hurry things along by sucking on the wound a little more than I usually do. Once I've had enough, I seal the puncture and blank myself from his memory. By this time, the phone's stopped ringing, but it starts again two seconds later.

An alley between two tall buildings is the perfect place for me to zip straight up without drawing too much attention to myself. Soon, I'm cruising back toward home—but an idea hits me. Calculus can wait an hour or three.

Minutes later, I glide in to land beside Glim on his favorite roof. As usual, he's sitting on the edge, feet dangling, gazing in the window of his ex-wife's apartment across the parking lot.

"Anything good on?"

"Ana's watching *Pretty Woman* again. I've seen it a hundred times." Glim leans back, turning his head toward me with a smile that would make most people (and some vampires) cry out in shock. Maybe I'm weird, but his overly pointy teeth don't bother me at all. They look 'right' for him. "What's on your mind?"

"Just some questions about 'how to vampire.'"

He chuckles. "Okay... Dalton's shirking his responsibilities again?"

"Well, one thing I sorta asked him and he avoided the question."

Glim holds up a finger. "I reserve the right to do the same if he had a good reason not to give you an answer."

"Fair enough." I sit on the edge of the roof next to him, let out a long, sad sigh, and explain how Sierra asked me to turn her into a vampire if something else killed her. Merely talking about it chokes me up.

Glim rubs my back. "That is quite a conundrum. The gift can do strange things if the recipient is too young. Have you wondered yet why you haven't run into anyone younger than yourself?"

"I just figured it was a really awful thing to do to an innocent kid... mostly the whole 'you have to die' part."

"Many feel as you do, yes. There are some places in the old world where our kind have organized themselves into a political system of sorts."

"Politics among vampires?" I fake gasp. "You're joking."

He grins. "Over there, it is considered forbidden to share the gift with one who has not yet reached physical maturity. Here in the States, third world countries, and the Middle East, not so much. However, it is still rarely done as it can have unexpected complications."

"Such as?"

"Ever see *Pet Sematary?*"

I blink. "They turn into little demonic psychos?"

Glim lets out a laugh that echoes over the parking lot and startles a stray cat. "It's a possibility, though perhaps my example was flawed. They will freeze as if in time, never maturing mentally from the state they're in at the time. I became aware of one such vampire in Iran who looked about nine or ten years of age, despite being two centuries old. The poor creature had no ability to understand time, nor his true age. It's not as if a vampire child would continue to mature mentally while being trapped in a body that cannot accommodate what their brains want to do."

I cringe. Of course, being eighteen, I take that sexually. Which then results in me having altogether horrifying thoughts about my siblings as they appear right now with fully adult minds. No. Brain bleach please. I whack myself in the side of the head like I'm trying to knock the idea physically out my left ear. Bad Sarah. Bad. Kid vampires are permanently stuck as innocent—but highly creepy—children.

"Most would consider it cruel," says Glim. "I'm inclined to agree."

"Yeah." I pull my legs up and wrap my arms around them. "Would it be crueler to lose them?"

"That's a comparison I don't think anyone can make. However, you shift the burden of cruelty from yourself to them. Instead of your loss, they potentially face a dichotic existence."

"But there's still a chance they could get like mentally stuck and remain a kid forever?"

He nods. "So I am told."

I swallow hard. "Look, I'm not at all going to turn anyone I know —or anyone I don't know for that matter—into a vampire just for the lols."

Glim pats me on the shoulder. "I believe that. You know, I've been thinking about what you said the other day on... bloodlines I suppose is the best word for it. Perhaps the circumstances of the Transference do have some effect on the type of vampire we become."

"Act of mercy?" I mutter.

"It's only a theory. Intent on the part of the existing vampire is important. Saeed El-Amin wanted a protégé, someone he could mold into an assassin. He said he chose me because I had the least fear among the entire platoon that night. The man took me like he selected the sharpest sword on the rack, and the blade had no say in the matter. He, too, was a Shadow, though some of our kind pass the gift on to others who do not join our numbers."

"He thought you were brave."

Glim lets out a sad chuckle. "I don't think I was any more courageous than anyone else there. Looking back on it, perhaps I was only naïve. The people around us seemed like anyone else back home. Just normal schmucks trying to live their lives the best they could in a shitty situation. Yeah, we had insurgents, people who looked like locals who'd kill us as soon as glare. A lot of the guys thought the whole country was like that. Me, I saw husbands, storekeepers, mothers, and children stuck in a situation no one should ever be forced to live in. I guess in a way I believed we'd gone over there more to fight for oil than defend the flag. I was just another poor idiot caught in the same meat grinder as the locals. So I didn't fear them. Probably dumb of me, but I figured whatever happened to me would happen, so being on edge all the time would only make me die tired."

"I still think that's brave. You could've been killed at any minute over there."

He laughs. "I technically was… but not by the enemy."

"Right."

"Blood."

"Already ate."

He shakes his head. "No, I mean to answer your question. Two things: blood and intent. In a traditional Transference, the vampire takes so much blood, the subject lapses into cardiac arrest. Before the living person finishes dying, the vampire cuts themselves and feeds their blood back to the person while desiring to pass along the gift."

I try not to think about doing that to anyone, least of all my sisters or brother.

"In your case, you'd already suffered a mortal wound, so Dalton skipped straight to the feeding you his blood step. And, of course, he desired to initiate the Transference."

"How long do we have? I mean… the only way I will ever possibly do that to anyone is if it's someone I don't want to lose, and they've asked me to do it. Like, do I have to give them blood before they finish dying, or can I drip it into someone who's been dead for a while?"

Glim puts a hand on my shoulder and fixes me with a stern look. "Do not, under any circumstances, ever feed your blood to someone who has been dead for more than a minute at most. The *best* result of that would be a Scrap."

I shiver. "Almost afraid to ask what the worst case scenario is."

"*Sefil*"—he says it with a foreign accent that kinda sounds Arabic.

"Right. That sounds bad."

"Heh. We are both vampires, but still ourselves. Our souls remain within our bodies. A *sefil* is created when an entity of darkness inhabits the remains after its soul has departed."

"Okay, right." I cringe. "Swear I'll never do that. I don't want to summon any demons."

"The *sefil* is worse. Demons make deals sometimes. Demons have reason." He winks.

Ugh. Right. There goes that idea. Odds aren't great I'm going to be right next to Sierra if something… not thinking about it. But, yeah. I'll just have to make sure she makes it to eighteen without a scratch. 'Cause, you know, I'm so good at preventing death.

"Is that guilt? You fear your being what you are will bring harm to them?"

"Not exactly. I mean, yes, but that's not what I'm mopey about this week."

He laughs. "Your sense of humor hasn't quit."

I manage a feeble smile. "Yeah I guess not. Sierra's obsessed with being shot at school. They did some drill and it totally freaked her out. I'm really surprised Sophia's taking it in stride. She's usually the one who worries."

"Children react in odd ways sometimes. When Stefan was six, he became irrationally terrified of this little ceramic owl my wife had in the living room." Glim holds his hands apart to indicate a statuette about eight inches tall. "He thought if he looked right at it, it would turn him to stone. I *still* have no idea where he got that from."

I chuckle. "Kids… but I bet his school wasn't doing active owl drills."

Glim whistles. "No…"

"Okay, second question." I try to push the gloomy thoughts away and sit up straighter. "How do vampires learn how to defend themselves with like claws and stuff? Like, is there a kung fu school for us somewhere?"

That gets him smiling. "I'm afraid not. I already had hand-to-hand training before I turned, so fighting came naturally."

"What kind?"

"Military close quarters focus. Little jiu-jitsu, little krav maga, bit of street brawling." He smiles. "Most of the time, a fight isn't like you see in martial art movies. None of that fancy, controlled back and forth stuff. Nine times out of ten, a fight's going to wind up rolling around on the ground inside of twelve seconds."

"Yeah, that's kind of how I remember it both times. I kinda feel like a cat on drugs whenever I get into a fight. Think you could maybe show me some stuff?"

He raises both eyebrows. "Are you planning something?"

"Nah. I only want to be left alone, but for some damn reason, the universe likes messing with me." I raise a middle finger at the sky. "Enough already, huh? How 'bout giving me a break." Sudden regret hits me out of the blue. "Wait. Hang on. Keep dumping on me if you want, just leave my family alone."

"Sarah..." Glim puts an arm around me. "You're not some kind of bad luck sponge. What happens to you has nothing to do with what happens to anyone else."

"Yeah, I know. But I'm just being superstitious." I smile. "I'm ninety-nine-point-a-billion-nines percent sure it's not going to matter, but on that tiny chance it does? What am I losing?"

"Just being guilty and miserable for nothing."

"Oh, so I'm Catholic now?"

He snickers. "Don't let Ana hear you say that. Okay, c'mon." He stands. "I can show you a couple basic things if you want."

"Cool." I grin.

"Unless you have somewhere to be."

"Nah. Just calculus homework."

He cringes and glides into the air. "I think I'd pull another tour in Iraq before taking that class."

"I'll take your word for that." I zip into the air behind him, hoping he doesn't kick my ass *too* hard. And yeah, Universe... if you're listening, please leave the littles alone.

9

PROFESSOR HEATH

If my little brother's karate class equates to 'yoga with screaming,' then what Glim and I did last night probably counts as 'highly aggressive mime school.'

I spent half the time picking myself up off the ground, but it was worth it. After an hour and a half, I've got a better handle on dealing with a single attacker coming at me from the front. And yeah, Glim threw me around like a doll while demonstrating defending against me pretending to attack him. When my turn came to defend, I started off 'combat hugging' him, but eventually worked out an arm lock takedown. No idea if it will really work against someone trying to kill me, but unless they're a vampire, too, I'm not all that worried.

The remainder of Wednesday night died as a sacrifice on the altar of calculus.

I wake up face-down in the book on my bed.

Ugh. Must've finished the last problem within seconds of sunrise. I don't even remember passing out. One second I'm doing homework, the next, my cheek is stuck to paper. It's almost three in the afternoon, so it's either kinda bright out or my 'fight' with Glim burned off more energy than usual.

After a brief period of feeling too tired to move, I finally drag myself out of bed and stumble to the door. The basement isn't too bad, but the top of the stairs to the kitchen throws off heat like a jet engine. Not that it's particularly warm out. This is all sunlight. Right. That's a big *nope* for going upstairs at the moment.

Tonight's class doesn't start until eight, so I have plenty of time. The sun's been going down around 7:30 p.m. the past few days, so I think I'm going to skip the car and fly. A little annoyed at the isolation, I plod back to my room and do a quick summary check of where I am with schoolwork. Wow. I'm all caught up. Amazing how much free time I have without a social life. Both of my friends and my boyfriend are all working and going to school. When I wake up, they're finishing up their last class and heading for their jobs. By the time I get back from my classes, they're all wrapped up in homework.

Wait, that's not totally true... Ashley has off one day during the week because she works on Saturday morning. I think that's tonight. Cool. Maybe we can do something. I shoot her a text to double check, then hop on the computer to burn some time with video games. Since I'm going in for programming, I may as well immerse myself.

I overhear Dad on the phone with the girls. They've decided to hang out at Nicole's place today and called to make sure it was okay— of course *after* they go there. Sam and his friends must be here since it sounds like a pack of elk on roller skates are having a dance off right above me. They wind up taking advantage of Sierra's absence and hitting the PlayStation in the living room on the big TV.

The afternoon is mostly uneventful except for an endless stream of foreign language cursing coming at me. Vampire reflexes plus first person shooter game equals I win. Or at least, I have the biggest kill count. Around half past five, I decide not to hop into another match and check light levels in the stairwell again. Still annoyingly bright but not 'Sarah burns to ashes' bad. I dart back to my room to throw on socks and sweat pants plus a long-sleeved sweater. Covering skin helps a little—at least it hurts less.

Mom's home already, and apparently in a good mood, so I head to the kitchen to help her with dinner.

"Hey, Mom."

She twists toward me, smiles, and gives me a brief one-armed hug. "Hey yourself."

"You seem happy."

"That contract went through. All the worry about layoffs is gone." She removes chicken breasts from a pack and drops them in a large, glass bowl. "And, Fowler called me into his office today to tell me that he thinks I'm vital to the team and is glad to have me. Might even get a promotion out of it."

"Oh, wow. Nice on that contract." I start slicing the veggies. "Lemon-garlic chicken?"

"Yep. Want me to throw in a piece for you?"

"I feel kinda bad wasting food."

She shrugs, and adds another piece to the bowl. "It's not wasted if you enjoy it. Food still tastes the same, doesn't it?"

I nod.

"So, umm..."

"I did not suggest that he give you a promotion."

Mom looks over at me. "So you *did* talk to him?"

"I can neither confirm nor deny rumors of a possible meeting."

She hugs me from behind, resting her chin on my shoulder. "I'd thank you, but I didn't ask you to do anything."

Her tone suggests she's being as evasive as I am, though I can't tell if we're messing around or if she really needs the plausible deniability to keep her conscience clean. "Of course you didn't. That would be unethical."

"In a theoretical situation where such a meeting took place, what do you think might have been discussed?"

I laugh. "Most likely that he would be foolish to lay off the best person working for him even if said best person refuses to kiss his ass."

"Best person..."

"Some shameless praise may have been involved."

She sighs and squeezes me. "We can't make a habit of this."

"Extenuating circumstances?" I grin.

"Right..."

Sierra and Sophia walk in. Soph heads upstairs while Sierra glides into the kitchen, heading for the fridge.

"Ooh, what's for dinner?"

"Chicken." Mom wags a garlic press at her. "It won't be long. Don't ruin your appetite."

While I tend to the cooking food, Mom runs upstairs to change. Sam's friends leave, headed home for dinner. He goes up to his room while Sophia and Sierra take over the living room. Sophia stands on one leg, pulling her other one as high up behind her back as she can get. I can just picture her losing her grip on her foot and kicking Sierra right in the face.

Watching her reminds me of the other night when she felt certain something had been watching her. Doubt the frog was responsible for that. I briefly wonder if Coralie might've been following me around... but she said she's trapped at the school. Hmm. Then again, Sophia waking up scared in the middle of the night isn't exactly a rare occurrence.

Dinner is nice. For a little while with the entire family around the table eating, talking—and in Sam's case, tossing bits of celery at Sophia—it's almost possible to forget anything supernaturally weird ever happened to me. I think I've finally even accepted that. Realizing I feel normal doesn't make me sad at all.

It makes me happy for the time I still have with them.

The littles zoom off as soon as they're done eating—another bit of normal that makes me smile. Since it's past seven, Dad shoos me off to school and takes on dish detail. Since I'm flying, I still have time... but hey, I'm not going to complain.

Having like twenty minutes sucks.

I mean seriously... it's too long to stand around waiting and too short to start doing anything interesting. Once I've got my backpack loaded, I change into another boring T-shirt and jeans ensemble, and add a hooded sweatshirt. My closet does have a couple nice things, but I've never been a clothes horse. Sierra's just like me in that regard. Our number one priority for clothing is 'keeps us from being naked.' Designer labels or trendy brands never really appealed to me. A $200 department store top covers me and is as warm as a $40 one from Marshall's or something. I'm sure the parents appreciate that. Sophia likes nice things, but to her, nice equates to frilly or pink. She doesn't really care about expensive.

The last fifteen-ish minutes before sundown I spend in the living room, sitting on the stairs with my sneakers on the 'shoe allowed' linoleum square and text-storming with Ashley, Michelle, and Hunter. Ash tells me all about this cat they had at the place she works today—stupid owners abandoned her for getting preggo. Michelle's on fire about one of the lawyers at the place she's interning at giving her attitude for making a comment about a case. Pretty sure it's not a racial thing or a female thing. Sounds more like the guy thinks interns should basically run around silent in the background until someone gives them a sock—or a law degree.

Hunter's day is busy and boring, so he mostly asks about me.

Eventually, the sun goes away enough for me to come online.

I send a ‹gotta go to school now› text to all three of them, do a quick run around the house hugging everyone 'see ya later,' and race out the door.

Barely a minute into the air, this deafening engine roar draws my attention to a car tear-assing down the street my cul-de-sac branches off from. It's an old school type sports car with a blower sticking out of the hood. Ooh. I bet that's the idiot that tidal-waved the littles. He's also driving like a complete reckless asshole, probably doing sixty down a street with a thirty-five limit. Guess he wants everyone to know he's got a shitty muffler.

I turn and follow him from the air until he pulls into a driveway not quite a quarter mile from the corner where my siblings wait for the school bus. Out of the corner of my eye, I catch sight of an orange pail in a backyard, already filled with muddy rainwater. Perfect.

Revenge time.

By the time I dive down to grab the bucket and get back up high enough not to be seen, he's opening the door to get out. Bombs away!

The muddy water splashes down on his head, splattering him, the white car, and the interior of the car, with brown while simultaneously hitting him hard enough that it knocks him off his feet. The dude as well as the car looks like they suffered the wrath of an incontinent pterodactyl, and he's soaked.

I put the bucket back in the yard I found it and proceed toward Seattle—but get distracted again when I spot a police car lurking in a side street a couple blocks west watching Avondale Road. After landing in the shadows, I walk up and say hello. During a brief innocuous conversation, I implant the notion that he wants to set up his speed trap on 197th ave tomorrow night and for the next couple days instead of here.

That done, I walk far enough that he can't see me, and take off again.

There's a lot less traffic flying to school than driving. Now *this* is seriously cool. My sneakers touch pavement about six minutes after I leave home. Whoever decided that school should happen during the darker parts of the year instead of summer seriously deserves a Twinkie or something. If only I could keep all my classes starting at eight. Though, once the clocks go back for the fall, it'll be dark even for my earliest ones, so I'll have a couple months of easy commuting.

Tonight's class is in the main building, downstairs one floor from ground level. Wow. Basement? Huh, okay. Whatever. Who am I to judge? After all, my bedroom is technically in the basement.

The room, other than not having windows, doesn't look much different from the other classrooms I've been in so far. Desks, shelves, whiteboards, that sort of thing. Again, no one would be able to tell what subject happened in here just from looking at the place. Unlike every other class so far, the professor is here before me, sorta-sitting on the front edge of his desk and talking to a pair of women in their thirties, both of whom clutch books to their chests like high schoolers.

He's in his later forties, pale, with salt and pepper hair combed back neat like a mafia don. Not sure what message he's trying to send by wearing a suit jacket over a dark blue T-shirt and dress pants. He *is* kinda old. Maybe he hasn't realized they canceled *Miami Vice* a long damn time ago. And yes, I know of it. Guess what one of my Mom's favorite shows was. Guess what's on VHS in a box in the attic now?

The professor keeps talking with the women, not paying much attention to the flow of students making their way into the room. Seems he's used to stragglers on the first day of a new semester as this room is a bit tricky to find.

At a lull in the new arrivals around 9:08, he slides off the desk to his feet. The women he'd been talking to head off to desks as he ambles over to the door, leans out, and looks both ways. Seeing no one out there, he eases the door closed then turns with a smile.

"Well, seems that's about it then. Apologies for the inconvenient room, it's all they had left. I hadn't saved up enough box tops."

A few of the older students chuckle.

What the heck do box tops have to do with anything?

"I'm Professor Peter Heath, and welcome to Who wants to *not* be a Millionaire."

More people chuckle.

He stops in front of his desk, hands clasped. "In all seriousness, welcome to my philosophy and sociology class. Now I'm sure you're all bracing yourselves for long, rambling, confusing lectures that take up the entire night and leave you just as lost about the meaning of everything as you were before you arrived... plus a whole bunch of mind-numbingly tedious work."

Murmurs sweep over the room.

Professor Heath holds his hands up, bowing his head slightly. "Well, I'm afraid I'll have to disappoint you in at least one of those areas..."

A few people make 'aww' noises.

"I'm not a true believer in work, tedious or otherwise. And life is mind-numbing enough."

Most of the students cheer.

"The point of my class, as I imagine could be said for any philosophy class, is to..." He raises both eyebrows as if some great profound knowledge is about to spill from his lips. "Sit around bullshitting for an hour."

Everyone laughs.

"Ideas." Professor Heath clasps his hands behind his back and proceeds to pace back and forth. "Since humans first realized they could think, we've been doing quite a bit of it. Though, perhaps not quite enough in these recent past few months."

More chuckling fills the room.

"In this class, we will consider ideas. Debate their merits, think about their meaning... and try not to let the administration find the weed." Before the laughter gets too loud, he raises a hand. "That, alas, was a joke. I'm not allowed to encourage such things, but who am I to tell you not to conduct any 'research' on your own time." He grins. "Speaking of life... Does anyone have any thoughts as to its meaning?"

Everyone's quiet.

He points at a guy in the front row, young twenties, short hair.

"Uhh, love?" asks the student.

"Love..." Professor Heath rubs his chin.

"Yeah, you know... find love."

Heath tilts his head. "Why?"

"I dunno. To get married, have kids. Procreate."

"Why?"

The guy shrugs. "To keep humanity going."

"Ahh yes, the usual routine." Professor Heath nods at him. "You've answered what people *do* with their lives. But what is the meaning of it?" He points at a girl a little older than me in a black leather jacket and blue wool cap. "What do you think?"

"Forty two," says the girl.

I laugh, as do about a third of the students.

"Fair enough." He winks at her and points at me.

Crap.

I'm about to feel awkward until we make clean eye contact for the first time and an astounding realization hits me.

The dude's a vampire. A trace of recognition shows in his broadening smile.

"What if there isn't any?" I ask. "No one asks what the meaning of a giant rock sitting in a field is. It's just there. What if life simply *is*? Not everything that happens or exists has to have meaning behind it."

"You know," says Professor Heath, rocking heel to toe. "In all the years I've been teaching this class, I've never had anyone come up with that answer before. An interesting concept. Why do you think humanity has been obsessed with the question of why we exist?"

I shrug. "Beats me. I'm only eighteen. I still think I'm immortal."

A few people laugh, mostly the older ones.

He holds up a finger. "Ahh, wait one moment. Our quest for immortality isn't scheduled until next month." Professor Heath gives me a subtle nod indicating he caught my pun. "We're not trying to be correct in this class, Miss…"

"Wright."

His eyebrows go up.

"Sarah Wright… with a w."

He laughs. "Ahh, clever. Well, Miss Wright. The questions floating around this class are ones that do not have specific correct answers, or what one may consider to be correct varies based on person and circumstance. The truth of perspective. Take a guess. What do you think is the reason humans have been obsessed with answering the 'why are we here' question?"

I make a series of faces while trying to come up with something. "Okay. I think it's part ego part curiosity. Curiosity in that humans are obsessed with learning and figuring things out, and someone a long time ago asked a question that's difficult to answer. Ego because I think we as a species feel so vastly superior to everything else—animals, possible aliens, the planet—that we can't accept beings like us simply happened by chance. Our ego demands that our existence have a reason for being. Why have a key if there's no door for it to unlock? They don't stop to think maybe it isn't a key at all."

Okay, now I know how Sophia felt at her dance recital. Everyone is looking at me.

"That's fairly deep for a woman your age," says Professor Heath.

"My mother's a lawyer and my sister has a PhD in sarcasm. I'm a master of weapons-grade bullshit."

"Do you believe that, err, 'weapons-grade BS' you came up with, or did you say something you think I wanted to hear or the class would enjoy discussing?"

"Well, you said take a guess. That's the first thing that came to mind."

He nods. "Interesting. Does anyone else have any thoughts on Miss Wright's theory that life has no meaning other than itself?"

A fortyish woman leaps at the chance to start talking about how God made humans.

"Why?" asks Heath.

"What?" the woman blinks.

"Why did god make humanity? Was he lonely? Did he need someone to give him a ride home from the bar if he had a little too much?"

A few people chuckle.

"It's in the Bible," says the woman.

A handful nod, a few roll their eyes.

"No one is disputing that. My question is still the same. *Why* did god make humanity? Or do you think Miss Wright has a point and he simply stubbed his toe on Jupiter and a bit of energy shot out when he said 'ouch' and created life?"

"I don't think any god made us at all," says a fiftyish guy with white hair and a fluffy beard.

Oh shit. Here we go.

The guy speaks for a few minutes about a random lucky mixture of environmental conditions and chemicals coming together on Earth that caused life to occur. God Woman counters by saying she thinks that still could be God's work, only over the course of millennia rather than an old man in a robe snapping his fingers. The next hour or so blurs by in a back-and-forth discussion about the meaning of life and possibly it not having any. I try to keep my head down, but Heath kinda threw me into the middle of the conversation, so I'm forced to chime in on occasion. True to his prediction, we engage in a roundabout discussion that meanders all over the place and never reaches any sort of consensus.

With about ten minutes left in the class, Professor Heath brings the discussion to an end. "May as well call it here. I'm sure you all wouldn't mind getting an extra couple minutes back in your day.

Next week, we'll take a look at some of that sociology stuff. Assuming a few of you actually bought the book in the syllabus, chapters two and three will be relevant to what we're talking about next week."

"Wait, does that mean we have to read them?" asks the twentysomething who thinks life equals procreation.

Professor Heath smiles. "My boy, short of breathing and eating, no one *has* to do anything. Well, I suppose those two are optional as well in the grand scheme of things. However, sometimes, the choice is fairly easy to make."

People get up and file out toward the door. Heath catches my eye and beckons me with a wave.

Sure he *might* want to talk about my thoughts on the meaning of life, but I think he's more interested in my thoughts on the meaning of death.

"Miss Wright."

"Yep. That's me." I smile.

"Sorry to take up more of your time, though I have a feeling you like to stay up late."

"What can I say? I'm a night owl. Bet you are, too."

He smiles. "Something of that sort."

I glance over at the door waiting for the last traces of sneakers squeaking on stairs to fade out. "Didn't expect to see another vampire in college."

"Nor I. You'd be the first. I imagine there's an interesting story behind it."

"Bit, yeah. I'm still kinda new. Happened this summer." I give him the short version of how I wound up with fangs.

Professor Heath shakes his head. "I'd comment about society, but man's capacity for violence hasn't changed… it's merely on Facebook now."

"Heh. What about you? What made you decide to be a teacher?"

He sits on the desk as he'd been when I first walked in. "I enjoy keeping the mind busy. As I'm sure you'll eventually know, it becomes difficult to routinely interact with people and not arouse some suspicions. Every forty years or so, I reinvent myself, move to a new state, new school."

"Guess it's working if you haven't gotten bored yet."

"It's my calling. Teaching truly sustains me." He wags his eyebrows.

I'm not sure whether to stare in horror or laugh. "You feed on your students?"

"Doesn't every teacher who loves what they do? Though, I dare say I'm somewhat more literal."

I chuckle.

"Ahh, the gloriousness of an open door policy and a private office. Nothing untoward happens of course, merely sustenance." He regards me with an almost sad smile. "I have shared my reasons for being here with you. Would you do me the honor of reciprocating?"

"Not that big a mystery. I'm just outta high school. Parents wanted me to go to college. I got into USC but after... yeah. Got like super clingy with my family. I guess I'm really here to feel as normal as possible."

"Well that does explain why someone so young would be attending night school. Barring a difficult home situation, of course."

"Difficult life situation. Or sun situation. How do you deal with it?"

"Notice my classroom has no windows? This basement area hadn't been intended for classrooms, but I persuaded the dean."

I nod. "Must make for an easy commute."

He chuckles. "That it does."

"Why the sad look before?"

"You're so young. But, I suppose it is better than your being stuck as an eternal child. Although, you could pass for sixteen."

I sigh. "Yeah. I know. Was talking to a friend of mine about kid vampires."

"Happens, but quite rare. Though, given the number of forty-year-olds I encounter wishing they could be children again and have no responsibilities makes me question if such a fate is truly as cruel as people think."

"To never grow up? What if they wanted to have kids or have a career or something?"

He regards me with a contemplative stare. "When you were small, how much thought did you spare to having children of your own, or a lucrative career?"

I shrug. "None, but I also wasn't stuck as a ten-year-old for eternity."

"And if your mind had thus frozen in the same thought patterns, wants, and desires as a ten-year-old? You would never consider anything else. They say ignorance is bliss. And a career isn't necessarily something to look forward to. Some people find happiness in their work, but for most, it's like looking forward to a prison sentence. Work is an artificial construct society has imposed upon the human condition."

"As opposed to meandering tribes?"

"I guarantee those meandering tribespeople never got a case of the Mondays."

I laugh.

"Child vampires. A rather somber subject. What's brought that out of you?"

"My sister…" I explain Sierra asking me to turn her if she ever got killed. "It's hard for me to even think about. And I'd only do it if something happened to them like what happened to me. Dying with no chance of survival."

"You should be careful not to attempt it if they have been dead too long."

"Yeah… I already heard about the *sefil*. And I *think* I know how to pass on the gift, but I don't think I'll ever do it unless someone really begs me and they're gonna die."

Professor Heath rubs his thumb and fingers together as if examining blood on his hand. "That is wise. Vampires made against their will often turn out a bit on the nutty side."

"A bit? Are you talking like hazelnut coffee 'bit of nutty' or Baby Ruth bar?"

"Varies."

I bite my lip, thinking about Glim. He doesn't seem crazy, but I get the feeling he'd come to terms with his death before it happened. If he'd survived that tour of duty, he would've been surprised. "Do you think I should do it if the situation ever occurs? Dalton didn't give me any choice—not that I really could've answered him at that point. But, like, is it better to save someone by making them a vampire or let them die? Even if they're too young?"

"Oh, vampire all the way compared to death. This is far too much fun to give up for whatever's on the other side."

"Other side?" I ask.

"Wherever ghosts go when they get bored. Or people go who don't become ghosts."

"What happens to vampires if we go foom?"

"Foom?" asks Professor Heath.

"Burst into flames? Die permanently."

"Oh. More than likely the same thing that would happen to anyone else."

"We're not evil? Our souls aren't destroyed by becoming vampires?"

He shakes his head. "I don't think so. True there are some religious folk who would call us agents of the devil or some such thing like that. Have you ever felt any strange urges making you want to do bad things?"

"Only when I get stuck in traffic behind some idiot doing ten under the speed limit." I fold my arms. "But I know what you meant, and no."

"No voices in your head telling you to kill, rob, steal, burn churches?"

"Nope."

"Light random priests on fire?"

I laugh. "Certainly not... though I did light my ex on fire."

He stares at me.

"Scrap."

"Oh..." He shudders. "Yes, that's completely justifiable."

We spend a little while having a philosophical discussion about the 'better to be a vampire or dead' thing, even if the person in question is 'too young.' Heath's all for doing it, especially since Sierra asked for it.

It's kind of a nice thought in a way... me and my siblings together forever, though I'd wind up basically turning into Mom unless I made the parents into vampires as well.

Of course, it's a nice daydream to think about having them forever, but it still feels wrong.

My siblings need to grow up and be normal. Wanting to keep them around forever is totally selfish on my part. Or at least thinking about them as permanent children is. They have their own lives and destinies and desires waiting for them. Professor Heath says he thinks 'The Universe' will leave them alone, at least since it already let me have both barrels.

Of course, I don't really think of it that way. Yeah, if Dalton hadn't been there, Scott simply murdered me... and 'game over, Sarah' happened, that would've been both barrels. But I hacked the matrix. Or, I guess Dalton hacked the matrix for me.

Whatever.

I'm still here and... major upgrade.

By the time our conversation ends, I'm in a great mood. Professor Heath is an awesome guy. Little eccentric, but he's a philosophy professor... that kinda goes without saying. And wow. Seattle Central College not only has a resident ghost, there's a vampire on the faculty.

While walking down the dingy grey hall to the stairs, I can't help but wonder... how much of the world is full of paranormal stuff like this? It's been around forever and like hardly anyone believes in it.

How many vampires could I have possibly run into before during my mortal life and never known? Wow, I could've even been fed on and not realized.

And... my brain is going crazy asking questions that have no answer. Well, I did just leave philosophy class.

Guess I learned something.

10

THE FUTURE'S SO BRIGHT

W hen I wake up Friday afternoon, I can tell from the leaden feeling in my arms and legs that it's another bright day.

That's not good.

Today's one of my early classes, and based on my sluggishness, it might just be too bright out for me to go. Crap. Not good to miss class in the first week. Though I *could* make the teacher forget I wasn't there. Still, I'm going to try my best to make it. Except for a really awful stomach virus when I was in sixth grade, I didn't miss a day of school except for snow when they closed the whole place down. If I had the choice, I'd have preferred being healthy and in school. At least I was so damn sick I don't remember much of it. Wednesday became Saturday afternoon in a blur.

No point even bothering to check my door, so I surrender to another hour drifting in and out of sleep before dragging myself to the computer desk. With my brain finally awake, I go back over my comp sci and calculus from Wednesday. Since I'm trapped in my room (or at least the basement as Dad tinted the windows) I may as well refresh my memory on classwork. You know that kid who's smart but lazy? Gets decent grades without even trying? Yeah, that's me. Or at least *was* me in high school. I'd been happy enough to get good grades with as little effort as possible. Never felt the urge to overachieve or be the valedictorian, though I came in third. I suppose having the third best GPA in my graduating class while barely trying means something—and not necessarily that I'm smart.

I read and go back over the calculus work, fixing a handful of problems where I catch slight errors. Guess I rushed a bit toward the end when the sun was coming up. Around five, I peek outside into the basement. It's still bright but doesn't feel like I'd turn into instant ash if I tried to go upstairs.

Time for some unusual measures.

Sunblock.

After smearing it all over my face and hands, I throw on the usual outfit plus a hoodie and sunglasses. I'd have worn gloves, but it's not *that* cold out and I don't need people staring at me like I'm crazy. Bad enough I'm a vampire. Well, no, that's not a bad thing. Having to hide it is annoying.

I step tentatively outside with my hood up... and I feel like I'm stuck in the Sahara desert. Even with shades on, it hurts to look at anything. Instinctively, I keep squinting and flinching away, ducking my head. And the sunblock is doing precisely nothing.

Silly me, trying to fight magic with science.

Well, driving to school is not going to work. I'm going to wind up causing an accident because I can't bear to keep my eyes open due to the painful brightness. I hop back inside and close the door a little hard, grateful to be in the much dimmer house.

"You okay?" asks Dad.

I shake my head. "Nope."

"What's wrong?"

"It's totes nuclear out there," mutters Sierra from her position in front of the PlayStation.

"Yeah. I can't drive right now. The light hurts my eyes too much to see."

Dad glances at Sierra, then back to me. "I could drive you in if you think you'll be okay once you're there?"

"Should be. I can sit away from windows. It's not exactly so bright I'm going to combust instantly."

"Okay." Dad leans into the stairwell. "Sophia, Sam?"

They scramble out into the hall.

"C'mon. We need to drive Sarah to school and I can't leave you three alone."

"Where's Mom?" I ask.

"Late at work. Some new important project she's in charge of."

"Oh." I put on a fake impressed face. "Fancy."

Dad grabs his coat and shoes. "She shouldn't be that much longer, but their set-up meeting took longer than expected."

The littles scramble over and grab their sneakers and coats. Even Sierra's not complaining about losing video game time. They're all kind of excited to see where I'm going to school. After we pile into the Sentra, I pull the drawstrings on the hood as closed as possible and stuff my hands in the hoodie's pockets.

Feels like I'm sitting in an oven.

Dad backs out of the driveway, turns around, and heads off.

"Shit," I mutter.

"What?" asks Dad.

Sophia gasps at my language while Sam laughs.

"I forgot you're driving. I should've allocated more than an hour to get there."

"Ha. Ha."

The ride into Seattle takes only a little longer than when I drive, which isn't all that bad. It sucks, by the way. Not the traffic, or my Dad's driving, or the Eighties music he has on the whole time. Actually, the music is okay. No, what sucks is feeling like a Barbie doll someone dropped in a deep fryer for thirty-two minutes.

"That's it?" asks Sierra. "It's just buildings. Aren't colleges like big or something, with fields and grass and stuff?"

"This is in the middle of the city. And it's more than just this building. A bunch of them around here belong to the school." I lean over and hug Dad. "Thanks for the ride. See you guys later."

"Need a ride back?" asks Dad. "Oh, sorry I didn't pack you a lunch."

"Duh…" Sierra rolls her eyes.

"Nah. I'll grab someone to eat while I'm here. And I can fly home." I grin. "Thanks, though."

Dad chuckles.

"Can we get ice cream?" asks Sophia.

"You haven't had dinner yet," says Dad.

"Gotta run. See you guys." I wave at the littles, hop out, slam the door, and run as fast as I can make myself move—about the stride of normal mortal me after falling asleep on the toilet for two hours—to the door.

Once I'm inside, the burn ratchets down from flame broiler to school cafeteria heat lamps. This really sucks… ugh. At least I only have an hour and a half to wait for darkness. I hurry to my comp sci class. It's mercifully on the east-facing side of the building, so the sun's not coming in directly. Walking into that room is like coming inside from a hot July day to air conditioning.

Okay, that wasn't *too* bad. I can tolerate this. Not like it could be any worse. The sun doesn't really become angrier than this in Washington, and if it *did* somehow get worse, my ass would stay home.

Good sign for the night: I feel like this computer science class is going to be too easy. Perhaps because I actually *did* the reading—twice —I spend the whole class mostly in a state of 'yeah, I know, can we move on to new stuff?' Professor Garcia keeps us a few minutes past seven to wrap up. It's still light out, but the sun has lost most of its fury.

I head to the cafeteria area again like I did Wednesday. Oh, damn. I forgot to joke with Dad about the arcade machines. Darn. I can do that tomorrow. Still, I'm not planning to feed quarters into retro video games when I can play them at home for free on my computer. The urge to feed is strong enough to be distracting, but it's still too light out for my fangs to work. I suppose I'd go online in the bathroom since they don't have windows… but there's that whole mental association thing. It's awkward enough biting a total stranger on the neck, but attempting it while crammed with them in a bathroom stall is worse. *And* if someone's recently demolished the atmosphere in there... gag.

Yeah, no. I think I'm going to skip bathroom feeding from now on. So, I'll wait for dark. Calculus starts at 8 p.m. That gives me a few minutes short of a half hour of break left after sunset. No point in rushing, so I'll grab a bite on the way home.

I finish about a third of the reading for comp sci, then head to Dr. Mercer's class. As soon as she starts her lecture, I remember her annoying habit of talking slow. Calculus is arduous enough without it taking super long while I'm hungry.

The class is supposed to be one hour long, so there's only a short break in the middle. Not enough time to feed without involving bathrooms. I only leave the room so I don't seem like a weirdo. During the break, I let people see me doing normal things like getting chips and a Gatorade from a vending machine after faking a bathroom visit.

Upon returning to my desk, I find Coralie sitting in the back row. She stands and walks over, taking the empty seat next to mine—not that anyone else can see her.

"Hey," I whisper.

She smiles. "Hello."

"Auditing calculus or looking for me?"

"I like to listen in on classes. It helps soothe the boredom."

Dr. Mercer resumes lecturing.

"Are you sure there's nothing I can help with?"

"Shh!" Coralie playfully swats at me. "Pay attention. You still have a future. I'll talk later. Meet me outside after class." Her expression shifts to pained hope.

Despite this woman being two years older than me—ghost age aside—I can't help but think of her as this lonely, lost soul in need of help. Something about the way she's staring at me feels too much like a battered wife trying to find the courage to ask someone to help them, and dreading she could be killed for opening her mouth.

I wait for Dr. Mercer to face the whiteboard and start writing before leaning close to Coralie. "If you need help, I'll do whatever I can."

"Shh," whispers Coralie. "I've been dead almost two centuries. It can wait another hour."

"The class is over at nine," I mutter.

"This is Dr. Mercer." Coralie gestures at her.

"Oh, right."

Dr. Mercer turns and looks at me, evidently having heard me talking.

Before she can make a quip about my not paying attention, I poke her in the brain with the urge to forget she caught me talking to an empty desk. Dr. Mercer steps away from the whiteboard, pointing, and begins explaining the equation she wrote.

I lean back, arms folded, and smile at myself.

Mind control would've come in damn handy a few years ago on this obnoxious teacher I had in eighth grade.

It makes sense now why the vampire community is hesitant to turn kids into vampires.

They would abuse the ever-loving heck out of it.

11

AFTER SCHOOL

C oralie didn't specify where she wanted to meet beyond 'outside.'

Of course, she decided to skip out on the last half of intro calculus and left while muttering something about how she can't believe society accepted teaching this 'crazy math' to women.

Okay, I get that she's like 200 years old, but still... grr.

That just makes me want to learn this shit even more. So, I focus as best I can given the plodding cadence of Dr. Mercer. It's not that she's monotone or boring, but listening to her makes me feel like reality is being played at seventy-five percent speed. It's like sitting behind a slow driver on a one lane road. The temptation to shout 'get on with it' is pretty epic, but I behave myself.

As usual, she runs late and class finally wraps up at 9:18 p.m. Still, it's an improvement from Wednesday even if only by a few minutes.

On the way out of the building, I take note of a clean cut guy in his early thirties wearing a business suit with the collar open and no tie. His day job might be sending him here to take a night class or two, or maybe he's trying to get a promotion. Either way, he's kinda isolated and I'm hungry.

Even though I didn't drive myself today, I decide to follow him to the parking garage and into the stairwell. Luck is with me as there's no one else around. I fake tripping, falling into him from behind. He spins, grabs me, and we make eye contact.

"Are you oka—?"

His expression goes blank as I basically hit the 'pause' button for his mind. Just in case someone else comes by, I pull the guy around into the space under the first set of stairs. If anyone *does* see us, they'll probably assume we're making out. And, of course, if anyone sees too much, I can always give them the *Men in Black* treatment. Maybe I'll make them think they work for the Post Office.

Trying not to giggle at that mental image, I pull the man's shirt out of the way and bite down.

I'm not sure what disturbs me more: that sinking my teeth into a person's neck has become as casual as having a biscotti with my coffee, or that the guy's blood tastes like chocolate cheesecake. Like seriously. Where in the hell did that come from? Nothing about this guy says chocolate *or* cheesecake... or even dessert.

Guess calculus derp-slapped my brain.

Oh well. Not what I was expecting to taste, but it's still yummy.

And yeah. I just referred to a person as yummy. I need help. Or I really need some cheesecake. Maybe both.

Going out in the sun this afternoon took a bite out of my energy reserves. Speaking of bite, once I feel sated, I lick the blood off the man's neck and think about wanting the puncture wounds to go away. And yeah, licking a strange dude's neck is only a *little* sexual in nature, but I'm not doing it for that reason at all. One, my tongue is already 'right there,' and two, the guy's shirt is too nice for bloodstains. And why waste blood.

Especially when it tastes like chocolate.

I drag the guy out from under the stairs, make eye contact with him long enough to erase myself from his memory, and leave him standing there staring into space. Hmm. I had been kinda hungry, so I took more blood than I usually do. We—vampires I mean—can sense the point where we approach taking 'too much,' and by that I mean a fatal amount. I didn't even come close to that with this guy, but he's still going to be a little woozy. On that note, I dive back into his head and implant a craving for orange juice and chocolate chip cookies.

Dunno if that actually helps, but they always give that stuff out at like blood donation places.

With my nutritional needs met, I head out of the garage and down the street, hoping I might find Coralie by that same church-shaped building. I'm not calling it a church because I still don't know if it's... oh, wait they have this sign out in the sidewalk. Looks like some kind of music/singing school. Cool. Guess I won't catch fire if I go inside.

Just kidding. At least, I'm assuming the holy ground thing doesn't work. When I asked Dalton about it, he just laughed. Right, so that's probably up there with crosses, garlic, running water, and all that other useless folklore stuff. Oh, stakes, too. They don't do anything beyond hurt—and ruin T-shirts that your kid sister gave you for Christmas.

Coralie stands up from where she'd been sitting on the steps of the former church and walks over to me. I stop, waiting for her, then turn and follow as she keeps going. She crosses Harvard Ave and heads right at the corner into the courtyard between the main building and the Science & Math building, the same spot we hung out at the other day... only this time, she goes past the corner and about halfway to the next street. I almost get the feeling she's hiding from something.

When she finally stops, she spins to face me with a nervous, fidgety demeanor that makes her look more like Sophia after she smashed one of Mom's glass figurines than a twenty-year-old woman with a serious problem.

"I'm guessing I don't know that much about spirits if there's something that can make you look that frightened," I say.

"Oh... well..." She sighs. "Yes, death is scary to the living. But there are worse things."

I raise both eyebrows.

Coralie shakes her head. "Not yet. I'm merely concerned they might happen. I'm still not sure if there *is* anything you can do."

"Won't know that until you give me a little more information."

"Yes, yes. I know." She emits a nervous chuckle. "My remains are being kept by a group of occultists connected to the school. I'm not sure if you would even have any way to help me escape from them, but... if you could, I would be forever in your debt."

"Heh. You realize 'forever' means something a little different to me?"

She laughs. Good. I *was* trying to make a joke there.

"Okay. I'll help if I can. So wow, you've been stuck in school for..."

"Over a century."

"Wow, that's... sorry." I cringe.

"It's not all bad. It's usually interesting here except during summer. Even then, there are a few classes going on and people around. Sometimes, I find someone who is sensitive enough to pick up on my presence, but you're the first person to ever really *see* me or that I could talk to. Except, of course, for the people keeping me. I've come to accept what I am, but I am tired of being imprisoned here."

I fold my arms, thinking. "So these, umm, occultists, can see and talk to you?"

"Not like you do. Only in a specific room that acts as a conduit between realms. Think of it as a window on the side of an aquarium tank."

"Have you spoken to Professor Heath? He's, umm... like me."

Coralie nods. "I know. He does not see me for what I am like you do. To him, I'm a shadowy apparition that frightens him. I do not think he will help me, so I have not bothered to speak with him."

"You're really what I see, right? No head games or stuff?"

"Since you didn't realize I was a ghost, I can only assume you see me as I appeared in life. I'm not trying to trick you, Sarah. Demons who play those sorts of games mimic smaller children."

"Wait... there's demons?" I blink. "Seriously?"

She nods. "That is the most apt name for them, though I cannot say with any certainty that any human belief system truly encompasses what they are."

"So, what about like God and stuff?"

Coralie shrugs. "If such a being exists, I have yet to see it. It is possible some manner of higher power is real. However, it either chooses not to show itself or doesn't exist as we would like to think of it."

"Huh?"

"A human-like figure. We could be like microorganisms coursing through the body of some vast, incomprehensible force."

"Right, okay. We're going off on a tangent now." I grin. "So, if I understand you correctly, some 'occultists' are holding you prisoner?"

She nods.

"What do you need me to do?"

Coralie edges closer, lowering her voice as if someone other than me might be able to hear her. "They are keeping my remains in a vault that is sealed both with physical locks as well as spiritual ones. If you could remove my remains from that place, I would be free."

"Ooh…" I grimace. "The last time someone asked me to steal something from somewhere, things went *way* wrong. I'm not a great thief."

"You're not stealing something." Coralie smiles. "You're rescuing someone."

"Fair point." Doesn't make me feel that much better about my odds of success, but it's a lot more 'noble' than pinching a spyglass Dalton tried to steal. "Okay. Where are you and how do I get in?"

She points back at the corner. "The old church. It's become a music school, but the lodge is underground, hidden behind a trick door in a storage room. Unfortunately, there are wards all over the place. Since you're supernatural, you can't go in the front door. There is another access in the school's main library, but it's probably warded, too."

It takes me a moment to process that. I set my hands on my hips and lean toward her, eyebrows scrunching. "Wait, so you're telling me that magic is real, these people have it, and because I'm a 'supernatural being' I can't even go in the building?"

"Not entirely. They only warded the doors and windows."

"Oh, okay. I guess I'll just bash a hole in the bricks."

Coralie winces.

"And hey, what if a vampire wanted singing lessons?"

She laughs. "They'd have to go to a different school."

"Ugh. So unless I somehow learn how to teleport, I'm screwed. What about the library one?"

"Follow me."

Coralie walks across the courtyard, down the street, and into the Broadway-Edison building. I act as casual as I can for someone walking *into* the building after 9:30 p.m., and follow her to the main library. Of course, it's closed at this hour. She phases right through the wall and keeps going. Short of ripping the doors off their hinges, I don't have any way inside. My new friend appears to notice this and stops, then hurries back over. She sticks her hand into the frame and the lock emits a sharp *click*.

"Ooh. That's a neat trick. Bet you're fun at parties. What's a little casual breaking and entering?"

She looks at me, confused, then walks in.

I slip in, pull the door shut behind me, and hurry down the shelves, chasing her into the back.

Upon reaching the end of a row of giant, old reference books, she points at a fat book on a shelf to the left. "Behind that. There's a brass fitting that looks like a shelf bracket. Push on it."

"Okay…" I tug the book out of the way and peer into the space behind it. Sure enough, a metal bracket juts out at the top corner. It appears to be an ordinary part of the shelf, but when I reach in and press a finger against it, it moves back a millimeter with a soft *click*.

The shelf straight in front of me at the end of the aisle swings inward like a door, revealing a cramped set of spiral stairs.

"Oh, ick. There's going to be bugs in there."

Coralie blinks at me.

"Yeah, yeah. I know. Vampire grossed out by bugs is kinda lame, but I'm still *me*. At least I'm not afraid of the dark."

She laughs.

"Well, okay. I *am* a little afraid of the dark, but nothing is dark to me anymore."

"You are a walking contradiction. A vampire afraid of the dark and bugs." She giggles.

"And the most evil thing I've done with my powers is compelling people to buy my kid sisters' Girl Scout cookies."

Coralie gapes at me. "They make cookies out of girl scouts?"

"Are you pulling my leg?"

"No, I am standing here."

I really can't tell if this girl is playing with me or not. She's got an awesome poker face. I guess you could say she's 'dead' calm. Ugh. There I go again channeling the spirit of my father. While making my way down the cramped stairs, I explain the whole cookie thing. She seems surprised that the girls aren't making them, and thinks it's sad that everything in the world is mass produced now. I don't bother saying anything about public health concerns and how people would freak out at kid-made cookies being sold to the general public. Bad enough they're conscripting children into a sales force, they don't need to set up cookie sweat shops.

Okay, that kinda gets me giggling to myself, picturing this Dickensian run-down warehouse full of beleaguered girl scouts slaving away over giant ovens and cookie sheets. Of course, in my head, all the grimy, hopeless little girls break into sudden song about how horrible a life they have in the cookie factory.

Yeah. Maybe I *do* need help.

I'm pretty sure we're in the basement by the time the stairwell corkscrews to a stop. This section of hallway doesn't look like it's normally part of the school... more like something from a World War II bunker. A few pipes run along the ceiling and the place smells like wet mold. Muddy footprints go in both directions, though not a great deal of them. Given the dampness here, I can't tell how long ago someone walked by.

Coralie leads me about forty feet to the end of the corridor and a right turn that ends at a big steel door reinforced with thick metal bands. An odd herbal-industrial smell hangs in the air, like someone roasting plants on a cookie sheet covered in motor oil. This thing looks like it belongs on the front of an evil mastermind's lair from the 1890s. The bronze handle is sculpted in the image of a dragon, wings tucked against its side. I grab it to pull, despite expecting the door to be locked. It's as hot as a boiling kettle. I yelp and jump back, waving my hand around. Once the pain stops, I look at my palm, dreading what I'm going to see... but it appears fine.

"Ow."

"Warded," says Coralie.

I sigh at the door, wondering if I can knock hard enough. Upon noticing a gap at the bottom, I flatten myself on the ground and peek. More corridor extends beyond it, something straight out of a medieval castle with armor on stands, statues on pedestals, and such. If I could somehow shrink myself to an inch tall, I could fit under the door.

"Wait a sec. Maybe..."

Coralie tilts her head.

I shove myself upright and hold up a finger. "I might have a way to do this. Let me check with a friend."

Her turn to raise both eyebrows. "I had been thinking of you using your mental influence on one of them and making them release me."

"Oh. Well, yeah I guess that *would* be easier."

She looks around as if worried about eavesdroppers. "Perhaps your way might be better. But they might have protections against mental influence. Better you avoid being seen and identified by them. Though..." Coralie smiles. "You are quite a bit more difficult to recognize than Professor Heath. If I couldn't *feel* your energy, I'd never know what you are by looking at you."

"Thanks." I gaze up at the ceiling.

"So... how long do you think it will take you to speak to your friend?" She flashes a hopeful smile. "Not being pushy, just curious. A little more waiting won't bother me."

"Well." I smirk at my backpack. "I did just get a shitload of calculus homework."

She nods.

"But... I have until next Wednesday." I grin.

12

FLEETING SHADOWS

F inding a gap under a door made me think of Glim and the
way he got us out of Petra's lair.

I'm hoping he'll be willing to let me 'borrow' that ability
the same way Dante loaned me his Fury. Then again, Glim is pretty
flashy with that stuff so I don't really know how much of all that black
smoke and such is illusion and which parts are real.

Still, he got in and out of that night club to take the spyglass and
we covered a *lot* of ground really fast when he did that umm 'shadow
jump' thing. I hope it's not like learning to fly an airplane or
something terribly complicated.

I fly to the roof he usually sits on, but he isn't there. Drat. Guess I
shouldn't assume he spends all his time sitting here watching his
family. At that thought, I sigh, feeling bad for him—and feel doubly
glad I decided to go home to my family instead of letting them
continue to think I'd died. Wonder what Glim is going to do when his
sons grow up and no longer live with their mom.

Knowing him, he'll probably rotate his time and haunt them all.

Kinda naïve of me to expect he'll be on this roof whenever I want
to see him. Maybe we should do the normal friend thing and trade cell
numbers. Not sure why it's never come up in conversation between

us. Now that I think about it, I've never seen him with a phone out. Maybe he spent so much time hiding underground in the Middle East he forgot about technology?

Though, Shadows do seem to have a way to communicate with each other. Maybe he doesn't need one? And really, who would he call? He makes Sierra look like an extrovert. So, on that note, I decide to head home.

Coralie did say she's not in any tremendous hurry, but does a soul's freedom rank higher on my list of priorities than the drudgery of math homework? I spend the few minutes the trip takes debating which of the two tasks is more difficult. Perhaps I should be worried that I can't definitely say stealing (or rescuing) the remains of a woman who died almost 200 years ago from an ancient mystical order is more daunting than calculus. It's definitely going to do more good for the universe as a whole. The odds of me ever actually *using* calculus are pretty low. But, after her comment about it being 'too much math' for girls, yeah, I'm gonna own that shit.

Really, it's my old laziness coming out. Schoolwork that I found tedious, I made out to be this great big task. Like physics homework and building the Giza Pyramids equated in difficulty. No, this homework isn't *that* bad. I'm just dreading doing it because it's the exact opposite of fun.

But at least I don't have to roam around the city to find my calculus book.

I land in my backyard and walk up onto the deck.

"Sarah," says Glim, while materializing out of thin air in a billow of shadows beside me.

Good thing my heart is only faking it, or it would've stopped.

"Shitrabbits!" I yell, jumping back.

He tilts his head. "Dare I ask?"

"Uhh, no idea where that came from." I take a few slow breaths. "You scared the hell out of me."

His attempt to hide his amusement fails, though once the shock wears off, I can't help but laugh. Ash, Michelle and I used to scare-prank each other a lot. Sophia's no fun, since she winds up crying and makes me feel guilty. Sierra takes revenge in other ways... like tying the laces of all my shoes together so tight I had to go to school in flip flops in the middle of December.

"You were looking for me?"

"Yeah." I glance sideways at the sliding patio door to the kitchen. Lights are on in the living room, which means the parents are still up watching TV. It probably won't bother them to talk out here unless I scream again. "So... I ran into this ghost at school."

I explain the situation with Coralie asking me to help her escape.

He listens, offering the occasional nod.

"Anyway, I was wondering about that weird shadowy thing you did when you carried me away from Petra. Is that teleportation? Could that get me inside this place?"

"Not exactly teleportation. It's stepping into the spirit world, traversing distance there, then crossing back into this world. We are still covering the same amount of distance, merely in a different place where the rules aren't exactly the same."

"Do you think it could get me inside there, past the wards? There's a gap under the door. If I could turn into smoke, I could fit in."

"Possibly. Are you sure she isn't manipulating you?"

"I don't think so." I shrug. "She seems so lonely and sad. And really, it's not like she's asking me to hurt someone or steal anything valuable... just get her remains away from the people holding her prisoner. That doesn't sound bad."

He nods. "If all she's requesting is for you to liberate her remains, I'm inclined to agree with you."

"Cool." I smile. "So, I was thinking... can I borrow that shadow hop thing like I borrowed Fury from Dante?"

He rubs his chin, his nails glinting in the moonlight. Even retracted, his claws are longer than mine fully extended. Of course, being eighteen, my brain jumps straight to what Hunter did with his fingers the other night and I involuntarily cross my legs in pain.

"Something wrong?"

"No. Just random bad thoughts of the painful kind." It's way too awkward to talk with Glim about intimate stuff, especially the kind of intimate stuff he couldn't partake in with those swords on his hands. "You seem hesitant. Is it dangerous?"

Glim bows his head. "I think so, yes. That ability is too close to our core nature. It would be like you loaning me your tolerance for daylight. Too powerful, and wouldn't last long. Also, if it faded at the wrong time, you could wind up stranded on the other side or disfigured."

I shiver at the word 'disfigured.' Maybe it wouldn't be such a great idea to mix such an intrinsic aspect of the most dead-like vampires with the most lifelike one. It's been awhile since I had chemistry class, but mixing exact opposites rarely ended well.

"Ahh. Hmm." I shift my jaw side to side while thinking. "Guess I risk mental influence."

"It would be too dangerous for me to feel secure in trying to loan you that ability temporarily. Better I go with you."

"Really? I don't wanna impose."

Glim's broad smile shows off his pointed teeth. "I'm not exactly running late for a business meeting. Besides, I'd rather go along and help than you wind up stuck in a prison cell again."

"Ugh, don't remind me. But these guys aren't vampires, and it's dark now so no one's kidnapping me. Give me a sec to put my bag inside?"

He nods.

I unlock the door, slip inside, and head down to my room to deposit my backpack on the bed. The parents don't notice me, and I don't want to keep Glim waiting while a long conversation happens... but I can't let them worry. Ugh. They're watching *Titanic* again.

"Hey guys. Just checking in. Be back in a little while."

"Going back out?" asks Dad. "How was school?"

"Fine. Dr. Mercer's a bit... I don't want to say long-winded, she just talks really slow." I hug them both. "And yeah, gotta go do some vampire stuff."

"What is this time?" asks Mom. "Another war between the elders?"

"Nah. Just going to try and help someone escape a bunch of occultists who're holding her prisoner for the past century or so."

Dad shakes his head. "Seattle's really going to hell."

I can't tell if he's making fun of the situation or didn't really hear what I said, but... Glim's outside. "Be back as soon as I can."

They nod.

"Have fun, dear," says Mom. "And try not to kill anyone who isn't already dead."

I blink. Whoa. Okay. I'm in another dimension now. My parents have gone to Mars.

"You guys okay?"

They both look at me.

"Fine, why?" asks Dad.

"I just told you guys I'm going to try and rescue someone from occultists and you're being like super casual about it."

Mom fidgets. "Well, I figure you know what you're doing with this *weird* stuff now... and, well, we are trying to be as supportive as we can. You're still our daughter and we love you."

"Guys, I'm undead, not out of the closet."

"We appreciate you scheduling vampiric shenanigans late enough that they don't conflict with taking your sister to dance class." Dad winks.

"Right... Umm, yeah. Got someone waiting on me so..." I point both thumbs toward the kitchen. "Gonna get going. See you guys soon."

They wave and un-pause the movie.

I'm half tempted to say 'the boat sinks' but they've already seen the movie. And well, anyone going into that film who is actually surprised that the boat goes down... I can't even. Mom's right. Our education system is failing.

Anyway... I head outside to meet Glim. He takes my hand and we leap into the air again. It's somewhat odd to see him flying. Well, it's odd to see a human flying in the first place, but for him, the lack of just poofing into a cloud of darkness is unusual.

"We're not jumping into the cloud of black stuff?" I ask.

"I'm not entirely sure where you wish to go."

I point toward Seattle. "There's a door in a tunnel under the library at Seattle Central College."

"Never been there. While I'm sure I could eventually find it, it will be faster for you to lead at the moment."

"Okay."

Not that there's a real rush, but I fly as fast as I can make myself go. It's pretty obvious he's barely working to keep up with me, which reminds me that I'm pretty weak among vampires. Both for being new and an Innocent. Tolerating sunlight is a huge deal, but other than that, my 'powers' are pretty tame. For what I want most right now—being with my family—it's perfect, but I briefly wonder if like two hundred years from now I might feel jealous. Like, once my parents, sibs, and friends are gone and I'm not so closely tied to any living relatives, would I really care about being able to wake up before the sun goes down?

Throwing cars around could be pretty fun.

Meh. I'm not unhappy with what I've become, not at all. This is still pretty damn cool. No sense grumbling about things beyond my control. And it's not like I'm Sierra playing an MMO. I don't have this drive to 'level up' and become the most über vampire in the world. I'll probably wind up collecting cat figurines or something and keeping to myself.

That gets me wondering if vampires like Aurélie ever imagined cars, airplanes, or space travel. Like, what is the world going to have when I've been a vampire as long as she has? Will androids and stuff be everywhere? Cybernetic implants? Could a vampire even use them? Okay, maybe I won't wonder about that. The idea of sticking computer bits inside my head is kinda disgusting. Maybe vampires will go mainstream and become another minority. Sure would be much less of a pain in the ass than having to keep secrets. Or probably not. People want to hate and kill each other for variances in skin tone that are meaningless. Something like society discovering vampires are real where there actually *is* a difference? Yeah, out will come the torches and pitchforks.

I fly us back to Seattle and land in a cluster of trees by the corner.

Despite it being after ten, there are still a few people here, but no one noticed us come down. That's gotta be Glim giving off some kind of 'don't see us' power.

He looks around. "Which one?"

"C'mon."

Still holding his hand, I hurry across the street and make my way back to the main building. The doors are still open, so we go inside and down the hall to the library. Coralie re-locked it on our way out, so I stop outside the glass doors.

"Go all the way to the back and left. At the end of the reference section, there's a secret door in the wall. That goes to a spiral stairwell, then a corridor underground. There's only one way to go there, so it should be obvious."

He nods.

Glim leans slightly toward the door and a whooshing rush wells up around us. For an instant, my stomach leaps up into the back of my mouth from the floor falling out from under me. Walls of shadow rise up on all sides and collapse over us, changing reality into this black-and-white, twisted version of the world. We lurch toward the narrow gap between the doors, which widens like a giant pair of ancient castle gates pulling apart. Shelves blur by in a torrent of shadows. Glim pulls me along, bobbing and weaving side to side with the weightless agility of disembodied eyeballs flying around. It occurs to me that I can't feel my body at all, and trying to move my arms or legs doesn't do anything. When I try to look over at Glim, my view rotates, but the only thing I see is a mass of darkness with a vaguely head-shaped part at the leading end. Oh, this is trippy.

Do people even say 'trippy' anymore?

Yay me for having a father stuck in the Eighties.

Glim's shadow form swerves to the left, pulling me along into a silent vortex of books and infinite darkness—sort of like being a librarian. I try to ask him how we're supposed to push the hidden button to open the secret passageway, but my voice ignores me. He doesn't slow down, flying straight into the bookshelf at the end.

A sensation akin to jumping naked into a bathtub full of tepid peanut butter accompanies us passing *through* the solid barrier into a nightmare version of the spiral stairs. On this side of reality, the metal railing appears to be covered in glowing blue marks, rune writing. Going down is *way* faster in this form. In mere seconds, we're at the bottom and cruising along the underground passageway. It's pretty hard to get lost in a corridor that has only one door.

We round the only corner and stop short at the sight waiting for us: the door is glowing bright blue. Circles appear, drawn in thin white lines, rising up from the door's surface and expanding out a few inches until they fade away. Each ring is lined with indecipherable writing in no script I've ever seen before.

But damn, it's kinda pretty and mesmerizing.

Glim dips low, dragging me along. What had been an inch-high gap at the bottom grows cavernous. We slide under a ceiling of roaring blue fire. I can't help but cringe away from it, feeling like a hunk of meat teased by a char broiler. The instant we're past the painful light, I stop short. A blurry, shadow-filled hallway in front of me appears to stretch off away from me along with a sensation similar to being drawn backward at high speed. The next thing I know, I lurch forward as if I've been fired out of a slingshot and land face down on solid stone.

"Ow," I mutter.

Everything is spinning so damn much, I can't even push myself up. I roll on my side, holding my gut and throwing up like I've never puked in my life. Only... I'm not actually throwing up. There's nothing in me to come out, which makes the convulsions way more painful.

Hands grasp me under the arms and gently lift me upright, holding on until the retching stops.

"Are you all right?" whispers Glim.

I cling to him, shivering. "No. What the hell happened to me?"

"The energy in this place interferes with my crossing. It is mild, but it has affected you more because you are neither acclimated to, nor supposed to experience that world."

"Right." I swallow hard, then lift my face away from his coat.

Sure enough, we're inside. The hallway looks like we've gone back in time to a medieval English castle. It runs on for at least a hundred yards with multiple branching passages on both sides, archways, and doors everywhere. Several suits of medieval plate armor stand on pedestals among tapestries showing a bunch of dudes wearing funny costumes. The outfits sorta have an Egyptian feel to them, but the men are almost whiter than I am. They've even got some swords hanging on pegs and some other weird symbols I don't understand.

Odder still, a heavy metallic quality in the air tastes like I'm sucking on a penny.

"I'm going to assume you don't know where specifically she is," says Glim.

"Nope."

"Keep holding my hand then in case we need to make a quick exit."

I nod. "No arguments here."

My confidence has taken a slight hit. It's easy enough to laugh off the idea that magic exists when someone's merely talking about it—even if that someone *is* a ghost—but I can't explain the funny feeling tingling over my skin, or the glowing door with arcane circles dancing around it.

"I don't think we're in Kansas anymore."

"Indeed."

Coralie walks out into view a ways down the hall, and waves at us in a beckoning manner. Her eyes are wide and she appears to be trembling.

"There she is. Can you see her?"

"Yes." Glim nods. "You are right. She looks terrified."

"Let's hurry up then before someone notices we're here." I jog toward her. "Do you think they live here?"

Glim glances around at the décor. "I wouldn't think so. This place has the look of a lodge. I'd guess they use it for meetings or rituals."

"That's good." I stop in front of Coralie. "Is there anyone else here?"

"No one alive." She bounces with excitement and nearly attempts to hug me, but catches herself, remembering she's not solid.

"Cool. Perfect. Umm, this place is a damn maze. Where are you?"

Coralie points at a set of wooden double doors behind her. "This way."

While she ignores them, I have to open them. Fortunately, these aren't locked. I step into a long, curving hallway with dark walls, burgundy carpeting, and a serious amount of medieval weapons on the walls. Every like twenty feet, a big alcove on the outside of the curve holds a leering gargoyle statue as big as a man. They're all the same: muscular male figures with eagle heads, angel-wings, and clawed hands. I'm sure they're meant to be menacing, but having them perched on pedestals like cats makes them look a little silly. People only adopt that posture for one reason... and they don't do it terribly often since the invention of the flush toilet.

My inner ten-year-old snickers at the row of pooping gargoyles.

Coralie breezes down the hallway, but stops short without warning, pointing at the wall. "Sarah. You should take that."

When I catch up to her, I realize she's gesturing at a shield.

"Are you serious?"

She nods. "Yes. But you won't have to carry it for long."

"Okay... whatever." I reach up and grab the giant thing from the wall, staggering under its weight. "Oof." Once I think about wanting to be stronger, the shield goes from as burdensome as a car door to a hunk of plastic. "Okay. Got it."

With the exuberance of a kid racing to the living room on Christmas morning, Coralie zooms off down the hall. She leads us through a series of turns—crap this place is big—to another passage that ends with a pair of ornate metal double doors that look fairly tough. Etched symbols cover most of the flat spaces in neat vertical rows, though I can't begin to read it.

"I can't go past here." Coralie turns to face us. "This is the vault. Turn left at the first room, follow the hallway around, and you'll find me in there. Mine is the only body in the place, so you shouldn't have any confusion."

Glim nods and examines the doors. "We'll need to jump past it."

"Is King Kong going to gut punch me again?" I shiver, nearly ready to say screw it.

"For such a brief hop, I doubt it."

I heft the shield. "What about this thing? This isn't going to fit under the door."

He laughs. "Neither should your body. Be glad I am a Shadow and not a Sybarite."

"Do I even want to know why?"

"Some of them can turn their bodies into fog... but only their bodies. No clothes or objects."

I smirk. "I've already put in my twenty-four hours of compulsory public nudity when I escaped the morgue. Not really in any hurry to do that again."

Glim smiles. A brief flash of shadow surrounds us along with a stomach-twisting moment of vertigo. I'm vaguely aware of something whooshing past us at high speed, and we're standing in another hallway of plain concrete walls.

"Oof." I press a hand to my stomach. "I'm okay. Just did a little flip."

"The Old Guard can transubstantiate into mist as well, but as I understand it, it takes them a long time to reach that level of power. Perhaps the Sybarites who are wonton libertines manage it more easily since it takes less energy for them when they leave all their possessions behind. I can't say I've ever cared to study it."

As soon as the cramp in my gut fades, I look up. A short distance in front of us, the corridor connects to a room filled with an assortment of giant trunks, cabinets, and shelves holding all sorts of things: books, globes, bottles, staves, and bundles of fabric that could be rolled up tapestries or enormous scrolls. The air in here is so dry and dusty I'm tempted to lick the floor to *improve* the flavor in my mouth.

The hairs on the back of my neck stand on end. I can't tell if it's due to nerves at breaking the rules, a genuine feeling that something is now watching me, or some unexplainable magical energy.

I cautiously advance down the plain hallway. "Wow, I thought that turning into fog thing was a made up story. What about wolves and ravens?"

Glim shakes his head. "Not that I've ever heard of."

"So," I whisper, still creeping forward. "How's that fog different from what you can do?"

"They aren't jumping into the spirit world. They're stuck drifting around only as fast as the wind pushes them."

"Oh that sucks. Guess it's really for quick escaaaaaaa—"

I'm flying across the room before I realize something smashed into me from the left with a loud *bang* of stone-on-wood. My body slams into the concrete wall on the right side of the room, then slides a few feet down until my sneakers touch the floor. It takes me a second to realize I'm peering over the shredded remains of that shield at one of those gargoyles.

Only… it's no longer squatting. The damn thing's *alive*.

And that shield is the only reason my head is still attached.

"Fuck!" I shout.

The bird-headed pale grey statue pivots and swipes its claws at Glim, who disappears into a puff of black smoke. Three stone claws as long as steak knives pull at the dispersing mist. The gargoyle shifts its head toward me. Blue light wells up within its eyes. I raise what's left of the shield to guard my face an instant before a strange buzzing crackle goes off. Something hits the shield with the force of a mild punch, and a corresponding *bang* comes from the right.

I glance over at a patch of blue fire burning on one of the shelves.

"Oh, of course it throws tiny fireballs from its eyes."

Azure beams like lasers shoot from its eyes, converging a short distance in front of its beak. Another little comet of blue flames forms and flies at me, but slows to an almost-creep once my reflexes slow down the world. It's almost trivial to swat it aside with the shield. This evidently annoys the creature as it comes storming at me, raising claws.

Glim grabs a giant quarterstaff thing covered in decorative feathers, beads, and other dangling junk. He rushes the gargoyle from behind, swinging to take its head off. The stick breaks on contact, though the hit does make the creature stumble. Glim eyes the broken staff with a contemptuous 'cheap piece of shit' smirk.

The fireballs are slow enough to my accelerated reflexes that I can dodge them with ease, so I toss the broken shield aside and run to the right, putting some distance between me and razor sharp stone claws. Coralie is probably losing her mind on the other side of the door at all the noise we're making in here. I wonder if she even knows about the —of course she does. She told me to take the shield.

Geez. It would've been real nice of her to warn me.

The gargoyle whirls on Glim with surprising speed for a solid stone statue. Again, it shreds a dissipating cloud of black smoke when he poofs at the last second. I have no damn idea what we're supposed to do to a creature like this. Our claws aren't going to scratch it. Weapon. Need a weapon... I start looking around at all the junk in here—taking note of three corridors leading out, one in each direction. Hmm. Maybe running is the best idea?

When the thing charges at me again, I race around the room in a wide circle.

"Hah! You might be strong and tough, but I'm still faster than you!"

It shoots another fireball at me.

"Cheater!"

I stay ahead of the first one, and stop short, letting the second fireball go past me in front. The gargoyle shrieks like an eagle someone kicked in the balls. Glim reappears in an inky cloud above and behind it, falling into a drop-kick that knocks the six-foot bird man flat on its front with a resounding *thud*.

"Okay... if there's anyone in here, they definitely heard that." I eye the left offshoot. "If there's anyone on the fourth floor of the school, they heard that. Shit, my parents probably heard that back in Cottage Lake."

Glim laughs.

A metallic gleam catches my eye from one of the shelves. I zip over and grab a broadsword from under a giant cloth scroll. But... it doesn't have the heft of a real weapon. More like a cheap ceremonial blade. It's not even sharp.

The gargoyle pushes itself up to kneel.

"Bleh. It's a prop." I toss it back on the shelf. "We're not going to be able to get her out of here with this thing in our way, are we?"

"Of course. Once we find her, it's easy to leave." Glim jumps on the gargoyle's back, knocking it flat again.

"Okay. Let's grab her and get the hell out of here." I run across the room, jump the gargoyle's legs, and haul ass for the hallway that would've been a left turn from the way we entered.

The gargoyle rolls onto its side and swats Glim with a wing, launching him into a tall shelf. He smashes into it, creating an explosion of dust and flying splinters. Grr. It lumbers back to its feet and turns toward him. He looks down at a large piece of broken wood sticking out of his chest that evidently impaled him from behind. That looks super painful. And it's my fault.

I skid to a stop, and by total chance, wind up eye-to-top with a giant metal candlestick. It's solid bronze or brass or something. Perfect. Even with my strength turned up to eleven, it's got obvious heft. I grab it like a baseball bat and dash back across the room, leaping into the air and bringing the metal club down on top of the gargoyle's head.

A dull *clonk* accompanies the candlestick bending. The gargoyle's head shatters into several large hunks of stone. The body ceases moving like living tissue, statue-rigid in an instant. It falls over sideways with another floor-shaking *thud*.

"Take that, bird brain."

"That was even more painful than this board." Glim sits up, stands, and walks over before turning his back. "Would you mind?"

I grab the piece of shelf sticking out of him and pull. "I'm really sorry."

"Oh, it's not that bad. Worst thing is having to get a new coat, but it's fine. We have an entire room full of brooding black trench coats back at the conclave."

"Hah."

Faint scraping draws my attention to stone chips vibrating on the floor. They gradually slide toward the gargoyle body.

"Shit. It's putting itself back together." I whack it in the head again to break more of the neck stump.

Glim flashes a toothy smile. "It appears you only, umm, knocked it out."

I use the candlestick to swat a softball-sized piece of its head across the room. "Hopefully that'll buy us a few more seconds. Wow, talk about a splitting headache."

"You are your father's child."

"Sorry, the puns are contagious." I jog to the corridor, spend a few seconds trying to straighten out the candlestick, and stand it back where I found it. "Maybe they won't notice."

Glim scratches his chest where the wood had poked out. "Worst part about wood injuries is they itch so damn much."

"Is that where the stake thing came from?"

"Maybe. Could be an allergy... most likely it's my body purging dust particles or tiny splinters."

The corridor only goes about twenty feet before it bends to the right and leads to an octagonal room with tall cabinets, most of which have fancy inlay patterns. This stash makes me wonder who raided the bedrooms of a dozen princesses... and at least one princess is wedged between two cabinets on the left side. Or at least, a former princess.

Surprisingly, for a woman who's been dead for almost two centuries, Coralie's body doesn't look that bad.

Her dress has rotted more than a little, but it's clearly the same outfit she's wearing as a ghost. Something weird and magical has to be going on here to preserve the body, since she doesn't look *too* decayed or dried out. Her skin's intact and white as paper, her waist-long hair light brown and reasonably healthy in appearance. A slight hint of withering at the mouth is the most obvious sign that she's dead, along with her sunken cheeks. She looks like a mannequin tilted to the left, her head against a cabinet and arms at her sides. The contrast between her perfect hair and slightly-not-right face makes her look more like an ancient doll than a corpse that's been sitting around since 1849.

I creep over to her and reach a tentative hand out, tracing my fingertips over her sleeve. Dry fabric at the verge of disintegrating crinkles at my touch, the arm under it as rigid as wood. Thankfully, the body doesn't give off much of any detectable smell beyond a faint floral perfume—which is pretty damn weird.

"Wow… you've aged rather well."

Glim walks up behind me. "They've turned her into a mummy of sorts. Preservation techniques I do not understand have been used on this body."

"Thank you Captain Obvious." I chuckle.

"I mean *remarkable* preservation. She's barely decomposed at all."

"But she's clearly dead." I fidget. "Ugh. Is this what I look like when I'm sleeping? No wonder I freaked Sophia out."

A loud scrape of stone sliding over the floor echoes in the hall.

"Here comes big bird," I mutter.

"Think we should bug out."

"Yeah. So how's this work?"

He wraps his arms around me from behind. "Pick her up."

You know, after tearing Scott up with my bare hands, touching a well-preserved mummy doesn't bother me at all. Without the slightest hesitation—a 1,200 pound homicidal statue is quite a motivator by the way—I grasp Coralie's body as gently as possible and lift her. I'm initially startled at how light she is, but then I realize I probably made myself strong enough to lift up one end of a car right before walloping that thing over the head. Guess it works in a way akin to vampire adrenaline… takes a few minutes to wear off.

"Okay. Got her."

A ring of blackness washes over me from behind as I fall backward down a well of endless darkness. The void closes around us, leaving me once more in a swirling, colorless world. Roaring wind fills my ears, so loud I couldn't shout over it even if my voice worked. I catch a vague glimpse of the gargoyle's glowing blue eyes turning toward us, but we're down the hall in seconds and bird man is gone behind the corner.

Glim must be flying upside down and backward. I feel like a

drowning swimmer being pulled to shore. It's super disorienting not to mention freaky as hell having no control over where I'm going while falling ass-first at the speed of a jet aircraft. Before I completely lose my shit, I close my eyes. The rapid swaying of turns bothers me much less when I don't have to see the twisting landscape awash in churning dark vapors going by.

Not that I have much of a sense of time, but it doesn't seem to be that long before all the motion and deafening whooshing cease. My head stops spinning a few seconds later with the realization that my feet are on the ground and Glim is no longer hugging me.

"You can open your eyes." He chuckles. "We're clear."

I risk a peek, and find myself standing outside my house. "Oh, wow. I didn't realize you brought me all the way back here."

"Much easier than conventional flying with a third passenger." He smiles. "And faster."

"No kidding. Thank you!" I set Coralie on her feet to free one arm so I can sorta-hug him. "I'm really sorry you got hurt."

"It's hardly the worst thing I've experienced since my Transference. I hope you never encounter a land mine. Regenerating an entire leg is not fun."

I cringe. "Ouch."

"Indeed. Well... I'm off to find something to eat."

"Okay. If there's ever anything I can do for you, please let me know."

He winks. "Perhaps you can visit me in the usual spot tomorrow or the next day and bring some beer."

I grin. "You got it."

13

A QUIET ROOMMATE

One thing I never expected would happen is to have my parents catch me carrying a dead woman into our house.

They're both still up watching TV, and glance over as I walk inside and nudge the door closed with my foot. I'm carrying Coralie sideways kind of like an ironing board under my left arm. She's a bit unwieldy after all considering she's about as flexible as my old high school's dress code.

"Hey guys," I say, like I'm not holding a corpse. "How was the movie? Did the boat still sink?"

Mom smirks.

"What's that?" asks Dad. "Aren't you a bit old for dolls? I thought you were over them around twelve."

"Coralie's not a doll."

Mom gasps, stares for a few seconds, then points. "Is that a... a..."

"Mummy dearest." I hold her upright so they can see her.

"Sarah..." Dad gives me his fake scolding look. "I thought we spoke about your bringing dead bodies into the house."

"Sorry, I know I said I wouldn't, but this is kind of an unusual situation. And I didn't kill her. I'm saving her."

"Shoes," says Mom.

I set Coralie down and lean her against the wall, remove my sneakers, and pick her up again. Before I can even take a step, Mom clears her throat.

"What?"

She points. "Your friend still has her shoes on."

I glance down at Coralie's boots. The leather's in worse shape than her skin. "Umm, Mom, she's a mummy. I don't think her shoes *can* come off."

Dad, the more adventurous of my parents, gets up and walks over for a closer look. "Oh, wow. Poor thing. So, umm... you're carrying a dead body into the house."

"Yep."

"Like it's completely normal a thing to do," says Mom.

I shrug, making Coralie bob up and down. "Yep."

"Umm, why?" asks Dad.

"Some people were keeping her prisoner, and she asked me to get her out of there. So, I did. Not sure where she wants to go since I haven't seen her in a bit, so I brought her here. She's not going to stay that long and she's a really quiet roommate. Won't make any noise or mess. Is it okay if she stays here for a little while?"

Mom pinches the bridge of her nose. "I don't think it's legal to have human remains in a house."

"Even if they've been dead for like two centuries?" I ask.

Dad looks back and forth between us with a 'don't ask me' face.

"I'm going to keep her in my room for now. If anyone finds her, I'll just make them forget. She won't cause any trouble."

Mom turns away, hands up in her 'I can't even' posture. "That's so unsettling. I don't know, Jonathan. I understand our daughter has certain new challenges to face, but I'm not sure about keeping a dead woman in the house."

"I'm sure there's a good reason behind this. Sarah wouldn't even ask if it wasn't important. You'll explain this in more detail soon, I hope?"

"I promise it's important. And yeah. I'll definitely give you the deets."

Mom points at me. "You will not let your siblings find, play with, or even see her."

"Promise."

Honestly? I'd rather they find Coralie than catch me with Hunter. The near miss with Sophia the other day was *beyond* embarrassing.

My parents resume muttering with each other as I go by, carrying Coralie into the kitchen and maneuvering her down the stairs to the basement. Damn. I had hoped they'd be asleep by now. After this, perhaps dialing back the weird is a good idea. Mom needs a nice couple months of everything being as normal as possible. Her dropping hints about mind-tweaking her boss should've been a sign that she's fraying at the seams. Or maybe she's not above a little manipulation of circumstance to keep from losing a job she's had for like sixteen years over things beyond her control.

Right so, just a dead woman coming over to hang out. Not a big deal.

I carry her into my room, look at the closets for a moment—too full—then, somewhat reluctantly, set her down on the floor and slide her under my bed. It's inglorious, but at least the littles won't see her there.

No sooner do I stand up than Coralie's ghost is right next to me with a dismayed expression.

"Eep!" I jump back and land seated upon the bed, clutching my chest. "Holy crap you scared me."

She looks at me like I just stole her lunch at school.

"Sorry. I know. Hiding under the bed is the first place someone will look. But, I can't put you in a chair without breaking bones... and I can't let my siblings find you."

Coralie bows her head. "It's all right. I'm grateful that you've brought me away from the influence of their enchantments. Even if I've been relegated to a space under your bed. You've done me a great service I am unsure I will ever be able to repay. For that, you shall always have my thanks."

I let myself fall back, and stare at the ceiling. "You're welcome."

There's a dead woman under my bed. Wow, my life has gone to plaid.

14

THE ORACLE

Coralie paces around my bedroom, her expression curious.
My mind spins with images of that stupid gargoyle. Did I really just see a live gargoyle? Is magic like an actual thing? Holy crap that thing nearly took my head off.

Speaking of which.

I lift my head up from the mattress enough to peer at her. "Coralie?"

She pivots to face me. "Yes?"

"Why didn't you tell us about that gargoyle? It would've been nice to know *why* you asked me to take that shield."

"Gargoyle?"

I explain what happened inside the 'vault.'

"Oh!" she gasps, covering her mouth. "I am sorry. I did not know exactly what would happen. Only, when I saw that shield on the wall I knew you should have it."

"That's really freaky. It saved my life... or, well... you know what I mean."

She giggles. "I knew it would, but not how. Now that I am free from the *Aurora Aurea*, I can speak openly. They used me as an oracle of sorts."

"What, so you like see the future?" I sit up, arms crossed in my lap.

"In a manner of speaking, yes. The same way vampires have different strengths from one to the next, so too do spirits who choose not to pass on, or cannot. My strength is receiving flashes of insight regarding future events."

"Oh. Is it because you died so young, you're not ready to go on yet?"

"No." Coralie sighs, shaking her head. "My husband was a member of that order. We met when I was only sixteen, though back in those days at that age, I was ready to marry. Our wedding happened about a year later. I'd been fascinated by the strange things he studied, and he told me that I had a gift. A few of the small tricks he showed me, I was able to do, so I wanted to learn more. He discovered a ritual and told me it would unlock a greater power inside me. Of course, I expected something quite different from what happened."

"He killed you..."

"The elixir they gave me did, yes. I do not think it was their intent to end my life, but in doing so, they bound me here as a spirit with the ability to see into the future. Their goal had been to create an oracle all along. Although my death surprised them, they weren't too upset by it. What happened did not deter them from using me as the tool they had hoped to create."

I rest my chin in both hands. "Ugh. I know the feeling."

"You do?"

"Well, my boyfriend killed me. Both men we thought we loved killed us."

Coralie sits on the bed beside me. "I'm so sorry. You are too young. Even younger than I was."

"I'm not as young as I look. I'm eighteen."

She tsks. "That is still too young."

"You died at twenty. Two years."

"I suppose I should pity myself then, too." She fake pouts.

"Right."

"Your boyfriend, he is a vampire?"

"Briefly, by accident."

Coralie blinks. "He did not kill you to make you into what you are?"

"No… He was just pissed that I dumped him, so he stabbed me in a fit of rage. He didn't stab me to make me into a vampire. The vampire who turned me only did it to save me. He thought I was a kid and couldn't bear to watch me die or something like that."

"Aww, that is so gallant."

"That's a word for it." I shrug, smiling.

"And your boyfriend?"

I explain how Dalton thought he killed Scott, but the asshole got back up as a Scrap and I wound up dealing with him. "Did you ever take revenge on your—oh wait, you said you didn't warn him of his death."

She nods. "It upset me most never having a family. I wanted children."

"Sorry. I dunno how I'd have felt if things had been normal, but I'm okay with not being able to. I guess because I was so much older than my siblings it kinda feels like I've already done the mom thing."

Coralie smiles. "That is sweet of you to take care of them."

"Ehh. I wasn't exactly the best big sister for the last year or two of my mortal life, but it's not like I was mean. Just busy, wanted to do other stuff. Really, what fifteen-year-old wants to spend all day hanging out with their eight, seven, and six-year-old siblings?"

"Families were much closer when I was a child. I had three older siblings and we did everything together." She wipes a spectral tear. "The worst part of dying was watching them lose me."

A giant lump forms in my throat. "Yeah… I can sympathize with that, too. It's why I came home instead of running off with Dalton."

"I demanded they tell my family I remained as a ghost and that they be allowed to visit me whenever they wished." Coralie fusses at her frilled sleeves. "There was a room at the old lodge that made it much easier for me to appear to the living."

I nod.

We spend a little while more commiserating about being murdered by men we thought we loved, and family stuff. She asks about what I meant regarding a disastrous attempt at stealing, so I tell her about that stupid spyglass. It's a much needed topic change from grieving relatives, that leaves us laughing.

I start to groan at myself over the mound of calculus homework, but it *is* the weekend and I'm caught up with everything else, so I have time yet.

"What should we do with your remains now?" I ask.

"Is your attic dry?"

"No, not really. I saw some mold on the window. You're probably better off in here for now. But… I'm sure you don't want to spend eternity under my bed."

Coralie scrunches up her face. "It makes me feel too much like a piece of ugly furniture tucked out of the way."

"What about a coffin and burying you somewhere?"

She ponders that idea for a little while, then shakes her head. "I think it would be too scary. Being shut in a box isn't nice. That is for the dead."

I tilt my head. "But you are dead."

"So are you. Would you care to be in a box?"

"No… that sucked."

She blinks. "You were?"

"Morgue cooler. Close enough. You're right. Screw that."

"They screw them closed?"

I laugh, startling her. "No, it's a phrase. You're right. Being in a box is too scary."

"I am happy enough to be free from the *Aurora Aurea* that I will gladly sleep on your floor for a while."

"The who?"

"No, not a band."

I smirk. "Now I know you're doing that on purpose."

She grins. "You may have heard of them referred to as the Golden Dawn."

"Nope. Sorry."

Coralie sighs. "Well, the world has largely thought them disbanded since 1903. I shouldn't be surprised you haven't heard of them. They are an order devoted to occultism, magic, and paranormal studies that have been around in one form or another since the late 1600s, though they did not always use that name. It was adopted in 1887, quite a while after my death, by a group of men in Great Britain when they attempted to bring magical studies into public awareness. It did not go well. I warned them that society would hunt down every last person with any scrap of magical gift and burn them to death. The masters of the order decided to allow the world to think of them as eccentric fools, and publicly disbanded as a show. They enacted internal laws of secrecy and forbid open displays of magic."

"Yeah, people probably loved the idea of magic about as much as they'd love vampires. Probably why we still hide."

"I'd imagine your kind would be *less* welcomed."

"You're probably right. Though the government knows about us."

She nods. "Yes. But they think they know more than they do."

"Hey, can you tell me if anything bad is going to happen to my siblings? Like my one sister is terrified she's going to be shot at school."

"So tragic what happens in this country these days." Coralie shakes her head. "Alas, my abilities don't work like that. I will, however, keep her in my thoughts. It is the least I can do for you."

"Keep her in your thoughts?" I scratch my head. "How will that help?"

"If something horrible comes along the thread of fate for Sophia, Sierra, or Samuel, I will see it ahead of time. Much like I saw the riots and burnings of the mystics." She inclines her head ever so slightly. "Something significant involves Sophia relatively soon, but I do not think it bad."

"Wait. Something's going to happen to her?"

Coralie nods. "Yes. Her path will bend in a way it had not originally been meant to, but you should not worry. It is not dangerous and I do not believe she will mind. She is adorable."

"You've seen her?"

"Yes. I followed you home some days ago out of curiosity."

"I thought you were stuck at the school? I think Sophia somehow felt you here."

"She did. The girl is sensitive."

"Heh. Yeah, no kidding. She cries at everything."

"Not that kind of sensitive." Coralie giggles. "You are correct. I was stuck at the school before you removed my remains. But a being such as yourself has enough energy that I was able to hitch a ride so to speak. I could not, however, stay away long before the enchantments dragged me back. Oh, it is so good to be free of it."

"You're welcome."

"I am happy to remain here as long as necessary, though I don't think your parents are too pleased with my presence."

"Yeah. Mom's a bit freaked out. Not sure if you talking to them would help or hurt that. But..." I sigh at the carpet. "For what to do with your remains... I'll figure something out eventually."

"I'm pleased it doesn't bother you to share your room with what's left of my body."

I shrug. "I don't have any trouble passing out at bedtime anymore. Yeah, it *is* kinda creepy, but I guess I technically am a corpse too when I zonk."

"We are mostly underground."

"Please don't call my bedroom a tomb." I flash a weak smile. "I'm trying to have a normal life."

"Normal." Coralie raises her eyebrows.

"Yes. As normal as I can be." I get up and grab my backpack. "Might as well do the nasty."

"The nasty?"

Laughing, I flop down at my desk. The next few hours are full of math and trying to explain modern phrases to Coralie.

Honestly, the calculus is easier.

15

PISSING OFF THE UNIVERSE

S aturday afternoon goes by in a blur of shrieking tweens.
Sierra invited Nicole over, Sophia invited Megan from her
dance class and her school friend Priya. Sam had Jordan and
Daryl over. To be fair, most of the shrieking came from the girls in the
living room. The boys aren't much for squealing in delight or
screaming when startled at whatever movie or video game is on. No,
most of their loud noises came from 'battle cries' in the yard involving
Nerf weaponry.

It was a clear day, so I wound up stuck in my room for a while
after waking up, dividing my time between the rest of my homework
and laundry. Since both parents had kid patrol, Mom carried the
baskets to the basement and I did the actual washing and drying for
her. Amazing the amount of clothing we go through in a week.

A little after six, the stupid fiery ball in the sky decided to chill out
enough that I could go upstairs. At that point, I took over 'mom'
duties, and the 'rents slipped out to deal with a couple errands and
shopping.

Coralie didn't make an appearance, so I figured she might be off
doing all the ghostly things she'd been unable to while trapped at the
school. The area has changed quite a bit since she arrived from

London. Evidently, the mystics brought her to the States due to her warning them about World War II. The building they formerly occupied didn't survive the war. They arrived about seven months prior to the rockets falling on London and spent awhile in Boston before something made them split into smaller groups. The main one relocated here, bringing her with them. Others went to Richmond, Virginia; Atlanta, Georgia; and Baton Rouge, Louisiana. The people who use the hall under the college haven't spoken much about the other 'lodges' in a long time, so she thinks there may have been bad blood.

Whoa. I guess even people who use magic have drama.

She did tell me a little bit about that, too. They're not like 'wizards.' I'm thinking these people throw fireballs or something, but it's *way* more subtle than that. According to her, they do rituals in the meeting hall and those rituals cause things to happen elsewhere. She called it 'manipulating fate.' I'm not sure if that's more or less frightening than the idea someone might come after me with fire flying from their hands, but, hey, at least Coralie is an oracle. If someone's going to mess with me, she'll warn me, right?

Eventually, the kids go home, we have dinner, and Dad throws on *Bloodsport.* Of course, we can't watch that movie without him telling us—again—about how he and his friends used to pick on this guy's movies. Like, in almost every one of them, he'll get into a fight and the other guy will like totally kick his ass. Then, out of nowhere, he gets this second wind and totally owns the other guy. Sierra and Sophia both find the one guy making his pectoral muscles bounce hilarious.

It's awesome to have a normal (well, as normal as it gets for me) day.

Around bedtime for the littles, Sophia creeps down the stairs and tells me she feels like someone's in her room with her. Pre-death me probably would've told her she's imagining it and sent her off with a 'don't be such a baby.' Not only has almost losing my family turned me into a squishy emo gummy bear, I now consider the quite probable truth that something really might be there.

So, I get up off the couch and follow her to the second floor. She hesitates outside her bedroom, afraid to go in, gripping the rug with her toes. Fully expecting to find Coralie standing in the middle of the room, I stroll right in.

Empty.

Okay, maybe it's frogs. Thinking I'm smarter than I am, I cross the hall to Sam's bedroom to check the terrarium before searching Sophia's room. If both frogs are in the tank, I won't need to look for an escapee. Both frogs are sitting there staring enviously at the jar of freeze-dried crickets right next to their enclosure. Hmm. I'm sure there's a metaphor there about being two impenetrable glass walls away from something you really want.

"It's gone," whispers Sophia. "It doesn't feel weird in here anymore."

I walk back over to her. "I'm helping a ghost. She might have been wandering around the house. It's okay. She's really nice and won't hurt you."

"I don't think she's here now." Sophia edges into her room, looks around, and relaxes. "Yeah. The creepy is gone."

My thoughts return to Coralie saying my sister is sensitive. Well, if she doesn't wind up doing makeup for Hollywood, she could always try tarot cards or something. I perform a cursory check around her room, find nothing of paranormal interest and shrug at her.

She hugs me. "Thanks for looking. I'm okay now."

"Night, Soph."

Once she's in bed, I head back to my room to change out of the tee and sweats I'd been slumming in all day. For a change of pace, I throw on a mini dress over yoga pants, which satisfies my 'no flying in dresses' problem. Add fuzzy socks and some boots that won't fall off in midair, and I'm good. I'd wear the Uggs for comfort, but they'll disappear as soon as I go past 100 MPH.

Now, to deal with the Coralie question.

She's still nowhere in sight. No point waiting around for her since I have no idea what she's up to. I head outside via the sliding door in the kitchen and leap straight up off the deck into the sky. After an as-perfect-as-it-gets-for-me day with the family, flying feels doubly awesome. I swear, this will never get old.

My house, the cul-de-sac, the whole neighborhood falls away below, leaving me with the quiet peace of open sky. Here and there, a roaming set of headlights drifts along a road. I spot a guy walking a small white dog, two boys I'm fairly sure are now seniors at my old high school, and an elderly guy out to stretch his legs.

Best of all, a certain white sports car is sitting on the side of the road in front of a police car with the lights flashing. Hah. Eighteen year old doing sixty-something in a thirty five zone? That's going to sting. Hope he gets the message before he hits some neighborhood kid.

I leave Cottage Lake behind and angle toward Seattle. The aerial view of the various lakes and waterways makes me want to take my phone out for pictures, but knowing my luck, I'll drop it. Something tells me that wouldn't be covered under the protection plan.

As tempting as it is to just hang up here and watch boats, I accelerate into the city and swing by the same liquor store I did last time. Of course, since I look like I'm fifteen, the guy behind the counter practically laughs when I walk in. I grab a six-pack of that cheap beer Glim likes and head over to the counter with it.

Mr. Mullet behind the counter is already reaching for the phone to call the cops on me. I set the cans on the counter and plunge into his brain before he can dial. As far as he's concerned, I look like Mrs. McMahan, the English teacher I had junior year. We both have the same long brown hair, which makes it easier to alter his memory. This dude is so lucky I'm like 'Follows Rules Girl' or I'd totally just shoplift this beer for his being a butthead.

Okay, well, technically speaking, I am still too young to buy alcohol. But simply explaining that I'm buying it for someone else who *is* old enough won't work. A teenager saying 'oh, I'm not buying this beer to drink myself; it's for an adult' is about as believable as a politician saying they care about average people.

At least the beer Glim likes doesn't cost much.

Ill-gotten booze in hand, I head back outside, duck into an alley, and fly. A few minutes later, I land on the roof at the apartment complex where his former wife and sons live. He's in his usual spot, legs dangling over the edge while watching whatever's on the TV in their place. At my arrival, he scoots back and smiles—as much as he can—at me.

"Hey." I plop down and set the six pack next to him. "Got you something."

"Busch… you remembered."

I smirk. "It hasn't been *that* long since you told me."

"Perhaps I underestimate the attention span of high school girls."

"I am not a high school girl." I fold my arms, thrusting my chin up. "I'm a college student."

Serious face lasts only a few seconds before I giggle. He laughs. I hold an arm out to him.

Glim gently bites me on the wrist and drinks a few sips of blood. I concentrate on wanting to loan him my ability to consume food, and a faint tingle runs down my arm. He cracks open the first can and takes a long, slow sip while making a face like a wine snob tasting from a bottle that cost more than most cars.

"Thanks again for helping with Coralie." I wrap my arms around my legs and gaze off in the general direction of his family's place. "How are Ana and the kids?"

"They're doing all right. Arcelio's becoming attached to the man she's seeing. Stefan's 'tolerating' him."

"Well, he is fourteen… and you're still doing that ghost writing deal with him, right?"

"Yeah." He takes another sip, then talks about his older son's exploits in school. The boy wants to join the military 'like Dad,' even though his father 'died' overseas. Glim's been trying to talk him out of it with the 'ghost writing.'

"What do you think I should do with Coralie? I can't exactly keep a dead body in the house." I whistle. "I really ought to get her out of there before Sophia finds her and uses her for a makeup dummy."

Beer froth flies from Glim's mouth on a laugh. I imagine if he breathed, he'd have been choking, but he simply shakes his head, trying to wipe dribble off his chin. "Where is she now?"

"At home, asleep. Or at least she better be."

Glim blinks. "I meant the mummy."

"Oh… duh. She's under my bed."

He laughs. "Seriously?"

"Well, it's either that or the attic. And the attic is damp. Dad still hasn't fixed that leak. And really, I don't want any of the littles to see her. She might be really well preserved, but she's still kinda gruesome in a way."

He makes thinking faces while sipping the rest of his first beer. "I can check around a bit and see if I can find a safe place."

"Thanks."

My phone tweeps.

I pull it out and find a text from Ashley: ‹Where the hell are you?›

"Oops."

Glim looks over at me. "What's on fire now?"

"I got so wrapped up in the Coralie thing I forgot I was supposed to hang out with Ash and Michelle tonight." I look up at him. "Hey, you wanna join us?"

He freezes like a statue, his face stuck in a 'you've got to be kidding' expression.

"Seriously."

"I'm a little old to crash a 'girls' night in' with your friends. Not to mention…" He gestures at himself. "I'm a little rough on the eyes."

"When you showed up at the house with the spyglass, you used an illusion or something to make us not see it. Can you make yourself look different?"

He shakes his head. "It doesn't quite work that way. Shadows or just making people not realize I'm there. I can't disguise myself."

"Aww. Bummer."

"It's all right. I understand you had prior plans, and I don't feel like you're bailing. You're all so busy with school you don't have much time to spend with them now. We can do this any time during the week."

"Okay. Sorry. I feel bad."

"Don't." He smiles, opening the second can.

"Monday night?"

He nods. "That sounds like a plan."

I text ‹OMW› to Ashley, then stand. "Oh, hey. Do you have a phone?"

Glim shakes his head. "Not since I stopped breathing, no."

"Ahh. Okay, I was gonna ask for your contact info, but..."

"If you need to get in touch with me, either come here or talk to the wind. I should eventually become aware that you're looking for me."

So creepy, yet so cool at the same time. "'Kay. See you soon."

He holds up his Busch as a toast.

UPON ARRIVING AT ASHLEY'S HOUSE, I FLOAT UP TO HER BEDROOM window.

No sense ringing the doorbell and bothering her mother. Mrs. Carter is usually asleep by nine or so. My friends are on Ashley's bed, sitting cross-legged and talking about random funny things that happened at school or their jobs. Like five minutes go by of me hanging there—quite obviously—at the window, and neither one of them even look at me. I tap a fingernail at the glass. They both turn toward me and scream at the same time.

Once they recover from laughing, Ashley opens the window and screen enough for me to slip inside.

"Hey. Sorry. Dealing with some weird stuff."

"What sort of weird stuff?" asks Michelle.

Ashley pokes her. "You have to ask?"

I pull off my boots and join them on the bed. "Oh, the usual. Going places I don't belong, nearly getting killed—again—and I've got a dead woman under my bed."

They both stare at me.

After a brief explanation of Coralie, we shift gears back to normal. Ashley throws on *Zootopia*, which gets Michelle laughing.

"What?" asks Ashley, hands on her hips. "It looks cute."

"We're not little kids." Michelle rolls her eyes.

"Come on, you know Ash likes cartoons. Besides, she probably wants to make sure we watch something that won't get her all revved up." I wag my eyebrows.

"Bad choice then. That fox is kinda hot." Michelle fans herself.

Ashley whacks me across the head with a pillow, laughing. "I think I'm over that."

"Dude." Michelle clucks her tongue. "You had it *bad* for a while there."

"Yeah I know. I'm good now." She flops on her back and stretches. "I'd ask how your days are going at work, but someone's a lazy ass without a job."

"Ha. Ha."

With the movie on more or less as background noise, Michelle rambles about one of her professors being hilarious. I tell them about Dr. Mercer and her irritating habit of talking slow. In the midst of our conversation without any mention of vampires, mummies, or paranormal weirdness, I almost forget anything bizarre happened to me. We're all hanging out acting the way we might've acted if I'd remained oblivious to the stranger side of reality.

Today's been an awesome day, first with my family, then my friends. And as cool as that is, and as happy as I am right now, I can't help but nurse a tiny flame of worry.

I'm *too* happy.

That's going to piss off the universe.

Something bad is going to happen soon.

16

NEAR DEATH EXPERIENCE

When I return home from Ashley's place, Coralie's hanging out in my room.

I explain that Glim is looking around for better living accommodations than beneath my bed. That seems to make her feel better, and we wind up talking about random crap. Aside from her once having an infatuation with obtaining magical power, she seems like a fairly normal young woman, albeit with a bit of a dated sense of things. I do bring up her remark about crazy math not being for women and point out a handful of prominent female scientists.

She's more surprised that the women were 'allowed' to study than they had the smarts for it. Admittedly, Coralie has been stuck in a small bubble, but you'd think she'd have figured some of that out being trapped in a college. I mean, sure, there's still plenty of patriarchal bullshit going on, but it's kinda gotten a little better for us compared to when she'd been alive. She tells me about a cat she had as a kid, and her parents, the house she used to live in... all like it had only been a few weeks ago. Fortunately, she skips the gloominess of her siblings reacting to her death again.

We talk until dawn sneaks up on me, and I barely make it to bed in time to avoid collapsing on the floor. Not that I'd really notice. I could sleep upside down headfirst in a giant trashcan and not have a sore back the next day. Once I'm out, I'm *out*.

Sunday is nice and overcast, so I head upstairs soon after my eyes open at 2:33 p.m. The girls have their friends over again while the boys appear to have gone elsewhere, as I don't hear them up in his bedroom, nor are they in the living room. More than likely, they're at Daryl's using his PlayStation since Sierra's claimed ours.

The girls don't give off any vibes that I'm intruding on their space, so I flop on the couch kinda-sorta hanging out with them while throwing most of my attention toward texts with Hunter, Ashley, and Michelle.

Tween conversation mostly goes in one ear and out the other.

Nicole mutters something about the bathroom before standing. She turns in place, eyeing the room. "Whoa. It feels kinda eerie in here now. Like there's something watching us."

"I made friends with an undead I met at school," I say in a toneless, unimpressed voice.

"A ghost?" asks Sierra.

"No. A grad student."

Dad laughs from his office, though the girls stare at me, blank-faced.

I grin at their expressions. "Just kidding. Yes, a ghost."

Priya gasps, clutching her hands (and the controller) at her chin.

"Whoa." Nicole, who's already pretty damn pale, gets a little whiter. "Serious? Like for real a ghost?"

I nod. "Yep. After my, umm… near death experience, I sometimes see them."

Sierra realizes Priya is no longer controlling her character and stops pummeling it, then pauses the game.

"You brought a ghost here?" Sophia shivers. "I felt it, too."

"Don't worry. She's friendly. Just lonely and wanted someone to talk to."

Priya's fear shifts to an eye roll. "She's teasing us."

"Umm. I dunno. It does kinda feel weird." Nicole takes a few tentative steps into the hall, heading toward the bathroom.

"It's all in your mind." Priya shakes her head and unpauses the game. "Hey, you kept hitting me when I wasn't even looking."

"Sorry. I was watching the screen, not you." Sierra opens a menu. "Restart?"

"'Kay," says Priya.

Nicole creeps down the hallway. Between her black hair, T-shirt, and leggings, she looks like some kind of suburban kid ninja. Or a tiny version of that woman in the vampire movie with the werewolves. I've met a few Old Guard who have more color than her.

"Hey, Dad?" calls Sierra. "Can we get a Oujia board?"

"No way," mutters Sophia. "That's a bad idea. Those things are evil."

Priya scoffs. "They're not evil, they're fake."

While the girls get into a debate over the 'legit-ness' of spiritual tools made by a board game company, I get up and wander to the kitchen, grinning at a string of texts from Ashley talking about a guy in her class who showed up drunk. Before I realize it, I've got the fridge open and I'm peering inside.

"Old habits?" asks Dad, right next to me.

"Gah!" I jump and push the door shut. Grr! I hate not having my super hearing active. It sucks being normal. "You snuck up on me."

"Yes, well, that was the intent." He wiggles his sock-covered toes at me. "Fridge surfing?"

"Old habits die hard or something like that." I shrug.

"Near death experience?" Dad raises an eyebrow. "That's *almost* a lie."

"Did we not agree that fibbing to conceal certain things is a necessary evil?" I ask.

He winks. "Yeah. Just teasing. So, about the, umm guest."

"I'm working on it. Friend of mine is scouting around for a good place."

He nods. "No rush. Just… your mother is a little unsettled at having a dead person in the house."

I raise an eyebrow. "That never stopped her from inviting Uncle Hank for Thanksgiving."

Dad cackles.

Like legit Wicked Witch of the West cackles.

Okay, so my great Uncle Hank—Mom's father's brother—is like eighty-nine and basically looks like a mummy without all the bandages. I wouldn't normally pick on a guy for being ancient and brittle, but he's not nice. Barks at me and the littles to be quiet even when we're already quiet, constantly complains about everything, even Mom's food. I'm really not sure why the heck she keeps inviting him over. Ooh. Idea. If he's back this year for the holidays I am *so* going to compel him to shut the hell up. I don't care if Mom yells at me for it, the old bastard's going on mute.

"Do you think I'm doing the right thing going for programming? I still can't decide. Maybe I should switch to English."

Dad wipes laugh tears away, then pats me on the shoulder. "Well, I know some part of your going to college is merely to make your mother and me happy. Neither of us have any illusion that you'll have a normal career considering. So, you should study whatever you enjoy. Don't take programming just because it's what I do. And really, if you decide going to college at all isn't working out for you, please don't feel forced."

I hug him. "Thanks, Dad. And I'm not in the programming track purely because it's what you're doing... it's something I can do from home. Okay, I'm not as much of a tech geek as Sierra is, but I don't hate it."

He takes a seat at the kitchen table. "What would you have studied if you'd gone to USC?"

Thinking of Ashley, I mutter, "Majored in homesickness with a minor in being pathetic."

Dad chuckles.

"But seriously? I dunno. I still haven't figured this stuff out. Probably would have taken core classes at first until something jumped out at me. Is it worse to have no idea what I wanna do with my life or be someone whose parents force them into a particular job from the minute they pop out of the womb?"

"Well, at least that kid knows what they're going to do." He snickers.

"Programming looks interesting, but I've never been *that* mathy."

"You're certainly smart enough, just a bit on the lazy side."

I stick my tongue out at him.

Dad looks like he's about to say something, but gets misty eyed. "It doesn't matter what you study. I'm just happy to still have you around."

"Aww, Dad…" I flop into his lap and hug him.

It takes him a moment to get his voice back. "Whatever you study, I couldn't care less. As long as you're happy."

"Ehh. You're right. I'm just lazy, and I guess I'm trying to go undercover as a normal kid."

"What?"

I grin. "Concealing my nerdiness. Wasn't terribly cool to be into computers, math, science… stuff like that. 'Course the only one I ever really fooled was Scott. Maybe that's why he treated me the way he did. Once he figured out I was the 'smart girl' and he was 'too cool' for me or something, so he considered being with me like some kinda charity thing."

"You are beautiful, Sarah. You don't need to disguise anything."

"I kinda do." I make a biting gesture at him. "But I think I'm confident enough to get my nerd on now."

He laughs.

The doorbell rings.

Sophia yells, "I got it" as if Sierra would bother getting up.

Dad starts telling me a story from his college days about the 'grand high wizard of nerdvana' who lived next door to him in the dorms.

Sophia walks into the kitchen with a robotic gait and a 'nobody home' look in her eyes. "Sarah. There's a man here to see you."

"Who?" I ask.

She stands there like a statue.

"Soph?" I snap my fingers in front of her eyes, but she doesn't react.

"Umm…?" asks Dad.

"Shit," I mutter. "That's not good."

17

A MUTUALLY BENEFICIAL ARRANGEMENT

Someone messed with my little sister.

I jump out of Dad's lap and grab Sophia's shoulders, shaking her. "Soph?"

She jostles around like a mannequin, oblivious.

"Soph!" I yell.

The girl ignores me. I pivot and push her toward Dad. "Here. Hold her. I'm going to rip someone's face off."

I storm down the hall to the living room, where Sierra, Nicole, and Priya remain absorbed in the PlayStation. A thirtysomething man in a fancy black suit that gives off an old-world vibe stands in the open door. Long semi-curly brown hair hangs down to his shoulders, and little round sunglasses perch low enough on his nose he can stare over them. Wow. The only thing missing is the horse-drawn carriage outside.

He shows no reaction to my scowl as I stomp over and get in his face. "What the hell did you do to my—"

"Obey me." The man waves a hand past my nose like he's trying to do some kinda Star Wars crap.

I raise an eyebrow. "Umm, dude. Hate to break it to you, but that shit might've worked like a century or two ago, but dating has evolved. And you're way too old for me." I nearly grab him by the neck, but catch myself upon realizing I'm offline and no stronger than a smallish eighteen year old girl with a minimal degree of physical fitness ought to be. "What the hell did you do to my sister?"

He blinks at me, looks me up and down, and makes that funny hand gesture again—thumb to ring finger, index and middle fingers pointing up. "Obey me."

"How about no?"

The man makes a face like he'd showed up for a gunfight and forgot ammo.

"Wait... you like legit expected that to work?"

"Ordinarily, yes."

I exhale. "Wow. You must really be a fun date."

He continues looking at me like he's never seen a girl before.

"Oh, hang on. This is about the mummy, isn't it?"

After clearing his throat and staring at me for another few seconds, he smooths his hands down the front of his shiny black vest and nods. "Well, since you are being so direct, yes. I shouldn't be at all surprised the charm didn't work on you if you somehow managed to get in and out without triggering any of the wards. Where did you study?"

"Umm. Seattle Central College."

He stares at me.

"What?"

The man leans closer, whispering, "The esoteric arts."

"Umm." I laugh. "I don't use magic."

Brows furrowed, he waves that funny hand gesture at me again. "Obey me."

"Dude. Really. That's even less effective than 'nice shoes, wanna fuck?'"

Sierra, Nicole, and Priya burst into giggles.

"Oooh!" says Sophia. "She said a bad word!"

Whew. At least she's back to normal.

The man leans in, eyeing the four eleven- and ten-year-olds in front of the TV.

No sooner do I get the inkling that he intends to threaten them, the previously not-too-bad gloomy daylight ramps up to painful heat. Without really thinking, I grab him by two fistfuls of his jacket, lift him off his feet, and step outside before swinging him around and planting his back against the house.

"If you, or any of your 'order' or whatever you are, do anything to my family, there won't be a wizard left anywhere in this state. I'll make the Salem Witch Trials look like Mario Kart."

He leans his head back, as much as he can with the house in the way. "Oh... you're..."

"Pissed off?" I narrow my eyes.

The man stares at me, whispering some weird language for a few seconds.

I keep holding him against the wall, trying to ignore the pain of daylight scorching up my back.

"Vampire?" he whispers.

"I've been called worse, but not since high school."

My flash of rage passes. The sun relaxes from burning to tolerable, and my arms lose the strength to hold the guy in the air. He slides back down onto his feet, though I don't let go of his suit.

"Oh, now that is interesting. You are rather adept at concealing yourself." He looks around. "How are you even awake during the day? And... how is it possible that you even entered the hall?"

"A girl's gotta keep some secrets." I let go of his vest and take a step back.

"Hmm. I find it most curious to be having a conversation with you like civilized people."

I fold my arms. "What were you expecting?"

"Much more blood."

"That can be arranged. Stay away from my family."

"Why did you take the mummy?"

"*Coralie* was tired of being a slave. She asked me to."

"Oh. So... you'll not be inclined to return her to us?"

"Not unless she wants to go, and I kind of doubt that."

He holds up a finger. "Perhaps we can come to a mutually beneficial arrangement then."

"Would that arrangement involve anyone losing body parts?"

The man smiles. "No. It shouldn't."

Crap. I know I'm going to regret this, but... I sigh. "Okay. I'll at least talk. What are you thinking?"

"Excellent. Please meet us at the Brass Tap next Wednesday night."

"Can't be too early, I've got class. And it usually runs long. Teacher's a slow talker. Ten?"

"Class?" He tilts his head.

I shrug. "Yeah, you know, like college?"

"All right. Ten then."

"This is such a bad idea." I sigh at the grass. "I'm walking into a trap."

"Oh, please do not worry. You have my word that we shall undertake no hostilities for the time being. It is an unusual circumstance to meet one such as you and discover they can be reasoned with."

"I'm also housebroken."

He emits a forced laugh.

"Do you have a name, or should I just go with 'hey dickhead'?"

His lips form a thin, flat line. "Darren Anderson."

"Inferring I'm an animal or creature aside, you did something to my little sister. Calling you a dickhead is getting off easy."

"I merely sent the girl to fetch you."

"Not big on *asking* are you? Are you and your friends going to 'ask' me to help you with something or should I expect to be charmed?"

He clears his throat. "I imagine there will be an offer made to exchange a favor in return for what you stole from us."

"I didn't *steal* anything. I helped a prisoner escape."

"Semantics. Either way, the oracle's usefulness had waned. I believe the others will be amenable to an agreement, provided you do a small favor for us in return."

"Such as?"

"We will discuss it Wednesday night." He backs up a step, then bows. "The Brass Tap. Ten o'clock."

"Right…" I stand there watching him walk off across the cul-de-sac. He takes a right at the end of the street and strolls out of sight. "I should've known nothing is ever easy or simple."

Dad appears at the door. "Everything okay?" He sniffs. "Someone grilling burgers in September?"

A distant car door closes with a *whump*, and an engine starts.

"Nope. I think you're smelling me." Hmm. That's weird. Guess I subconsciously eased back my vampiric abilities from defense against sunlight to free up the power to make myself a little stronger. "Some jackass was about to threaten the littles."

Dad pales.

"It's dealt with." I shoot a glance toward the sound of a departing vehicle. "At least for now."

"You going to kill anyone?"

"Not if I can help it."

"If you have to tear someone's throat out to protect your siblings, go right ahead. But you should skip the part where they beat you to a bloody pulp first."

I lean against him, laughing. "Dad, this isn't an action movie."

"No, but if your sisters and brother are in danger, you do whatever you have to in order to protect them. Except for one thing."

"Mix Skittles with M&M's?"

"Okay. Two things are on the forbidden list." Dad kisses me on the head. "That, and disappearing. None of us want you leaving 'to protect us.' You got that? We'll find a way to handle anything unlife throws at us."

I hug him, surrendering to feeling like a little kid again for a moment. It's so strange to think that little ol' me has become my family's protector, way more than either of my parents could be. But it's kinda my job.

At least, it is once the sun goes down.

18

GHOSTLY WANDERING

I am the exact opposite of happy.

It's a little after ten Sunday night and I'm stuck at home. Hunter's bingeing homework, I think Michelle is worn out and asleep, and Ashley got roped into a graveyard shift at the vet clinic where she's not-quite-interning. I have no idea why they have her there at this hour since all she can really do for them is clean floors and cages, dole out food, and sing to kittens. I guess she's a body at the front desk in case someone runs in the door with an emergency.

Someone's gotta be there to call a vet.

So, yeah. I get to be alone with my anxiety. It's only a *little* worrying that those mystics came straight to my door. Guess I really do fail at sneaky. I should consider myself lucky they had no idea their command, uhh, 'spell' wouldn't work on me.

I'd been hoping for a little Hunter time tonight, but I don't want to be the reason he fails out of school. Thinking about him starts putting me in the mood. Though, I'd have to go to his place. It would feel too strange trying to be romantic in here with a dead woman under my bed. For the same reason, I decide not to take matters into my own hands.

And that makes me laugh at the thought.

How many people touch themselves with ghosts watching and don't even realize it?

Ugh. I need to distract myself somehow or I'm going to go nuts. I eye the computer. Video games to the rescue I suppose.

My door creaks open.

Sophia enters, stops two steps in, and looks around like she's never seen my room before. Upon turning all the way around, she spots the light switch and turns it on, then repeats her slow scan.

"Soph?" I ask.

The girl ignores me, gazing at my closet, the desk, my bed, me, and the wall with my life-size poster of my former upstairs bedroom window. Without a word, she walks out.

Okay, that was weird.

"Hey, Soph?"

I listen for a moment, but she doesn't reply.

Shit. What now?

I hop off my bed and follow her out into the basement. She roams down the hallway to the mini bathroom, opening all three closet doors and looking inside each one. Honestly, the girl's like a cat that's been relocated to a new house—if cats could do more than scratch at doors they wanted to get past. Wait, no. A relocated cat would be under the bed for days. Let's go with dog.

"Sophia? Are you sleepwalking?"

She pads across to the alcove that holds the washer and dryer.

Hmm. I don't remember. Is it bad to wake people up when they're sleepwalking?

"Mommy!" screams Sophia—from upstairs. "Help me!"

Say what? I gaze up at the ceiling.

"Daddy!" Sophia shrieks. "Guys, stop ignoring me!"

I stare at Sophia who's wandering the basement ten feet away from me while simultaneously hearing her shouting upstairs. Okay. This is too messed up.

"Someone help me!" yells Sophia, again from upstairs.

The Sophia in front of me continues exploring the basement. When I step in front of her, she calmly moves around me. Okay, so she's not sleepwalking. Or maybe she is? Can sleepwalkers see? Again, Sophia screams from upstairs, this time just a long horror-movie type 'girl sees monster' kind of shriek.

What the hell is going on?

I decide to leave zombie-Sophia alone for the moment and run upstairs.

Mom and Dad are on the sofa. He's got the news on while Mom's reading her Kindle. Sophia's standing between them, wearing the same pink nightie she had on down in the basement and flailing like one of those guys from an airport, only she doesn't have the funny flashlights with the orange batons on them.

"Mom! Dad!" shouts Sophia. "Stop ignoring me! Something's happened!" She tries to grab Mom's arm, but her hands go right through without grip.

Mom rubs her wrist. "Did the heat stop working? There's a draft in here."

"Feels fine to me," says Dad.

I walk over. "Soph?"

She peers up at me. "Sarah?"

"Last time I checked."

My parents both look at me, confused.

Sophia bursts into tears and runs at me. She attempts to jump into a hug, but whiffs right on by like a cold breeze and staggers to a halt a short distance away, still bawling. I turn to face her. "Shh. It's okay. We'll figure it out."

"It's not okay!" wails Sophia. "I'm dead! I'm a ghost! I don't wanna be dead!"

"You aren't dead. Something weird is going on."

"Sarah?" asks Mom. "Who are you talking to?"

I hold a finger up. "Let me get back to you on that."

Another Sophia emerges from the basement stairs in the kitchen and walks placidly down the hall. The spectral Sophia tries to grab onto herself. Solid Sophia twists in response to being grabbed, like the ghostly hands have somewhat of a grip, though not enough to stop her.

"Sarah! Help!" screams ghost-Sophia.

"What are you doing out of bed?" asks Dad. "Do you know what time it is?"

"Uhh, guys, Sophia's not home right now." I step back as she goes by, rounds the banister at the end of the staircase, and goes upstairs.

"Is she sleepwalking?" asks Mom, her voice quivery. "Oh, no. We should make an appointment as soon as possible."

"Mom." I gesture at her like I'm trying to stop traffic. "She's not sleepwalking. She's astrally projecting or something."

"What?" asks Mom and Dad at the same time.

"Her ghost is outside her body."

"Fix it!" screams Sophia. "This is too freaky!"

I run for the stairs, grab the banister post to swing around, then sprint up to the second floor and my sister's room. Sophia's lying in bed as if asleep. A cloud of silvery-white light rises up from her chest and coalesces in the middle of the room, taking on the shape of an indistinct adult woman.

"What the hell are you doing?" I yell.

The figure faces me for a second, then collapses into a cloud before racing out the window and shooting off across the sky. Ack! It's probably not a good idea to leave her body soulless for too long. I scoop Sophia up, momentarily alarmed at how little she weighs, and carry her downstairs. Ghost Sophia, evidently too freaked out to move away from the parents, hovers beside them, trying and failing to hug Mom.

She looks up as I thunder down the stairs with her noodly body in my arms.

"What's going on?" asks Dad, sounding freaked.

I rush over to them, having no better ideas than trying to bring the two Sophia's together and hope something happens. The instant her foot makes contact with her spirit, the apparition blurs into a smear of light that absorbs into the body. Sophia snaps awake with a heavy gasp, coughs twice, then clamps her arms around me and erupts in a fit of wailing tears. I sit on the couch between the 'rents and hold her as she sobs.

"I'm sorry," I whisper over and over.

Our parents pat her on the back, hold her hand, and repeat assurances that she's safe and okay.

"What happened?" asks Dad.

"The people who had Coralie want her back, and they found me. I think they did something that let one of them steal Sophia for a while to search the house." Unable to contain myself, I laugh. "I can't believe they didn't look under my bed. That's like the first place anyone would check."

"I don't wanna be dead," whimpers Sophia.

"You're not. Not even close." I squeeze her. "Someone who is going to soon be in a lot of pain kicked you out of your body and, uhh, borrowed it."

Sophia blinks. She looks back and forth at the parents, finally aware that they can again see and touch her. The realization calms her more, and she stops crying, though continues shivering.

Mom brushes a hand repetitively over my sister's hair. "Why her?"

"I don't know. Coralie said she's sensitive. Maybe it was easier to get in. Could be because the man who rang the bell this afternoon used magic on her already."

"What?" asks Sophia.

I explain how he must've used that 'obey me' thing on her to send her to get me.

"That's stupid." She frowns. "I would've told you someone was here for you if he asked."

"Are you okay, sweetie?" asks Mom.

Sophia sniffles, but nods. "That was really scary. I was standing here yelling and you guys didn't even see me."

I squeeze her again. "I'm sorry they scared you, Soph. It's my fault. I helped Coralie escape some not nice people and one of them just… used you to spy on us."

She ponders this for a moment while wiping tears from her face. "If you bite them real hard, I won't be sad."

"Yeah. I'll bite him hard… or something." I stare guilt at the floor.

"Sarah, this isn't your fault." Dad takes my hand.

I let my head fall back against the sofa. "I know. But it's not fair to you guys that the 'weird stuff' keeps affecting the whole family."

"We told you we'll deal with it." Mom play-punches me in the shoulder. "You just need to make them understand they have far more to lose messing with us than they could possibly gain."

"Mom?" I blink. "Are you seriously suggesting I go off on a murderous rampage?"

"That's not what I was implying. We'd appreciate it if you kept the wonton killing to a minimum."

I give her the side eye. "Are you in shock or teasing me?"

"Will you accept yes as an answer?" A weak smile flickers to life on Mom's lips.

"Cool. I don't think I could handle you seriously asking me to do that."

Sophia folds her arms. "Somewhere out there is an ass that needs kicking."

The 'rents gasp.

Hearing my little sister in her frilly pink nightie curse is too much on top of everything that just happened. I can't stop laughing. This is the kid who blushes when *I* swear. Once I get control of myself, I pull her in for another hug.

"Oh, yeah. There's definitely an ass out there I need to kick."

Her face mushed into my shoulder, Sophia mutters, "Sorry for swearing, but extenionating circumstances. I've never been outside my body before. It's okay if you ground me."

No one bothers to correct her; we're too busy laughing.

ONCE WE GET SOPHIA BACK TO BED, I EXPLAIN EVERYTHING REGARDING Coralie to the parents.

That done, I head downstairs to plot my next move. Mostly, this involves me daydreaming various scenarios in which I kick down the door of this Brass Tap place and start twisting the heads off anyone in a funny suit. Of course, I have no idea if they'll be there tonight or if they'll only show up for the meeting at the appointed time. For that matter, why would they even possess my sister after we made arrangements?

Oh... maybe it's another lodge. Coralie did mention that they'd broken up into several different groups and probably had some bad blood. I wonder if other parties know she's been liberated and they want to take her. The entity that stepped out of Sophia's body didn't look like Darren Anderson. Honestly, it barely looked like a human. But I'm mostly sure it wasn't him.

Argh! Once again, there I go doing something I think is good for someone, and my family winds up in the middle of the supernatural crosshairs. Maybe I should shut myself into my room and only go out to feed. If I don't do anything at all until the littles are grown and out of the nest, maybe then I won't feel like a completely horrible, reckless big sister.

I seriously need to blow off some steam. Guess there's *Call of Duty*, but I'm not in the mood to be cursed out in Russian, German, and Finnish. Always seems like I wind up in a game with Europeans at this hour, and as soon as I start winning, the swearing starts. At least, I'm *guessing* it's swearing. Every time I kill someone, the screen goes crazy with foreign language text.

Bleh.

A light knock comes from my door.

"Dad?" I ask, as he's the only one I can think of who would bother knocking.

"Not exactly," says Glim.

"Oh!" I run over and open it. "Hi."

He bows in greeting. "Is this a bad time?"

"No. It's actually a good time. I need someone to talk to." I pace in circles while ranting about what happened to Sophia.

Coralie picks that moment to finally make an appearance.

"There you are!" I say. "They attacked Sophia... just like you said they would."

She tilts her head.

"Well, you said something would happen to her and it wouldn't be dangerous." I grab two fistfuls of hair and barely manage not to scream in frustration. "Please tell me that couldn't possibly have hurt her?"

"Given the circumstances of the moment, no. She was perfectly safe." Coralie smiles.

"What's that supposed to mean? Circumstances of the moment?"

Glim's eyebrows tick up a notch in curiosity.

"It means that someone with the proper equipment might have trapped her spirit and allowed another entity to permanently inhabit her body... at least until the spirit was released. But, that was not their intention."

"Wait." I walk up to her. "Those people can just grab someone out of their body and stuff the spirit in a box, stealing them?"

"Not exactly. Someone would have needed to be physically here with a soul trap, and a displaced spirit that belongs to a still living body can kick out any foreign entity with ease."

"Didn't look like it." I shake my head. "Soph tried to grab her body but couldn't get back in."

Coralie sighs. "She did not try hard enough. If all she did was grab, it wouldn't have worked. She would have needed to think about jumping back in. I believe they were only able to take her for so long because she was scared and didn't realize she could take ownership of her body right back."

"Oh. Well. That's not exactly the sort of thing kids learn in school."

"Maybe it should be?" Glim chuckles. "If I may interrupt. I have some news."

Coralie and I look at him.

"There are four possible options for her to choose from, two of which aren't terribly good."

"Okay," I say. "Let's hear 'em."

"One, and least desirable, we could break into a mausoleum somewhere and place her in state. However, the people who once kept her would likely find her with ease."

"They will." Coralie shakes her head. "That is how they found this house. They have several items that I once owned in life. With those things, they can locate my remains wherever I may be."

"Ugh. So what do we do?" I ask.

"Not quite done yet." Glim pats me on the arm. "Second option would be I bring her to the Cathedral of Shadows."

"That sounds kinda scary." I fidget.

Coralie raises an eyebrow. "What is that?"

"It is a place where we find solace and a sense of community. However, it is only accessible to those like me. It's also on the other side, so she would be stuck there with only other Shadows to talk to."

That sounds almost as bad as being trapped at the school, but at least the Shadows won't force her to do the oracle thing.

"The other two options?" asks Coralie.

"Both Arthur Wolent and Eleanor St. Ives have expressed interest in Coralie's remains."

"Oh, forget St. Ives." I hold up a hand.

"Yes, she would most definitely try to exploit her. Then again, so would Wolent, though in a much friendlier way." Glim picks at his elongated fingernails. "Either of those two choices would have political ramifications. You could discuss it with them to see what they might offer."

I shake my head. "No. I can't. That's not me. I can't bargain like I'm trading an object. Coralie is a person. If it's not the ones who used to have her, I think another group is hunting for her. We don't have time to just wait for an ideal situation. It's Coralie's decision, but I think Wolent would be the best choice. Taking her to the Cathedral of Shadows wouldn't cause any political issues, but that's like locking her away forever. I... can't choose this. It's up to her."

Coralie stares into space.

My door opens. Mom sticks her head in, mouth open as if to speak, and stares right at Glim. "Oh. Hi."

Glim flinches.

Mom blinks. "Where'd he go?"

"Who?" I ask.

"That man who was just here." She points at where Glim still is. "I heard you talking to someone and got worried. Everything okay?"

"Yeah, Mom. He's a *friend*." I show off my fangs.

She nods and backs out, closing the door.

"Sorry." Glim scratches at the back of his head. "Reflex. My appearance is a bit much for most people."

"I understand. My mother's used to dealing with *actual* monsters… insurance company lawyers."

He snickers, still with a note of sadness. I lean against him since I know it makes him feel better.

Coralie snaps out of her trancelike state and nods at me. "I believe asking this Mr. Wolent to watch over my remains would be the best outcome. St. Ives would be… bad. Going with the Shadows sounds quite lonely for me. I have been shut away so long, I would like to be able to see the world."

Glim relaxes somewhat and puts an arm around me. "We're not as gloomy as you'd think. Shadows are basically introverts from hell. We hate drawing attention to ourselves in public, but among ourselves, we're a pretty fun crowd."

"Okay so…" I scratch my head. "Do I need to talk to Wolent?"

Glim nods. "Yes, but he's overseas. Should be back on Tuesday."

"Ugh. What about St. Ives? How much does she know?"

"Only that Coralie is out there somewhere and in need of a secure home."

I un-lean from Glim and resume pacing. "Two more days? What if something else happens?"

Coralie clasps her hands in front of herself and smiles. "I'm sure it will be fine."

Great. Okay. I guess I don't have much choice but taking her word for it. All I can really do is wait—and worry.

19

ANOTHER FAVOR

Monday's another annoying bright day.

I hide in my room until it's time for school. Sophia, still a little freaked out from last night, heads down to my room as soon as she's home from school. I take that opportunity to pass along what Coralie said about how she could've taken her body back whenever she wanted to. Sophia's confidence seems to return at hearing that, but she still wants to be clingy.

Pre-death me probably would've become a little frustrated with having her stuck to my side, but now I find it cute. She will eventually—at least I hope so—outgrow that at some point. It will be so weird having this little old woman following me around like an adoring kid sister. She takes clingy to literal heights for the rest of the time I'm home before having to leave for class. I've become a vampire pillow.

The sun today is unrelenting. Dad has to give me a ride in, and I'm half tempted to crawl into the trunk. I don't, instead making do with a hood, sunglasses, and gloves. To avoid being stared at as the weird kid, I leave the gloves in the car and run inside.

English Lit class is awkward due to the first ten or so minutes having entirely too much daylight for my liking. By 7:32 p.m., it's completely dark out so I can relax. Or at least I *could* relax if I wasn't worried about those mystics messing with my family.

Class starts with a discussion of our opinions on the stylistic change in Poe's work throughout his writing career. Fortunately, we don't need to read our essays out loud, but Professor Kendall asks us questions. Everything is reasonably normal until this one late-forties white woman randomly accuses Poe of being a racist, citing he chose the raven as a symbol of evil because it's black.

What is the sound of nineteen heads slamming into nineteen desks at once?

Professor Kendall—who is black—blinks. "That is an interesting and unique theory. Ravens are regarded as harbingers of doom in several cultures. Does anyone have any ideas what Poe's raven represents?"

A man on the left side of the room around Dad's age says, "What if he just meant it to be a creepy talking bird? He was writing popular things for the day trying to make a living."

"Yeah, like a writer describes the walls as being painted blue, it doesn't *have* to be an allegory for sorrow. Maybe the room was just blue." A twenty-something woman in the front row looks around in search of other people agreeing with her. "How much of what we think is symbolism never even crossed the mind of the person who wrote it?"

That discussion carries us past first break and well into the second half. Eventually, Professor Kendall pulls us back on topic. By the time class is over, I've got a bunch of homework studying literary terms, as well reading Hamlet.

As soon as I'm free for the night, I dash off into Seattle and grab a cop for a quick snack since I spot him wandering down a dark alley alone with his flashlight out. His blood almost makes me gag since it tastes like cheeseburger—reminds me of my first meal as a vampire: a thermos of Scott's blood. Still, for expedience sake, I force myself to drink it, erase his memory of the past few minutes, and leave.

While flying home, I risk taking the phone out to call Aurélie.

"Allo *mon cheri! 'ow 'ave you been?*"

"Ugh."

"That does not sound good."

I change course and land on the roof of a five story building that offers a decent amount of privacy. After taking a seat atop a giant air conditioning box, I explain everything about Coralie while gazing into the stars overhead. "Since it could go political, I wanted to check with you before doing anything that might spill over onto you as well. What do you think?"

"Hmm. Well, Arthur has the resources and power to protect her, but then again so does Eleanor. I think this ghost might be 'appy with the Shadows despite how gloomy it seems. Of course, since she has been so isolated for so long, perhaps she would not enjoy it. Arthur will no doubt use Coralie's abilities for his benefit, but the man is generally fair. Eleanor already dislikes you, and I do not think giving her the remains would change that too much. Arthur, on the other hand, would be inclined to think more fondly of you."

I sigh. "I'm not trading Coralie's body based on what I can get out of it. I want to do what's best for her."

"No one solely acts for the benefit of others, especially among our kind. In time, you will come to learn how to do what is best for you while appearing to also do what is best for others. However, in this case, they are one in the same."

If my cell phone had a cord, I'd totally twist it around my finger right now. But, hey... I have long hair. That'll work. I don't think I could ever consider another person—even if they're a ghost—as a resource to be exploited for my gain. Hope that doesn't mean I'm going to fail at vampire. I may *already* be failing at vampire.

"That's good," I say. "Makes it easier. Can I ask an awkward question?"

"You can ask anything you like. Few things are awkward to me."

I manage a nervous chuckle, thanking nothing in particular that Aurélie didn't make any reference to what she and Ashley did together. "Nothing really that bad. I was just wondering how it is that so many other vampires I run into seem rich."

Aurélie laughs. "Well, for me, I was born into some degree of wealth. However, I married several men who had accrued fortunes, and outlived them."

"It's not exactly easy to get a rich guy inter—wait. Never mind." I wince. "I'm nowhere near as gorgeous as you, nor is the guy I'm into rich. He's actually quite the opposite."

She emits a cute little giggle. "Oh, *cheri,* you have plenty of time yet to acquire money and no real need of it. I do not think you are the sort of girl who desires to surround herself with an obvious show of wealth."

"Nope. Not at all."

She makes a *pff* noise. "Then do not worry yourself about it. When we truly need something, we can take it. You are no Fury, Beast, or Shadow."

"True, but... okay? What does that have to do with money?"

"They are the weakest with mind tricks." She emits a soft 'ooh.' "Oh, Sarah, would you do me a favor?"

"Not another haunted doll is it?" I let out a nervous giggle. Speaking of... the vampires I met in Portland were far from rich, too.

"No..." She draws the word out, and the smile in her voice is obvious. "Dolls perhaps may be related. I would like to paint a portrait of you and your sisters. They are *so* adorable."

"Umm." I hesitate. Of course she wouldn't bite them. Probably shouldn't even ask that since it might insult her. "You know if I ask Sierra to put on a frilly dress, she might try to stake you."

Aurélie laughs.

"Though, you do have a ginormous television. Some time on a PlayStation hooked up to a screen the size of an entire wall might be a trade she'd accept."

"A what?" asks Aurélie. "PlayStation?"

"Yeah. It's a video game system."

The next twenty or so minutes go by of me trying to explain not only what a PlayStation is, but video games in general.

"Oh. Interesting." Aurélie emits a series of pensive hums. "I shall look into it. Do ask them for me? It would be such an adorable painting."

"Yeah. I'll do that. Thanks for the opinion. Sounds like Wolent is the best choice."

"Quite so. He is a nice man when the fury does not have him."

"Bye for now. I'll call you again once I run the painting idea past the girls."

"Ta."

I whistle in my mind. Yeah. Nice men generally don't randomly kick chairs out windows and launch them a hundred yards onto the back field. But... to be fair, the man's a Fury, so he can't really help it. Even women in that bloodline are prone to fits of random violence.

So... here goes nothing.

20

SUPERNATURAL COMPLICATIONS

U pon returning home, I run around checking on everyone.

Satisfied the littles and both parents are safely asleep, I head downstairs. Coralie's out and about I suppose as her ghost isn't there. Her body remains under my bed, undisturbed. She hasn't been stolen or turned into Ronald McDonald's stunt double. It occurs to me that I mentioned her being under my bed in front of Sophia, though since the body isn't wearing cosmetics and Sophia's not screaming, I'm going to assume she'd been too freaked out by the ghost thing to really grasp what I said.

I *really* want some quality time with a bath bomb, but I can't shake the feeling the minute I'm in the tub and vulnerable, something messed up is going to happen. Meh. Screw it. I grab a towel, bath bomb, and my Kindle, then head upstairs by way of the kitchen to put the e-reader in a Ziploc bag.

For the next oh, hour and change, I'm good friends with Hamlet and a 'blueberry dreams' bath bomb. Unfortunately, my being slick by leaving the light off since I can see in the dark backfires. Sierra wanders in, feeling around at the walls to make her way to the toilet. She gets about halfway across the room before she stops and sniffs.

"Blueberries?" She looks toward the bathtub, but it's too damn dark for her to see me. "Sarah?"

"Yeah."

"Oops. Umm. Mind if I go?"

"That depends."

"Just peeing."

"Okay."

I continue reading Hamlet while she fumbles her way over to the toilet.

"Pretty weird of you to sit in the tub at night in the dark."

"It's not dark to me."

Five seconds of silence. "You can see me?"

"I could if I wasn't looking at my Kindle."

"You're *reading* in the dark?"

"Uhh, yeah. Complete darkness is as clear as daylight used to be."

"Well… keep reading then."

She yawns a few times, eventually flushes, and trudges out of the room. That's probably a good sign that it's time for me to get out of the tub. I hop out and lock the door before toweling off and pulling on a knee-length T-shirt. No sooner do I walk out into the hall than Sam emerges from his room and goes to the bathroom.

"Ugh. Why's it smell like blueberry yogurt in here?"

His tone doesn't sound like he's expecting an answer, so I just keep going downstairs. Once again, I'm glad vampires jump straight from awake to not. I'm way too nervous to sleep normally. Normal Me would've spent all damn night staring at the ceiling.

I hop in bed and keep reading until the sunrise knocks me out.

TUESDAY NIGHT CAN'T COME FAST ENOUGH.

At least my bio class is interesting. That Professor Connolly is only slightly less boring than televised golf doesn't help, but the material holds my interest. I have always found science interesting. Not that I need the added distraction, but it gets me wondering about maybe changing my major to something science-based. Though, it's considerably harder to work in any sort of lab field while having a serious sun allergy.

I rush out of the building once class ends, not even caring that I took a critical hit from the homework cannon—ugh, seriously this class is going to be a shitload of work—and rush to the parking garage. The Sentra is here since I had to drive in, but I'm in too much of a hurry at the moment to tolerate a twenty-five minute ride.

Less than a minute into the air, I have an unexpected intimate meeting with a pigeon. As in, I take one straight to the face.

At 140 miles an hour, it kinda stings.

Probably stings the bird a bit more—no wait, he didn't feel a damn thing. I swat at the explosion of feathers, stunned from impact, and scream when I realize I'm seconds from crashing into a giant red and white radio tower. There's three of them right next to each other. Still screaming, I twist to the right and manage to zip between two of them, then wave my arms to level off.

Damn bird.

Aww. And crap. There's a smear of pigeon poop down my front. Sigh.

My broken nose knits in seconds, the pain disappears a minute after that. Grumbling to myself, I zoom home as fast as I can, focused on carrying Coralie to Wolent's place. If those mystics want to mess with him, they're more than welcome to. Something tells me he's far less conflict-averse than me.

I arrive home in about four minutes and hurry inside.

Dad looks up from the couch and laughs as I trudge by. "What happened to you?"

"Hit a pigeon. Why, am I a bloody mess?"

"There's a little blood on your face, but you're covered in feathers."

"Great…"

He gets up and walks over. "I'd ask if you're okay but…"

"Right."

"How's the bird?"

"Detonation."

He cringes.

"What? He came in from the left too fast for me to see. I was going kinda fast."

"Wait, didn't you drive in? Is the Sentra still at the school?"

"Yeah." I scoot past him. "I need to change. I'm covered in bird shit and feathers. Gonna go back for the car as soon as I deal with the Coralie exchange."

Dad nods.

Mom, sitting at the kitchen table with her laptop, looks up at me as I walk in. She blinks, but doesn't say anything as I go by and head down to the basement. A shower is tempting, but I'm in a hurry. I rush changing my shirt and jeans, then pull Coralie out from under the bed. Once again carrying her like an ironing board, I go back upstairs.

She coalesces beside me in the kitchen and follows. "Where are we going?"

"Wolent's place."

"Oh. Yes. I think I will miss it here. Your family is cute."

I smile at her. "Thanks. But you're not going to be trapped at this guy's house. You can roam around wherever you want."

Coralie blinks. "You're right. It has been so long, I didn't even think of that."

"What's that?" asks Sierra... sitting in front of the TV.

Crap. I really should've driven home.

"This is Coralie."

"Oh cool. Is that a dead body?"

"No, it's a giant Barbie." I sigh. "Of course it's a magically preserved 200-year-old mummy."

"I'm only 189." Coralie playfully tosses her nose in the air.

Sierra runs over, wide-eyed. "Can I touch her?"

Okay, that I was *not* expecting. I glance at Coralie. "Up to her."

"If she is gentle, I don't mind."

I nod to Sierra. "Be careful. She's very old."

Sierra brushes her fingertips down Coralie's arm. "I bet that dress used to be pretty. She's pretty, too. Sad she died so young."

"Thank you," says Coralie.

"Speaking of pretty dresses…"

Sierra narrows her eyes like a gunslinger about to kill someone.

"How would you feel about wearing one for a couple hours to satisfy the whims of an elder vampiress with a craving for cute?"

"I am not cute," says Sierra.

"On that we shall have to disagree." Dad leans on the corner where living room becomes hallway to the kitchen.

"Grr. I'll think about it." Sierra stomps around the sofa and resumes playing her game.

"Be back in a little bit."

Dad nods at me.

I head over to the door and try to leave, but Coralie bounces off nothingness in the doorway. The third time I ram her into what I can only describe as a force field, she yells at me to stop.

"What the heck is going on?" I ask.

"I dunno," mutters Sierra.

Coralie's ghost hurries over to stand beside me. "I think the mystics did something."

I blink at her.

"Well, obviously they did something. That was silly of me to say. I believe they've warded your house to trap me inside."

I slouch, staring at the floor. "Why the hell would they do that instead of oh, stealing you?"

"They are only mortals, no more apt to break into someone's house than anyone else. And, they are perhaps afraid of you."

"Do you think this is Anderson's people or some other lodge?"

"Hmm." She walks over to the door. Her spirit appears to also be stuck behind an invisible wall. "Most likely, this is the work of the lodge you rescued me from. Another one would not seek to trap me inside but take me."

I shake my head at the ceiling. "Why…"

"To make sure you will do whatever favor it is they ask of you."

"That was a rhetorical why."

"Oh." Coralie clasps her hands in front of herself. "Sorry."

"You better hide her again before Soph sees her or she'll lose her sh —mind," says Sierra.

"Close call there." Dad chuckles.

Sierra pauses the game and twists around to look at him. "There's a dead person in the house. We're talking about killing people, kidnapping people, and oh yeah, Sarah's a vampire. Am I really still going to get in trouble for swearing?"

"Yep." Dad smiles.

"Ugh. *So* not fair." She sighs, and resumes playing.

I carry her back down to my room. Again, Mom sits there in stunned silence watching us go by. After sliding Coralie's body under the bed again, I prop her head up on a small pillow.

"Thank you, but it doesn't make much difference." She smiles. "However, I appreciate the thought."

"Right. So, what now?"

"You should talk to Anderson. I don't feel it will go badly for us. My ability to give them information was not what they hoped it would be."

I sit on the edge of the bed, head in my hands. "What do you mean?"

"I cannot make it happen every time they ask. They originally thought I would be like some sort of crystal ball. Ask a question, receive an answer about the future. Sometimes, I receive information via whispers from the spirit world or see visions of things that will come to be. There is no control over it. The universe decides."

"The universe has a sick sense of humor."

Coralie lets out a wistful breath. "That it does."

"Crap. I gotta go get the car."

THE RIDE HOME—AGAIN—IS NOT TOO STRESSFUL AND MERCIFULLY pigeon free.

I while away an hour or so texting with everyone, then stare at my biology textbook. That makes me think of Hunter and how badly I want to work on another kind of bio project. But... that has to wait for the weekend. Ugh. My schedule sucks. Debate rages in my head for a little bit between goofing off with video games or starting on homework.

Time to take a bit of Dad's wisdom here. When in doubt: do both.

The more schoolwork I do now, the less I'll have to do later in the week. I budget some time to unwinding with a game first so I have the ability to concentrate on work. I'm in the midst of running around in *Skyrim* when Sophia creeps in. I spin, ready to pounce on her in case she's been hijacked, but she makes eye contact.

"Who was that woman who said sorry?" Sophia yawns and rubs her eyes.

"Huh? Where?"

"In my room. I woke up and she was standing next to me. She said I'm sorry they scared you, and walked into the wall." Sophia looks up at me and scrunches up her nose. "Why are you glowing?"

"What?" I look down at myself.

"It's pretty. There's like this light around you."

I examine my arms, seeing nothing out of the ordinary. "Umm. Did you eat something weird?"

"No. Why would eating something weird make me see white light?"

"Umm. Never mind. Forget I said that." I peek into her head and... sure enough she sees a thin aura of white light around me shimmering above an even thinner layer of black. A little further back in her memory, I find Coralie standing in her room. "Wow. You saw Coralie."

"Who's that?"

"It's way past your bedtime. C'mon. I'll tell you on the way."

I take her hand and walk with her upstairs. "Coralie is the ghost I've been helping and, I guess, she decided to appear to apologize for the man who kicked you out of your body."

Sophia yawns again. "Okay."

She crawls into bed and is pretty much out cold before I can even tuck her in.

While it's quite possible Coralie appeared to her, that doesn't explain why she saw light on me. Oh, no way. I sneak back into Sophia's room and gently peel her eyelids open so I can root around in her head a little more.

My sister didn't see any strange light on Sam or Sierra, nor the parents.

"Oh, shit," I whisper. "What if she can see vampires? Dammit. I'm endangering my entire family with supernatural bullshit."

Sophia reaches up and hugs me. "Don't even think about leaving. Please stay here."

"Why are you seeing auras? That's kinda not normal. What if something else happens to you, or Sierra, or Sam... or our parents?"

"I'm not scared." She sticks her tongue out. "You have an aura, but it could be better."

"Better?"

"It's not pink. White is pretty but it's kinda plain."

I furrow my brows. I'm an Innocent. What other color could that possibly be but white? Grr. Now I'll need to try and convince Glim to —wait. Aurélie wants to see them. If my sister sees an aura on her but no one else, that'll prove she can spot vampires.

It'll also prove this supernatural crap is corrupting my family.

"Ugh."

"What's wrong?" whispers Sophia.

"Go to sleep. It's way too late for you to be awake."

"I can't sleep," she whisper-whines.

"Why not?"

She limply hugs me again. "Because I'm scared you're gonna run away."

"Shh. Go to bed. I promise I'm not going anywhere."

Sophia smiles at me in a dreary half-awake sort of way. In seconds, sleep takes her again.

After backing out of her room and easing the door closed, I mime banging my head on it a few times before trudging back to my room, chanting 'Coralie said it wouldn't hurt her' to myself mentally the entire way downstairs until I fling myself on my bed with all the drama of a fourteen-year-old breaking up with her boyfriend for the first time.

I'm worried to bits, but I can't leave home. Scott killing me wasn't my fault, but ditching my family to hopefully shield them from all the strange stuff would totally be on me. Not sure if it's selfish to listen to both my parents and Sophia telling me to stay here, but I can't disappear. No way could I do that to them. Guess I'm going to have to keep a super low profile for the next ten years or so. I'll just go to school and hide under my bed...

As soon as Coralie moves out.

21

A SMALL REQUEST

To avoid poking any sleeping dragons, I don't make contact with Wolent—or anyone else.

No point making arrangements while Coralie is trapped in the house. Glim, or whoever actually made contact to sniff around, didn't tell anyone *where* she is or who has her. It wouldn't do anything but invite more trouble to say anything before I'm even able to bring her out the door.

Wednesday night after calculus, I leave the Sentra in the parking garage at the school despite rain, and fly the couple blocks southwest to the Brass Tap. The place kinda looks like a hipster bar. Wood covers the walls on the outside, styled in that 'fake old' way that some people think looks cool. I can't tell if the owners are trying to give this place an Old West feel on purpose. At least it's got a real door, not saloon-style swinging ones. The interior is dark and cozy, and whoa. I haven't seen this much brass in one place since I went with Dad to the lighting section of Home Depot. Damn... railings, trim on the walls, coat hooks, switch plates, light fixtures, plaques, and yeah, the entire bar area is practically metal. Wow, the light switches are like those giant lever things from *Frankenstein*. Maybe they're going for an attempt at 'steampunk.' I'm honestly not sure where the line between hipster and steampunk falls, but I don't see anyone wearing needlessly complex, pointless goggles.

The bar area takes up about a third of the building, but the place mostly appears to be a restaurant. That probably explains why no one's tried to kick me out yet. I don't simply look 'too young' to buy alcohol. I'm squarely in the 'oh, this is obviously a joke, where's the camera' category.

A late twenty-something guy with dark brown hair so over-styled it could probably deflect bullets approaches me. Based on his black polo and pants, I'm guessing he works here.

"Hi, sweetie. Are your parents hunting for a parking spot? How many in your party?"

Okay, maybe there *is* something that I don't like about my new vampiric existence. If I ever snap and go crazy after however many decades of immortality breaks my mind, being called 'sweetie' one too many times will probably be the trigger.

"No, just me. I'm meeting someone here."

He bites his lip. And, naturally, he thinks I'm thirteen and got tricked into a date with a grown man I met online. Sigh. I push my thoughts into his head, delete the idea that I'm a kid being victimized, and search his memories for Darren Anderson. This guy—Nate according to his shirt—remembered seeing Anderson walk in a little while ago with two other men. I give him a mental nudge to take me to their table, then back out of his head.

"My friends are already here," I say.

"Oh, yeah. Those guys." He turns toward the seating area, nodding to the side. "Right this way, miss."

I follow him past the podium, down a short hall, and up three stairs to an aisle with tall wooden booth seats on both sides. He stops and indicates a round corner table, encircled by one continuous bench seat except for a gap to get in and out. Anderson as well as the other two men I saw in Nate's mind pause their conversation to look at me. One guy's in his later forties with greying black hair and a short beard, the other one's a little younger, paler than I am (which says a lot). Longish curly blond hair hangs draped over his shoulders around a 'pretty' face. All three are dressed in suits that look like they're from a hundred years ago.

Anderson's sitting at the left end of the bench, close to the entry while the other two are in the corner.

"Wow, you guys are inconspicuous." I slip into the booth on the right, on the opposite side of the gap from Anderson.

Nate sets a menu in front of me and walks away.

"Menu ninja. Where the heck did he get this from?"

"Inconspicuous?" asks Darren.

"Those suits are from like 1890. The three of you look like fancy vampires about to go exploring New Orleans."

The older guy raises an eyebrow at me. "Anderson, are you sure this is the young woman you spoke of? She doesn't seem at all like what you described."

"Forgive me." Anderson places a hand over his frilled chest and bows his head at me. "Allow me to introduce my associates: Landon York"—the older dude nods—"and Callum Bailey."

The blond man also nods in greeting.

All three are wearing amulets that consist of metal discs inscribed with weird symbols. Darren keeps fidgeting with his, though the other two don't appear as nervous. I'm guessing they don't believe I'm a vampire.

"Okay, so was it you guys who warded my house to trap Coralie?"

"Yes," says Darren. "Mostly because we became aware of another lodge discovering she is no longer within our vault."

I lean on the table, arms crossed. "So you guys aren't the ones who possessed my sister?"

Callum and Landon glance at Darren questioningly.

"Possessed?" asks Darren.

"Yeah. Someone knocked her out of her body. Looked kinda female." I explain Sophia walking around like a zombie searching the house while her ghostly self had a panicky meltdown.

"I suppose it could have been Meredith," mutters Callum. "The woman's rather skilled with astral projection. Though, she wouldn't have been doing so by our request. She's not with our lodge."

I exhale out my nose. Not good news to learn I now have to worry about *other* mystics coming after us, but it's at least a small point in Darren's favor. They kept their word. As much as I can tell from the tip of their thoughts, they aren't lying. They even seem surprised at the idea someone would do that to Sophia. "Well, someone borrowed her and scared the hell out of her. If you find out who did it, please let me know. Promise I won't kill them."

They all seem confused. Callum shrugs.

"This might've gone farther than we thought," says Landon. "If the expatriates are involved."

"Word of Coralie's ability is overstated." Landon fidgets at his water glass. "But they have only old tales at their disposal."

"Yeah. She told me *it* doesn't work like you guys wanted it to. Kinda random. So, what's this favor you guys want me to do for you in order to leave her—and me—alone?"

Landon leans forward, eyeing me. "Are you sure you haven't lost your touch, Anderson? This girl doesn't look at all out of the ordinary."

"Verum apocalypsis," says Darren.

"Whoa." I hold up both hands. "No one's apocalypsing anything, especially me."

All three of them chuckle.

A waitress with reddish purple hair who can't be more than a month past turning twenty-one interrupts us, asking if we're ready to order. Considering it's after ten, I'm surprised they're still serving food. Struck with a sudden craving, I order some buffalo chicken nuggets. The men request an appetizer sampler platter, a snack more than a meal.

She collects the menus and whisks off down the aisle.

"It is an incantation that reveals the true nature of things." Callum grasps his amulet and holds it up, peering over it at me while whispering something in Latin that's way too fast for me to follow. His eyes flare wide. "Well, that is most surprising."

"I told you," says Darren, before taking a sip of wine.

Landon's black-and-grey eyebrows creep up. "Most impressive how normal you appear."

"Perhaps a side effect of her tragically young age?" asks Callum.

"Hi." I wave at them with a fake smile. "I'm sitting right here."

Darren clears his throat. "Please forgive my associates. You are the first of your kind we have encountered and have already shown yourself to be quite contradictory to what we had previously believed."

"That I'm sitting here like a normal person talking to you instead of like climbing the walls and tearing throats out?"

"Essentially, yes," says Landon with a hint of high-society aloofness in his voice.

"This presents a unique opportunity to us, one that—dare I say—would be well worth trading Coralie." Darren smiles.

"You can't trade in people. She's not a thing."

Callum holds up a finger. "The woman has been dead since 1849. Her remains do not possess personhood under any sense of the law anywhere."

"Not entirely true." Darren flashes a small smile of victory. "They issued a passport to Ramses II in the seventies when they sent him to France."

"One example does not precedent make," says Callum.

"*Au contraire mon ami.*" Landon grins. "A single example is precisely precedent. But precedent is not precept."

Callum narrows his eyes at him.

Darren clears his throat. "Fair point. Instead of in trade for Coralie's physical remains as an object, consider it a matter of soothing the trespass of your breaking into our vault."

"That's kinda like kidnappers being angry at the police for kicking in a door to save someone." I subconsciously pick up my water glass and drink—mostly because it's there.

All three of them stare at me like I conducted a demonstration of cold fusion using only household items.

"What?" I ask.

"You're consuming water?" Callum reaches over and gently grasps my wrist. "She's warm to the touch, as if alive."

I glance at his hand, still around my wrist. "Easier to shop for food while blending in I guess." A twinge of unease circles my gut from fighting the urge to explain that I just want to be normal. Even talking about Innocent vampires seems like a bit too much information to give away. These guys don't need to know that, and having them somewhat afraid of me so they think twice about screwing me over is a good idea. Scaring them *too* much would bite me in the ass.

"Look, I don't think you guys really want to sit here all night and debate the semantics of right or wrong about what happened. I'll do your favor if it means you'll leave my family alone and consider Coralie a free person. She doesn't even really hate you guys. She objected to being trapped."

The waitress returns with the food. "Here you go, hon." She smiles at me and sets a basket of orange nuggets with fries in front of me, then places a huge plate of various random stuff in the middle of the table. "Any refills on the drinks?"

Landon requests another wine, but the other two pass.

"You got it." The waitress nods and walks away.

"As I was saying..." Darren adjusts his ascot. "Your nature provides us with a unique opportunity. I assume you don't need to breathe?"

I shake my head.

"Perfect."

"In the early 1900s, a sailing ship, *Enigma*, went down in the Graveyard of the Pacific." Darren opens his suit coat and pulls out some folded papers.

"Oh, yeah. That's such a small area. Should be super easy to find. By the way, the closest thing to diving I've ever done is swimming in my friend's pool."

"We were hoping your nature obviates the need for any experience or equipment. You have advantages that the living do not possess." Darren stares at me for a moment. "Or, at least, we *think* you might."

I smile. "Your information may not be accurate considering you believed us all animalistic fiends."

Darren opens the folded papers, photocopies of old maps. "Are you able to see in total darkness?"

"Yeah."

"And you don't need to breathe." He smiles. "Shall we assume that the chill of the deep ocean won't bother you?"

I stab a nugget with a fork, pause long enough to say, "No idea. But probably not," then eat it. Sitting underwater in my bathtub to hide from the world for two hours isn't exactly the same as deep-sea diving, but it makes for a decent proof-of-concept that keeps me from laughing and walking away. Wow, these things are actually hot. Restaurant 'hot' is usually what I'd call 'mildly spicy,' but these things aren't playing around.

"How long will that food remain down before you... become sick?" asks Landon.

"Couple hours, and it goes out the usual way. This is probably stupid of me. It's going to burn later."

They squirm.

"Ask invasive questions, get uncomfortable answers." I wag my eyebrows at them and eat another nugget. While hot, they do taste pretty amazing.

"Right, well then." Darren pushes the maps closer. "*Enigma* sank somewhere within this circled area. It carried an enchanted trunk containing irreplaceable unique books."

"When you guys came over from England? Well, not *you* three. But your order?"

They nod.

"Is that stuff about Crowley true?" I ask.

Landon scoffs. Callum rolls his eyes. Darren sighs.

"The man was an utter lunatic," says Landon. "He only wanted s— umm. Well, he was not a well man."

"I'm not as young as I look. You can say the word sex around me."

"Absolute mockery," mutters Callum.

"Perversion even." Darren shakes his head. "He had a little power and a few interesting theories, but he mostly wanted women."

"Fancied himself a divine being." Landon rolls his eyes.

"Okay so…" I pick up the copied map and look at it. "How the hell am I supposed to find this thing? Like thousands of ships sank there."

Darren leans closer. "Being what you are, you don't need to breathe. You can survive the cold temperatures and likely pressures of the deep. You can stay down as long as needed to find the ship and the trunk. Retrieve it for us and we will forget entirely about Coralie. As well, you and your family will be far from our thoughts."

"So, you basically want me to go find a box that could be anywhere on the sea floor over a swath of like two hundred square miles? I'm not even sure I can see underwater."

"Have you tried?" asks Callum.

"No. Not exactly. I mean, I know I can stay underwater for hours."

All three give me curious looks.

"Bath bomb," I mutter. "Expensive one. Didn't wanna waste it."

"What does that have to do with being underwater?" Darren helps himself to a stuffed potato skin.

I shrug. "Nothing really. Just hid under the foam to hide from the world. I had some issues to sort out and wanted to be alone for a while. Anyway, I'm open to doing this for you, but I don't want to spend the next century with Coralie's body in my house while I roam back and forth across the ocean floor looking for a wreck that might've disintegrated to toothpicks by now. I've got way too much studying to do."

"You're a mystic as well?" Landon's eyebrows go up for the second time tonight.

"No. I'm a college student."

They stare at me.

"No shit. I really am eighteen. Kinda new at the whole deadly powerful immortal thing."

"Hmm." Landon rubs his beard. "All right. Give us a little time. We may be able to come up with a way for you to locate it more easily."

"What are you thinking?" asks Callum.

"The enchantment placed on the trunk should still have at least some residual energy within it. If it has become unstable, it would only be more readily located."

Darren and Callum nod at him.

"Sound logic." Darren pulls a business card out of another pocket and hands it to me.

It's plain white with only a phone number on it.

"What's this for?"

"When you receive a call from that number, please answer it. Once we work out if it is possible to assist you in locating the trunk, we will contact you." Darren nabs a buffalo nugget from the sampler plate that looks exactly the same as the ones I ate. When he tosses it in his mouth, he turns red and coughs.

"They're a bit spicy," I deadpan. "Like I said, that's going to hurt on the way out."

I sigh to myself. That's an apt metaphor for my vampiric life. Oh, this tastes great—ahh, damn, it burns! Why did I do that to myself? Just like picking up a doll for Aurélie, or helping that guy escape that crazy bitch Petra, getting a flower for an older vampire... or helping a sad, lost ghost named Coralie.

They all seemed like the right thing to do initially, but now my butt is on fire.

And you know what the worst part of this is? The next time I stumble across someone in need of help, I'm going to fall right into the sucker trap all over again. Honestly, I should start worrying about who I've become if I *don't*.

I just hope my ass can take the heat.

22

TESTING THE WATERS

Waiting sucks. Even if you're immortal.

Thursday is super overcast and gloomy, raining more than not. I used to have little reaction to weather. If it was nice out, cool. If it rained, cool, excuse to stay inside. For obvious reasons, I'm starting to prefer bad weather, but it makes me worry. Years ago, Ashley said something about people who love rainy days are depressed. She might've been kidding, and I'm pretty sure it's not true that only depressed people like the rain. In fact, it's quite possible that many depressed people hate the rain because it makes them feel worse.

No, I'm not being a sad sack. I have an actual, practical reason for preferring rainy days. And hey, it *is* an excuse to curl up in a blanket with a hot cup of tea.

I get out of bed and head to the bathroom to deal with the inevitable downside of eating normal food. Only, those chicken nuggets don't qualify as normal. You know how most living humans like *digest* stuff? Yeah, well… not me. Whatever went in, comes out unchanged. So that yummy but too hot sauce? Yeah.

Let's just say the screaming brings Dad to the basement bathroom door. He asks if I'm okay a couple times, but all I can do is moan and cry—and bite my arm to muffle more screaming.

Oh... never again.

By the time I'm done, I stagger bow-legged to the door and open it. My T-shirt is spattered with blood, my hair's a mess, my eyes are red, and I've got blood dribbling down my arm from where my fangs dug in.

"Good grief, Sarah!" Dad grabs my shoulders. "Are you okay? What the hell happened?"

I wipe my face on the back of my right arm. "They cancelled *Firefly*."

Dad gets misty eyed, nods, and sniffles on my shoulder.

Sad thing is, I can't tell if he's kidding. "Remind me *not* to eat super spicy stuff now."

"Oh." He cringes.

"I'll be fine in a moment. I think the pain's mental at this point. I got over a broken spine in a couple minutes."

Dad pushes me out to arms' length. "What?"

"Oh, I didn't tell you about that, uhh, troll?"

"On Facebook?"

"No, Dad. Actual troll."

"Oh, the cave thing." He nods. "Yeah, you did tell me about that."

I stiff-leg it past him, heading to my room. "Got some homework to finish up."

"Ouch, hon. You sure you're okay?"

"Yeah. The fire's already going out." I lick my arm to close the bite wound, then clean the blood off my hand. "The worst part is, I honestly don't even know why I ordered that."

Dad laughs. "Sometimes people do strange things. Live and learn, right?"

"One for two?"

He walks up behind me and wraps me in a hug.

"Sorry."

"What?" asks Dad.

"For reminding you. Hey, I'm not dead. I'm better than that."

He manages a weak chuckle, then holds me in silence for a little while before Sierra's shout of, "Fuck!" reaches us downstairs along with a couple hard stomps on the floor.

"Wow. Someone really must've pissed her off," I say.

Dad looks at the ceiling. "She is so lucky your mother isn't here right now."

"You're gonna let her slide?" I blink at him in shock. "That was a hard f-bomb."

"Well, I could say I didn't hear it down here, but I think the Perry's next door heard it."

"Hah."

"Sounds like it's time for a talk on managing anger. Let the bargaining commence."

I salute him.

Once he walks out, I turn my attention to homework. It only takes me about an hour to finish it, so I head upstairs. Sierra's on the couch looking glum, Dad sitting next to her. She looks up at me, teary eyed.

"Sare!"

Dad's expression is a mixture of worry and frustration.

"Hmm? What happened?"

"This guy on the other team got mad at me and said he knew where I lived and he was gonna do stuff to me. I got scared and started dying a lot and..."

I flop down next to her and put an arm around her shoulders. "Yeah, I heard."

"Is someone really going to come here to kill me?"

"I sincerely doubt it. Idiots like that just say stuff to scare people."

Dad pats her on the arm. "Someone who had the skill or the equipment needed to figure out where we are wouldn't waste the effort over a couple virtual deaths in a video game. And the most they could probably do is grab the IP address, which isn't going to give them our exact location."

Sierra sniffles and nods, then looks around like she doesn't know what to do with herself.

Since the PlayStation is already off and packed away, I'm guessing she's been grounded from it for at least the rest of today.

It's too rainy to go outside. "Board game?"

Dad smiles. "She needs to clean her room up first as part of our agreement."

Sierra nods and slides forward to scoot off the couch.

"I could help?"

She hangs her head. "Thanks, but that feels like cheating. I should probably clean it myself... but you can hang out."

The way she looks up at me while saying 'you can hang out' makes it more of a plea than a suggestion. So, I head upstairs with her and sit on the bed while she runs around tidying up. Honestly, her room (my old one) needs it bad. She's exploded all over the floor between clothes, shoes, gadgets, and school stuff.

Sierra drags a laundry basket into the middle of the room and starts tossing stuff into it. "How can someone get so mad over a game they wanna hurt someone?"

"No idea. Probably because they're not too sane to begin with."

She scoots around the floor on her knees, collecting clothes. "Dad was surprised I already had the PS4 off. First time I ever rage quit."

"That idiot broke your concentration. Happens to everyone sooner or later. Nothing to beat yourself up about."

Sierra twists back to look at me. "I was scared. Like a little kid. I thought he was really going to hurt me." She smirks. "Don't say it."

I raise an eyebrow. "I wasn't going to make a joke. It's shocking enough to hear you admit to being scared."

She grumbles. "You were gonna say I *am* a little kid."

"You're a kid, not a *little* kid." I wink.

"Thpbpbpbt!"

Sierra's been on edge ever since the school did that drill for active shooters. Grr. I hate seeing my 'tough' sister scared like this over some idiot halfway around the world who probably forgot all about her as soon as the match ended. I hate that she's eleven and so worried about dying.

So, I try to take her mind off it by talking about stuff she likes. Mostly video games and movies.

Eventually, her room is reasonably clean. I do help a little by carrying the laundry down to the basement. She overloaded the one basket, making it a bit heavy to manage herself. Sophia looks up from her Kindle when we collect in the dining room.

A rainy afternoon of board games and hanging out with the family later, I decide to drive to school anyway despite the darkness.

It's effing pouring.

Showing up at school as wet as if I'd jumped in the lake would suck.

Hang on. Jumped in the lake...

Sounds like I know what I'm doing after philosophy class.

Practice.

I run downstairs to change, grab my books, and haul ass out the door to the Sentra in the driveway. That short sprint nearly soaks my hoodie. Damn. I might not even need to locate a body of water for experimental purposes. Simply walking outside almost requires the ability to hold my breath for an infinite amount of time.

Driving in heavy rain is going to stink in a big way, too. But less so than showing up at school in a bathing suit and changing in the bathroom. I really wouldn't have any good explanation for that and I can't spend all night mind-wiping witnesses.

So... I hit the road.

Fortunately, this being the Seattle area, people are pretty used to driving in the rain. The ride is longer than usual, but I'm not late since I still over-budget an hour for travel. Professor Heath is in a good mood. I wonder if he was kidding about staying in the school or if he's got a place somewhere. You'd think *someone* would eventually discover a vampire sleeping on campus during the day.

Tonight we lean toward the sociology aspect. It's mostly a lecture this time—as opposed to a meandering class-participation talk—on the 'sociology of gender and sexuality.' The guy is an awesome presenter, somewhere between a stand-up comedian and a motivational speaker. As captivating as his class is, the two huge chapters of reading for next week plus 2,000 word essay required is less cool.

But, hey, I signed up for this.

Again, he asks me to linger a moment after class. So, I wander over to his desk while the rest of the students file out the door.

"Just checking up, hoping everything is well."

"Little weird, but not bad."

Heath tilts his head. "How so?"

I'm not getting any bad vibes from this guy, like he's trying to mine me for information or anything, so I tell him about Coralie. Not being a *total* naïve idiot, I omit that I've got her at my house, and say only that I'm trying to figure out where best to put her remains for her benefit.

"Interesting. Have you considered a museum?"

"No. Honestly didn't. She's not Egyptian. And the people who are trying to grab her would eventually get her back from a museum without too much difficulty."

"Ahh. All right. How are you holding up?"

"Fine."

He smiles. "That's good. Not missing the sun then?"

"Oh, nah. This is pretty damn awesome. Why would anyone get all emo over it? Does that really happen or only in movies?"

"Seems to be more of a trend among new additions as of late. Something about the young people. And when I say 'young people' I'm talking about twenty, thirty years of age, but I suppose millennials have enough to be emo about already without undeath."

"If you say so." I shrug.

"Forty or fifty years ago, a girl your age could wait tables or some such thing and earn enough to pay tuition at a private university."

"Yeah right. There's no way in hell I could ever have paid my own way at USC. I *might* be able to swing this place under my own power but I'd be working so much overtime I'd barely be able to do homework."

"Exactly my point, dear." He chuckles. "Well, I wanted to say feel free to ask if you have any questions about your new self. Since it hasn't been long since your Transference, I'm sure there's much you haven't learned."

"Thanks. Okay, yeah. Weird question: can we survive the deep ocean? Like, the cold and pressure and stuff?"

"Well, I can't say that I've ever personally visited the sea floor. However, unless you are considering visiting extreme depths or arctic locations, it shouldn't be a danger. We are still rather capable of freezing solid. Resisting it is possible to a point, though it... well I suppose it would be like your special relationship with the sun."

I nod. "But the ocean off the Pacific Coast isn't *that* cold that a body would freeze solid is it?"

He shakes his head. "I wouldn't imagine so. Might I inquire as to why you're asking?"

"Sure." I lean on his desk. "The mystics want me to hunt down a shipwreck and look for something their order lost. If I do that for them, they'll leave me and Coralie alone. I'm kind of worried because... if we can do that sort of thing so easily, why don't we?"

"Our kind don't usually make the news." He wags his eyebrows. "I know of at least one who found a considerable fortune from locating a stash of gold coins in a wreck."

Well, that's promising. Not that I plan on going all Jacques Cousteau. My luck, I'll wind up eaten by a giant squid. "Duh. That was kinda dumb." I wave a hand suggesting a headline. "Vampire discovers treasure off the coast of Spain. Full story at ten."

Professor Heath grins.

We chat a little while more about nothing of consequence. Turns out he *does* have a small place within walking distance of the school. He mind-whammied the landlord to completely forget the room he's using exists. Once he moves on from this area, he'll remove the mental block.

I head outside to find it still raining but nowhere near as hard as earlier.

The ride home is boring—hey, I'll take boring. It beats having vampires dropping out of the air onto the hood again. No cops or anyone else bother me on the way back home. I park the Sentra in its usual spot, then head inside to my bedroom, where I change into my two-piece swimsuit and put my T-shirt and jeans back on over it. Meh. I'll skip shoes. One less thing to lose.

Okay time to commence Operation Dumbass.

Well, at least the dry run for it. Or 'wet' run technically.

Mom and Dad are on the couch watching one of the newer James Bond movies... not sure which one. I scoot by without being noticed and head outside via the kitchen. The deck is wet and slippery after a day of rain, but I only take two steps before I'm in the air. I'm not entirely sure why I bothered putting anything on over the swimsuit. It's still raining and my clothes will wind up wet anyway. Maybe it's for stealth? I've gotten a bit paler since I became a vampire, and if I fly around in a bikini, someone will definitely see me. Then again, no one spotted me the first night when I didn't even have a bikini on. But yeah... I'm not exactly in a hurry to do that again.

It takes me only a moment to fly to Cottage Lake. By some subconscious pull, I wind up landing in almost the same spot where that guy, oh what the hell was his—River! That idiot. Yeah, this is the same spot I pulled Ashley out of his car.

Since no one's nearby, I pull off my shirt and jeans, stash them up a tree where the rain's not quite able to reach, then fly out over the lake. Hope no one sees me out here. Swimming in September is really weird. So weird in fact, I think people would wind up not even noticing that I'm flying and fixate on 'what the hell is that dumb girl doing in a swimsuit?'

I gaze down at the surface rippling along below, and gasp at the bizarre appearance. While the dirt and such suspended in the water prevents it from being clear, it's not entirely opaque. Oh hell. The longer I fly around above the lake, the more chance someone's going to see me.

It's probably not a great idea to hit the water while flying at like forty miles an hour. I stop to a hover, then—for reasons I can't even fathom—take a deep breath and lower myself into the water. And holy shit it's cold. What the hell am I doing? Those mystics are out of their damn minds. Feels like I've jumped into a bag of needles.

That nice big breath I took? Yeah, I scream it out into a bubble. Or several bubbles. It takes the realization that I'm not panicking about not breathing back in to remind me I'm no longer alive—simply good at faking it.

Okay, I'm *epic* at faking it.

Still, I can barely move since I'm freezing.

At the moment, I feel no different from a normal person jumping in a Washington State lake in early September. Wait. Normal people wouldn't do that. But I'm not normal people. It's debatable that I even count as 'people' anymore, but I'm going to be an optimist there. I'm still enough of a sap to feel guilty over a ghost to once again put my family in the middle of supernatural bullshit.

I'd sigh, but the lungs are empty.

Right. I can do this.

My body simulates warmth because I'm Innocent. When I wound up in the morgue, I didn't feel cold until after I escaped into a much warmer room. Really, that felt like going from normal to 'too warm.' Until I adjusted. So, maybe I just need to wait a moment?

I hang in place underwater, maybe three feet below the surface, forcing myself not to fold my arms, shiver, or act as cold as I feel. True, the most diabolical thing I've done with my vampiric powers is make people buy Girl Scout cookies, but dammit, I am a fearsome creature of the night. A little cold shouldn't bother me.

Roughly two minutes after going under, my muscles decide we can be on speaking terms again.

Okay, progress.

The remaining discomfort is mostly due to being wet and having a mental hang up that I *should* feel cold being out here in a lake at this time of year. I spend a moment focusing on the idea that I'm a character in like *Skyrim* or something who can go swimming in a snowbound lake while wearing full armor like it's no big deal. Hypothermia is for mortals.

First good thing to know: night vision works underwater. I should probably get a pair of goggles or a diving mask at least before I go into the ocean. I can't see too far with the water in my eyes, but I can still see.

Flying still even kinda works, though I'm nowhere near as fast as I am out of water. I experiment for a bit, though with my limited visibility (about thirty feet) and not being deep enough to see the bottom, I can't really tell how fast I'm going. The instant I sense my swimsuit preparing to rip off my chest, I try to stop—but wind up drifting. Oh, that's weird. Aha! Unlike air, the water filling in behind has enough mass to push me. Another good thing to know: if I sprint, I can't quite stop on a dime.

Since no one can see me down here and I'm pretty sure 'fly-swimming' too fast is going to tear off my bikini top, I slip it off and wad it up in my fist. The last thing I want to do is have my bathing suit randomly disappear and lose it down here. I'd never find it. I don't think my bottoms are in as much danger, but... losing them would suck even more than the top. I really ought to test this out to prevent accidents.

Staring at my lower half, I resume attempting to 'fly' as fast as possible. Arms at my sides, my body rigid, I pull the 'meat torpedo' routine. It's a bit like falling down while water skiing, and within seconds, the water rushing by rips my bottoms off.

Crap!

I whirl around and zoom back the way I came. Fortunately, I spot the pathetic scrap of electric green fabric tumbling around in my wake, and grab it. Dammit. Yeah, now that I think about it, I remember someone saying rip currents can sometimes tear a bathing suit off. While I've never been caught in one of those, I'm pretty sure 'flying' at however fast I'm going down here is subjecting me to water pressures way past a rip current. Since a dash tore my bottoms off, I don't even try testing the top.

Well, I'm already out of my suit, so I clutch half of my bikini in each hand and do the nudist mermaid thing as a speed test. Without my iPhone on me, I can't tell exactly how fast I'm going, but I do get up to a speed that makes it impossible for me to keep my eyes open.

I've learned a few valuable things: I need a wetsuit for this as a bikini isn't going to cut it. Also, I should probably get a mask or goggles. Then again, if my suit won't even stay on at even a quarter of the speed I'm capable of, a facemask is likely to rip right off, too. If I have to swim so fast I can't see, chances are I'll be running away from something like a shark, so it'll be straight up.

Okay, now that testing is done… I'm a child. Admittedly, I spend an embarrassing amount of time playing in the water by moving my body around to see how it affects my speed or steering. Like, while doing the human torpedo thing, I can move my hands like the flaps on the side of a submarine and steer. Kinda like a little kid sticking their hand out the window of a car. *Why* that's so amusing, I have no idea.

It's a little awkward *carrying* my suit instead of wearing it, but compared to how fast I can swim down here, the speed at which the water rips it off me feels like crawling. Once I've got a decent feel for 'flying' underwater, I dive straight down until I land on the bottom. With no air in my lungs, I don't start floating back up. And yeah, it does feel weird to 'hold my breath' with an empty chest. Even when I hid in my bathtub, I did so with full lungs like any normal person holding their breath, only for like two hours.

The lake bottom is super icky to walk on—so I don't do it for long, deciding to fly again and practice 'looking around for a shipwreck.' I do find a few, but only small rowboats. There's a car tire or two and even a full toilet. What the f—. All right. As bizarre as it sounds to be hanging out at the bottom of a lake, this 'fishing' expedition is starting to sound almost plausible.

I'd say sorry for the pun, but I'm not.

Okay, time to go home and get warm. For me, cold is evidently a state of mind. A morgue cooler felt fine until I realized what it was, then I became chilly. Right now, I want my bed and blankets.

I fly straight up to the surface and catch myself before pulling the drunken dolphin backflip out of the water. Giant splashes are the opposite of subtle. So, I come to a near halt, slip my bathing suit back on, and breach the surface. It takes me a few seconds to figure out where the hell I am and fly back to the tree in which I stashed my shirt and jeans. Since I'm drenched, I don't bother putting them on and carry them with me on the maybe forty second flight home.

While flying in over the house, I notice the front door open and an unfamiliar blond guy in a grey blazer struggling to back outside like he's attempting to steal our sofa without anyone helping him. The hell? I can still hear the television on, which means I haven't been gone so long the 'rents went to sleep. Shit. This is not good.

My thoughts leap to Sierra and that guy who threatened to kill her over the PlayStation.

I swoop down on the front lawn. Within a second of my feet touching grass, I realize this guy and another one inside are slamming Coralie headfirst into the ward over and over again. Her spirit is standing behind the inside dude screaming at him to stop.

Oh, these must be those other mystics who scared the shit out of Sophia…

Eyes narrowed, I dash in and try to kick the outside guy in the balls hard enough to launch him onto the roof. Both men unstick from slow motion time. The guy nearest me spins to face me at normal speed, even a bit faster than me. He catches my leg at the shin and I wind up hopping on one leg when he doesn't let go.

We lock stares.

Beard, neat hair, grey suit jacket over a white shirt with tight pants. Ugh. This guy's so hipster it's painful—and he's a vampire. He's giving me a somewhat surprised and confused look mixed with a dash of 'go away, kid.' The other guy's wearing a legit suit, but he's also got a beard halfway down his chest and like this Indiana Jones type hat. Both are maybe late twenties, and reek of craft beer and incense.

"Oh." I hop. "Sorry. Thought you were someone else. You must be St. Ives' people."

He lets go of my leg.

I lean to the right enough to peer past him at my parents, catatonic on the couch. Ugh. Seriously? That's so not cool. Bad enough when Dalton did it; I can't have random vampires showing up and switching my parents off.

"Guys, really? What the hell are you doing?" I flail my arms. "My parents?"

They look at each other.

"Umm," says the one in the back. "Nothing permanent, you should know."

I point at Coralie. "You can't take her."

"You're going to stop us?" asks the blond one.

"Well, I actually meant that in a more literal sense as in you are physically incapable of removing her remains from the house at the moment due to a magical ward."

"Will you *please* tell them to stop mashing me into it? I've got a headache now," yells Coralie.

Both men sigh.

"So you *can* see her?" I fold my arms. Yeah, I'm so totally intimidating standing here sopping wet in a bathing suit. At least when I have clothes on it's not so painfully obvious how un-muscular I am.

"Tell her to drop the wall and we'll be on our way," says Inside Man.

"Give us the body." Blondie steps up on me, though he feels more like he's trying to order a kid sister around than threatening real violence. "Now."

"I can't get her out the door either. Aren't you listening? Go complain to the mystics."

"Okay..." Blondie does this weird Buddhist meditation breathing thing for a few seconds, like he's trying to keep himself Zen. "Give us the body... or we'll twist the head off one of your little thralls."

I toss my shirt and jeans to the grass to free up my hands. "First, they are not my thralls. Second, do I have to remind you again that if you touch my family, Aurélie will rip St. Ives' uterus out and beat her to death with it."

They both lean back, blinking.

"Well, that was needlessly graphic," says Blondie.

"How the hell did you even find her here?" I ask.

Inside Man shrugs. "Shadows work for favors, too. Not only for friends."

"But... I thought they were like one big community or something."

"Your friend must not have asked them to 'guard the knowledge' or whatever it is they call it." Blondie scratches at his beard. "Look, kid. We—"

"Need to leave before I remember you threatened to harm my family. Maybe we won't be able to perma-kill each other, but do you really want to deal with having the shit clawed out of you?" I stare at his crotch. "I'm not above fighting dirty since I'm small. And claw wounds hurt like hell for days."

They squirm.

"Look," says Inside Man. "It's not personal."

I rake my hands up over my hair and bite back the urge to scream in frustration. "Why does that woman have a bug up her ass? Will you two please just go away? Tell her that Coralie is stuck here for the time being and *can't* leave. And, if she's got some grand idea of using 'The Oracle' to see the future, it doesn't work like she's daydreaming it works. She has no control over what she sees or when she gets a look at the future. St. Ives can't feed her questions and win the lottery—or whatever it is she wants to do. Why do you think the mystics are so willing to let her go?"

The guys exchange a glance.

Inside Man bonks Coralie into the force field again, shrugs, and sets her down leaning against the wall like an ironing board. She—the ghost—balls her hands into fists and fumes, unable to do much but scream and fire off nasty looks.

I take a step back to let the men go by. They look around at the cul-de-sac, and evidently confident no one is watching, glide into the air. Wow. They really just left without a fight. I really ought to go inside before someone notices me out here in a bikini. Grumbling, I pick up my clothes and head inside.

"You are drenched," says Coralie.

"Wrong turn at the lake on the way home."

She opens her mouth to say something, but just winds up staring at me.

"Kidding. Experimenting tonight." I nudge the door closed, secure the deadbolt, and pick up her body. "They didn't hurt you, did they?"

"No. The preservative enchantment makes me quite robust, and the ward is not exactly solid."

I start to carry her down the hall to the kitchen, but stop short, realizing my parents are still catatonic on the sofa.

Sigh.

"Dammit."

23

A TENTATIVE TRUST

I ease Coralie's stiff-as-a-board body back under my bed, and pull the spread down to hide her.

As if.

Eleanor St. Ives' people know where she is. Not sure how they realized *I* had the body. As far as under the bed goes, they might've mined that out of my parents' thoughts. No way they lifted it from my siblings' heads. They didn't know the mummy was even here.

My siblings.

Shit.

I dash upstairs to find the girls in Sierra's room on either side of a layout of *Magic* cards. Sophia's on her stomach, chin on her hands, one foot up. Sierra's sitting cross-legged, scowling at the cards in her hand. Both of them stare into space with a little drool rolling down their chins, like they've been exposed to a fourteen-hour marathon of *Jerry Springer*. For an instant, I get so furious my claws pop out... but since neither appears hurt, I calm myself and take a knee to peer into their eyes.

Sierra has a blurry spot in their memories, likely the vampires erasing their presence. Sophia, however, remembers seeing the two and knows she's been zapped paralyzed. In her head, they both had auras, one yellow, one dark blue. Both glows have a thin layer of black under them. I don't see any compulsions in either girl other than to zone out for a while. Their eyes flutter after I remove that command, and they resume playing cards like nothing happened.

At least for the two seconds it takes them to notice me crouching beside them.

Both of my sisters scream.

Sierra jumps back, throwing her cards in the air. Surprisingly, Sophia realizes it's me *before* she starts crying from being scared, and just sits there clutching her chest.

"Crap!" yells Sierra. "Don't do that!"

Okay, do I take the blame for scare pranking them or let them know what really happened? Meh. Sierra's already walking on eggshells over that shooter drill, then the PlayStation threat. I can't wind them both up in fear that vampires might just walk into the house at any time and mess with their heads.

"She didn't," says Sophia. "She un-froze us."

Sierra asks "Huh?"

Damn, Sophia remembers it... but how?

"A couple bad vampires made us sit still for a while. Sare just fixed us."

The look on Sierra's face says she wants to kill someone, but I know that expression—she's terrified.

"One had yellow light and one Dark blue." Sophia pushes up from being flat on her belly and hugs me. "I didn't wanna do what he said, but I couldn't break out."

I pat her back. "Well, crap. Sorry you guys."

"What happened?" Sierra narrows her eyes.

"One of the elders who is a bit of a bitch tried to kidnap Coralie." I explain the mummy situation to them, but don't mention where she is. "I'm trying to get her to a safe place. You guys don't have to worry about it, okay? Aurélie is like the oldest vampire in the area. She's protecting us. Well, you guys at least. If someone messes with *me*, it's different. But my family is off limits."

"That's the one who wants to stick me in a dress, isn't it?" grumbles Sierra. "I'm eleven. I shouldn't be extorted like that."

I laugh. "You don't have to. Her protection isn't conditional."

Sierra nods and proceeds to collect the cards she threw all over the place.

"And, let me go check on Sam."

The girls resume their game. I head across the hall and find my little brother in his computer chair, staring at the lobby screen of *Overwatch*. He, too, has been 'paused.' To avoid a similar awkward conversation after scaring the crap out of him, I erase the compulsion to be catatonic, then dash out of the room as fast as I can go.

"Huh. Stupid game kicked me out," mutters Sam.

Whew. Okay. I really need to relocate Coralie somewhere safe.

I rush back downstairs, zoom past my catatonic parents to the kitchen and... *don't* go down the basement steps. I catch myself on the doorjamb, hang my head, sigh, then trudge back to un-pause the parents.

"Gah!" yells Mom. "Please don't jump scare us like that."

Dad twitches, glares at me for a second or two, then cracks up laughing.

"It's not funny, Jonathan. You know I used to hate it when you did that to me. Wonder where she gets it from?"

"Guys." I sit on the sofa between them. "Some vampires who work for St. Ives showed up looking for Coralie's remains and tried to steal her. They basically paused everyone."

"Paused us?" asks Mom. "Are Sierra, Sophia, and Sam okay?"

"Yeah, they're fine. And you know, like a movie? Paused."

Dad shakes his head. "Young lady, we've spoken about your friends coming over at all hours and mind controlling us."

I open my mouth to protest, but he laughs again.

"Really, Jonathan?" Mom rubs the bridge of her nose with both hands. "This isn't a joke."

"Sorry." I look down. "Why is it every time I try to do something nice for someone it blows up in my face? Guess I should've realized helping a 200-year-old ghostly prophet escape a sect of mystics would've put my family in danger."

Both parents stare at me.

"It's probably an entirely inappropriate reaction, but I find it kind of exciting." Dad smiles.

"Life isn't an Eighties action movie." Mom smirks at him.

He gestures at me. "It's coming pretty darn close. And no, sweetie, you're not in trouble. I'm just making light of the situation."

"Still. I need to re-home her as fast as possible. You guys okay?"

Mom's expression says she's not, but she collects herself after a moment, then nods.

"I don't imagine there's much of anything any of us could've done about what happened," says Dad.

"That doesn't make me feel better." Mom reaches for the TV remote on the coffee table.

"If I was here, they wouldn't have done it." I stand. "Gonna go call them."

"The vampires?" asks Dad.

I shake my head. "No, the other 'them.' The mystics. They need to drop that ward and let me move her."

"And if you were here, they probably would've just waited until you weren't." Dad puts an arm around Mom. "And you've got entirely too many 'thems' these days."

"There's got to be *something* we can do." Mom's glare at the wall nearly burns a hole in it. She hates not having control of a situation.

"Those guys?" I grin and make a throwing motion. "Just toss a thing of beard cream to distract them and run the other way."

Dad snickers.

"Okay, let me try to deal with this." I point at the hall, then hurry to the kitchen. The instant my hand touches the knob, Sophia starts screaming like someone's trying to stab her.

"I got it," says Dad.

Nodding, I keep going downstairs. As soon as she shifts from shrieking to shouting "Get Mom or Sarah" I'm pretty sure this is an already-in-the-bathtub-plus-frog issue, so I allow myself to relax. I have bigger problems... like trying to figure out which pair of jeans on the floor of my bedroom has that mysterious business card in the pocket.

I crawl around grabbing anything denim.

Coralie walks out of my closet. "Ugh, what is wrong with those two?"

"Assuming you mean the guys trying to grab you? A lot."

She points. "It's in that pair. And, I mean why did they continue bashing me into the ward over and over again. Did they honestly think it would break?"

"Thanks." I pounce on the jeans she indicated and pull the plain white card out of the pocket. "This is going to sound silly, but I'm pretty sure ninety percent of vampires think magic is made up."

Coralie folds her arms.

I flop on the bed with the iPhone and dial. The line rings for about a minute before someone answers. Two seconds pass in silence.

"Hello?" asks Darren, hesitant.

"Hi. It's Sarah."

"It's only been one day. We're still working on—"

"I know. It's not that. Look, can you guys drop the ward? I really need to get Coralie's body out of my house before some idiots cause problems."

Darren emits a long-suffering sigh. "And move her somewhere we cannot reach her?"

"Isn't that technically true right now? Otherwise, why did you ward her into my house? Listen, I'll do your thing... find that box or whatever. Just, don't be assholes about it 'kay?"

"If she is presenting problems, you could simply return her to us."

I shake my head at Coralie. "She doesn't want to be there."

"What? You spoke to her?"

"Ugh. Of course. Why do you think any of this happened? Aren't you guys supposed to be like smart or something? Do you think I just randomly figured out you existed, had a dead woman's body stuck in your vault, and decided to help her escape?"

"Incredible," says Darren in an awed voice. "You can see spirits."

"Yeah, well. I kinda got one foot in the door of the afterlife." I sigh. "Look, just please turn off the ward thing, okay? I promise I'll help you find the books as soon as you come up with a way for me to locate them."

"What guarantee do we have that you will?"

"Umm…" I twirl some hair around my finger. "How about I'm like super honest and never lie?"

Darren laughs.

"No, I'm serious. Ask my mom. I suck at lying. Besides, you clearly know where I live and I just want to go back to living relatively normal. The last thing I need are a bunch of angry mystics trying to mess with me. You guys don't screw me, I'll keep my end of the deal."

Coralie puts an intangible hand on my arm. "Tell them I will agree to share my visions with them if they release the ward early."

"No." I look up at her. "I can't let you be trapped again… not after all this."

She smiles. "They do not need to possess my remains for me to speak to them. Without it, they cannot *control* me, but I can visit them if I choose."

I relay her offer.

Murmuring comes over the line for a moment.

"Fine," says Darren in a reluctant tone. "You certainly don't act like any vampire I've ever seen."

"Umm. How many have you seen?"

"That's beside the point."

"Just me, huh?"

He grumbles. "Yes."

"Well, you watch too many movies. Only a couple of us are like what you usually see there."

"Hmm. Well. We shall agree to your—and her—terms in the hopes you are as honest as you claim."

"Thank you."

"I'll call you once it is done."

"Awesome."

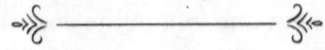

M Y PHONE RINGS A LITTLE OVER AN HOUR LATER, INTERRUPTING THE start of my sociology reading.

Well, okay. Texts from Ashley, Michelle, and Hunter were doing that already. But, yeah… they'll be asleep soon so I don't regret it.

I swipe the thing to answer. "Hello?"

"Miss Wright," says Darren. "The ward has been removed. You're welcome. Now, please remember not to ignore our next call."

"I won't… unless I'm in class. Gotta turn the ringer off. Any time after nine should be okay except on Wednesday or Friday since Dr. Mercer has a habit of going late."

"Right. Understood. We'll call you soon."

He hangs up.

Ugh. I flop face down over my desk. Why do I feel like I just sold my soul?

24

CUSTODY DISPUTE

C oralie fidgets with anxiety as I get dressed again.

My parents and sibs are asleep, leaving the house so quiet I feel like I'm making a ton of noise even though I'm not. I throw a hoodie on over a plain T-shirt, but I need a break from jeans so I do a cute black skirt—with yoga pants since I intend to fly.

Once dressed, I ease Coralie out from under my bed and check her over for damage. She seems to be in good… okay, can't say health. But she's only slightly creepy. The magic preserving her body is weird. She almost looks fake, like I'm holding a life-sized doll. Not sure if it's my vampire-ness letting me tune in on something beyond human sensing, but she *feels* like a genuine corpse.

Satisfied the idiots didn't hurt her, I carry her upstairs. Her ghost follows as if walking.

"Are you sure you're okay with going to Arthur Wolent's place?" I ask.

Coralie nods. "Yes, I believe that remaining outside the normal order of the world by residing with a vampire would be preferable to ending up in a museum where I would be vulnerable to another lodge, or worse. While I have grown fond of this place, my presence here may attract danger to your family." She smiles. "And I'm sure you don't want the young ones to see my remains."

"Well, honestly…" I hold her body out to arms' length and look her over again. "You're not *that* bad. They've seen worse in movies. But, St. Ives will keep trying, I'm sure. Damn, now I feel kinda guilty."

"For what?" Coralie tilts her head.

"Feels like I'm getting rid of you and you want to stay."

She steps through the glass onto the deck. "It does not matter where my remains are. I can visit whenever I care to now that I am free from the vault's enchantments."

I look back and forth between her and the body a few times. "If that's true, then why does everyone care so much about taking your remains?"

"The mystics have ways of using it to control me, and those other vampires don't know much about me other than some vague notion of my being able to offer predictions and warnings of future events." She clasps her hands in front of herself. "Once they learn how hopelessly random and spontaneous it is, I'm sure they will lose interest as well."

"Okay." I pull the patio door open and step outside. "If Wolent ever wants you to leave, you can come back here."

"I appreciate that. Perhaps I could remain here, though this house rather lacks suitable accommodations. Under your bed is inconvenient for you and somewhat awkward for me. Nor did I care much for being leaned against a wall in a vault like some object. My presence here is also altering the energy of this area. A few children were staring at your home this afternoon, thinking it creepy like a haunted house."

"Are you sure that's just not me?" I grin.

"Yes." She offers a wan smile. "I will be comfortable and safe. Now, let us go. You have homework to finish."

"Okay. One sec."

I pull my phone out of my pocket and call Aurélie.

"Hello, *mon cheri*. I hope you are well."

"Hi. I'm sorry to bother you out of the blue, but would you mind contacting Wolent and letting him know I'm bringing Coralie to his place?"

"Of course. And no bother."

"Thanks. Oh, hey I think Sierra might be warming up to the idea of the painting. She's *not* a big fan of frilly/girly stuff. But I'm working her up to it."

Aurélie emits a wistful sigh. "It is all right. Do not force the poor dear to do something she is uncomfortable with. I would adore to paint the three of you, but it is not required."

"Okay. I'll let you know. Going to leave now for Wolent's. Call me back if there's a problem bringing her there tonight?"

"Why the rush? Did you not have to do some favor for the mystics?"

I explain the two guys who tried to steal her. "St. Ives lost patience."

Aurélie clucks her tongue.

"It's all right. They didn't harm my family or anything."

"Be careful. I shall speak to Arthur right away."

"Thanks again. Talk soon."

I hang up, stuff the phone in my pocket, and carry Coralie's body outside. Her ghost blurs into a smear of energy that seeps into her remains—and the mummy starts giving off the creepy-as-hell sense that I'm carrying a live person who happens to be paralyzed.

Yeah, that's not weird at all.

Considering Coralie is a little taller than me and as stiff as wood, flying with her is a bit awkward. At least she doesn't weigh much. Can't put her on my back since her arms are stuck at her sides, and I don't feel like tying her on like a pack. Carrying her sideways causes too much drag, so I wind up hugging her to my chest and trying to ignore her hair whipping me in the face.

Finding my way back to North Hill isn't too difficult. The big statue of a medieval knight in front of Wolent's manor house is super obvious. I cruise in over the reflecting pool around the statue and land in front of the huge mansion.

The instant my sneakers touch paving, several bodies crash into me from behind. The hit is hard enough to send Coralie flying out of my grip and flings me face down on blacktop. As I stand back up, a guy and a woman grab at my arms while a third man beelines for Coralie's body. The dude holding my left arm's got a beard down to the middle of his chest that resembles a sugar snake from chemistry class—too damn round. The woman on my right side is dressed like she came from a corporate office.

I grab a handful of beard, her hair, and slam them together in front of me. A spritz of blood sprays from where their faces meet along with the cracking of bone. Can't tell if it's noses or teeth, but something's in more pieces than nature intended it to be. "First kiss is usually painfully awkward."

Beard staggers one way, hands clamped over his face while the woman falls on her ass, stunned.

Ignoring them both, I turn my attention to the blazer-and-T-shirt guy grabbing Coralie, but Wolent's door man—the Moroccan Hulk—beats me to him. This dude is seriously effing huge. He's like two people wide and I'm barely as tall as the middle of his chest.

The big guy leads in with a hell of a right hook. His fist connects with a crunch like a coconut going under a truck tire. St. Ives' dude rockets off headfirst, doing a spot on impression of a lawn dart in the dirt at least fifty yards away. His Jack Purcells are still on the ground next to Coralie.

"You missed the water," says another man in a black suit behind him.

"Was trying to be nice." The huge guy tugs at the lapels of his suit jacket.

My brain can barely wrap itself around the idea that this guy launched a man—even a skinny one—that far from one punch. Then again, he is ridiculously large, nearly inhuman. I'm too busy gawking at him to notice the fist coming for me until my jaw breaks with a loud *crack* that echoes inside my head. Executive Bitch apparently objected to my playing cupid.

Her punch doesn't send me into the air like a missile, but it does knock me a few steps to the left. Yay for vampire agility. Beard zips past us both, grabs Coralie, and goes straight up. Executive Bitch leaps at me again. I grab her arm the way Glim showed me and flip her. She might be a vampire, but she still only weighs like 130. That's why vampire fights tend to, uhh, migrate and cover a lot of ground. Massive strength, but we aren't any heavier than mortals. However, I don't toss her for distance, instead driving her straight into the ground to keep her from hitting me in the head and smashing my brain.

As soon as I let go of her, I leap into the air after Beard. Carrying Coralie slows him down enough that a short vertical sprint brings me close enough to get a hold of his legs. Unfortunately, he's a stronger flier than I am and even with me trying to full reverse, he's still inching higher.

"Get off!" yells the guy, struggling to kick at me.

"Fuhh oo!" I scream back, despite my smashed jaw. Wonder if Dad would consider that an f-bomb?

Executive Bitch drags herself back to her feet and eyes us, though she doesn't zoom up to grab me. Probably afraid that'll drag the whole party back to the ground. Or she's waiting for her left shoulder to un-break. I strain, trying to fly backward, and sink my claws into his calves to make sure my grip doesn't fail.

He screams in agony, and I don't blame him. Vampire claws sting—a lot. Burn even. I think I'd rather eat those buffalo nuggets again than be clawed up. As horrible as that was, it passed in a few minutes. Claw wounds linger for days. An irritating high-pitched squeal comes from my jaw as the bone mends, everything sliding and grinding back into place.

"Grr!" I growl, pulling backward with all I have.

Executive Bitch shouts, "Look out!" Then screams in fright.

Boom.

Beard's head explodes in a shower of gore. In an instant, creeping upward becomes zooming straight down. I barely have time to process the need to stop before smashing flat on the parking circle in front of the porch, Coralie's body sandwiched between me and the headless vampire. Since I didn't hear anything break—in me or her—

I'm fairly sure I managed to slow down enough for my landing to merely hurt like a bastard.

Arthur Wolent steps down from his porch, a giant military style shotgun held sideways across his chest. He's flashing a huge grin like he just achieved the high score at the clay pigeon range. The Moroccan juggernaut has Executive Bitch held off the ground by a fistful of her shirt, the nice suit jacket bunched up around her neck.

"Your friend mentioned you'd be coming," says Wolent. He hands the shotgun to a smaller—normal sized—man in a black 'Secret Service' suit.

I shove the headless guy off me to the side. Thick, dark red blood oozes out of his neck stump. His foot-long beard and a flap of face are draped over my leg. Gah. I swat it away. That's even more ghastly a sight than the lasagna at my old school. "Ugh. Is that guy dead?"

Wolent laughs. "Nah. Simply taking a long nap." He gestures at Executive Bitch. "You have five seconds to grab him and get the fuck out of here."

The big dude sets her down standing. Executive Bitch is an inch and change taller than me, but she still looks like a child next to this monster. He brushes his hand at her jacket, attempting to flatten out the wrinkles he made.

"Thank you, Aziz," says Wolent.

I blink, snicker, cover my mouth, and... burst into laughter.

Wolent, Aziz, the other security guy, and even Executive Bitch all look at me like I'm insane.

"Thank you, Aziz," I squeak in between laughter. "Holy crap, you have an Aziz?"

Aziz flattens his eyebrows.

"I feel as though I've missed an important piece of information," says Wolent.

Executive Bitch picks up the headless guy and struggles off into the air under his weight.

"Sorry," I rasp once I can speak again. "Line from a movie my Dad loves. This archaeologist has a kid with a mirror... light. Keeps saying 'thank you, Aziz.' Just struck me as funny."

Wolent chuckles, though I can tell he's faking it. At least I didn't piss him off. "So, this is Coralie?" He looks the body over. "Pleasure to meet you. Come on inside."

The Secret Service-looking guy with the shotgun scurries off somewhere. Aziz opens the doors for us on the way into the manor house and walks with us to a small, but nice bedroom deep in the back of the house on the ground floor. When Wolent indicates the bed, I set Coralie down like she's sleeping on it.

"Excellent." He nods once at me. "I'll have a proper casket made and set her up somewhere quiet where she won't be disturbed. Wherever in the house she fancies."

Coralie appears beside the bed. "Thank you."

"Welcome to my humble abode." Wolent holds his arms out.

Yeah. I'm not saying a word.

"Forgive the less than pleasant reception. I hadn't expected her to be so brazen." Wolent glances off to the side.

Sensing imminent rage, I try to distract him by asking, "Who made up that story about decapitation killing vampires?"

"No idea." Wolent makes a spitting gesture to the side. "Pricks. It may have originated from a legend involving a specific sword that was probably enchanted. Or, most likely, we started the rumor as misinformation."

"Okay, that makes sense. So fire really is the only way to kill us for good? No, I don't wanna kill anyone. Just want to know what to avoid."

"Not only fire. Complete destruction of the remains. Sunlight, fire, strong acid, lava—well, I suppose lava is fire." Chuckling, Wolent holds an arm out like he's inviting a daughter in for a hug. "Come, let us talk."

Ugh. Wonderful. How lame would I sound saying I have to finish homework? Saying 'no' to a Fury this old is also risky in general. And... I don't need to finish that assignment until at least next Wednesday morning.

Good, 'cause I think I'm going to be here all damn night.

I put on a mostly genuine smile and allow him to pull me into a one-arm hug. He's throwing off something between 'dad vibes' and Mafia don, so it's not at all creepy in an old guy with young girl way. It's creepy in a 'say the wrong thing and I die' way. Aurélie likes him, so maybe I'm overreacting to his whole presence.

Bleh. Suffering a night of conversation with people I don't feel like I belong hanging out with is a mild price to pay not to have to worry about anyone raiding my house to steal a mummy. And Coralie is here, so I have at least one person I can talk to freely.

"Okay. Thanks again for protecting me, and giving Coralie a safe home."

He walks me out into the hall, then releases his grip around my shoulders. "Think nothing of it. Can I offer you a drink perhaps?"

I rub my jaw. "Yeah. That would be great. Thanks."

25

THE IRONY OF TIME

With Coralie safe at Arthur Wolent's mansion, I can stop living in a perpetual state of crippling dread over what might happen to my family at any minute.

I'm merely in a state of severe worry.

However, since the only *extra* things that could happen at the moment are the mystics contacting me to cash in that favor and the outside chance St. Ives might be upset enough to seek revenge, I can breathe easy.

Or well, okay. Maybe not *breathe* easy, but whatever.

All I have to do now, other than homework, is wait for the mystics to call me and keep an eye open for retaliation. I'm reasonably confident that St. Ives is afraid of Aurélie enough not to mess with my family, but that doesn't mean she won't attack me directly. The woman's a scientist, so with any luck, she'll decide that the effort it would take to kill me isn't worth it for simply not giving her Coralie's body. It's not like I stole anything from her, or even stopped her from stealing from Wolent again. She had no claim to the remains.

So yeah. I've been worrying a *lot*.

Though, it's Friday night and I should be having some fun. So, instead of lying in bed staring at my ceiling, I'm presently lying in

Hunter's bed staring at his ceiling. Neither one of us bothered getting dressed after we finished making love a while ago. We both really needed this time together, but for different reasons. I'm not sure if I wore him out or if I should blame his schedule, but he passed out maybe a half hour after we finished. I don't think I'm *that* boring a conversationalist. But, it's nice to just be here with him.

He has almost no free time between school and work, and barely gets enough sleep. My problems are a bit more out there. Despite that, I do feel guilty that he's busting his ass so hard while I've got plenty of free time—just not at the same time anyone else does. Hunter doesn't want me 'tweaking' anything to make life easier on him because he knows it would bother me. Hell, I couldn't even handle the guilt of pranking someone in Portland by moving a lawn statue two houses over. I also told him about the PIBs being aware of me, and I'd be lying if I didn't say the idea they'd come after me for abusing my abilities isn't in the back of my head.

Which makes me wonder if there is some kind of 'acceptable limit' of exploiting things before they get involved. Maybe making life easier with a bit of money wouldn't bother them at all and they're only concerned with vampires who go off on killing sprees? Could be their role is purely to keep the public in the dark about supernatural things. Whoa. Could that mean aliens are real, too?

My superhero identity, Follows Rules Girl, barely managed to encourage Mom's boss not to lay her off, and only because it would've been based on ego bullshit. She won't kiss his ass, so the dick would've let her go first out of spite. Something like that doesn't bother me as much.

And okay, I guess I did compel people to buy Girl Scout cookies. Is that an abuse of power?

Thump, thump thump.

The unmistakable sounds of a small boy approaching come from the hallway.

Eep!

I leap up from the bed and scramble into my clothes as fast as I can move, nearly tearing the fabric. Being able to hover in midair makes getting pants on fast super easy. A quick grab-and-toss covers Hunter up to the neck with blankets. No sooner does my butt land on the bed than Ronan, the younger brother, pokes his little blonde head in. He's the same age as Sam, nine, but looks smaller.

Fortunately, I managed to put everything except my socks and boots on before he made it down the hall. He looks at me, at his brother, then back to me.

"Hey, bud," I say. "What's up?"

"What'cha doin?"

I scoot my feet back and forth on the rug. "Hanging out. Your brother's kinda tired, so I was going to head home and let him sleep. He needs it."

Ronan steps into the room and points to the left. "The bathroom light's not working."

Hunter shifts and yawns. "Gimme a sec, Ro. I'll get it."

"Hurry. I gotta go."

"I can change a lightbulb." I pat Hunter on the leg and get up, following the boy to the end of the hall and a small closet.

If not for him watching me the whole time, I'd have skipped the stepstool, but being normal is easier than erasing memories. Once the bulb's changed, I head back to Hunter's room and find him up, in sweat shorts and sitting at his computer desk, though it's not on. That computer will never turn on again after his shithead of a father broke it. Hmm. I can probably find a bargain laptop somewhere. He's going to need it for school.

He swings around in his chair, smiling at me. "How many vampires does it take to change a light bulb?"

I roll my eyes and plop down to sit on the foot of his bed. "Ha. Ha."

"Sorry for falling asleep like that." He runs a hand up over his head, mushing his hair around.

"It's fine. You're working yourself too much. Not your fault my schedule puts school late in the day. It's annoying it cuts into the time I can spend with you." I stare down, wondering for the hundredth time if having a relationship with him is unfair since we'll never have anything close to a normal life together.

"Yeah, but it's only a couple years." He grins. "Kinda ironic for you to complain about not having time. You got plenty of it."

I sigh at him. "Yeah, but you don't."

"I'm busier than hell, but the time I get to spend with you makes it all worth it." He holds his arms out in a come here gesture.

I move to sit in his lap, smiling at his words despite the doubts swirling around in my head. As soon as he kisses me again, the overwhelming happiness radiating from him pushes my hesitation aside.

"Are you sure this is a good idea?" I ask when we come up for air.

"Positive. I can do homework tomorrow."

FOR THE SECOND TIME THAT NIGHT, I WIND UP NAKED ON HUNTER'S bed staring at the ceiling.

I decided to let myself enjoy the time we have together. He certainly doesn't seem to care about the unusual dynamic between us. Suppose it probably is premature for me to obsess about 'our entire life' together. Honestly, people our age only stay together 'happily ever after' in stories. I can't think of anyone I know whose parents met around eighteen and are still together. Heck, Mom never met Dad until she was like twenty-six. Granted, they fell for each other hard. She wound up pregnant with me before they married.

So, yeah. Before I work myself up over 'stealing' Hunter's life, I need to relax. For all I know, we might not work out. Then again, he *does* have an entire notebook full of doodles and poems about me. If he'd have managed to find the courage to talk to me in high school, I might not have been killed. Of course, in that case, I'd still be able to get sick, grow old, and die for good.

I blow a raspberry at the ceiling.

Vampirism is pretty damn cool. I get why most of us leave their mortal families behind now. Constant risk to them is the only thing I regret about what happened to me. If I knew for a fact that they'd be hurt, I'd wish myself back in time like none of it ever happened. But just for myself? Nah, hell with that. This is awesome. I can make this work though. Just keep my head down and not piss off any elder vampires until the littles are no longer little. Not that I'm planning to start trouble the instant Sam moves out, but I'll be able to relax at that point. I hope.

I lay there for a while brushing my hand back and forth over Hunter's chest. He fell asleep again. Okay, perhaps he had a little help in that regard. It's almost one in the morning now and he's got to wake up in time to do homework before his job. So, I may have 'encouraged' him to sleep. The plush Snoopy I got him sits prominently on the shelves above his desk watching us. Wonder what he thinks of us being together. Probably doesn't mind since he's still smiling.

The pleasant silence dies a sudden death when my iPhone explodes ringing.

Once again faster than humanly possible, I fling the covers off and dive to the floor where my pants lay in a heap, and fish the noisemaker out of my pocket.

"Hello?" I whisper.

"Sarah, *mon cheri*," says Aurélie. "I hope you are well."

"Yeah, I'm okay."

"Why are you whispering?"

I bite my lip. Do I tell her I'm kneeling on the floor of my boyfriend's room with no clothes on, a potential embarrassing situation due to roaming parent or little brother inches away at any loud noise? Nah.

"I'm at my boyfriend's place and he's asleep. I was just about to head home. Don't wanna wake up his parents." I snag my underpants and pull them on.

"Oh, *mon dieu!* Why did no one ever tell me about these PlayStation things? This machine is rather addictive."

"Yeah." I chuckle and slide into my jeans before grabbing my T-shirt. "They can really soak up time."

"I am looking forward to meeting your sisters. When do you think you will be able to bring them to see me? I am sure Sophia would adore my dolls."

"Oh, yeah… she'll either be in heaven or wind up in therapy for the rest of her life. Some of those dolls are creepy. Do straitjackets come in frilly pink?"

She laughs.

I set the phone down on the rug long enough to get into my shirt. "Umm, maybe tomorrow or next Friday. I can't keep them out late on a school night."

"All right."

"And I gotta make sure my parents are okay with it."

Aurélie keeps quiet. Hmm. Is she surprised I'm like actually asking permission instead of just taking them?

"Still there?"

"*Oui. Un moment. Montée dangereuse dans le jeu,*" she mutters in a distracted voice.

"Umm. What?"

Another few seconds of silence go by before she sighs. "Oh, forgive me. I'm playing the game. The climb was dangerous so I had to concentrate. Yes, of course, make sure it is all right with your parents. They are still children after all."

I decide not to mention St. Ives people attacking me at Wolent's place. Maybe the bitch will take my lack of complaining as a peace offering of some kind, and I also don't wanna be that kid who runs to mommy whenever someone gives me a dirty look at school. Besides, Wolent knows who sent them. That'll cause her enough trouble. No need to involve Aurélie. Of course, she probably knows already.

"Cool. I'll let you know as soon as I do."

"Perfect. Good night, *mon cheri.*"

"Night."

I hang up, pull on my socks, then slip into my boots. Feels a little weird having shoes on inside, but Hunter's mother doesn't care about that at all. Not like my mother. The way Mom reacts, you'd think we tracked live Anthrax around the house if she catches us wearing shoes inside.

After kissing Hunter, I whisper, "Night. Sleep well."

On the way out, I pause by his mother's bedroom door. I could be super lazy and bite her, but nah. Feeding on my boyfriend's mom just feels wrong. It would be awkward even in an emergency with her permission. Not that she'd give it since she doesn't even know what I am. Yeah, not going there.

I let myself out a second-floor window and fly off toward Seattle in search of someone to eat. Oh, and I should probably buy a wetsuit while I'm in the city. The 'rents are going to bite my head off for spending money on something like that without asking first, but my father is fond of a phrase that applies here.

Easier to ask for forgiveness than permission.

26

ALL EMO AND STUFF

I awake in my bed Saturday afternoon still smelling like shower soap.

Yeah, going twice with Hunter and getting dressed without a shower happening put those clothes in the actual hamper. My laundry is divided into several floor piles. Basically, I've got the 'could still wear all day' pile for stuff I only put on for like an hour or so. Pile two is 'too dirty to wear outside, but fine at home.' Pile three is 'better this than naked.' I don't have a pile four. Anything I would put into an even filthier category goes straight into the bin. Really, I haven't had a situation to wear pile three clothes once, so I should probably scale it back to two piles. I mean, my room is literally fifteen feet from the machines. No excuse to be lazy anymore.

Not having any plans yet, I ditch the long T-shirt I slept in for a tee and sweat pants from pile two, and head upstairs. It's a moderately cloudy day, but not quite gloomy. Leaving my sanctuary of darkness before sunset is going to make me hungry by nightfall, but I want to spend time with my family.

It's about quarter to three when I make it up the stairs. Everyone's in the dining room around the table playing a haunted house board game. Sophia's sniffle-crying while trying to keep herself as quiet as possible. Sierra's eyes are ringed with red like she'd been crying recently, but her expression has settled midway between furious and like she lost a pet. Sam is neutral, apparently oblivious to their emotional state, and focusing entirely on his arrangement of story cards.

Strangest of all, my sisters have their chairs together and they're sorta-hugging.

Both girls look at me like they want me to insert myself into whatever family love fest is going on, so I head over there. Soon, we've got three chairs touching and I'm being hugged from both sides.

"Umm..." I glance at Dad and Mom. "What did I miss?"

"Sierra screamed the F word at the TV," says Sam, matter-of-factly. "She's grounded off video games for a week."

Sierra sniffles and looks apologetically at Dad.

"I offered to play a board game with her," whispers Sophia, "but she got mad at me, too. I said something kinda bad."

"It wasn't bad," mutters Sierra in a tone indistinguishable between surly or somber. "Just depressing."

I'm assuming that since Mom hasn't said a word, she's got a lump in her throat.

"Sierra started to stomp upstairs but Soph yelled at her to stop." Sam rolls dice and moves his figure around the map tiles. "Soph said like 'please don't be mad at me. What if you die like Sarah did and the last thing we did was fight?' That made Sierra cry."

I choke up. "W-what?"

"I'm sorry." Sophia hangs her head. "I shouldn't have said that. It was mean."

"No, you're right. Any of us could die whenever," says Sierra while staring into the table. "We almost lost Sarah. What if me or Sophia or Sam don't come home from school someday? We shouldn't be crappy to each other."

And... I'm done. I squeeze them together and sniffle right along.

The parents both cringe. Neither one of them have said much about their fears concerning a lunatic showing up at the littles' school, but they have to be thinking about it. I'm sure they're also well aware how much it's affected Sierra. I'm tempted to erase the idea of it from her head but I can't keep doing it every time the school runs a drill. As freaked as she is now, if I got rid of the very concept that someone could hurt her at school, the next time they run an exercise, it would completely traumatize her.

Mom dabs at a tear while Dad gets up and comes around the table to give us all a squeeze. At that, she also clings to the group hug from behind.

"I'm getting diabeetus," says Sam. "Will you guys stop being like all emo and stuff?"

I sputter into a giggle.

Dad lets out a heavy breath.

Sam puts his cards down and crawls under the table to add himself to the family hug by climbing into my lap—but only for a moment before he slips down and scrambles back to his chair.

"Sorry for swearing, Mom," says Sierra barely over a whisper.

"Another idiot say something in the game?" I ask.

"Nah. The controller died in the middle of a match." She takes the dice when Sam pushes them close to her. "We're out of apples."

I snicker. "Not sure that would've helped. Or were you already having a bad match?"

"Nah. I *was* doing okay 'til it stopped working."

The game's well into progress, but I add a character and draw a hand of cards anyway. Ooh, enchanted crowbar—the best weapon. Dad mentioned it was a reference to an old video game, but I don't remember which one.

Mom and Dad return to their seats and we resume playing. Sophia stops crying, though she's hanging on me like we're adrift at sea. Sierra goes back to her normal personality in a few minutes, or perhaps a slightly more vulnerable version thereof. She keeps leaning against me, and even tolerates my arm around her shoulders while I'm not moving pieces or rolling dice.

The game ends in a little less than an hour with everyone in much better spirits.

Mom glides over to us as we're packing up, giving us each a brief back pat. "I'm thrilled to see you three getting along so well, but"—she looks at Sierra—"you're still grounded for a week."

Sierra draws in a breath to snap back at her, but holds it.

I stare at Sierra, trying to see into her thoughts. The ambient light in the room dials up from ugh to 'shit! ouch!' for a few seconds. Fortunately, it's dim enough inside that I don't need to be in a life-and-death (or should I say a death-and-deathier) situation to redirect power from shields to primary weapons so to speak. Still, it hurts like hell, so I only manage a brief peek before my brain snaps back like a hand off a hot pan. Sierra wasn't *acting* nice in hopes of changing Mom's mind about grounding. Sophia's remark about any of us—well them—dying at any minute stabbed her straight in her anxiety gremlin over school shootings.

"She wasn't playing nice to get off being grounded." I grab Sierra and hug her despite the squirming. "You just really hurt her feelings."

Mom cringes. For an instant, she looks guilty, but covers it up with a cough. "Sarah, don't read your sister's mind."

"Yeah," says Sam. "It's below your grade level. You should read something harder."

Sierra raspberries him.

"Sorry." I try not to glare at my mother. "Exigent circumstances. You really didn't need to poke her about that."

That Sierra hasn't yelled 'get off me' by now is roughly equivalent to Sophia bursting into tears.

"I..." Mom sighs at the rug. "You're right. I'm sorry. I'm not even sure why I said that. Stress from work probably."

"At least you don't have to worry about being laid off." I smile.

"You messed with your mother's job?" asks Dad.

"I claim plausible deniability. A conversation may have happened, but it was just some random girl dropping off Girl Scout cookies."

"Okay..." Mom walks over and collects Sierra from me, hugs her, then pats her on the shoulders. "I'm sorry for hurting your feelings. How about a compromise offer? Instead of a week of no video games, you vacuum all the carpeted areas and help me with the windows tomorrow instead? Your choice."

Sierra thinks it over for about eight seconds. "I'll do it."

"Hey, it's Saturday. Sarah doesn't have class." Dad claps his hands. "Movie time?"

"What particular strain of Eighties cheese are we to feast upon tonight?" I ask.

"I was thinking *Ice Pirates.*" Dad rubs his chin.

"Can it wait an hour? I gotta vacuum stuff," says Sierra.

"That sucks," mutters Sam.

Sierra and Sophia groan. Mom facepalms. I giggle. Dad scoops him up like he just scored his first touchdown.

"He punned!" Dad fake-sniffles. "I'm so proud."

"C'mon." I pat Sierra on the shoulder. "I'll help move stuff out of your way."

27

SMALL PRICE

Sierra finishes vacuuming the house, including the main basement room, with a few minutes to spare before dinner.

That means *Ice Pirates* waits until after we eat. And, being that Mom made spaghetti, I don't at all feel guilty about 'wasting food.' Hmm. I might as well throw this out there now while everyone's in the same place.

"Umm, Mom? Dad? Aurélie asked if the girls could visit."

Sierra gives me side eye from hell.

"Why?" asks Sam.

"She's a painter, and thinks we'd make for a nice picture."

"You're leaving something out," deadpans Sierra.

"She's not gonna bite us?" Sophia claps her hands over her neck.

"Absolutely not. I wouldn't even ask if I thought that." I glance at Sierra. "She's going to dress us up like dolls first."

Sierra narrows her eyes. "You've done this before, haven't you? Tolerate humiliation from the ancient vampire so she's nice to you."

I shrug. "It makes her happy. And she's lonely. And she's got a crapton of dolls."

"Ooh!" chirps Sophia, wide-eyed.

"Yeah." Sierra laughs. "You're one of them."

"Apparently. Oh. Did I mention she's got a 120-inch television with a PlayStation?"

Sierra points. "That's not fair."

"What kind of dolls?" asks Sophia, interest clear in her voice.

"I'm not sure about this." Mom fidgets. "Why would an elder vampire be interested in them?"

"Maybe she has a sweet tooth?" asks Dad.

Mom swats at him. "Jonathan!"

Sophia gasps. "She's really not gonna eat us?"

"No. She likes cute things and she wants to paint our portrait. It's only a painting." I look over at the 'rents. "And she didn't say you guys couldn't come along. I can't fly carrying both of them. Well, I could, but I'd be too afraid of dropping them."

Sierra twirls her fork into her noodles. "Okay. I'll wear a silly dress for a little while if it keeps her happy and wanting to help us."

Dad puts a hand on Sierra's forehead.

His turn for epic side-eye.

"When is this supposed to happen?" asks Mom.

"I suggested maybe tonight or next week, Friday or Saturday."

Dad chuckles and grins. "We should probably do it before she changes her mind."

Sierra looks up, a few noodles sliding into her mouth. She stares at him like she wants to say something but waits until she finishes chewing. "There will be no photographic evidence."

"She's painting us," says Sophia. "There's gonna be evidence."

"A painting can be made up. I have plausible deniability." She grins.

"You're sure this is safe?" asks Mom.

"Yeah. The drive into Seattle is riskier than being around Aurélie, though she might have an... effect on Dad." Ugh. Now there's a thought I never *ever* wanted in my head.

"Effect?" Dad blinks.

"She's... magically charming." I can't even look at him.

"Would this woman do anything inappropriate?" asks Mom.

"Only if she's asked to," I say before thinking. "Oops. Sorry. Just kinda spat that out."

Both parents stare at me in shock.

"No. You guys… That's not what I meant." Ack. I can't tell them about what Ashley did. Especially not in front of the littles. My face has to be bright red. "I'm just going to go to my room and shove a stake into my chest."

Sophia gasps. "No!"

Dad's expression goes from shock to inquisitive.

I sigh, then lock eyes before speaking mentally to him. *No, Dad. Not me. Ashley. Aurélie is like a Wood Nymph. Anyone attracted to women who sees her has to make a save roll against mind control.*

Now there's an unanswerable question: what's more embarrassing? That my Dad wondered if *I* did something inappropriate with Aurélie, or that I admitted Ashley did.

"Well, I'm sure it'll be all right." Dad squeezes Mom's hand. "No radiant charm is stronger than your mother's."

Sam makes a gagging noise.

"Are you guys gonna kiss?" asks Sierra. "Please warn me so I can look away."

"Aww," says Sophia. "They're cute."

"They're your parents," says Sierra in a toneless voice.

Sophia nods. "I know. That doesn't mean I want to *see* them get cute. But they're cute."

Mom and Dad chuckle at each other.

"On that note… should I call Aurélie then?" I ask.

Mom's cheeks pale. "I… don't really know how I feel about this, but if that woman is the reason we're relatively safe? Sitting for a painting seems a trivial request."

"Okay. I'll go call her." I hop up.

"Sarah?" asks Dad before I can take three steps down the hall.

"Yeah?" I whirl around.

"What's the $98 charge for?"

I clasp my hands in front of myself and flash a cheesy smile. "A wetsuit."

"Why did you buy a wetsuit?" asks Mom.

"Umm. Because stealing one would be wrong."

Both parents stare at me.

Sam laughs.

"What did you need a wetsuit for?" asks Dad.

"Those mystics want me to recover some ancient lost chest from the bottom of the ocean. A wetsuit won't disappear straight off me if I swim too fast."

"Oh. Okay." Dad nods.

Mom looks at him like she can't believe he gave up that fast. "That seems kinda frivolous to just go out and buy a wetsuit you'll use only once."

I shrug. "Not like I'll outgrow it. And, it was that or going bare-assed."

Dad fidgets. Sierra snickers. Sophia blushes. Sam keeps laughing.

Mom shakes her head waving at me, her usual reaction when she can't think of anything to say.

I grin, then run back to my room.

Wow. I spent a pile of money without asking first and my parents didn't yell at me for it.

My life has seriously become weird.

MOM DRIVES US ALL TO SEATTLE IN THE YUKON AFTER A MINOR argument about how to dress.

She'd wanted the girls to dress 'nice' to visit someone of Aurélie's status, though Sierra parried by saying we would be spending most of the time there in whatever she made us wear for the painting anyway. So... the 'rents got dressed like they're going to a fancy restaurant and the rest of us look normal.

Aurélie's sitting on her couch when we walk in, absorbed by one of the *Assassin's Creed* games. Can't tell which from the scenery. And wow. She's still wearing clothes like she belongs in early 1800s France, yet she's playing a video game. The anachronism is hilarious, but I cover my mouth to avoid laughing.

Of course, the 120-inch mega-screen makes Sierra's knees weak. She lets out a gasp of awe. Dad, too, can't help but stare at it. Mom, on the other hand, is too busy taking in the giant apartment to even notice it has a TV. I can practically see her doing the math trying to guess how ridiculous the rent on a place like this is.

At least, until Aurélie notices us, pauses the game, and stands.

You know what sucks about being a vampire? I can *hear* my father's heart pick up speed the instant he takes in the woman's supernatural beauty. Even Mom lets out a somewhat unsettling noise.

"Ahh, *mon cheri!*" Aurélie swoops around the end of the couch and glides over.

"Hello," says Mom.

Dad merely stares at her.

Sam's gone platter eyed, but he's way too young for her aura to have its usual effect. He stares at her the way a nine-year-old might react to being given a real fire engine as a Christmas present.

"It is such a pleasure to meet you. I am Aurélie Merlier. Sarah has told me so much about you. Oh, pardon me." She glances at Dad.

His eyes flutter in response and he seems less stunned. "Hello."

Mom accepts a handshake. "It's nice to meet you as well. Thank you for watching out for Sarah."

"It is a pleasure. She is such a delightful young woman. Please, make yourself at home. Excuse me just a moment."

Sierra walks up to the TV like a primitive tribesperson visiting a shrine to their most powerful god. I half expect to see her sink to her knees and bow at it. My parents head over to the enormous sectional and sit.

Soon, Aurélie returns with a tray of wine and cheese, which she places near my parents.

Mom eyes the wine glasses. "Sarah, you can drive us home."

"Sure. No problem."

"Come, girls." Aurélie reaches one hand toward me, one toward Sophia.

Sam walks over to the parents, still transfixed by her.

Aurélie whisks us through the ornate white double doors, down a short hall, and into the room full of wardrobe cabinets. She's already set out two frilly dresses, both white, that look roughly the right size for my sisters… and a matching one that's got my name all over it.

Sierra looks around like a mouse locked in a room with cats.

I kick off my shoes and strip down to my undies. Sophia follows suit.

Sierra stares up at me. "Sare… we're supposed to like, just get changed here?"

"Yeah."

She blinks. "But we're all in the same room. And she's right here."

"Models change outfits in front of people all the time. Sometimes, they even take their underwear off in front of people," says Sophia.

Sierra's face goes scarlet—until she gets a good look at the dress. "Ack. It's so *extra*."

"Oh, come on." I nudge her. "It's cute."

She begrudgingly sighs and removes her sneakers and socks, then shirt and jeans.

Aurélie helps us into the elaborate gowns, which are genuinely impossible to put on alone. Sophia adores the fanciness and is the first one to finish changing. She stands by a full length mirror admiring it the rest of the time Sierra and I fight with fabric. Aurélie stuns Sierra mute by doing Sophia's hair up with ribbons in about four seconds, her hands a complete blur.

Sophia squeals in delight.

The look on Sierra's face when it's her turn for hair-fancying would be appropriate were she about to be executed, though she keeps still and says nothing. I tolerate the decoration with a mostly straight face. When I'm her age, maybe it won't feel so strange to use vampiric abilities for something as lame as putting ribbons in people's hair. Then again, I am the cookie whisperer, so perhaps I'm not one to make fun of her. That done, Aurélie hits us with a little rouge and a slight hint of lip color.

My little sisters totally look like live porcelain dolls.

When Sierra goes to check herself in the mirror, she blushes hard. "Oh. My. Gawd. You will *not* let anyone who knows me ever see me like this."

I walk up behind them. "You guys are too adorable."

"'Tis a shame you do not appreciate finery." Aurélie brushes the back of her finger at Sierra's cheek. "You are *so* cute. I do appreciate what you are doing for my benefit. Thank you."

Sierra sighs down at her bare feet. "You're welcome."

"Please, follow me." Aurélie glides out of the room, turning left.

"Wow. You're not complaining?" I pat her on the head.

Sierra shrugs. "She's protecting all of us, right? Feeling ridiculous for a little while isn't a big deal." She hugs me, then points a finger at my face. "If you tell Nicole I dressed up like this, I'll… I'll… Be mad at you."

"I won't tell anyone."

Sophia's still looking at her gown, twirling side to side. Fair odds she's going to beg to keep it.

We follow Aurélie out of the dressing room and down the hall to a large study where she already has a giant rectangular canvas set up on an easel near a divan. She arranges us sitting in a row with me in the middle. While she's fussing at our outfits and making slight adjustments to where we have our hands or how we lean, Sam walks in.

He goes right up to Aurélie. "Can I be in the painting, too?"

She looks at him, tapping a finger to her chin. "Hmm. I don't have anything for you to wear."

Sam shrugs. "I can wear a dress."

"Uhh, that's a little weird," says Sierra.

"It would probably bother him less than you," whispers Sophia.

Sierra smirks.

Aurélie gingerly grasps Sam by the shoulders and positions him standing in front of the divan to Sophia's left. "Oh, I think I can imagine an outfit on you. Can you stand still for a while like this?"

Sam nods.

Sierra turns her head to stare at me. The look on her face is pretty obvious as 'if she can just imagine outfits on us, why am I stuck in this thing?'

Mom and Dad walk in, each with a wine goblet and small plate of cheese. From the look of it, Mom's already had a glass or two. Perhaps being around Aurélie is just a bit too much for her, or more likely having *all* of her children in arms' reach of an elder vampire is stressing her out. At least Dad appears unfazed by the charm in the air.

The parents stare at the three of us. Dad's expression is 'wow' while Mom kinda looks like Ashley seeing a giant fluffy rabbit.

"Ack," says Sierra. "They can see me."

The 'rents gawk at her for a moment before gushing over how cute we all are. I'd expected begging to come from Sophia tonight in regard to being allowed to keep the dress she's posing in, but Mom surprises me by pleading with Sierra for her to tolerate a photo or two —hundred.

"She better not show Nicole," mutters Sierra, before saying, "Okay."

"She won't." I smile for Mom as she goes for her phone. "But Dad will definitely show them to anyone you bring home on a date in six years."

Mom's first picture captures Sophia's gaping mouth. The second is a great shot of her punching me in the shoulder. Picture three has all of us laughing, and the fourth one looks probably as normal as the painting will.

"All right," says Aurélie after taking up a position behind the canvas. "Please try to sit as still as you are able."

I feel like I'm in stuck inside a bizarre techno-magic device from a steampunk world. I've got extreme joy radiating from Sophia and extreme 'ugh' radiating from Sierra. The two emotions are creating a powerful energy field. Though Sam is calm enough to act like a control rod.

Aurélie blurs into a flurry of motion, her arms like hummingbird wings.

A LITTLE OVER AN HOUR LATER, AURÉLIE STOPS BLURRING, EYES US, blurs a little more, then stops again.

"There." She smiles. "Thank you for sitting for me. I can finish the scenery without you needing to remain there."

Released from our need to sit totally still, we all get up and stretch except for Sam, who collapses over the Divan. He's had enough of standing for a while.

"Sophia, would you like to see the doll room?" asks Aurélie.

"Ooh! Please?" She bounces on her toes.

To keep my parents' sanity intact, I accompany Sophia and Aurélie deeper into the apartment. Watching an elder vampire lead their ten-year-old daughter off alone would've exceeded their tolerance. They take Sam and Sierra to the living room so Sierra can cash in on her 'payment' for putting up with the frilly dress: an hour or so of 120-inch screen time on a PlayStation. Granted, an hour is going to go by in a blur. So maybe they'll let her stay a little longer.

Aurélie shows us to her doll chamber, a large, open room with blue carpeting and ceiling, white walls. A few cushioned chairs occupy the middle on either side of a dainty table. Shelves with padding like bench seats the same blue as the rug encircle the chamber. She's got to have 200 or more dolls in here. Sophia squeals with glee at the sight.

"Be gentle with them, sweetie." Aurélie pats her on the head. "You can pick them up if they like you, but be careful not to drop them. I'll be right down the hall finishing up the painting." She gives me a 'please keep an eye on her' look before gliding out.

Sophia walks around the shelves, whispering and chatting with the dolls. Creepily enough, a few times, I swear she reacts to something being said back. She eventually picks one up and carries it to a chair where she sits and has a conversation.

I ease myself down in a chair, sharing a bit of Sierra's feeling ridiculous at being so overdressed. I'm half tempted to perch on the shelf with the rest of the dolls. My brain runs away with some twisted nightmare scenario of Aurélie locking my sisters and me in here as more dolls for her collection. The bizarre energy in the room isn't helping that worry at all. For all I know, maybe she *does* do that. Eek. I need to stop thinking dark thoughts.

Taken by a sudden urge, I get up and roam the shelves until I locate Rebecca. Though the doll has no capacity to make facial expressions, I have the weird notion she's happy to see me. I can't remember the last time I played with dolls. Still, I reach to pick her up, and upon getting the sense she doesn't mind, do so, and carry her to a chair.

"I hope you're happy here," I say. "It's nice to see you again."

A feeling of contentment radiates from the doll.

"Looks like you've got quite a few friends now."

She gives off an emotion that makes me think 'mostly.'

Sophia takes the doll she picked back to its place and wanders the shelves again, complimenting other dolls on their hair or dresses. Once or twice, she giggles and says "Thank you." She seems to avoid the rear right corner of the room, which has a fair number of dolls in dark colored clothing. Looking in that direction stirs an uneasy feeling in the pit of my stomach—probably why Soph's avoiding it. She finds a doll that's wearing almost the same dress as hers and starts pretending to talk like she showed up at some party and ran into someone in a matching outfit. Only, she's not jealous, she thinks it's great.

Honestly, my kid sister in that outfit with the hair ribbons does look so much like these dolls, my sense of discomfort about this entire situation grows. Aurélie could be way darker than I ever imagined. Or, more likely, the woman just *loves* dolls and finds it adorable to dress us up like this.

After a while, Sophia walks up to me with an eyebrow up.

"Everything okay?" I ask.

"Hi, Rebecca," says Sophia, waving at the doll in my lap. "And yes. Most of these dolls are alive. They have auras."

I blink. "And... you're not screaming?"

She grins. "No, they're friendly. Little creepy, but nice. Well, Lucy over there doesn't like me because I can still walk around, but the others are telling her to leave me alone. Lucy doesn't like people."

Aurélie breezes into the room.

"Oh, your dolls are so lovely," says Sophia in a faintly British accent, a huge grin on her face.

"*Oh! Tu trop mignon!*" Aurélie clasps her hands beneath her chin. "If my heart was not so soft, I'd want to keep her."

I chuckle. "Did you do that on purpose?"

"Do what?" Sophia asks, all innocence.

"Use that accent. We're not actually in a creepy manor house in the English countryside circa 1802. We're only dressed like it."

She giggles.

"Aurélie?" I ask.

"Hmm?" She pivots toward me.

"She's started seeing auras. Do you know how that happened or what it means?"

Sophia nods. "Hers is dark blue with a bit of white at the edges. And I see ghosts, too."

Aurélie glides closer and sits on an ottoman so she's eye-level with Sophia. "May I?"

Sophia shrugs, then nods.

They stare at each other for a moment.

"Your sister has been affected by magic. Someone displaced her spirit and took her over." Aurélie narrows her eyes. "Who did this?"

I explain the mystics, the rival lodge that probably used her to search our house for Coralie's body.

"Ahh. Perhaps. Being exposed to this magic unlocked something inside her. It has always been there, though she may not have ever known or been able to access that part of herself without the touch of supernatural energies."

"Cool," whispers Sophia.

"So it's harmless?" I ask.

"*Oui.* The only risk to her is possibly seeing something she cannot handle. Not all spirits are… pleasant to the eye."

Sophia turns a little paler.

We return to the living room, where Sierra—surprisingly still in her doll dress—is engrossed in the video game. Our parents are on the sectional, Sam between them, out cold. Sophia dashes over to the relatively open area nearer the door in and proceeds to try dancing while wearing such a fancy gown.

Aurélie vanishes back down the hallway.

I head over and sit by the parents.

"You look so beautiful," says Dad. "The three of you. Like something straight out of a fairy tale."

"We look like characters from one of those boring movies Mom likes," says Sierra.

"Oh, Sierra," calls Sophia in a passable British accent. "Come and see the garden! I bet there are faeries."

Mom smiles, then giggles.

I glance at her, then dad, and hold up three fingers.

He holds up four.

Is she that worried? I ask in Dad's mind.

He shakes his head, thinking, *No. The wine is amazing. Expensive stuff. She kinda overdid it.*

I grin. Okay, at least Mom's not having a stress attack.

Aurélie returns carrying the large canvas. She brings it over and turns it so we can see her work... and wow. Dad was right. We *do* look like something straight out of a storybook. Sam's depicted in an outfit like that painting *The Blue Boy*. Kinda weird she painted him wearing shoes, but I guess a barefoot boy in a painting looks more like a pauper than 'innocent.' The way we're posed resembles a painting of some king's brood.

Sophia, predictably, gasps in glee and gushes about how beautiful it is. Much to my surprise, even Sierra appears impressed. Mom and Dad whistle, in awe of Aurélie's skill. I'm sure neither one of them expected to see a painting that looks like an old master did it.

"That is beautiful work," says Mom. "You really painted that in... two and a half hours?"

I wag my eyebrows. "She works fast."

"Thank you." Aurélie curtsies at Mom. "I am glad you like it."

"It's fabulous. You've got an amazing talent." Mom, no longer seeming quite so tipsy, leans close and studies the canvas. "It's nearly photographic."

"You are far too kind." Aurélie fakes a blush. "Oh. If you like, I can create a copy for you."

"No, please," whispers Sierra.

"It's all right. I'd love that, but I couldn't ask you to go to the time or expense." Mom fans herself. "Is it warm in here?"

"Yeah, it's eighty... four-glasses-of-wine degrees." I poke her in the side. "I'm wearing this elaborate thing and I'm not even uncomfortable."

"You're also a vampire," says Sierra.

"Are *you* overheating?" I raise both eyebrows at her.

"Only my face from blushing."

Aurélie waves at Mom as if dismissing a triviality. "It is no bother. I insist."

"We can hang it right in the living room," says Dad with a huge smile. "Right above the TV."

"Please no," whispers Sierra. "Everyone will see it."

I throw an arm around her. "It's not bad. You look so adorable."

"But, I'm not adorable."

Dad gives her a 'yeah, you are' look.

"Are you really that upset by it?" I ask.

She shrugs. "I just don't wanna be teased."

"No one will tease you for wearing a dress. You're a girl." Sam yawns. "They'd tease me if I had a dress on."

Sierra gives up with a long sigh. "Fine. Just... not the living room, please?"

Dad nods. "Okay. Dining room."

I lean down and whisper in Sierra's ear. "If anyone teases you, I'll blot the painting out of their memory."

She grins. "Awesome."

Aurélie sits with Sophia and me on the left side of the sofa, and I can't help but feel like my sister and I are dolls at the table of a giant child having a tea party. Sierra keeps playing the game, so engrossed in such a massive screen she's almost forgotten how frilled up she is. Or maybe she's just tolerating a dress she can't stand because she can't remove it without help.

The parents mostly watch the video game while having wine and cheese. Yeah, I'm going to need to drive us home.

28

THE GRAVEYARD OF THE PACIFIC

Sunday is an irritatingly sunny day, so I spend the daylight hours in my room doing schoolwork.

At least until Ashley shows up. She's got a rare day off work and has no classes on the weekend, so she comes over. Michelle's bogged down with stuff to do for school, and Hunter's both working and drowning in studying as well.

Other than my being stuck in the basement, the day feels pretty close to old times hanging out with my best friend. We even break out the ping pong table... though Ashley gets frustrated fast when I start exploiting my reflexes without even thinking about it. I can't *not* do it, so rather than play for score, we devolve into her just trying to send a ball past me.

We laugh like idiots the whole time.

The parents invite her to stay for dinner. She's unusually hesitant, citing her mom's been on the lonely side lately. As kids, we'd often randomly eat dinner at the others' house. Ever since her parents divorced a couple years ago, her mother has been growing increasingly quiet and withdrawn. Ashley having dinner here means her mom eats alone. Since our moms are close friends, my mother says she's going to invite Mrs. Carter over, and runs off to find her phone.

Dinner is nice, especially with Ashley's mom being in a good mood.

Ashley decides to go home and spend some time with her mom. So, I head downstairs to throw the rest of the night at homework. Since Sierra kept up her end and helped Mom wash windows all day, she's on the PlayStation. Sam goes upstairs to his room for computer games while Sophia drapes herself over the couch to read her Kindle.

Alone, I no longer have a need for pants, so I change into just a long T-shirt and flop at my desk to read more sociology.

Not quite a half hour later, my phone rings. Great. The universe must really not want me doing homework.

The caller ID shows the number on Darren's card.

Oh, goody. Tonight's going to be cold and wet.

I pick up and swipe at the screen. "Hello?"

"Sarah?" asks Darren.

"That's me."

"We have created a tool that should assist you in locating the books we need."

I scuff my toes back and forth over the carpet. "Great. How's it work?"

"It's an ordinary compass that we've enchanted to react to magic instead of magnetism. It should point toward the strongest source of magic in an area."

"And I'm guessing there isn't too much of that on the ocean floor."

"Doubtful. When do you think you would feel inclined to uphold your promise?"

"Might as well do it tonight." I stare at the ceiling. All my life, I've always hated having assignments hanging over me. The sooner I deal with this, the sooner I can stop worrying about mystics.

"Excellent. I'll stop by your house in about an hour with the compass."

"Okay."

He hangs up.

I spend a moment wondering if I'm supposed to wear anything under the wetsuit, but decide to change into my bikini, then slip into the wetsuit. It covers everything but my head, hands, and feet. I bought one toward the midrange that the place had in terms of cost. Hopefully, this thing will hold up to me swimming at vampiric speed. Oh, I checked Google. Riptides that move at five miles an hour are 'unusually fast.' Riptides can steal swimsuits. So yeah… I had to be doing at least fifty underwater at my fastest.

Eventually, my phone *tweeps* with a text from Darren's number: ‹I'm outside.›

It's like two hours after dinner, so everyone's still awake. Guessing he didn't want to disturb the family—or be seen. I head upstairs and go out the front door, not bothering to put shoes on. A small dark silver BMW sports car sits in the middle of the cul-de-sac.

Darren and Landon get out as I walk over. Both raise eyebrows at me.

"What? Never saw a wetsuit before?"

"It is a bit unusual to see someone wearing one in the suburbs. Especially at this time of year." Darren chuckles to himself, then offers me a camouflage metal compass.

I take and examine it, underwhelmed. "This? It looks like you ordered it off Amazon."

"We did," says Landon. "An object does not need to be unusual or precious to absorb an enchantment."

"Though it helps." Darren points at it. "Look more closely."

When I glance back down at the compass sitting in my hands, it hits me that the needle appears to be gold, with a tiny diamond at the tip. "New needle."

"Indeed. Please try not to lose that. We would appreciate it back if at all possible." Darren gestures at it.

"Okay. Let me, umm… go start looking then."

Landon waves his hand around in a weird gesture that reminds me of something a priest might do when blessing a person. He mutters a few words in Latin, then switches to English. "May Poseidon guide you."

"Thanks." I force myself to smile, but don't fire off a wiseass comment. Hey, I'm a vampire, and this guy did something to the house that trapped Coralie in there. If he wants to invoke Poseidon to help me, whatever.

After they get back in their little car, I return to the house and find the parents plus Sierra and Sophia in the living room still.

"Gonna go out for a bit."

Everyone except Sierra—who's glued to the PlayStation—looks at me.

"In a wetsuit?" asks Dad.

"Yeah." I hold up the compass. "Got the device that's supposed to find the missing trunk. Gonna go roam around the bottom of the Pacific for a while, searching shipwrecks."

"Okay, dear," says Mom. "Try not to stay out too late."

"Watch out for sharks." Sierra pauses the game. "You're supposed to do the biting, not be eaten."

I give her a thumbs-up. "That's my plan."

"To bite sharks?" asks Dad.

"No..." I roll my eyes. "To come home without being shark food."

"Be careful." Mom stands up and walks around the end of the sofa to hug me. "Call us if you need anything."

"I'm not bringing my phone. Don't want it to die. And this thing doesn't have pockets."

Mom tugs at a small zipper at the stomach. "What's this?"

Upon further examination, I come to the realization that the wetsuit *does* have a pocket. "Oh, neat. Well, I can put the compass in there."

"You need a knife," says Dad.

"Why?" Mom twists back to look at him. "What on Earth would she need a knife for?"

Dad peers over his book at us. "All divers carry knives. It's just what they do."

"Dad..." I hold up my right hand and sprout claws. "I *am* a knife. Besides, I'm going out the door now. Amazon doesn't deliver *that* fast."

"Give 'em a few years." Dad resumes reading the Kindle. "In fact, they probably heard me through this thing and a diving knife is already on its way here."

I laugh. "Okay, guys. Be back as fast as I can."

Mom hugs me. "I'm going to be a nervous wreck until you're home."

"Heh. So will I. Never done anything like this before."

"Hey." Dad looks up from the device again. "Can you get the bends?"

"Umm. I don't think I'm going down *that* deep. But I'm not sure." I decide not to mention that I regenerated from a broken spine, so the bends probably won't kill me—again. "I'll take it easy."

They nod.

I head out via the kitchen patio door since the backyard offers more privacy for takeoff. It's pretty easy to figure out which way is west, and once I've climbed up to a thousand or so feet of altitude, I can kinda match up the shape of the coastline with the maps Darren gave me. Yeah, it's a giant area of ocean, but I'm hoping this compass will give me some clue of where to be before I go under. I can cover *much* more mileage in the air in less time.

We're about a hundred miles from the Pacific Coast, so I'm looking at almost an hour just to fly *to* the shore. Luckily, the Graveyard of the Pacific is right up against the land, so I won't need to go out to the deep ocean. As best I can tell from their notes, the boat carrying the books never made it to the Strait of Juan de Fuca, so I'm looking at an area from the mouth of the strait south to around Astoria. So it could be anywhere within a rectangle like eighty miles potentially out to sea and 140 or so south.

It's probably around nine when I reach the coast. Some planes went by overhead, but I'm low, small, and slow enough that I doubt anyone saw me. Also, all-black wetsuit helps. From this altitude, it's super easy to find the strait's mouth and head for it. This modified compass is useless for actual directions, so I have to guess from here.

The scent of sea salt fills my nostrils as I descend to skim a couple feet off the surface of the water. Honestly, whether I tease the waves this close or go a little higher probably won't make that much difference in the compass picking up magic at the bottom. The fifth time an icy spritz of seawater hits me in the face, I pull up a bit.

What the heck am I thinking?

Am I really going to swim in the ocean and go down to the bottom? The idea of it is terrifying. Even though I know I can't drown, there's just something about the sea. Especially a location where so many people have died. Maybe this area is charged with bad energy.

I never imagined I'd ever be out at sea at night, alone like this. It's simultaneously sad, creepy, scary, and awesome.

Of course, I also never imagined I'd become a vampire—or that they even seriously existed.

Waves froth and churn over a seemingly endless expanse of darkness below me. Ugh. Salt water isn't the same as lake water. I have no idea how well (if at all) I'll be able to see when I go down. Again, I remind myself that a face mask would never stay on me as fast as I'll be going, so I don't feel like too much of an idiot for not getting one.

I start off watching the compass to see if the needle reacts to anything, but after an unexpected wave slaps me in the face, I pay a little attention to my surroundings as well. Ugh. Being soaked makes me feel half frozen already. For well more than an hour, I fly back and forth from east to west, going south for ten seconds each time I reach the coast or my estimation of the outside edge of my search area.

Eventually, the needle stops drifting around aimlessly and seems to want to point to my left. I lean into a gradual turn until it orients straight ahead, then fly in that direction for a while until it drifts left. I stop and watch it, and the needle keeps going all the way around until it's pointing the exact opposite way.

Ugh. It's reacting too sluggishly to pinpoint anything, probably because of distance. I peer east. Okay, it looks like I'm only about twenty miles from shore here. Screw it. I could go back and forth for hours above the surface, constantly chasing a point that moves after the fact. It would be like playing an online game with tons of lag. In short: frustrating as hell.

Here goes nothing.

I lower myself into the water, and shiver for a minute until my body adjusts to the ocean temperature being normal. It's pretty obvious when that happens as the wind blasting over my face starts to seem warm and cozy. Well, if nothing else, that means getting out of the water later will feel great. I already miss my bed, but... I promised. Due to force of habit, I take a deep breath.

Down I go.

Once I'm under, my eyes adjust. If it hadn't been obvious to me before that I'm no longer a normal, living human, being submerged in the ocean confirms it. I can kinda see, and the saltwater doesn't sting my eyes *too* much. I can't call the sensation pleasant, or anything I'd even want to experience if I could avoid it, but it's tolerable when I have no choice. Kinda like house music.

Specks of unidentifiable stuff drift around in my vision. Could be little shrimp or fragments of debris, or even plants. They're enough to convey a sense of motion and that I'm going downward. My surroundings are *way* darker than I'm used to, almost reminding me of what it felt like at night before my Transference.

After a few minutes of descent, the diamond at the tip of the compass needle begins emitting a faint green light. Ooh, that's kinda cool. Soon, I can perceive a darkening up ahead, which I'm fairly sure is the sea floor. This close to the coast, the depth can't be too severe. I remember something about a continental shelf or some such thing where the ocean gets super deep. Can't say I remember how far off the coast that is, but I'm hoping I haven't gone past it.

The greyish world around me is like an alien planet. The seabed appears to be about fifty or sixty feet below, so I figure that's approximately the limit of my vision. How I wind up being able to see farther in saltwater than the lake, I have no idea.

Unless that Poseidon blessing actually did something.

I'm about to roll my eyes at the thought, but... again, I'm a vampire at the bottom of the Pacific using an enchanted compass to track down a box of magic books. Am I really going to laugh off the idea that he might've cast a beneficial spell on me?

Admittedly, I'm sometimes tempted to laugh at the idea of vampires still, but... yeah.

Okay, thank you Lord of the Sea. And if you could keep the sharks busy, that would be awesome, too.

I turn, line up my facing with the compass needle, then fly. Well... swim. Not sure. I'm projecting myself forward by sheer force of will instead of paddling my arms or kicking, so I'm going to call it flying even if I'm not technically in the air.

A few minutes into chasing the needle, I glide over a fragment of a ship that's been down here a long damn time. It's barely recognizable as anything more than a pile of lumber—though the mast gives it away as a former sailing ship. Here and there, I spot flashes of silver or blue from fish, though none are brave enough to get close. And I'm totally okay with that. Make you guys a deal. You don't bite me, I won't bite you.

Shipwreck after shipwreck goes by below, in varying states of decomposition from a couple of stray boards to a metal boat that probably went down in the sixties. And yeah, I'm totally guessing there. For all I know, it sank yesterday. The compass diamond grows brighter, so I keep going in that direction.

The glowing needle leads me to a smooth patch of seabed. From like five stories above the bottom, it looks like a river of silt flowing between rippling dunes on either side. That must mean there's a current here. The area contains about ten recognizable ships, most wooden and well-covered by various barnacles and crusty greenish stuff.

I steer downward and make my way toward where the needle points. My destination winds up being a bit of a toss-up between two boats that came down almost on top of each other. The larger one landed completely upside down, so it resembles a weird house from a fantasy movie. It's also the more intact of the two, so I head for the smaller one, assuming it to be older.

A cannon port on the side lets me into the hull.

Some manner of eel comes right at me out of nowhere. Only my vampiric reflexes save me from having most of my face taken off by razor sharp teeth. I dodge to the side, its slimy side brushing my ear as it races on by and goes out to the ocean.

Unable to scream in shock, I wind up giving it the finger.

I hang there with a hand over my heart for a moment to calm down.

Exploring this boat doesn't take long since most of the inner decks have collapsed. It's obvious I'm in the wrong place. Even at the far end of the wreck, the compass is still pointing me past the wall. So, I fly back out another cannon port and land on my feet. I wonder how many people in the world have ever stepped barefoot on the bottom of the Pacific Ocean. Probably not too many. I should be long dead—or at least in deep poop—from hypothermia.

It's kinda nice oozing between my toes actually. Feels like really wet beach sand.

And it would totally suck if it got into my wetsuit.

Two laps around the larger boat confirms the only apparent way in is a gap between the hull and the seabed at the midpoint of one side. It's weird that the thing doesn't have any windows or cannon ports. There's plenty of ruined rope netting, covered in that crusty stuff and barnacles, but the only way in is the space between the wall and the sand. The boat is a pretty decent size, maybe three stories tall, and the compass is locked on it.

Okay. This is why I'm here, so only choice is onward.

I flatten out on the bottom and pull myself forward into a 'chamber' between the outer deck and the ground. There's only about three feet of clearance at the tallest point, and a shitload of crabs hiding in here. I don't see any sign of a navigator's wheel. All four masts are either stuck way deep in the sea floor like spears or they broke off while the boat sank. I do, however, spot a door in the 'ceiling' near the back end of the area. Eager to get away from the crabs, I fly the length of the ship with my back brushing the wood above me, and zoom over to the old hatch. Upon reaching it, I grab the edge and roll over to pull myself headfirst into the opening.

Wooden steps lead down (or up in this case) to the second deck. Aside from being upside down, ruined, full of water, and covered in oceanic crust, it looks pretty much like it did before going down. Stuff is everywhere, which I suppose happens when a boat rolls over and over while hurtling toward its grave at the bottom of the sea.

The compass leads me forward. I ease my way down the hall, peering into rooms so far gone I can't even tell what they'd once been used for. Fragments of barrels, bunks, scraps of cloth, even a human bone or two sit around in disarray.

I can't help but feel like I'm not supposed to be here, or that I'm desecrating a sacred place. But, I don't see any angry ghosts. It's gotta be in my head. Logic says that if the men who died on this ship remained in any form of existence that could object to me being here, they'd be some kind of apparition I could see.

Pushing unease aside as a product of imagination, I keep going.

The compass reverses itself after about fifty feet. I stop and back up. The needle flips around right away, not like at the surface. Also, the diamond is glowing super bright. So, I must be directly over (or under) the trunk's location. Ugh. Guess I go down one more deck. Err, Up. Dammit. Why did this ship have to roll over? This is too effing confusing.

I cruise back to the stairs and swim through the hole to the next deck. Unsurprisingly, the rooms are smaller, since the outer hull is narrower. Scraps of unidentifiable cloth float by, along with some papers and at least two quills. A thick wooden door at the end of the corridor gives me hope. That looks like an important door, the kind of important door that people use to guard important stuff.

Though, honestly, who the heck would try to steal a trunk full of books on a boat while out at sea? Where would they hide it?

It's tempting to invert myself so I'm right side up to the boat, but that would feel too bizarre. So, I approach the door and grasp the encrusted iron ring serving as a doorknob. Naturally, it's locked. I swing my legs up and brace my feet against the slimy, encrusted muck on either side, grab the ring in both hands, and pull as hard as I can.

A dull *crack*, surprisingly loud, breaks the stillness as the door gives way. Being underwater, I *feel* the sound as much as hear it. The pull ring comes off in my hands and I go sailing backward. The door, free from the lock, drifts open a few inches. I smirk at the ring and toss it aside before swimming to the four-inch-thick door and pulling it out of my way.

The room beyond it stretches the full width of the boat and about thirty feet deep. All sorts of decaying boxes and crates litter the former ceiling. One stands out due to it being intact: a steamer trunk with brass metal bands and a dark jade green inlaid surface. It's probably not a great sign that this box hasn't developed a layer of crud like everything else down here. It's even freakier that it looks old in terms of style but not in condition. And, I haven't exactly had the best luck with steamer trunks.

A twinge of memory pain pokes at my upper front teeth.

Okay. There you are. Time to go home.

Since I no longer need the compass out, I tuck it into the wetsuit's pocket, pull the zipper closed, then drift into the room. The trunk's about four feet wide, three tall, three deep, almost the same size as Ashley's. So bizarre that it doesn't look at all the worse for wear after spending so long under the ocean. Metal plates on the top seem to have some kind of engraved pattern on them, though it's difficult to make out under the layer of silt. Bleh. I'm not here to admire stuff. I stretch down to grab the handle on the left side. The instant my skin touches the metal, a whole bunch of little symbols and carvings on the brass bands light up with a dark emerald light. The same glow illuminates the gunk coating the plate at the center of the lid.

Ooh, that's pretty.

At least, I think it's beautiful until the debris between me and the door erupts into a beige silt cloud. Bony hands reach out of the junk, shoving it aside as three moving skeletons drag themselves upright.

Oh, and the door I came in? Yeah. It's closed again... somehow.

Skeletons? Seriously? Are you effing kidding me?

All three rise to their feet, advancing toward me with wicked, rusty rapiers.

Shit.

29

SHARP, NASTY, POINTY THINGS

T he sight of skeletons moving under their own power leaves me dumbstruck.

This room has no windows and only the one door, which slammed itself shut. Seems unlikely those guys are going to stand around idle while I try breaking my way out the hull.

And they've got swords. Thin, rusted-to-hell rapiers to be exact.

I glance down at my brand new $98 wetsuit that I miraculously didn't get yelled at for buying. Not that I've ever been a diver, but this thing *is* kinda nice, and I haven't exactly had the best luck as a vampire with clothing surviving crap trying to kill me. The skeletons keep advancing, their motion somewhat sluggish due to the water. I zip backward to the corner of the room, hoping to buy a few seconds. As fast as I can move my arms, I peel the wetsuit off and kick it toward the floor.

Stripping is probably not the usual reaction someone has to three skeletons with swords coming after them. At a guess, I'd say it's not even on a top twenty list of things to do when confronted with the unexplainable. But I just bought my wetsuit and Dad would kill me if I came home with it shredded. It drives him nuts when we 'don't take care of our stuff.' So glad I decided to wear my bikini under it, but something tells me these guys are way beyond caring if my boobs are covered or not.

They all come around the left side of the trunk, closing in on me, so I head around the other side and hurl myself at the door. It doesn't break. How tough can old wood be? I pound at it, but succeed only in embedding tiny splinters in my hands. If I can get past this door, maybe the skeletons will follow me out to the ocean. I'll lead them off a good ways then come back for the trunk before they—wait. Would they follow me straight to land? That trunk might attract them like a homing beacon.

Grr. I can't drag this crap back to my family.

The door is surprisingly tough. I rear back and kick at it with both legs, but it holds. My strength is nowhere near the high end of what vampires are capable of—thinking about Aziz—but I should at least be able to kick a hole in ancient, waterlogged wood.

Ugh. Magic.

A thin, corroded rapier blade sprouts from my chest—along with a stream of tiny bubbles, air leaking out of my lung. I involuntarily try to yell in pain, though I succeed only in creating an even bigger bubble. The skeleton behind me attempts to pull the weapon out, but the narrow blade is so heavily encrusted with rust and 'ocean crud' that it refuses to come loose from my body. A sharp, searing pain accompanies each tug, so painful I can't even do anything but stare in shock. The fourth time the skeleton pulls, the blade snaps off with a jarring *crack* that reverberates in my bones.

I whirl around and punch that skeleton straight in its lack of a nose, driving my fist into the skull around a cloud of splintering bone fragments. Dark muck—whatever had been inside its empty brain case—billows out of its eye sockets. It flails its bony arms, one hand clutching the basket hilt of a rapier with only a few inches of blade remaining on it.

Skeleton Two stabs at me, but I fly left to avoid the incoming weapon, then stomp-kick the skeleton in the ribcage. My foot punches through its ribcage up to the calf and gets stuck. Trying to pull my leg out brings the whole skeleton closer to me. He tries again to spear me with his sword, but I catch his wrist in both hands.

Of course, Skeleton Three takes that moment—while I'm hopping on one foot and holding the other one's sword away—to stick his rapier into my chest from the side, under my right arm. The corroded blade grinds over my rib and comes out the other side, piercing everything on the way. Holy shit that hurts! Ooh, that's bad. It had to hit my heart, at least I think it did. This rapier's got so much crud caked on it that I may as well have been stabbed by a stake covered in broken glass.

Skeleton One stabs his four-inch blade into my back and leaves the basket hilt hanging there.

Again, I try to scream, and in that instant of blinding pain, Skeleton Two's bony arm slips my grasp and his sword pierces me under the left collarbone. He goes to yank it out, but the blade's so rough and cruddy it won't come free. I think I black out from pain for a second or two since the next thing I know, the skeleton's drifting few feet away with a broken rapier hilt in its hand. The fourteen-inch fragment of blade is still sticking out of me.

Argh! I'm not a goddamn pincushion!

Growling in my head, I whirl on Skeleton Three. It tries to bite me, but I grab it around the neck in one hand, my other on its shoulder. Make a wish, buddy. A sharp yank disintegrates the spine and the skull floats off, separated from the rest of it. Of course, the arms keep raking at my face, shoulders and chest. I shouldn't be surprised really. It's not like they are seeing with eyeballs.

Searing pain burns into my right side.

I glare down at a rusty table knife. Skeleton One continues trying to push it in deeper. I grab its hand, squeezing until I crush it, then ram my elbow into its face. The jawbone sails across the room while pieces of the smashed skull glide to the floor.

If we'd been out in the air, these skeletons would probably be flying all over when I hit them, but the water density basically holds them in place, so instead of knocking them over, I'm punching holes in them. Speaking of which. I grab the rib cage of the other skeleton and rip it apart so I no longer have one leg stuck. Skeleton Two disregards its near total lack of ribs and lunges in, trying to bite me.

No idea if a skeleton can be surprised, but it stops moving after I reach out and rip its jaw off with a blurry-fast swipe of my hand. I'm sure if it could do facial expressions, it would be gawking at me.

I give it the finger. No sword, no jaw. Now what are you going to do to me?

Skeleton Three's still scratching at me with its bony fingers. I grab one arm, break off its hand, then snap the forearm in half, before breaking the upper arm in half, then ripping the remaining stump out of the shoulder socket. The whole time, it rakes at me with its other hand.

A rusty cutlass blade stabs up through the floor *way* too close to my left foot.

Oh, shit. How many skeletons are on this boat?

Wow. If I wasn't already dead, being inside a flooded shipwreck on the ocean floor would be terrifying.

I swim up enough to avoid any more floor blades, and continue tearing the skeletons apart. Naked bones are not terribly tough compared to my strength, so it's like I'm under attack from a pile of kindling sticks. They're shredding the shit out of me, but they don't exactly have claws, so the scratches are healing almost as fast as they inflict them.

And yeah, it hurts like a son of a bitch. But not quite as much as my heart still pumping while it's got a rusty, encrusted rapier blade jammed through it. These guys would be way more effective defending their trunk from living people trying to take it. I have a nasty habit of not dying when stabbed in the heart.

Pain similar to a wasp sting bites into the back of my right shoulder. I snap my head that way and blink in confused surprise at a rusted fork sticking out of me. Seriously? Wow, these guys are getting desperate. I can't even tell which skeleton is behind me anymore other than it being headless. Guess he volunteered next to be disarmed.

It makes no effort to get away from me, continuing its mindless assault as I systematically break it to progressively smaller pieces.

Cutlass Boy pulls a floorboard down, but the hole it made isn't anywhere near big enough for it to get into the room. Instead, it reaches one arm in, waving its sword back and forth at me. The skeletons already in here follow me as I drift away, though the one in the floor keeps trying to get at me with no comprehension it's impossible.

I drift by the trunk amid a cloud of flailing bones, and glare down at the stupid thing. The disturbance of fighting around it has blown the silt off the lid, revealing a thin glowing green line tracing the shape of a skull on a metal plate, surrounded by more glowing writing. It flickers and emits a tiny orb of pale light that glides off into the floor.

Pain gets me in the back of the left ankle.

One of the loose skulls is biting me.

Argh! Bastard. I kick my leg around until the skull slips off, then stomp-crush it.

Every time the raking bony fingers bump against one of the blades jammed into me, I want to scream, but my lungs are already quite empty. Wait... no they're not. They're full of water.

Son of a bitch.

I rip the leg off one skeleton and use the femur as a club, but it's slowed too much by swinging it in water to be effective. Snarling—mentally—I go full crazy kitty on the moving bones. Only, I don't use claws since it seems silly to attempt cutting bone. Grabbing and breaking works well enough. A blurry moment later, I'm surrounded by a mess of smashed bones sinking to the floor. I'm 'breathing' hard only as an instinctive reaction to feeling like I exerted myself. The sensation of water blowing in and out my nose is beyond weird.

Swords clatter against the door, and Cutlass Boy in the hole is still trying to reach me.

I stare down at myself—finally noticing that my bikini top is gone. Red lines in varying degrees of healing from quarter-inch-deep gouges to cat scratches crisscross my skin, too many to count. Three broken rapier blades, one basket hilt, two table knives, and a fork stick out of me at random places.

Ugh. This is going to hurt.

A piece of hand bone slides over my toes, on its way to rejoin a gathering pile of fragments.

Oh hell no. They're going to get back up?

The skull-faced drawing in the trunk stares up at me in spite. Pretty sure each time it emits one of those little light pulses, it's waking up another skeleton.

What if...

I grab one of the table knives, pull it out of my side... and spend the next maybe thirty seconds paralyzed in pain. Not sure what hurts more: encrusted not-quite-sharp blade ripping loose or saltwater entering the wound.

The constant clatter of swords and bony fists on the door snaps me out of my agony trance. No one ever told me if being sliced into small pieces will kill a vampire, but I *really* don't want to find out. I drift down to kneel over the box and rake the knife at the metal plate with the skull engraving, grinding at it with as much strength as I can summon. The blade crumbles away from the force, but I'm scratching the plate. Breaking the skull drawing doesn't seem to do much, so I turn my attention to the writing around it. I can't even recognize the language those symbols came from much less what it says. It looks like the sort of thing game developers put on magic scrolls, all fancy and squiggly.

As soon as I gouge the text, a bright camera-flash of emerald light explodes from the metal plate along with a faint *pop* noise.

All the clattering falls silent.

I twist to my right. A cutlass sits on the floor near the hole, no sign of the skeleton.

Whew. That was easier than I thought... then again, a normal person—much less a girl my size—probably wouldn't have been strong enough to scratch steel.

My attempt to breathe a sigh of relief hurts.

Ugh. This is going to suck.

Trying to pull these things out is going to be torture if I do it slow. Of course, doing it fast is going to hurt a bunch, too. I grab the second table knife that's probably in my left kidney, take a few seconds to psych myself up—and yank.

I finally have one complaint about being a vampire: we can't faint from pain.

We can, however, curl up into a floating ball and cry for Mommy and Daddy.

Once I get control back, I grab the fat end of the sideways rapier blade that pierced my heart and both lungs. About an inch of it sticks out of my right armpit, preventing me from lowering my arm all the way. Damn, that is super annoying. It's a trefoil blade that's thicker toward the hilt and tapers to a needle point. Each of the three edges had once been sharp, but the metal has such a thick layer of ocean crust on it that even the point isn't all that sharp at the moment. And yeah, it's like tearing sandpaper spikes out of my body.

A sharp yank rips it clear with the agony of a red-hot saw blade. I clamp one hand over the hole on the right side, shuddering from pain while debating how many mystics I'm going to kill. They could've warned me about these stupid skeletons. That gets me wondering if they knew about it and sent me down here in an attempt to kill me, or if they genuinely wanted these books and had no idea the trunk is a spiteful piece of shit.

I extract the last two rapier fragments out one after the next, as well as the four-inch blade still attached to the basket hilt, while mentally screaming F-bombs over and over. After, I just hang there in the water for a while, clenching my jaw while my body restores itself and forces the saltwater out. Tiny particles of whatever that crust is also grind their way to the surface. It's an obnoxious sensation a little shy of painful, more an itch *inside* that I can't reach to scratch—ants digging tunnels in my flesh.

Time loses meaning, but eventually I feel pretty decent—other than being topless and trapped in a shipwreck at the bottom of the Pacific Ocean. I drift over to the wetsuit, shake it out to clear it of silt, then pull it back on. I can't even tell where my bikini top went—or how many pieces it's in—and I don't feel like staying here long enough to search for it. It's easy enough to replace, and it isn't like I have plans to go to the beach any time soon. Hmm. Back in Aurélie's day when vampires ran around in those fancy, elaborate dresses and suits all the time, did that make them hesitant to fight? Replacing a cheap swimsuit top is one thing, but those outfits had to be expensive .

One last pull snugs the zipper up to my neck. I set my hands on my hips and stare at the trunk.

Now, how the hell am I going to get that thing out of here?

A LITTLE BIT OF REALITY

Whatever magic sealed the room broke when I scratched the writing on the plate.

One kick knocks the door open, revealing about twelve more skeletons—collapsed on the floor. Well, ceiling since the boat's upside down. With luck, the trap and the magic that protected the books are different. But, I can't say I honestly care too much if the contents survive. All I want to do now is spend some quality time with a peaches and cream bath bomb, then curl up in bed under an excessive amount of blankets.

The trunk isn't too heavy, though I am abnormally strong and we're underwater. No surprise it's easy to move. I tow it down the hall over the mess of bones, down two sets of stairs, then into the space between the upper deck and the seabed, sending small bluish crabs scrambling to get away from me.

Naturally, the trunk is way too big to fit in the gap I slipped in, so I lose some time kneeling in the sand while digging it out enough to get the trunk past it. And, I'm not the most patient girl in the world at the moment. Perhaps a board or two had to break.

I swim out first and pull the trunk after me, beyond grateful to be outside the wreck. Few things on this Earth are as frighteningly claustrophobic as the inside a shipwreck at the bottom of the ocean. Dad once watched this documentary about a submarine that went down, its crew trapped alive inside. Ugh. I can't even imagine how horrible that would've been for those guys. I *can't* drown and I can see in the dark—and it still freaked me out a little.

Since I've completely forgotten which way is east or west, I glide straight up. Whether or not vampires can suffer the bends would depend on gases dissolved in our blood. We don't aspirate like living things, so I'm not sure what exactly our blood is like. It is a bit thicker and darker than normal human blood. Meh. No sense inviting *more* pain tonight. I've had plenty. I take it reasonably slow going up.

My head breaches the surface into a breeze as warm as a clear August day. Yeah, my hands right now have to be cold enough to cause heart attacks if applied to the back of someone's neck. Ashley does that all the time. Oh, look how cold I am—grab.

Why must people do that? Like do they think we won't believe them unless they make us squeal to prove it?

I invert myself, feet in the air, and let all the seawater drain from my lungs. While I no longer have any *need* to breathe, my body decides this is a great time for a horrendous coughing fit. I choke and gag on ocean water, which also streams out of my nose, burning like hell. Somehow, I manage not to lose my grip on the trunk and send it racing back to the sea floor.

Seriously, this thing is not in the mood to float. Trying to pull it into the air doesn't work, it's both unwieldy and heavy. Okay, so this box weighs more than Ashley. I could fly with her on my back, but she's like 120 pounds. Ugh, taking this thing home is going to be a pain in the ass. It's either full of seawater or packed to the brim with books. And it's huge. Yeah, not exactly 'packing light.'

A passing wave douses me, causing an involuntary shriek at the cold.

Damn. I've adjusted to the air being normal temperature, so the sea is once again frigid.

Time to go home.

There's only one thing I can really do in this situation, since neither air travel nor swimming are feasible. I grab the handle on one end while draping myself over the trunk and flying as fast as I can without smashing it apart. Basically, I'm turning it into a giant skipping stone. Other than having to occasionally swerve to ride the edge of a wave too big to plow through, I head straight for shore. Though the constant icy splashing chills me way worse than being all the way at the bottom did. When everything is the same temperature, I don't notice. But mixing like forty degree air with splashes of much colder water is hell.

Something tells me that vampire who went treasure diving probably brought a boat along to help him carry stuff.

The *Enigma* went down reasonably close to shore, so I only have to put up with the personal watercraft from hell for about fifteen minutes. As soon as the sea becomes shallow enough for me to walk, I lift the trunk over my head and trudge up onto the beach. I'm tempted to sit there for a while and rest, but that's an echo of past instincts. The kind of tired I feel won't be helped by idleness. I'm effing hungry.

Picking the trunk up with my feet on solid (mostly) ground is easier than I thought. It's noticeably heavy, but compared to my new strength, it's no worse than an overloaded laundry basket was to my mortal self.

I trudge from goopy, waterlogged sand, to dry sand, then to grassy sand, and finally grass, having no idea where I am. I don't feel like lugging this trunk into the forest that's straight ahead of me, so I stop, look around to make sure there's no one here to see me, then float straight up for a better view. A road not too far north of me leads from the beach to a small strip of civilization. Deeper inland, past a narrow lake that stretches a long ways north and south but only a short distance east, the road connects to a highway that looks like it will take me home—or at least closer to it. I know I went mostly south while hunting for this trunk. Further east is all forest. Ugh. The road I want to be on appears to be about a mile away. Not too big a deal to walk, but I'm barefoot.

Oh well. If I cut myself, it'll heal.

Heh. Cut myself. Nothing on the ground is going to hurt anywhere near as much as rusty rapier blade.

I land, pick up the trunk, and start for the road. A sandy path leads from the beach to a paved circle with a road leading east from it. I'm still clueless as to exactly where I am, but following the road is my best bet. Fortunately, at whatever time it is, the area is deserted.

This strip of paving doesn't have much of a sidewalk, so I pad along in the middle of the right lane. No chance a car could come from behind me without teleportation being involved. I pass an empty parking lot on the left. Otherwise, I'm surrounded by trees for the next few minutes of walking.

Eventually, I pass a couple houses, a few with lights on but no one seems to notice me. The first cross street I reach is labeled Clark Road. Apparently, I've been on Sunset Beach Road. Still, no idea where I am. I keep going, just an innocent girl in a wetsuit carrying a trunk down the street at like two in the morning in the middle of September. Nothing at all unusual here.

Soon after I pass an RV park on the right, I hit a bridge over that narrow lake. Still haven't seen a single moving car, which I suppose is both good and bad. More houses go by on the right, open field... maybe a golf course, on the left.

My mile-long hike brings me to the end of Sunset Beach Road, a T-intersection with the north-south road I saw from the air. I'm ninety percent sure I need to go north. Make that ninety-nine percent. It's odd that my toes don't feel like they want to fall off from the cold. Even odder is my not feeling tired after hiking a mile. Well, *more* tired. I'm sure I burned a bunch of energy preserving myself in the extreme cold of the deep ocean, and the skeletons didn't help much.

A sign by the intersection identifies the other road as Oregon Coast Highway. Shit. I'm *way* south. That's a problem. By sheer time alone I'm probably not going to be able to make it home before sunrise. At least, not on foot. I suppose I could stash this box somewhere, fly home, and drive back down here tomorrow to get it—assuming Mom lets me take the Yukon. This thing isn't fitting in the Sentra.

Do I have too much dignity to hitchhike? No not really. All I have to do is get someone to stop and make eye contact, and they'll drive me wherever I want them to. Getting them to stop could be a problem. However, I'm a young-looking girl alone at night. If a creep tries to abduct me, I get a meal *and* a free car.

Hmm.

I walk across the highway—not sure how anyone can call a two-lane road a highway—and start heading north while debating if I could bring myself to kill a guy who intended to murder me. Like, Scott was already dead, so I didn't so much *kill* him as cremated an existing corpse. If I ran into a dude who wanted to like kidnap, abuse, and kill me… Yeah. You know what? I think I could. In fact, I think I *would*. Someone who'd do something like that to a girl 'my age' doesn't even qualify as a human being. So, yeah, it's not murder. And I'd rather have the potential guilt of doing that than the worse guilt of wondering who else he'd hurt if I left him alive.

One of the old movies Dad likes has a guy in it who calls assassination the greatest public service, or something like that. In this case, I'm inclined to agree.

A few cars go by over the course of the next maybe half hour, but none stop. Guess this is an interesting part of town if a girl in a wetsuit with a giant trunk isn't weird enough to make them at least slow down to stare.

The heavy rumble of a tractor-trailer shakes the road under my feet a few seconds before I hear it. Not wanting to be steamrolled, I step onto the shoulder to give traffic a lot of extra room and turn to look back. A big rig trundles down the street, the headlights so intense I squint.

It slows to a stop right beside me, amid the hissing of pneumatic brakes and the reek of diesel exhaust. The passenger side window opens, and a fortyish guy with a beard and a red ball cap leans up to check me out.

"Hey, you okay? Need a lift somewhere?"

My intent to simply compel him to drive me home wanes when we make eye contact. Wow. This guy isn't even considering anything creepy at all. He thinks I'm like fifteen, ran away from home, and shouldn't be out on the road alone after two in the morning. The wetsuit confuses him though.

"Uhh, yeah. I'm going home. Guess I look like a runaway or something, but I'm not." I smile, futilely trying to puff a strand of hair off my face. "You heading to Seattle?"

"Olympia. I can get you at least that far." He hops over the seats, opens the passenger side door, and climbs down. "I'm Mike. Here, let me help you with that."

As soon as I let go of the trunk, it drags him to the ground. He gawks at it.

Oops.

When he looks up at me in bewilderment, I make him forget trying to hold the like 300-pound chest.

"Where can I put this?" I ask.

He opens a storage compartment on the side of the cab that's just big enough for it. I ease the trunk inside, then climb up into the passenger seat. Mike jogs around the nose end to get in via the driver's side door. Once he's got the rig rolling again, he smiles over at me.

"Kinda odd seein' a little thing like you out here on her own this hour."

"What time is it?"

"2:19 in the morning."

"Damn. Any idea how long it'll take to drive to Seattle from here?"

He runs a hand down his beard. "Well, if we were goin' straight through, reckon about three and a half hours."

Umm. Sunrise is around 6:40 or so this time of year—the weird things my new life makes me study. I *could* make it, but it's going to be damn close.

"What are you gonna do in Olympia?"

"Just drop a trailer off, then sleep. I'm a vampire."

I glance at him. He most certainly is *not*. But, I'm guessing he's talking about sleep schedule. I giggle and flash an innocent smile. "Me too."

He shakes his head, chuckling. "Kinda have to be one for this job. Never did much care for gettin' up early. Drivin' at night's a lot easier. Less traffic."

"Yeah." Now there's a thought. If I was totally alone, a night-drive trucker might be a career choice. Constantly moving, no shortage of feeding grounds, no worries about people recognizing me. But, I have a family... at least for the next eighty or so years.

"So how'd you wind up out here all alone in a... what happened to your shoes?"

"Epic Jet Ski mishap."

He blinks. "Come again?"

"Oh, just kidding. I was on a boat with some friends and fell overboard when Ricky accelerated too hard. They were, uhh, kinda drunk so didn't notice. I had to swim back to shore."

Mike looks at me like I'm speaking Swahili.

Ugh. Forget it. I rewrite his memory of that conversation to something about me being a college student who broke down and he picked me up on the side of the road. He also now believes I'm wearing jeans, a T-shirt, and sneakers. I'm super tempted to feed from him since I'm so hungry, but he's driving and he's also a genuinely nice guy.

The ride to Olympia takes about an hour and a half. Mostly, Mike talks about his wife and two daughters back home in Astoria. He likes the job because it lets him spend some time with his kids before going to work after they're in bed. He's also thinking of moving to Portland, or at least the suburbs.

When we arrive at the shipping yard he's going to, I thank him for the ride and hop out while he's dealing with the security guard at the gate. Neither of them notice me remove the trunk from the storage compartment and set it on the sidewalk. It makes for a decent place to sit while waiting for him to finish. Once the rig pulls in and disappears among the rows of other trucks and cargo boxes, I approach the security guard.

Wonder if he's going to taste like donuts.

I WAKE UP STARING AT THE DUSTY CEILING OF AN UNFAMILIAR BASEMENT.

Oh, right. I'm like three blocks away from that shipping yard. Yay for my first ever time breaking and entering. Well, charming and entering anyway. The first house with a light on at almost four in the morning drew me like a moth to a candle. I knocked and made the guy let me in. He was also kind enough to feed me and let me use his shower to de-salt myself. Staying in a wetsuit for hours after diving itches like mad.

The guy who lives here, Ernie Lewis, works nights but had yesterday off due to it being Sunday. When he wakes up, he'll have completely forgotten I exist. It's tempting to use his phone to call my parents, but I don't want to create any evidence of my having been here. It's probably on the paranoid side since I'm not planning to do anything more illegal than crash in his basement uninvited. However, if this guy turns out to be the type who goes over his phone statement line by line and wants to know why there's a random call to a mobile number from Cottage Lake, pointing this guy at my family will create problems I don't need to deal with.

I could steal a car, but I don't know how to do that. I could steal a car by virtue of mind controlling the driver. There's always Uber, but I don't have my phone or wallet on me. I can't walk from Olympia to Cottage Lake. Okay, best idea is probably leave this trunk stashed here in the basement and fly home to get the Yukon.

After an extremely boring hour or so lying around the basement, sounds of activity come from the house. Ernie's up. I listen to him make something to eat and watch TV. Later, he showers, and goes back to watching TV.

Ugh. The worst part about being stuck here right now without powers of mind control is that I know my parents (and siblings) are undoubtedly freaking out that I've been gone all night into today. And *dammit*. I have class. Crap. Maybe I should've tried to beat the sunrise going home? Nah. I can make a teacher forget an absence. I can't make reality forget melting me into a pile of ashes.

Oh, shit. Idea. Possibly evil, but, it might work out. My powers of mind control only stop working when I'm exposed to sunlight. There's no sunlight down here.

I bang on something, making noise. The TV gets quiet. I bang again.

The basement lights flick on and Ernie comes down the stairs with a handgun out. "Someone here?"

With a burst of supernatural speed, I leap out and pounce on him, grabbing his wrist and pushing the gun away to the side. He barely has time to start screaming before I'm in his head. Ernie's going to be a super nice guy and drive me home before he has to be at work tonight. He's got plenty of time since his shift starts at nine.

I lean hard on the mental implant since I'm going to be pretty much helpless once I'm out in the daylight. Well, no more helpless than an ordinary girl my age would be, but still. Can't afford to make an error.

A few minutes later, I'm curled up on the floor of Ernie's pickup truck using bath towels to somewhat shield my head, hands, and feet from the sun. It's not *too* bright out, but it's still in the realm of ouch. Between the two of us, we managed to get the trunk loaded in the bed. Holy shit that thing is heavy to a mortal.

A little after five in the afternoon, Ernie backs up to my driveway. Dad leans out the door, no doubt confused by some random person pulling in. When he sees me slip out the passenger side door, he runs over and grabs me like he's helping war wounded limp to the hospital.

"Sarah!"

"Sorry for disappearing. Got stranded by the sunrise. Took longer than I figured it would."

As I programmed him to do, Ernie gets out and walks around to help me unload the trunk. Dad grabs the other side for me since I'm a bit out of sorts in the light. Ernie sets his end down on the driveway and gets back in the pickup.

"Hey, umm..." Dad stares at him while gesturing at the garage.

I put a hand on my father's arm. "Don't. I only gave him a limited instruction set."

Dad raises an eyebrow.

"He's going to go home now and forget ever driving here. Can we put this thing in the garage for now?"

Ernie drives off.

Dad helps me lug the trunk into the garage. That done, I head down to my room to enjoy the darkness.

And get the hell out of this wetsuit.

AT 9:30 P.M. MONDAY NIGHT, I'M SITTING ON THE TRUNK AT THE END of my driveway.

After almost twenty-four straight hours in a wetsuit, I opted for a dress today. Thanks to Ernie, I was able to not miss a class on only my third week of school. The *Aurora Aurea* guys can wait a couple more hours for books they've been missing for centuries. My family found the story of what happened last night fascinating. I glossed over some of the stabbier details since Sophia was listening in, but they at least understand why I disappeared and how sorry I am for not making contact. Dad agreed that I made the right decision not using that man's phone or computer to contact them. Mom focused more on agreeing with my decision not to play chicken with the sun.

"Better late than baked" was Sam's nugget of wisdom.

Of course, Sierra had to make a marijuana comment in response, which didn't go over well with the 'rents.

Anyway, Darren sounded ecstatic when I called him about the trunk. Whether or not I'm going to metaphorically rip his head off over the skeletons is still a matter of debate. I kill time playing a mobile game while waiting.

At 9:41 p.m., a nondescript black van pulls into the cul-de-sac and backs up to me.

Darren and Landon hop out along with Callum. They still look like they're dressed to film a movie about vampires in the early 1900s. Wow. No idea why they do that, but whatever. You'd think a sect of actual mystics trying to remain unnoticed wouldn't dress like that. Or maybe they do it on purpose so people think they're just weird in case they let something slip they shouldn't.

"Miss Wright," says Darren, while bowing in greeting.

The other two swarm over and examine the trunk I'm sitting on.

Darren notices my bare legs and lack of shoes. "Are you not cold?"

"After the ocean?" I hop off the trunk and glare up at him. "Did you know this thing had a... trap?"

All three of them ask, "Trap?" at the same time.

I explain the skeletons.

They are sufficiently clueless that I don't scream at anyone. "Well, it had one. And it sucked. But, here it is. I haven't opened it."

"Excellent." Callum traces his fingers over the metal banding. "This glyph on top is destroyed."

"That was the trap," I deadpan.

"Oh." He stands and bows to me. "Yes, yes. No harm done then. The preservation enchantment is intact."

Landon and Callum grab handles and groan as they lift it. It nearly kills them to haul it the ten feet to the back end of the van. Then again, they've got the rocking physique of science nerds. Both of them gasp and wheeze while pulling the doors open. I smile to myself, wander over, and lift the trunk into the van for them. The guys stare aghast at me.

I pat Callum on the bicep. "Don't feel too bad. My fitness plan is to die for."

Darren groans.

"So?" I face him. "We're even now?"

"Indeed." Darren looks around. "Might we have the compass back?"

"Oh. Hang on. It's inside." I run back to my room to fetch the compass from the wetsuit pocket and bring it back out to them. "Here ya go."

He slips it into his vest. "Thank you, Miss Wright. A pleasure making your acquaintance."

We shake hands.

The men get back in their van and drive off.

Gee. I hope I didn't just hand 'World Domination for Dummies' to a pack of nutcases.

"Perhaps I should have asked what's in those books before agreeing to do this. And wow, magic. I thought an enormous troll was the weirdest thing ever—but that didn't really happen. I didn't go through a reality portal in some cave and fight a giant monster in an alternate dimension. Trolls are one thing, but magic? Seriously?"

Coralie appears beside me. "I believe the creature you confronted in those caverns *did* happen."

"Nope. Total dream. I reject that reality and substitute my own."

She tilts her head at me. "I didn't realize you were a politician."

I laugh. "But really… that seriously happened?"

Coralie nods. "There are dimensions and worlds within worlds. The vast majority of people in *this* world remain ignorant of that. You have only seen—oh, what's the phrase? The tip of the iceberg? Merely a fragment of what's out there."

"Ignorance is bliss." I fold my arms and stare down at my toes. "Time for a new coat of polish."

"Sarah?" Coralie rests an immaterial hand on my shoulder.

I look up at her.

"If you could go back and alter fate so you would still be a mortal, would you?"

"Umm." I pick at a spot on my chest where a corroded rapier blade stuck out of me not a full day ago. That didn't kill me. I consider flying, getting to know Glim, even making friends with Aurélie and how I'll never grow old. "Nah. This is pretty cool."

Coralie smiles. "I never was quite able to accept my fate. I've always regretted being murdered. But I cannot change the past, so I've come to *tolerate* what I am. It fills me with joy to see you're at peace with yourself, even happy over what you've become. Thank you for breaking their hold on me. I shall always be your friend."

"Glad I could help." I start to smile, but a scary thought hits me. "Crap!"

She gasps. "What's wrong?"

"I have bio class tomorrow."

"Why is that bad?"

"There's a test!" I flail my arms. "I haven't studied!"

Coralie giggles. "I've audited Connolly's class at least twenty times. Come on. I will help you study. It's the least I can do."

A woman born in 1829 is going to help me study for an intro to bio test.

Yeah… everything's back to 'normal' all right.

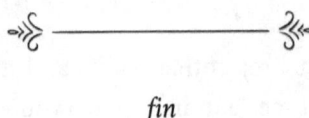

fin

ACKNOWLEDGMENTS

Thank you for reading The Phantom Oracle!

I'd also like to thank Alexandria Thompson for the wonderful cover and interior art.

ABOUT THE AUTHOR

Originally from South Amboy NJ, Matthew has been creating science fiction and fantasy worlds for most of his reasoning life. Since 1996, he has developed the "Divergent Fates" world, in which *Division Zero, Virtual Immortality, The Awakened Series, The Harmony Paradox, and the Daughter of Mars series* take place. Along with editing for Curiosity Quills press, he has worked in IT and technical support.

Matthew is an avid gamer, a recovered WoW addict, developer of two custom RPG systems (paper & dice), and a fan of anime, British humour, and intellectual science fiction that questions the nature of reality, life, and what happens after it.

He is also fond of cats, presently living with two: Loki and Dorian.

Visit me online at:
    Facebook: https://www.facebook.com/MatthewSCoxAuthor
    Pinterest: https://www.pinterest.com/matthewcox10420/
    Goodreads: https://www.goodreads.com/author/show/7712730.
Matthew_S_Cox
    Twitter: https://twitter.com/mscox_fiction
    Instagram: https://www.instagram.com/mscox.author/
    Email: mcox2112@gmail.com

OTHER BOOKS BY MATTHEW S. COX

Divergent Fates Universe Novels

Division Zero series

- Division Zero
- Lex De Mortuis
- Thrall
- Guardian
- Harbinger
- The Shadow Fixer
- Neuroshock

The Awakened series

- Prophet of the Badlands
- Archon's Queen
- Grey Ronin
- Daughter of Ash
- Zero Rogue
- Angel Descended

Daughter of Mars series

- The Hand of Raziel
- Araphel
- Ghost Black

Virtual Immortality series

- Virtual Immortality
- The Harmony Paradox

Prophet of the Badlands Series

- Prophet's Journey
- Prophet's Mercy

Divergent Fates Anthology

(Fiction Novels - Adult)

The Roadhouse Chronicles Series

- One More Run
- The Redeemed
- Dead Man's Number

Faded Skies series

- Heir Ascendant
- Ascendant Unrest
- Ascendant Revolution

Temporal Armistice Series

- Nascent Shadow
- The Shadow Collector
- The Gate to Oblivion
- The Queen of Discord
- The Burning Alchemist

Vampire Innocent series

- A Nighttime of Forever
- A Beginner's Guide to Fangs
- The Artist of Ruin

- The Last Family Road Trip
- The Phantom Oracle
- How Not to Summon Demons
- Ordinary Problems of a College Vampire
- A Vampire's Guide to Surviving Holidays
- An Introduction to Paranormal Diplomacy
- A Vampire's Guide to Adulting
- How to Stop a Vampire War in Six Easy Steps
- Ancient Vampire Death Cults and Other Annoyances
- Hunting Vampires for Fun and Profit
- A String of Seriously Unlucky Events
- The Summer of Completely Usual Strangeness
- Demonic Crisis Management for the Modern Vampire

Standalones

- Wayfarer: AV494
- Axillon99
- Chiaroscuro: The Mouse and the Candle
- The Spirits of Six Minstrel Run
- Sophie's Light
- The Far Side of Promise anthology
- Operation: Chimera (with Tony Healey)
- The Dysfunctional Conspiracy (with Christopher Veltmann)
- Of Myth and Shadow
- The Girl Who Found the Sun

Winter Solstice series (with J.R. Rain)

- Convergence
- Containment
- Catalyst
- Catacombs

Alexis Silver series (with J.R. Rain)

- Silver Light
- Deep Silver
- Silver Quarrel
- Silver Crucible
- Silver Heart

Samantha Moon Origins series (with J.R. Rain)

- New Moon Rising
- Moon Mourning
- Haunted Moon

Vampire For Hire series (with J.R. Rain)

- Moon Master
- Dead Moon
- Lost Moon
- Vampire Destiny
- Infinite Moon
- Vampire Empress
- Moon Elder
- Wicked Moon
- Moon Blade

Maddy Wimsey series (with J.R. Rain)

- The Devil's Eye
- The Drifting Gloom
- Dark Mercy
- Primal Wrath

Samantha Moon Case Files series (with J.R. Rain)

- Blood Moon

Immortal Operative (with J.R. Rain)

- Broken Ice
- Broken Wing

Four Elements series (with J.R. Rain)

- The Elementalist
- The Black Rose
- The Wakefield Curse

Witches series (with J.R. Rain)

- The Witch and the Hangman

Zeb Clemens series (with J.R. Rain)

- The Beast of Devil's Creek
- Wanted: Undead or Alive

Young Adult Novels

The Eldritch Heart Series

- The Eldritch Heart
- The Cursed Crown
- The Sapphire Soul

Evergreen Series

- Evergreen
- The World That Remains

- The Lucky Ones
- Nuclear Summer
- The Nuclear Frontier
- The World We Make
- The Threat Unseen

Progenitor Series

- Out of Sight
- Out of Mind

Diary of a Teenage Fey

(Short story series)

- Elder Horror
- The Hag of Barrow Falls
- Babysitter's Nightmare
- Lharakki
- Bauble for a Soul
- Simulacrum
- Amorphous
- Manticore

Standalones

- Caller 107
- The Summer the World Ended
- Nine Candles of Deepest Black
- The Forest Beyond the Earth

Middle Grade Novels

The Adventures of Ubergirl series

- My Dad is a Mad Scientist
- Aliens Ate My Homework
- The End of all Halloweens
- Dr. Infinity and the Soul Smasher

Tales of Widowswood series

- Emma and the Banderwigh
- Emma and the Silk Thieves
- Emma and the Silverbell Faeries
- Emma and the Elixir of Madness
- Emma and the Weeping Spirit

Standalones

- Citadel: The Concordant Sequence
- The Cursed Codex
- The Menagerie of Jenkins Bailey